ADVANCE PRAISE

Cozy, warm, mysterious, enchanting. Although *Eternal Enchantment* is the much-anticipated prequel to *The Knowing*, it stands on its own beautifully. Kimberly Patton has pieced both stories together seamlessly while giving readers an entirely new world to lose themselves in. A world of intriguing magic—both light and dark, deep familial bonds, whimsical love, and the coziest sisterhood.

— MISSY MILLER, AUTHOR OF *UNDER THE GYPSY MOON: THE LAND OF THEE*

Eternal Enchantment is a captivating prequel that immerses you in a world of lore and magic from the first page. The magic is spellbinding, but it's the strong, layered friendships between the women that truly make it special. It's a must-read for fans of fantasy with emotion, suspense, and unforgettable relationships.

—JORDYN FLEMING, AUTHOR OF *BLADE OF QUEENS*

An enthralling dark adult fantasy that weaves together themes of emotional, forbidden love, and inherited power. This captivating tale is impossible to set down, showcasing exceptional storytelling from a skilled author. A truly remarkable reading experience!

— DEBORAH FONTAINE, LITTLE FREE LIBRARY 85340

A stunning prequel to Kimberly Patton's debut novel, *The Knowing*, *Eternal Enchantment* was exactly the follow-up I wanted. Vivid ambiance, inventive magic, and mounting tension make this story so much more than an origin tale. The trauma and obstacles the characters face are gripping and original in their own right, driving the story forward rather than simply laying groundwork for what comes next. Mathilda, who was mysterious in *The Knowing*, comes fully alive here. Patton gives her immortality rich color rather than simply charting a timeline, making her one of the most compelling characters in the series. Dynamic, well-crafted, and utterly absorbing, *Eternal Enchantment* more than delivers.

— CHARISSA COSTA, FOUNDER OF CHARM CITY READERS

Beautifully written and compelling, *Eternal Enchantment* is a medieval cottagecore origin story with everything I love— profound magic, forbidden romance, and a sisterhood—that left me wanting more.

— ASAD ALI, AVID READER

Eternal Enchantment pulls you in fast and doesn't let go. As Mathilda discovers the true extent of her father's evil, her mother's power, and the role she is predestined to play, she is drawn into a battle she never asked for and cannot escape. Dark, gripping, and emotionally charged, this origin story delivers fierce sisterhood, high-stakes clashes between good and evil, and devastating choices that linger long after the final page.

— ANNE WADE, AUTHOR OF *STORYSHIFT*

Lush and atmospheric. *Eternal Enchantment* transports you into the bewitching world before *The Knowing,* where one must decide between family forged by blood or family forged by magic.

—ASHLEY PHAM, READER

Eternal Enchantment combines fairytale-like storytelling with the magic, rage, and femininity of a Florence and the Machine album. This book is for the witchy ones who crave a cottage in the woods.

—KAITLYN COLLIER, READER

ETERNAL ENCHANTMENT

ETERNAL ENCHANTMENT

KIMBERLY PATTON

HIGHLANDER PRESS

Header image by AlexArt and licensed via Creative Market for commercial use.

The Highlander Press logo and Highlander Press are registered service marks of Highlander Enterprises, LLC.

ISBN: 978-1-956442-71-7
ebook ISBN: 978-1-956442-72-4
Library of Congress Control Number: Applied for

Published by Highlander Press
501 W. University Pkwy, Suite B-2
Baltimore, MD 21210

Cover design: Patricia Creedon (www.patcreedondesigns.com)
Editor: Kris Faatz (www.krisfaatz.com)
Managing Editor: Deborah Kevin, MA (www.deborahkevin.com)
Author photo: Marjorie Stallard

For all my "sisters." You know who you are.

1

The forest was blessedly awake after the long hush of winter. Several finches chased one another through the trees, and somewhere in the distance, a thrush sang a graceful melody. The new life that had unfurled many weeks ago had finally grown denser between sunrises, carrying a vibrance that wove between the hazel branches and through the verdant canopy of the towering giants overhead.

Mathilda Longhurst kept to the rough-trodden path, still wet with morning dew that darkened the hem of her green tunic in a wide band around her ankles. She freed a snagged section of her long, honey-golden hair from a limb and paused, taking in her surroundings. She had walked these paths for seventeen seasons, and the beauty of the woodland still passed before her eyes in wonder. Everywhere her eyes fell, droplets hung from leaves, shimmering in the sun like thousands of sparkling diamonds. Her heart swelled with love for this place. Her place. All of nature was her home.

As she walked deeper into the forest, nature responded to her presence. Like magnets, the leaves pulled to her when she brushed past them. A deer lifted its head momentarily, unperturbed by her sudden appearance, before returning to the vegetation along the forest floor. Mathilda smiled, recognizing the light in the creature's eyes, the same light she recognized in herself and everything before her.

A fluttering sound below a thicket drew her attention. Bending down, she lifted the branches, prompting a startled shriek from the injured blackbird thrashing wildly beneath the leaves. Mathilda reached in and gently cupped the bird between her hands.

"What happened to you?" she asked.

She closed her eyes, and a scene began to unfold in her mind.

Trees blurred past the blackbird. It could sense the hawk closing in. Faster, it flew, its heart racing at a furious pace to survive. An opening in the branches ahead appeared, and the bird swooped low, but the hawk followed. The bird twisted and dipped into the thicket, pain shooting through its wing. It had escaped the hawk, but instinct told the blackbird its fate was still sealed.

Mathilda's breath caught, the bird's horrific plight tangible in her mind. She opened her eyes and gazed at the small creature in her hand. Its racing heart slowed as a gentle peace settled between them.

"You poor thing," Mathilda soothed. "Here, let me make you better."

She pulled out the injured wing and blew a gentle breath over it. The bird fluttered, regaining its strength. "There, all is well. Be careful of predators, little one."

Mathilda kissed its head and released it into the sky. She shielded her eyes from the sun and watched it fly out of sight.

"Rescuing the injured ones again, I see?"

Mathilda smiled at the familiar voice behind her. "I found it under the thicket with a broken wing."

The sunbeams streaking through the trees highlighted her mother's head like a shimmering crown. Unlike other women, she wore her hair unbound most days. Long, golden waves, nearly the same shade as Mathilda's, though with more red tones, cascaded to her waist, below the belt of her rust-colored tunic.

"You are a compassionate girl, Mathilda." Her mother smiled, deepening the fine lines at the edges of her mouth and around the same blue-green eyes that matched Mathilda's. "And your powers are growing stronger. The Goddess grants you the healing talent that most witches covet. Keep your innocence and peace with the earth. Others will try to corrupt you for their own gain. You must never allow such a thing."

Mathilda met her mother's firm gaze. "I won't. I swear it."

"Good. Wisdom, caring, and a giving heart, my dear child, are what give you your strength. Now, come," she said, reaching out to cup Mathilda's chin with a work-strong hand. "We must finish our preparations for the Beltane celebrations. You must be ready for the Goddess to grant you her gifts."

Mathilda followed her mother back down the path toward their home at the upper end of Whitsby Village. Their house was situated near the woods, and a large field stretched between her home and the village, far enough away from the bustle that Mathilda felt they were not part of the village at all. She noticed a raven pulling at a reed from the thatched roof of their stone dwelling as they approached.

"Maelen!" her father bellowed from inside.

Mathilda and her mother exchanged an anxious glance.

"I am here, Aelle," her mother called, hurrying into the house.

Aelle loomed over the cluttered table, a severe look on his features, darkened by the black he wore constantly, which matched his hair, eyes, and demeanor.

"Do something about that wretched bird upon the roof. I cannot think with that thing scratching about."

"Yes, husband."

She reached for the broom by the door and beat it against the stone facade, scaring the raven away.

An anxious pit settled in Mathilda's stomach as she looked

toward her father, and the peace she had gained from being in the forest faded away under his harshness. He had been kind once. Before his sick desire for power corrupted him and twisted his mind and his tongue into sharp and hateful weapons. She gazed at him, searching for any hint of that kind man, but kindness only lived in her memories, leaving her choking on bitterness.

The lid from the large, wooden chest behind the table banged against the wall, jarring Mathilda from the past. Her father rifled through its contents, then went about the room searching for something, his potions, written spells... The empty ledge running along the length of the wall beneath the window brought another scowl to his lips, though she could not begin to guess why. He stomped back to the table, nostrils flaring, then, in a fit of anger, he overturned the table. Potion bottles crashed to the floor, spilling their contents, splintering into shards of broken glass. Mathilda's mother rushed over to clean up the mess.

"Leave it!" Aelle roared. His pulse beside the bulged vein in his neck beat furiously, mirroring the racing beat of Mathilda's heart.

"Come, Mother," she beckoned toward the bedchamber. "We should prepare for the festival." Years of practice kept her voice light despite her fear and anger toward her father.

Midmorning light flooded her mother's bedchamber, warming the tones of the wood floors and glinting off the sewing needles resting on the table. Mathilda grabbed one and settled into the small wooden chair by the bed and readied her thread. The Beltane dresses lay stretched across it, awaiting their final touches. She reached for the sleeve on her dress and began to stitch another row on the band she had already begun, while her mother worked on the dress next to hers. Sewing felt monotonous to Mathilda at times, but the repetitive motions took the edge off her nerves at least.

"Why do you stay with him, Mother?" Mathilda said, keeping her voice low. "We should leave. I doubt Father would even notice."

Her mother gave a look that was almost humorous as she glanced up from her work.

"Oh, but he would. As soon as he needed something done, that is when he would notice." She glanced toward the door as Aelle let out a string of curses, her expression turning firm and unyielding. "I will not leave. This is my home. Besides, soon he'll be off to the bed of that woman, Gundred, and leave us in peace."

Mathilda cringed. "Why do you allow him to leave your bed? I know you. You have spells that would put Father in his place."

Her mother paused, needle in hand, and an odd smile touched her lips. "Did it ever occur to you, Daughter, that I do not want your father in my bed?"

Mathilda kept silent at that. She thought of the many nights that she would watch her mother slip off into the darkness, no doubt to the arms of Fulk, the smithy. Her mother often gave him smiles that seemed too familiar. Mathilda was glad her mother had someone who truly saw her; her husband certainly paid her little heed. He was rarely home enough to remember he even had a wife. Were it not for having to appease the church when he *was* home, to remain free from their suspicion by attending the occasional mass, claiming he had been away working, he likely would never return.

Mathilda remembered seeing Fulk at last year's Beltane festival. Tall, broad, and fair-haired, he was full of laughter, and the opposite of Aelle in every way. Fortunately, her father kept away from the village, wrapped up in his mistress and his dark magic miles away, keeping him ignorant of Fulk's attentiveness. The way Fulk touched her mother when he thought no one was looking. They were looking.

However, no one dared to speak of it. Everyone loved her mother. She was a great healer and compassionate to all. But as much as they loved her, they equally feared for her. Feared what Aelle might do to her or Fulk if he ever found out. He was powerful and ruthless in his cruelty, and everyone knew he was no longer married to Maelen in body or mind. He had been visiting the bed of the witch, Gundred, for as long as Mathilda could remember.

Gundred was cunning and manipulative but not strong in power, though she had a burning desire to become more powerful than any woman of her kind. She practiced dark and forbidden magic and used Mathilda's father to gain more power through his knowledge of spells.

There were rumors of a child from their union, an old rumor that someone supposedly had seen Gundred swollen with babe; however, Mathilda had never seen proof of any such child, and neither she nor her mother dared ask Aelle. He forbade them to even speak of Gundred. The darkness in him, which had started to poison him even in Mathilda's earliest childhood memories, grew stronger by the day. Mathilda could sense it. She hated the fear he raised in her mother. If only they could be free of him.

"Ow!" Mathilda put her needle down and wiped the drop of blood from her finger.

"What is it, child?" her mother asked.

"I was thinking of Father. He is so spiteful."

Her mother's face filled with compassion and understanding, but a hard determination shone in the depths of her eyes. "Yes, but do not waste your time fretting over him, Mathilda. He brings out the worst in anyone, and I will not have you darkening yourself over him. Now pick up that needle and pay attention to your work. You have a dress to finish." She slipped her own needle into a sleeve, smiling. "You will be the most beautiful maiden at the festival by far."

Mathilda couldn't help smiling back. As she returned to her sewing, her thoughts turned to the festival and the ritual she would go through. "Mother, what gifts will the Goddess bestow upon me?"

"I know not," her mother said, completing her final stitch. "The Goddess looks into every witch, granting her additional gifts according to her deeds and strength of powers. Of the five of you coming of age now, your powers are the strongest. Your gifts will be unique, my child."

Mathilda wondered how her mother knew this as she thought of the four other girls participating in the ritual with her. Each one approaching or in their eighteenth year, like Mathilda, and all maidens from surrounding towns and villages near Northumbria.

Regina was the only one that Mathilda could remember in some detail from past festivals. She was from a wealthy, titled family and very beautiful, with a liveliness about her that drew everyone in.

Ramona, Mathilda knew well enough. She was a beauty with hair so dark it often appeared black and eyes to match. She had fair skin and a certain Romanesque look to her features. Mathilda remembered that Ramona had a keen skill for reading into a person's mind. She also had a stony personality and rarely let anyone get too close. Mathilda wondered what gift could possibly be bestowed upon her. She couldn't readily recall the faces of the other two girls, as it had been many years since she had seen them.

She finished the last stitch on the band of her sleeve and put the needle down.

"Let us see your dress," her mother said.

Mathilda laid the dress across the bed, noting how flat the mattress had gotten. It needed more feathers as soon as they could spare the coin. She smoothed out the dress and moved to stand by the wooden headboard to inspect her work. The dye from the woad was an even shade of pale blue. The warp and weft weaving was tight, and the small floral embroidery band at the sleeve and hem was straight and tidy. The matching belt was embroidered with the same floral pattern and not overly embellished, to keep the sumptuary laws per the status of the lower classes.

Her family once had the means to afford some of the luxuries allowed to the middle classes from her father's work as a master stone carver, but in his pursuit of dark magic, he had abandoned his occupation. It was now because of her mother's talents as an herbalist, weaver, and dressmaker that they occasionally had the means for some niceties within the law.

"Very good, Mathilda. You are almost as good as I am. To the untrained eye, this dress is finished. But I see a loose stitch at the hem. Repair that, and you are my equal."

Mathilda flashed her mother a proud smile and settled in to

repair the stitch. The cottage door banged closed, and she froze, listening. "Father must have left us."

Blessedly, the main room was empty. Aelle had gone, taking his dark energy with him.

"Good," her mother said brightly. "Shall we go into the forest to gather our offerings for the festival?"

"Yes. I'll fetch my basket."

Mathilda's mood plummeted when she saw the broken potion bottles and their contents still on the floor. Her father always left his messes for them to clean up. She sighed and lifted the small hand broom from the nail on the wall and knelt to sweep up the broken glass, working her way toward the mortar that lay upside down with the pestle trapped beneath it. As her fingers touched the stone mortar, she gasped. A darkness slammed into her mind. Her vision went black, and a sickening bile rose in her stomach, roiling and threatening to spill. Screams of pain and suffering filled her ears. She felt something hot—a tear?—slide down her cheek. Death was all around her.

What was her father doing?

Then her mother was crouching beside her. "Mathilda? Child, what is it?" Her voice sounded urgent. The vision winked out, and Mathilda blinked, gazing at her mother's blurred and frightened face.

"I—I don't know." She rubbed her eyes, trying to rid them from the haziness still lingering. "I felt evil and suffering when I touched Father's mortar and pestle. I've never felt anything so horrible," she said, still trembling. "What does it mean?"

Her mother touched her fingers to the pestle and made a hissing sound. She took a basket and placed the mortar and pestle inside, frowning distastefully at the items.

"Come with me. I want to show you something. Quickly, now."

Mathilda got to her feet, found her balance, and followed her mother into the forest, her thoughts troubled as they ventured deep into the wood.

Her mother had veered from the path, and the new scenery

began to register, pulling Mathilda out of her head. Dark, angry clouds gathered overhead, threatening rain. She was about to ask where they were headed when her mother suddenly stopped along the edge of a large clearing that Mathilda had never seen before. Something about the place felt peaceful and familiar to her. The landscape looked mystical to her, as if the trees stood like sentries over the clearing, somehow causing nature to thrive here under their careful watch.

Her mother reached her arms out slightly, palms up, and closed her eyes. A haze-like atmosphere rippled and fell away, revealing a small, stone cottage. Mathilda gasped, realizing it had been here all along, shrouded beneath her mother's magic. A weathered bench rested beneath the window to the left of the door. Songbirds flitted over the thatched roof and between the foxglove and chamomile growing at the edge of the stone wall to the right of the door. Mathilda smiled. This little cottage and its clearing were perfectly enchanting, and she loved it at once.

"Come," her mother said over her shoulder, walking toward the door. "You must tell no one about this place. Do you understand?"

Mathilda nodded, still taking in every detail of the clearing, wondering how she never known of its existence.

It began to rain as they reached the cottage's front stoop.

"Hurry inside," her mother urged. "Light the candles."

Mathilda lifted her hands, and flames danced on wicks, bathing the room in warm, golden light. Ledges and shelves on the walls held apothecary jars and herbs. Magical items to enhance spellwork and offer protection, such as a wooden rod and cuttings from various trees, a small statue of the Goddess, and a lone grimoire filled one shelf alone. Extra candles, parchment, and books filled a small chest in the corner. A table sat near a window to the right of the hearth, and baskets of various sizes hung from the ceiling above it.

Her mother took a jar of herbs and a fat candle from the ledge, along with her husband's tainted mortar and pestle, and walked toward a door at the back of the room into a small sleeping chamber.

A rush mat covered part of the stone floor. Mathilda watched as she pulled it aside, revealing a deep, blackened etching of a magical circle.

"Sit quietly and watch." Her mother settled onto the floor with her belongings. Her presence was commanding by nature, but when her magic sparked to life, it transformed her somehow. It was the way a storm could be both beautiful and destructive at the same time—felt, like the energy gathering before the lightning strikes.

Reaching into the jar, Maelen sprinkled a pinch of herbs over the candle and spoke a single command: "You will yield your secrets unto this faithful Guardian."

Mathilda shivered at the power encircling the room. Her mother's eyes were now closed, and she looked deeply troubled. The flame on the candle suddenly shot up, and she convulsed and slumped over.

"Mother!" Mathilda lurched from the bed. She dropped to the floor and brushed aside the hair concealing her mother's face, watching her anxiously.

Maelen slowly stirred and propped herself up, leaning back onto her forearms.

"What did you see?" Mathilda asked.

"Your father is completely overtaken with darkness." Her voice was as strained as her features. "The Goddess is no longer with him. He has found a way to obtain vast power, but it required spilling the blood of an innocent."

Shock reeled through Mathilda, and she struggled to speak. "Who...?

"A peasant girl," her mother answered sadly. "Her spirit communed with me just now. She told me that your father is working on something terrible, but we were separated from each other before she could say more." Her mother shook her head, leveling Mathilda with a weighted look. "That poor child was only twelve years of age."

Mathilda's throat constricted, and her breath came quick and shallow. Her father had become a monster.

"I never imagined Aelle could do such a thing. Something must be done." Her mother's fierceness had returned. She stood up. "I have to send word to the other Guardians. Quickly, child. A piece of parchment..."

Mathilda pulled the quill, ink, and parchment from the chest and sat them on the table. Her mother hastily wrote a few words and rolled the parchment up. As she tied a crimson ribbon around it, she whispered something Mathilda couldn't catch.

"Mother, what is going on?" Mathilda asked, growing more anxious. "Who are these Guardians?"

"I had planned to tell you everything before the ritual, but I will do so now. Listen closely, Mathilda, for this is your legacy."

The magnitude of the situation washed over Mathilda with a heaviness that suddenly made her weary. She sank into a chair and waited for her mother to continue.

"I belong to a coven of five witches who guard against the usage of magic for dark purposes. You already know them as my old friends, although it has been many years since we were all in each other's company. There have been accusations of witchcraft in recent years, and it is growing increasingly dangerous for us to meet in these times. We rarely come together except to celebrate at occasional feasts and pay homage to the Goddess, or in situations like this, when we must protect the innocents from dark magic.

"Our coven is an age-old lineage that goes back beyond memory. My mother was a Guardian; now I am. Someday you will be. The girls who will be going through the ritual with you are the daughters of my coven sisters. As part of the ritual, each of you was to begin receiving from us the full knowledge of the Goddess from our traditions, in addition to her gifts of powers. I am telling you this now because of your father." She reached for Mathilda's hand, suddenly seeming frightened. "You *must* protect yourself at all costs. Do nothing to anger him. If he were to lash out at you and harm you, the line would be broken."

Mathilda was numb. She nodded in answer.

"Now, I want you to take my letter and place it in the hollow of the druid tree and return home immediately. Here," Maelen said, reaching overhead. "Take this basket and fill it with herbs along the way for the festival—as many as you can. We must not rouse your father's suspicions about where we have been. I will be along shortly."

Mathilda found her voice. "What will you do?"

"I need to raise the veil and conceal this place and then, like you, get a gift for the Goddess. Now run along. We will discuss this again soon."

Mathilda took her basket and went out into the wood. Her mind reeled from her mother's revelation. How careful she had been meeting with her sisters. Brief encounters at gatherings, hushed words exchanged with peaceful features to mask their true intentions. Not to mention her show of devotion at mass. A chill ran through Mathilda. If the church ever found out what she and her mother were, they would likely burn.

She wondered what the Guardians would do about her father as her feet led her to the great white oak, known as the druid tree. It stood on a slight knoll behind the intersection of the Three Paths, a sacred place ingrained with the ancients' magic they harnessed from the Goddess, a place that still held secret gatherings.

The tree had stood witness to rituals, worship, and travelers along the path for countless centuries. Its massive size alone was a thing of wonder. The branches gnarled and twisted outward as if each carried a wealth of knowledge. A hum of energy imbued the massive tree, calling to Mathilda like a sentient being. She took the letter from her basket. Standing on her toes, she reached up as far as she could to place it in the deep hollow where the great branches met. Once she was sure it was tucked in, invisible, she set off again.

A loud screech stopped her in mid-stride. Whirling around, she saw a large owl fly off with the letter clasped in its talons. She had heard of these winged messengers assisting witches, from her mother's lore, but had never witnessed one until now. Mathilda watched it fly off on silent wings, until it was out of sight, then she hurried for home, gently plucking the best herbs and berries she could find along the way.

When she arrived home, her mother was already there, sweeping up the rest of her father's mess. The mortar and pestle were neatly replaced on the ledge.

"Has Father returned?"

"No, he hasn't. Did you deliver my letter to the druid tree?"

"Yes. An owl took the letter from the hollow."

"Good."

Mathilda glanced around the room, suddenly feeling lost. "What do we do now?"

"Wait for a sign of response," her mother said, placing the rush mat back on the floor.

"How will we know what the sign is?"

"Listen for the cry of the owl's return. It will signify that a response has come. I see you filled your basket," her mother remarked as Mathilda placed it on the table. "These look free from blight. They will make a fine offering."

Mathilda smiled, pleased at her mother's appraisal. "And did you find a suitable offering as well?"

"Yes. Come, I will show you."

Mathilda followed her mother into the larder at the back of the house, where the herbs and food were stored. Above the scrubbed larder table, two plump rabbits hung by their feet.

"They will make a fine offering," Mathilda said.

Her mother glanced up at the rabbits. "Indeed, they will."

"Maelen!" Aelle's bellow startled them both. Mathilda's jaw clenched.

Her mother pinned her with a firm gaze and whispered, "Remember what I told you. Do not anger him."

Mathilda's nod brought a look of relief to her mother's face. "I am here, husband," she called out.

Aelle stepped into the larder, blocking the doorway. His malicious eyes scanned over the room, over Mathilda and her mother, searching for some fault to accuse them of. Mathilda felt his black energy filling up the space.

Finding nothing fit for argument, his cold eyes turned to his wife. "I am hungry."

"The herring will be ready soon, and so will the beets," she answered placatingly.

He pointed at the rabbits. "I will have those."

"But they are for the Goddess," Mathilda blurted, forgetting her mother's warning.

"Shut your mouth, girl," he snapped. His stony eyes bored briefly into Mathilda before disregarding her altogether.

"No matter, child," her mother interrupted. "I can find more in time for the celebrations."

Mathilda looked on in hatred at her father as her mother took the rabbits down from the hook. She placed a hand gently on Mathilda's arm. "Come, help me with these. You and I will eat the herring tonight."

MATHILDA STABBED ANGRILY at her fish. She focused on the repetitive sounds of her own chewing to drown out the angry thoughts of her father. She watched him finish the last of the meat. He gulped down the rest of his mead and wiped the back of his hand across his mouth before stalking out of the house.

"Well, he's gone for the evening," her mother said lightly.

"I hope he never returns." Mathilda snatched her father's plate from the table and stormed toward the larder with it.

"My dear, please do not say things like that. You are not a hateful person."

Mathilda sighed. "You are right. I'm sorry, Mother. What will you do about a gift for the Goddess? The eve of Beltane is tomorrow."

"You let me worry about that. Now, let us clear this mess and then off to bed. You will need your rest for the festivities."

Mathilda lay in bed, listening to the sounds of the nighttime creatures. Leaf shadows danced along the far wall, lulling her closer toward sleep. As she drifted off, she heard an owl's call and her mother's footsteps walking out into the night.

2

Shortly after dawn, Mathilda slipped out of bed and quickly dressed, anxious to find out where her mother had gone in the night. Her father's absence from the cottage made for a cheerful morning already. She found Maelen in the larder, skinning a rabbit. Three more hung on the hook above the table.

"I see I worried for nothing," Mathilda said.

"Yes." Her mother tugged the skin from a hind leg, briefly glancing up to meet Mathilda's gaze. "What did I tell you? Not only did I replace the ones your father took, but I was also rewarded with two additional rabbits. The owl dropped both at my feet at the druid tree. A kind heart, Mathilda, will be rewarded."

"What response did the owl bring?"

"Ramona, Katrina, Isobel, and Regina all now know their purpose. We have decided that the Guardians' gift of knowledge will be passed to each of you tonight. It is imperative to bestow this knowledge now. Your father's instability insists upon it."

Mathilda's eyes flicked warily toward the door. "I wonder when he will return?"

Her mother glanced up, eyes bright and pleased. "Your father will not be back for some days."

"How do you know this?"

"I saw it in a vision," she said coolly, swiping the scraps into a wooden bucket. "He is in the arms of Gundred even as we speak."

Mathilda scoffed. "How do you speak so calmly of this woman? She has taken your husband, corrupted him…"

"As I said before, Mathilda, I care not what your father does. Now help me with these rabbits. We have much to do before the feast."

Mathilda met her mother's eyes, amazed at her strength and resolve as she reached for a knife.

"When will the others arrive?"

"Ramona will be here with Leticia at midday to help with the preparations. The others will arrive before dusk. While we work, I will tell you more of these women and their daughters that you will meet again."

Mathilda took off her apron and hung it outside the larder. Having finished the vegetables for a meat pie, her mother had told her to go rest for a while. The sun was nearly overhead, and she settled on the worn, wooden bench beneath the window, pressing her back against the stone facade, enjoying the warmth for a time.

She had just dozed off when she sensed something she recognized. A powerful force thrummed all around her. It was comforting, and it tugged at her consciousness.

"Greetings, dear Mathilda," a woman's voice sang out.

Mathilda opened her eyes. Ramona and Leticia stood before her, holding baskets laden with supplies. Though she had not seen them in some time, she knew them both at once.

Leticia wore a deep-blue linen tunic with a leather belt wrapped around her waist. Her dark hair was neatly parted down the middle, and the tail of her braid hung across her left shoulder. She had kind eyes that shone with wisdom. Her daughter's features were similar, though her demeanor was aloof. Her dark-gray dress seemed to fit her expression.

Aside from herself and her mother, Mathilda had never sensed this heightened pulse of magic. As Guardians, their magic was Goddess-given, and Mathilda knew its pulse as well as she knew her own name. She quickly stood and embraced them both.

"Greetings, Leticia, Ramona. I trust you are both well?"

"Indeed, we are," Leticia replied. "Is your mother inside?"

"Yes, in the larder. Come with me."

A smile lit up her mother's face upon their entrance. She quickly wiped the flour from her hands. "Leticia, so kind of you to come help with the preparations," she said, kissing Leticia on the forehead. "And look at you, Ramona. What a beauty you are," she added, repeating the kiss. "I have everything nearly ready, save for the tarts. Mathilda, you and Ramona go into the woods and pick primroses for the head wreaths. My sister and I must speak alone."

"Yes, Mother."

Ramona's dark eyes boldly met Mathilda's. She was attractive despite the harshness of her features, which she wore unapologetically. Mathilda took two baskets and gave one to her.

"Shall we?" Mathilda asked.

"Lead the way."

Neither of them spoke again, and soon, a heavy awkwardness settled in the air, which Mathilda tried to ignore by filling her basket with the flowers she found along the way. She strove to keep her features impassive, but she found herself growing increasingly uncomfortable. She wished Ramona would say something to break the deafening silence between them.

"Why do you feel so uncomfortable?" Ramona said right on cue. "You have no terrible secrets hidden away. Refreshing, for once."

Mathilda felt a flush of crimson bloom on her cheeks as she recalled Ramona's gift of mind reading.

"You are not the first to be uneasy in my presence," Ramona said, dropping her flowers in the basket. "Those who know my so-called *gift* fear I will see something they don't wish revealed. I have grown used to being alone in my own company." A flash of emotion crossed her face that betrayed her iron mask.

Mathilda softened. No wonder Ramona scoffed at the mention of her gift. How sad to be ostracized. At least now she knew the reason behind Ramona's stony personality.

"I am sorry," she said.

"Why should you apologize? As I said, I don't mind."

The expression that Mathilda caught a moment ago said that Ramona did mind. She dropped a handful of primroses into her basket. "Are you looking forward to the festivities?"

Ramona shot a flat look. "I am a mind reader attending a gathering. I'm likely to have a headache before the night is through with all those people's thoughts running in my head."

Mathilda flinched. "That is dreadful."

Ramona shrugged. "What about you? Are you looking forward to tonight's events?"

"Yes. But I am afraid, too. After learning about my father and what we are to do against his kind, I do not know if I am ready."

Ramona's brows raised. "Of course you are. It has been the way of our ancestors since the olden days. Besides, you have no choice in the matter. It is in your blood. You cannot escape."

Mathilda sighed. "No." She glanced at their baskets, recalling their task. "We had better hurry back and start weaving our crowns."

As DUSK APPROACHED, Katrina and her mother, Katherine, arrived at the house. Katherine carried a large basket, its contents swathed in thick linen. She was a striking woman who had exotic features with big, dark eyes and full, high cheekbones that rounded beautifully with her smile. Katrina stood just behind her, fairer in coloring than her mother. Mathilda noticed her apprehension and the way her muddy green eyes darted nervously across the room. No doubt she, too, worried about her future as a Guardian.

Two more figures shadowed the doorway, and Mathilda recognized Isobel and her mother, Annora. As Annora said her greetings, Isobel's eyes fell on Mathilda, and she smiled. Isobel was of African descent from her mother's side, Mathilda recalled from her mother's earlier talk. Mathilda had never seen anyone else with Annora's or Isobel's warm-honey skin and long, thick hair. They were stunning beauties, and Mathilda couldn't help but stare.

Quick introductions were made, the women talking over each other in excitement to be reunited after so long, and the baskets everyone brought were set on the table to free arms for embraces.

The sound of a carriage drew Mathilda's eyes toward the door.

"That must be Philippa," her mother said. Mathilda glanced out the window. The driver had just climbed down from his seat and was making his way to open the door for the occupants. Mathilda stepped away before she could be seen spying.

Voices carried from outside the window, growing louder as they approached the door. Lady Philippa Darnley swept in like the noblewoman she was, in a silk brocade dress the color of wine. Her pale hair was intricately braided and held in place with a fine, golden crespine.

Regina followed behind, looking even lovelier than Mathilda remembered. Fair, like her mother, she wore a beautiful green gown, not as ornate as the one Philippa wore and unadorned, save for the floral banding around the hem and sleeves. Her pale hair hung in loose waves down her back, and a golden belt hung around her waist. Regina had a look of serene confidence. When her eyes fell on Mathilda and the others, she smiled warmly.

"And I thought Annora was the one descended from queens," Mathilda's mother teased, eyeing Philippa. "Shall we bow, my lady?"

"I'll have none of your nonsense, Maelen," Philippa retorted, lifting her chin even higher. "This is a feast day, and I wear my finest to honor the Goddess."

"Speaking of which, we had better prepare our girls," Annora said.

"Yes," Maelen agreed. "Follow me." She motioned toward the bedchamber, where the five dresses she and Mathilda had made lay stretched across the bed with the flower crowns placed by each one. Mathilda eyed Regina, wondering what she thought about them. They weren't nearly as elegant as the one Regina now wore.

"She likes them," Ramona whispered.

Mathilda flushed, embarrassed, but she couldn't help noticing Regina's smile. Ramona was right. The girls and their mothers took their dresses and the flower crowns and went out into the main room, leaving Mathilda and her mother alone in the bedroom.

"Mathilda, turn around," her mother said. "We still have your hair to tend to."

She picked up the comb and meticulously worked through the tangles, softening the golden waves cascading down Mathilda's lower back. Once satisfied, she settled the flower crown, fixing it in place.

"Now. What did I say about you?" Pride shone in her mother's eyes as she lifted Mathilda's chin and gazed appraisingly. "You are beautiful, my daughter. And it is time we were on our way." She glanced beyond the door. "It looks as if everyone is ready," she added as she stepped into the main room. "Mathilda, take the cheese and wine in your basket. The rest of you, take what you can and follow me. We will meet near the Three Paths after the feast, so don't go far," she said, glancing pointedly at Mathilda and the rest of the girls.

An indigo sky stretched across the horizon, with billowing clouds the color of a bruise. There was a hush of anticipation in the air as they stepped outside. Voices from the lower end of Whitsby Village carried from the spring celebrations, but Mathilda and the others would not be attending that festival. Instead, they slipped silently into the cover of trees, away from the village.

Flickering flames atop candles, shadowed by the cupped hands of other secret devotees of the Goddess, moved like phantoms along the path, deeper into the wood. Mathilda's mother led their group until they reached the site of ancient gatherings.

A fire blazed. Regina's father, Lord Darnley, had provided a deer for the feast; it was already roasting on the iron spit. Other wealthy devotees had contributed pheasants and various meats. Many tables had been pulled from homes and adorned with the best fabrics each household could afford. Benches were lined in straight rows down the length of the tables, and some rough-built stools were placed where the benches would not reach.

A crow's caw sounded over the noise. The crowd parted, and Mathilda saw the large black bird hopping, wings stretched as if clearing the way for a cloaked figure leaning heavily on a bent staff. Though stooped, something about this figure commanded attention.

An aged hand pushed back the hood, revealing Goda, the old Druidess. The firelight yellowed her long, wiry white hair while casting the other side of her in shadows. The crow flew up to perch on the tip of her staff, and Goda took her place at the head of the table, signaling a respectful quiet from the participants as they moved to join her at the table.

Goda's unsettling, cloudy eyes roved intently over every face as if she were committing their features to memory or seeing something only visible to her. Mathilda noticed a few who shifted beneath her unseeing gaze. Perhaps they sensed that Goda saw plenty despite her blindness. Or perhaps they were bothered by the crow, who seemed to be more than just a pet to the old woman.

"We are grateful for this feast and the upcoming growing season," she said in a voice like aged leather. "I see many familiar faces, along with a few new ones. Let us treat one another kindly and remember this gratitude in the months ahead." Her features suddenly shifted, ominously stern, as her milky gaze swept down the length of the tables, and when she spoke again, it was like a low, rumbling thunder. "Heed my words: Double your plantings, for I have foreseen a coming blight." Her eerie eyes fell on Mathilda, pinning her where she stood. The crow let out a sharp caw, making several people jump, including Mathilda.

"Now, let us make merry," Goda said lightly, turning toward the shocked faces still gazing at her.

Mathilda let out a pent-up breath. She saw others exchanging wary glances, tucking Goda's warning away. Then, as the old Druidess lowered herself into her seat, light conversations began, and before long, laughter came as rich and poor alike sat as one to share in the Beltane feast.

Mathilda reached for the wooden cup sitting before her. As she brought it to her lips, something akin to a magical force tugged at her attention, prompting her to look up. To her left, about midway down the tables, she noticed a dark-haired young man boldly staring at her.

He flashed her a roguish smile, the kind that likely got him anything he wanted. His chestnut eyes held a good-natured mirth in their depths, and he had an ease of confidence that she immediately felt. She guessed his age at about five and twenty years. The patterned tartan he wore over his léine indicated he was a Celt. His gaze held hers like a powerful spell, and a light flutter arose in her chest and settled low in her core. A plate of food was placed before her, breaking their gaze.

Flushing, Mathilda turned to her food, wondering at the force that urged her not to break eye contact with this stranger. Her body's reaction to him unsettled her. When she looked up again, his eyes were still upon her. The corner of his mouth lifted, and he dipped his head. She nodded back, quickly turning away, curious at his thoughts yet angry at his boldness.

Next to her, Ramona frowned. "You do not want to know what he is thinking?"

"Is it bad?"

"No, but you would be embarrassed if you knew the depth of his thoughts."

"Well, if it is not malicious or harmful, then I would rather you not tell me," Mathilda answered, stabbing at a potato.

"He wants to know who you are."

"Ramona, I don't care."

Ramona's eyes sparkled. "Your thoughts betray you, Mathilda."

Mathilda banged her knife on the table, flustered at her reaction to the handsome stranger, and embarrassed that she couldn't hide it from Ramona. "Would you stop that? You are intruding."

Ramona shrank back in her seat, her teasing smile gone. "I apologize."

"No, I'm sorry," Mathilda said, adjusting her tone. "That man has bewildered my senses, and I should not have taken my frustration out on you. Let us eat in peace." She gave Ramona a reassuring smile and carefully kept her eyes turned from the man gazing at her, though it wasn't without difficulty. She picked up her knife and gave her plate her full attention.

With the feasting over, it was time for everyone to collect their offerings for the Goddess. Mathilda gathered her basket of fruits and berries while her mother removed the extra rabbit from the spit. The crowd of devotees reverently set off a little way through the trees toward the Three Paths, where the festivities would truly begin.

A carved wooden fertility statue stood at the intersection of the Three Paths, bathed in shadows and light from the nearby fire. Everyone moved in close to lay their offerings around it. Goda took her place in the center by the statue and struck the ground thrice with her walking staff, nearly unsettling the crow. Upon her cue, hands connected, making a large circle around her.

Goda closed her eyes and lifted her palm out. "May the Great Goddess grant our soil's renewal so that the earth may bear forth an abundance, feeding us through the long winter. May your women's bellies swell with the future babes you've long hoped for. Let it be so." She struck the ground one final time. The crow squawked, and an excited roar rose across the circle. The celebration had now begun. The crowd dispersed, most going toward the casks of ale, others settled down on stumps or at tables. A few men stacked logs near the fire to build it up when needed.

From across the path, the young man's eyes found Mathilda's. She flushed and turned away before he could see more of her discomfort.

The pull she felt toward this stranger was unsettling. She found she suddenly wanted to know more about him. Ramona was beside her again, and Mathilda saw the girl grinning. Unspoken questions flooded her mind. She broke away from the crowd, pulling Ramona with her. Her curiosity could no longer be ignored. "You must tell me everything."

Ramona seemed to be swallowing a laugh. A hint of mirth twitched her lips as she gazed at the man in question. "Very well," she said. "He thinks you're beautiful, and he wants to know if you are intended for another."

"Oh," Mathilda said. A heady feeling settled in her body. "Who is he?"

"They call him Duncan. His father recently died, and he is the new chieftain of the Ferguson clan."

"There you are, my child," Mathilda's mother said, flustered. "I told you to meet behind the Three Paths after the feast."

Mathilda caught a glimpse of Philippa's bright dress beyond the trees. Everyone else was already standing near the Paths, waiting. "I am sorry, Mother. I got distracted."

She nodded. "Come along; we are ready for you. Ramona, you too."

Mathilda glanced over her shoulder as she followed her mother away from the celebration around the fire. Duncan stood watching the flames as sparks shot up from the added wood. Somehow, she felt he still saw her, even with his back toward her. Hopefully, he would not follow.

Her mother pushed back a section of a hedgerow, and Mathilda stepped through into a large clearing with the others. The four other mothers—Philippa, Annora, Leticia, and Katherine—stood with torches in hand beside a stone-encircled stack of wood prepared for a small fire. Mathilda's mother joined them, and they dropped the torches, setting the wood ablaze.

Maelen turned to the girls. "Lie down around the fire with your heads to the flame and feet facing away. Touch fingers to fingers in an unbroken circle." The firelight turned her golden hair the color of the flames and heightened the intensity in her eyes.

Mathilda reveled at knowing the Goddess would personally touch her during the ceremony, yet she was still frightened, unsure what would happen. She clung to her mother's reassurance that no harm would come to her as she lay on the ground beside Ramona.

The Guardians picked up several long staves, stretching them toward one another to form an unbroken circle around the girls. Ramona's hand squeezed Mathilda's reassuringly, calming her as their mothers moved around them. The power radiating from the women as they spoke their sacred rites bore down upon the clearing. It moved in waves along the grass and settled as a thick haze in the atmosphere. Had Mathilda not already experienced this magic herself, she would have trembled before these women.

Four times, they circled to the right, and on the fifth time, Mathilda felt a sudden jolt. The right side of her body tingled, from her shoulder to the sole of her foot. It seemed as if even the right half of her brain became a thrum of energy, honing sounds and vibrations. It was as if she were somehow separated from the left side of herself, fully enlightened on the right. Then, the Guardians circled to the left. As before, on the fifth time, Mathilda's left side tingled. In a rush, it joined with the right side, thrusting her into some otherworldly realm.

Blackness filled the deep places of her mind. She felt as if she were flying through the unknown spaces between the stars. A flood of energy coursed through her body, settling acutely in her mind. She was deeply connected to everything around her. She felt vitality thrumming through the roots beneath her and in the life-giving waters forming in the clouds. The intense pull of the moon's energy and rhythms were also felt. The spirits of the ancestors surrounded her. They spoke in a rush of a thousand voices, like the roar of a river in spring, yet somehow, she heard each one distinctly as if their words were imprinted in her mind. They spoke of secrets and darker things that she did not understand. Then, a blinding light came over her, reconnecting Mathilda to the present. Stirring slowly, she sat up, noticing the looks of stunned confusion on the other girls' faces.

Her mother stood, gazing down on her, not motherly, but looking every bit the powerful Guardian she was. "What did you see?"

Mathilda sat up straighter. A reverent bewilderment briefly stole her words as she recalled her experience. "The ancestors of old came to me. It was as if we were all one being. I was in the air, everywhere at once. The secrets of the universe were made a part of me. I sensed the great Spirit in the earth, and I was part of it." She saw the other four Guardians look at one another in astonishment.

But her mother said nothing yet. Instead, she stood and turned to Katrina, on Mathilda's right side. "And what of you, Katrina?" she asked. "What did you see?"

Katrina looked pale, as if her stomach would empty. She met Maelen's eyes. "I saw blood dry up and disease removed. I was the one who made it go away."

Maelen nodded, moving past Katrina. "And you, Isobel?"

"I was standing before a great cauldron. It started to boil and bubble until it began to run over into me. It was as if I were a vessel taking the contents from the cauldron. Then, I had vials and jars before me that suddenly became full."

Mathilda looked on, stunned by the other girls' visions as her mother paused again.

"Regina?"

"Men were standing before me. Each one of them was vile and wicked. I paced before them, weighing their hearts until I saw an outcome I wanted. With my words, their tongues were ripped from their mouths."

Mathilda saw a slight flash in her mother's eyes, which she interpreted as impressiveness, but it quickly faded as she stood before Ramona.

"And what of you, Ramona? What did you see?"

Ramona's eyes were fixed on the ground, her brows furrowed in worry. She raised them to Maelen. "I was standing before a crowd, and all their voices rang through my head at once. The pain made me stop up my ears. Then, somehow, my ears opened again, only the noises no longer hurt. I also felt a weight over me, as if I could distinguish day from night, good from bad, man from woman, but I already knew these differences, so I could not understand the meaning." Ramona paused, fretting with the end of her belt. Her brows were pinched with confusion, and her gaze was distant. "But another part of me, far away, took a different meaning from those things, and that part of me understood."

A gentle smile touched Maelen's lips as she gazed at Ramona.

"Listen closely," she said. "Each of you was granted a gift. I will tell you the meaning of your visions." She stooped before Ramona, taking her hand. "Ramona, the gift of sight that you had before was a burden. You constantly had the thoughts of others running through your mind. You have worked hard to hone them to a single individual, but sometimes, it still comes at once."

A tear slid down Ramona's cheek, and Maelen gently brushed it away. "Your isolation was noticed, and the Goddess took pity. You now have the gift to search others' thoughts of your own accord. The weight you felt was wisdom to know the hearts of man."

Ramona nodded, relief plain upon her features. Maelen patted her hand and moved to stand before Isobel.

"Isobel, the cauldron you saw represents knowledge, and the vials and jars before you were filled by your hand from the knowledge you gained in potion making."

Maelen moved before Regina next. She gazed long at her before speaking. "Regina, you were granted the ability to coax anything necessary from a person for the greater good of the Guardians. The Goddess took note of your way with others and honed it for the purpose of manipulation. Use this gift wisely, and it will remain with you. Use it foolishly, and it will be stripped away."

Regina's widened eyes searched out Philippa's as Maelen moved on.

"Katrina, you were granted the power of healing. Any potion you use in treatment will be amplified through you. As you grow in your role as Guardian, your power will also grow stronger, and most times, you will not need elixirs in your healing."

Mathilda noticed the proud smile Katherine shared with her daughter as her own mother suddenly paused before her. Mathilda's anxious gaze lifted. Her mother's eyes were firm and intense.

"My child, your gift is complex. The Goddess highly favors you. The knowledge and old ways from the ancestors are now in you. The feeling of being the air and earth was your great connection with Spirit and the earth. The energy in the universe will be yours to harness at your will, and as you grow in knowledge, these powers will grow and adapt around you. The earth shall be entrusted to your care and protection, and you will lead your sisters henceforth."

Stunned, Mathilda could only nod. *Why did the Goddess choose her to lead?* She looked for any signs of bitterness from the other girls or their mothers, but they all seemed comfortably resigned to the declaration.

Her mother stepped back. She scanned the girls intently. "You are now a coven of five. You will look after each other. Your sisters' trials will be your own. You will work together for the gain of the coven and the good of the earth." There was a fire in her mother's eyes. It was mirrored in the gazes of the other women standing near her. "If darkness threatens the peace and harmony within the earth, you will act as one to dispel it at all costs. You will live in the shadows as we do. Gone are the days of open practice. There is yet another movement to crush out the witch. You must not allow that. You will preserve the ways of old and pass them on to future generations."

Mathilda's heart pounded as she listened. Her mother was right. Whitsby Village only knew her mother as a healer. If they knew what she could do, the power she wielded, they would tremble and rise up against her. As if sensing Mathilda's fear, her mother gave her a reassuring smile.

"You may all go and enjoy the evening's festivities," she said lightly.

Ramona surprised Mathilda by catching hold of her hand. "Come," she said, tugging Mathilda along. "Come, Sisters, the night is ours."

Regina caught Mathilda's other hand, and Isobel and Katrina joined them. Mathilda's apprehension faded, left to the confines of the clearing as a giddiness overtook her. They pushed through the hedgerow and danced along the forest path, their giggles ringing merrily through the wood. The raucous celebrations grew louder as they drew closer to the main bonfire. The fertility celebrations had begun. The men ran naked through the fires, and many of the women joined in. Others were fully engaged in sexual acts amongst the sacred groves.

Regina stopped to take in the sights. Unfazed by the wildness around her, an amused grin played at the edges of her lips. The drunken revelers ignored her chime of laughter.

"Come," she said, taking the lead and leaving Mathilda to the back of the line. Regina's laughter came freely as she led them toward the Three Paths. Her joy was infectious. Mathilda found that she had as much laughter in her as Regina did as she was pulled around the druid tree.

A strong, calloused hand suddenly grabbed Mathilda's, yanking her away from her sisters. Ramona cast a glance over her shoulder and surprised Mathilda with a sly grin as she continued along with the others.

Mathilda stumbled, nearly falling before two steady hands caught her wrists, and backed her against the rough bark. She stifled a scream, opening herself up to her magic to unleash on the broad figure standing mere inches in front of her, before realizing it was Duncan who had pulled her away. Ramona must have seen that he meant her no harm for her to leave with the others as she did.

Mathilda's lungs heaved with adrenaline. His eyes lowered, taking in the quick rise and fall of her chest, lingering briefly before they slowly dragged up to meet hers. There was a hunger in his gaze that she had not seen before in a man. His closeness startled her. She became aware of his scent, earthen, like wild game, and the heady smell of the woodland. Her body reacted to his nearness; she felt the odd fluttering again in her core, making her blush. A part of her wanted this, wanted *him*. She was losing control of her senses, and it frightened her.

"Let go of me," she said with as much force as possible, feeling the tangle of her skirts around her ankles and the tree against her back, barring her escape.

"I must know," he replied in a thick brogue. "Are you intended?"

"You speak our language well," Mathilda bit out, giving him a haughty look to disguise her chaotic emotions.

He raised an eyebrow. "Did you think me a heathen, then?"

Mathilda met his eyes, rich tones of amber encircled by darker rings, and saw something akin to hurt and amusement in their depths.

"No," she said, lowering her gaze in a flush of shame. "For I am one too."

His fingers grazed her chin, tipping her head up. She kept her eyes fixed on his chin, avoiding his gaze, noticing that her head reached his nose, that he had a tiny freckle to the right of his mouth—anything to avoid the intensity of his gaze. He nudged her chin again, and she raised her eyes. His gaze was all-consuming, and she felt her heart pound loudly in her ears.

"What is your name, lass?" His voice was low and wanting.

She started to give a false name but felt compelled to speak the truth. "Mathilda."

His lips curved into a smile. "Mathilda," he said as if savoring the taste of her name on his tongue like wine.

"Are you intended for another, Mathilda?" he asked again, more intently this time. His hands still held her arms by her sides with a gentle firmness, and he unconsciously stroked Mathilda's left wrist with his thumb.

Her heart raced wildly. Duncan set her afire with his touch, with his words. His eyes held hers, and a connection the like of which she had never felt before tethered her to him. Her tongue felt heavy in her mouth, unable to shape any words.

He leaned in closer, his trimmed beard brushing her cheek. She felt his breath against her neck as his mouth moved close to her ear, and with barely a whisper, he asked again, slowly, reverently, "Are you intended?"

Mathilda's breaths were quick and shallow. A fire seemed to blaze in her chest. Her voice caught in her throat as she tried to answer. "No," she managed to whisper.

Duncan's gaze turned ravenous, and he pinned her tight against the tree. His hair fell over his shoulders, curtaining her face, and his mouth was on hers, hungry and possessive. All the resistance Mathilda clung to earlier melted away in the fire of his kiss. She was stunned at the willingness with which her body responded to him, and it alarmed her that she could yield so easily to his touch. He felt dangerous to her suddenly. She struggled against him, tried to pull her arms from his hold.

"Do I frighten you?" he asked, looking surprised as he pulled away from her lips with a heavy breath.

Mathilda raised her chin in defiance. "Nothing frightens me."

He suddenly grinned. "You have spirit within you. Good."

"I must return to my sisters."

His amber eyes roved over her face, memorizing it. He brushed the back of his fingers across her cheek and let her go. As she stalked away, he called after her, "I will have you, Mathilda."

His words stopped her in her tracks. Anger streaked up her spine as she faced him again.

"No man will have me, for I belong to the Goddess."

He threw his head back and laughed. Mathilda's fingers itched to pick up a rock and fling it at him, but it seemed the rich sound of his laughter had found a way into her heart, easing her ire. She fought away the smile that touched the corners of her swollen lips as she left him standing there.

She found her sisters gathered around the Three Paths, listening to Goda talk of the ancestors. Thankfully, Ramona was the only one to notice her. Mathilda motioned Ramona to join her behind the gathering and sat with a breathless, giddy sigh.

"Your mother was looking for you," Ramona whispered, scooting closer. Her eyes fell to Mathilda's reddened lips, and she flashed that same sly grin from when Duncan pulled her away.

Mathilda glanced toward where her mother sat alongside Leticia, and she thanked the Goddess that she hadn't been caught with Duncan. "What did you tell her?"

"I told her you went to fetch us a drink." Ramona absentmindedly smoothed the wrinkles from her lap. When she lifted her eyes again, they were troubled. "I'm sorry I abandoned you to Duncan. I knew you were curious about him, and once I saw that he meant you no harm, I thought you would want privacy. Was I wrong?"

"Did you not read my mind?"

"No. I failed to intrude upon your thoughts as he led you away."

Mathilda smiled. "You are not wrong. Not entirely. And I am delighted for you, Ramona. I know you must feel lighter having that burden lifted from you."

"Yes. I do." She regarded Mathilda thoughtfully. "What transpired between you and Duncan?"

"You do not want to know."

Ramona's eyes widened. "Did he defile you?"

"No. He kissed me, then claimed that he would have me."

"And will he?" Ramona asked, her face questioning yet teasing.

"No. I belong to the Goddess."

3

Three days had passed since the festival, and Mathilda's power had already strengthened beyond what she could have expected. It thrummed beneath her skin when she closed her eyes and focused on the feel of it. How much more her magic would grow remained to be seen.

Her mother had gone into the village earlier, leaving Mathilda alone in the cottage to tend to the midday meal. She was grateful for the silence. It gave her the peace she needed to attune to her magic.

The cottage door was suddenly yanked open, jarring her from her thoughts. She turned from the cooking pot as her father darkened the doorway. He seemed different. More confident. He had an ease about him that suggested whatever had troubled him days ago had been resolved. Yet an underlying danger emanated from him, filling the room with an overbearing bleakness.

"Where is your mother?" he demanded.

Mathilda ignored his rough tone and spoke politely. "She took some weaving into the village to sell."

"Did she now?"

He stepped toward her, and Mathilda's skin crawled at his nearness. She hated how his height afforded him the ability to loom over her. She met his eyes unflinchingly despite the suspicion swirling in them. Her mother's warning came to mind, but she could not manage to keep the bite from her tone. "I speak the truth, Father."

"Mind your tongue with me!"

She clenched the ladle between her fist, the metal digging into her palm. "I speak to you in the same manner in which you speak to me." Her power flared. It ached to be released. She longed to hurl it toward him, but she held it back.

He reared his arm back to strike her, but an unseen force stopped his hand. His eyes rounded in shock.

She glared triumphantly, projecting her voice into his mind. *Yes, Father. It was I who stopped your hand. The Goddess protects me.*

He quickly masked the new shock of hearing her voice inside his head. "How dare you use your powers against me," he said, his voice deceptively calm, almost gentle. He paced in slow circles around her, like a wolf with trapped prey.

Tingles ran up Mathilda's spine each time he passed behind her. His silent stare washed over her like filth; however, she refused to shrink beneath his dark gaze.

He stopped at the hearth, peering into the cooking pot of porridge her mother had put on before she left, and sneered down at the contents. "Am I expected to eat this?"

"We did not expect you home," Mathilda managed to calmly say. "It was intended for Mother and me."

"Am I not home now? You will prepare meat for me."

"There *is* no meat, Father. That is why Mother went into the village—to buy meat with the money from the weaving."

He flung his arm out toward the spoons hanging by the cooking pot, knocking them to the floor in a clang of metal. "Then bring me bread!" he roared. Spit flew from his mouth.

Mathilda flinched, but he did not notice, thanks be to the Goddess. She calmly wiped the spit from her cheek while her father yanked out a chair and sat expectantly. She went to the larder and unwrapped the bread, grateful for a moment away from him to calm herself. Slicing off a chunk, she put it on a plate, then filled a cup with ale and returned to place it by her father's arm, standing near as he ate.

He took a mouthful of ale and spit it out. "You expect me to drink this swill?" He slammed the cup down. More liquid sloshed on the table. "The ale is old."

Mathilda reached for the cup and tasted it herself. "The ale is fine."

He whipped his head up to glare at her. "You dare go against my word?"

"I speak the truth."

His fingers curled into a fist in his struggle to control himself.

"The Goddess is in me, Father," Mathilda warned. A surge of connection to her flared inside Mathilda as confirmation.

"The Goddess is *weak*," he spat.

Mathilda's anger won at last. "No, *you* are weak!"

The chair overturned with a crash. Aelle jumped to his feet, raising his fist.

Mathilda should have felt fear, but a strong authority inside her heart bolstered her. "You once feared the Goddess. Would you dare to strike me, dare defy her? Bring her wrath upon your head?" She felt his silent rage.

Hatred blazed in his eyes, and his next words spewed like venom from his mouth. "You will pay for your defiance toward me, *witch*."

Mathilda did not break eye contact, nor did she show any fear toward him. With a growl, he turned on his heel and stalked out of the house. She gazed at the place where he had just stood, wondering when his hatred for her began. Sighing, she wiped up the spilled ale and took the empty plate to the larder. Her mother came through the door several moments later, carrying two small quail.

"Was that your father I saw going toward the wood?"

"It was."

Her mother's gaze was penetrating. She seemed to glean that

something had occurred between Mathilda and her father. Worry creased her forehead as she noticed the overturned chair. "Oh, child, tell me you did not anger him."

"Mother, I could not help myself."

Maelen went to the larder first and laid the quail on the table. When she returned, she placed the chair upright and sat, turning her attention to Mathilda. "Tell me everything."

Mathilda took a deep breath and explained how Aelle had complained about the porridge and ale. "But the worst," she finished, "was that he insulted the Goddess."

Her mother's eyes were intense, searching. "You are keeping something from me."

Mathilda inwardly flinched. She had disobeyed her mother, broken her promise to keep the peace with her father. "It was nothing, just Father's usual hatefulness."

Her mother's face turned to stone. "No, that is not all. You will tell me, Mathilda. Now."

Mathilda had never been able to lie to her mother, and she wasn't sure what possessed her to try. Her father's evil was clouding her senses. "Very well. Father tried to strike me. I stopped his hand before it reached my face, and it was evident that my power caught him off guard. He said I would pay for my defiance."

Her mother sighed. Her expression turned thoughtful as she leaned back in the chair. "You are fortunate indeed, child. The very fact that you showed your powers to your father may be what saves you from him. You must never speak to him like that again, Mathilda. If he loses control, he may not care about the wrath of the Goddess. He might do more than strike you. Now go take the quail and pluck out their feathers. After that, you may have some porridge."

"Yes, Mother."

THAT NIGHT, Mathilda woke up to her father's voice, shouting from the main room.

"Is that what you teach her while I am absent? To defy her father, threaten me? You despise me as much as she does, only you hide it better."

Her mother's reply was calm and assuring. "I do not teach her defiance. I reprimanded her over her behavior toward you already."

"You lie!"

Mathilda heard the slap and a crash. She jumped out of bed, yanking her tangled nightshift down around her legs, and rushed into the main room. Her mother was splayed on the floor, her burnished hair around her in a wild, tangled mess. The stunned expression on her face was still fresh, and there was a vagueness in her eyes that showed a helplessness Mathilda had never seen before. Her nightshift had ridden up over her knees in the fall, and the rivulet of blood running down her chin from her split lip dotted the front of it.

Her father had never struck her mother before, and a scorching rage swept through Mathilda at his cruel audacity. She rounded on him. "You will *never* lay a hand on my mother."

"Ah, the defiant one comes to defend you." The dying embers in the hearth still lent enough light for Mathilda to see the hatred in his eyes. He was dressed in his usual black attire, which meant he had just gotten home and caught Maelen still awake. "This is between husband and wife. You will not interfere, *Daughter*." He spat the word with a mouthful of disgust.

Maelen pushed herself to her feet, leaning against a corner of the table. "Mathilda, go to bed. Now." The vagueness had left her eyes. She sounded calm, but her expression pleaded for Mathilda to listen.

Mathilda stood up straighter, wishing she could make her own body a shield. "I will not leave you."

"Oh yes, you *will*," her father said. "Or my hand will not be stopped the next time."

Mathilda caught her mother's firm shake of the head, not to

argue. What did she know? Had her father's powers grown? A tingle of waning ran up Mathilda's spine.

"Leave us, Mathilda," her mother softly urged.

Reluctantly, Mathilda turned to go back to her room. Before she could take a step, her father said, "Yes, *witch*. Away with you."

Mathilda's back stiffened. Rage tore through her like a rushing river. She turned around to see her father smiling at her, taunting. That mouth was an ugly, twisted thing. Full of hatred.

Mathilda lost all control. A stool was in her periphery by her father's side. Without taking her eyes off him, she released a burst of her magic into the stool, causing it to hurl toward her father's head. He dodged it right before it made contact.

Enraged, he lunged toward Mathilda with his fist drawn. Mathilda stumbled back, fear tingling in her chest. She felt her father's power rolling off him in filthy, sickening waves. It was strong, and he had been masking it somehow.

"No!" Her mother caught the iron candleholder off the table and struck her husband over the head with it. He stumbled into the table, stunned. A thread of blood ran down his forehead.

His face contorted, red with rage. He swiped at the blood, smearing it in his hair. "You filthy *bitch!*" He raised his hand, fingers curled, as if squeezing some imaginary object in his grip.

Maelen coughed and gasped for air in awful choking heaves. She grabbed at her throat, clawing desperately as a deep red flush spread over her face.

Mathilda rushed at her father, the magic sparking to life in her veins again, but before she could unleash it, he lifted his other arm, and a force she had never felt before slammed her high against the wall and held her there in an iron grip. She had never dreamed he had this kind of power. Anguish burned in her throat.

"Father, *please!* Don't hurt Mother." Her voice was raw, and she nearly choked on her words. "I am sorry. I will never do it again. *Please* let her go."

He merely tightened his grip on the power choking his wife.

Maelen's eyes were wide, her face now purple. The horrible gagging sounds that filled the room were her last attempt to hold onto the life now slipping away.

"Mother," Mathilda sobbed. "I am sorry. I am so sorry I did this to you. I love you. Mother!"

Maelen, her eyes huge with terror, turned from her husband toward Mathilda before falling limp.

A scream ripped from Mathilda's throat. "*No!* You killed her!"

"No, Mathilda." Aelle's voice was a hiss. "*You* killed her. You know that. I warned you that you would pay for your defiance. Perhaps now you will watch your tongue in my presence."

He released his invisible hold over Mathilda. She slid down the wall, helpless. He stepped over her mother's body like she was nothing more than a broken cup and left the house.

As soon as she was free from her father's invisible grip, Mathilda scrambled across the floor and pulled her mother close.

"Come back. Come back to me. *Please* do not leave me," she begged. "I sense your spirit. Come back into your body. Father is gone now. It is safe."

The dying fire popped. Shadows danced across the floor. Mathilda rocked her mother back and forth, smoothing her hair. *Maybe this needs a healer's hand.*

A wool blanket draped from a nearby chair. Mathilda reached for it and balled it up beneath her mother's head, then got to her feet. She hurried to the chest and took out the parchment, quill, and inkpot, and a ribbon, then sat down at the table to write. Her mind felt numb, and the words she needed to relay refused to materialize. She glanced at her mother, then dipped the quill and scribbled the first thing that came to her.

Mother is in need of a healer. Please hurry.

Mathilda

She rolled up the parchment, then tied the ribbon around it before rushing into the wood. Briars tore at her ankles and ripped her clothes, but she barely felt them. When she reached the druid tree, she whispered Katrina's name over the letter. Standing on her toes, she stuffed it into the hollow and prayed to the Goddess to send her swiftest owl, and for Katrina's new powers to be enough to revive her mother.

Returning home to see her mother's body on the floor was a fresh rip to Mathilda's heart. The blood on her lip had long caked, and Mathilda couldn't bear to see her in such a state. She went into the larder to fetch a pitcher of water and a cloth, then returned to clean her mother's body before Katrina arrived.

She dressed Maelen in an emerald-colored tunic with white hawthorn flowers embroidered around the neck, and a matching belt and shoes—all gifts from Philippa on her recent visit. After retrieving a comb and a blanket, Mathilda laid the blanket lovingly over her mother, before settling on the floor and running the comb through her mother's long waves.

Despair and hope flared around the numbness in Mathilda's heart as she worked through the tangles. She combed for hours in the darkness, lost in her misery as the final hearth embers turned to ash, leaving the pale moonlight as her only source of light.

Near midnight, Mathilda heard the call of the owl. She caught up the small stone lamp by the table. "Fire." The flame caught on the wick, and she stepped out into the darkness, unsure what to do. Movement in a tree across the clearing caught her attention. An owl, perched on a low branch, leaped into the air and swooped gracefully toward her. Its talons were curled around a parchment, which it released as it glided overhead. Mathilda caught it and quickly unrolled it, holding the lamp close.

We will be there by dawn.

Katrina

Relief washed over Mathilda. Stepping inside, she placed the lamp on the table and lay down beside her mother, pulling the blanket over them both.

"I do not feel your spirit anymore, Mother." Fear made her throat tight, and her voice cracked with emotion as she took her mother's hand. "I beg you not to leave me. Katrina will be here soon, and all will be right once more."

A tear streaked down Mathilda's cheek, running along the edge of her nose and over her lip as she rested her head against her mother's shoulder. Her eyes fluttered closed, and soon she was asleep.

A KNOCK CAME at the door, jerking Mathilda awake. Her mother's hand felt cold and uncomfortable, and Mathilda released it with alarm. Exhaustion from what little sleep she'd had clouded her mind, and it took a moment to register that it was a knock she had heard. A rush of relief had Mathilda scrambling to her feet. Katrina was here. She would fix everything; she would bring her mother back.

The door swung open, having gone unanswered, and Katherine stepped in ahead of Katrina, carrying a large basket. It slipped from her hand, spilling out various herbs and tonics when she saw Maelen on the floor. Her face went ashen, and she turned to Mathilda with a sharp, panicked tone. "Why did you not say that your mother was dead, child? How did this happen?"

"My father did it," Mathilda replied gravely. "Come, Katrina. I need you to work your healing magic." Mathilda turned anxiously to her mother. "Katrina, you must hurry," Mathilda urged. "My mother's spirit is slipping away beyond reach."

"Maelen!" The voice, sharp with horror, was Leticia's.

Mathilda turned toward it. Ramona lingered by her mother's side, looking pale in her dove-gray tunic.

Leticia stepped into the room. Her hands anxiously bunched the sides of her kirtle as she looked with shock at Maelen. Leticia dragged her gaze to Mathilda, and a tear spilled from her eye. "What has happened to your mother?" she asked, wiping the tear from her jaw.

"My father strangled her," Mathilda impatiently answered. There was no time to explain. She turned back to Katrina. "Katrina, quickly. You must do your part."

"What do you mean?" Leticia asked.

"I want Katrina to heal my mother's body so her spirit can return."

Leticia's expression went from shock to pity. "Oh, you poor child. She cannot do that."

Mathilda glared back. *How could she not understand?* The Goddess herself gave Katrina her powerful healing magic.

"She *will!*" Stalking over, Mathilda grabbed Katrina by the wrist and dragged her across the room, pulling her to the floor. She ignored Katrina's whimper as she lifted her mother's hand. "Do it, Katrina."

"Mathilda, come away from your mother at once," Leticia commanded.

"I will *not*. Not until Katrina has done her part."

A sob broke Katrina's silence. Leticia crossed the room in two steps and gently took hold of Mathilda's shoulders.

"Look at me, child. Your mother is with the Goddess. She is happy there. She is free."

"No... she is here," Mathilda answered in a shrill, desperate voice. "Mother is here with me."

Leticia cupped Mathilda's cheek. Her expression was full of empathy. "Look again, child," she softly said, gazing across her right shoulder.

Ramona and Katherine stood behind them, silent except for the rustling fabric of Katherine's tunic as she rubbed her hand over Katrina's shoulder to soothe her sobbing daughter. Mathilda reluctantly followed Leticia's gaze.

Her mother's radiance was long gone, leaving behind this cold, gray shell of a body. Her eyes that once danced with laughter were glazed and fixed on the ceiling. Leticia was right. Her mother could not come back. The tight knot of grief that had held firm in her chest cracked. It welled up into her throat and broke free in racking sobs.

Ramona hurried to her side. She pushed her skirt out of the way as she crouched and smoothed Mathilda's hair from her tear-dampened face. "I am so very sorry for you, Mathilda. Let me get you away from here. Come and take in some fresh air with me."

Mathilda nodded and took Ramona's hand. They saw Isobel and Annora coming up the path as they stepped outside.

"Mathilda?" Annora said. "Katherine sent a letter that your mother had taken ill. Has she worsened?"

Ramona shook her head, asking her to leave them alone.

Annora hurried into the house. She let out a wail that carried beyond the door, "Maelen! This cannot *be!*"

Isobel gazed through the open doorway, a look of shock slowly registering on her face. There were tears in her eyes when she turned back to the girls. "I am sorry, Mathilda."

Mathilda couldn't answer. She stood numbly, watching as Isobel followed her mother into the house to join the weeping women.

"Do you want to talk about what happened?" Ramona asked.

Mathilda shook her head. Ramona guided her to the wooden bench beneath the window.

"Then let us share silence together."

Time had seemed to stand still from the moment Mathilda stepped outside, despite the sun that had been climbing steadily over the treetops. Her grief tied her to the bench, to Ramona, whose silent presence was like a lifeline, to the clearing, the cottage, and the towering trees beyond the clearing, that offered a quiet peace that had slowly seeped into her heart, easing the worst of her pain. After Regina and Philippa arrived, Mathilda eventually rose from the bench in solemn numbness to join them and the others inside.

"We must bury her," Philippa was saying. She had the look of a woman about to take charge.

Mathilda stopped in the doorway. "We have no shroud to bury my mother in, nor any money to buy one." Her lip trembled. Admitting this to these women—especially Philippa—was mortifying.

Philippa turned. She studied Mathilda for a moment, then stepped past her. The silk of her pale-blue skirts swished around her ankles as she went outside. Several village children played in the field below Mathilda's home.

"You, boy," Philippa called.

A dirty little thing, not much older than seven winters old, thin and sickly-looking, came running to the door.

"Go to the silk merchant. Tell him a lady sent you to purchase a burial shroud—the best one he has. If he has none, go ask the priest."

The boy looked warily toward the doorway where Mathilda stood, fretting with the hem of his dirty sleeve. "Is it for the angry man who lives here?"

Philippa's face turned sad. "No. It is for his wife." She dug into her purse for three coins. "These are for the silk merchant, and this one is for you when you return with the shroud. Hurry back with it as fast as you can, and I will give you two coins."

The boy's eyes bulged, and he nearly stumbled as he darted back toward the village.

Philippa stepped into the house. "Mathilda, dear, go and change into your finest gown. We will give your mother the burial she wanted."

"I will help you," Ramona said. The other girls followed.

Mathilda opened the chest at the foot of her bed and took out the dress she wore to the Beltane festival.

"Here, allow me," Regina offered. She spread it out over the bed, a small comforting smile playing at the edges of her lips as she proceeded to remove Mathilda's tunic.

Ramona helped her into her dress, her presence a strong, silent support, her gaze one of solidarity, as Katrina wrapped a belt around her waist.

"May I?" Isobel asked, reaching for the comb on the small wooden table by the bed.

Mathilda nodded and sat. She felt numb throughout the process, barely feeling the comb as it passed through her hair. After she was dressed, Ramona placed a gold ring on Mathilda's index finger. The setting was a small emerald, raised in a pie-dish bezel, which her mother had given to her upon her sixteenth birthday.

In the months before she had bought the ring, her mother had woven a beautiful tapestry unlike any Mathilda had seen her make before. The colors were rich with birds and flowers that she said would sell quickly to a fine lady. She was right. Her mother used the coin she earned that day to buy the ring. Mathilda's heart stung as she gazed at it.

She absently ran her fingers over the stone as she allowed the pain of the memory to fill her up. She was now as ready as she could be to let her mother go. She made her heavy feet carry her back to the main room.

Philippa and Leticia stood in the doorway. Just outside was the constable, a large, harsh man, whose features tended to stay in a perpetual scowl. He held tight to the boy Philippa had sent to buy the shroud. Behind him was a monk, and several villagers who had followed them to watch the spectacle unfold.

"The boy is telling the truth," Philippa was saying. "Tell the merchant he did not steal the coins. I sent him to buy the shroud. The mistress of this house is dead. She was a friend, and I will see her properly buried." Her tone brooked no argument.

The constable looked briefly affronted. He glanced from Philippa to the boy, releasing him when he could find no reason to detain him further. Philippa dropped the promised coins into the boy's hand, and he darted away.

"If you'll excuse me, lady," the monk said, now occupying the space where the boy had been, "What happened to Maelen Longhurst, if you don't mind?" He had a look of genuine concern, and his eyes were wide with worry.

Leticia turned to Philippa and nodded subtly.

"Her husband murdered her," Philippa answered bitterly.

At this, the constable brightened, angering Mathilda. A few villagers started weeping, and one ran back to the village.

The monk wore a look of shock. "Constable, it seems you are needed after all."

"Aye, Brother Alphonso." His voice sounded gravelly, and he smiled, showing blackened teeth. "I will report this to the bailiff, Lady." He turned to leave without a bow of respect to Philippa or a word of comfort to Mathilda.

Mathilda somehow knew her father would not return. The constable was wasting his time.

"And I must go tell Father Muncey and have Mistress Longhurst's grave prepared," said the monk. "I will return shortly with him," He gave a small bow before turning to go.

Panic seized hold of Mathilda, and she reacted before she could stop herself. "No! My mother will *not* be buried in your grounds."

The monk gave a sharp gasp. He turned, gaping with a horrified, angry expression at Mathilda that made her reel. He quickly recovered. "She *must* have her rites."

Philippa turned abruptly, a disapproving look on her face as her eyes went wide, silencing any retort Mathilda might have. Mathilda shrank beneath the gaze. She hadn't meant any disrespect, but she could not allow her mother to be buried in this village, the place where she was so wrongfully murdered.

Philippa turned back to the monk with a soothing smile. "You must forgive Mathilda, Brother Alphonso. She is beside herself with grief. The priory at Lindston will be giving the rites. Mistress Longhurst's wishes were to be buried there amongst her kin."

Mathilda frowned in confusion, but she kept silent.

"Of course, my lady." The monk gave Mathilda a sympathetic glance. "I will speak to the merchant and see that the shroud is delivered shortly." He turned his gaze to Philippa then. "Forgive the earlier misunderstanding with the constable. The boy has been known to steal." He bowed, and his tonsured head shone beneath the midday sun before he straightened and turned to go.

"Brother," Philippa said, stopping him. "My servant is in the tavern having a quick meal. I need him to return. Would you get word to him on your way through the village? His name is Eldrid Guillaume."

"I will."

Mathilda watched the monk cut across the field, the hem of his coarse brown tunic brushing the grass.

Leticia stepped closer and wrapped her arm across Mathilda's shoulders. "Are you all right, my dear?"

Mathilda nodded. She turned her gaze to Philippa. "I am sorry I spoke out of turn to the monk. I panicked. I could not allow the church to take my mother's body. She has a secret cottage. I want to bury her there."

"We know of the cottage," Philippa said, clasping her fingers together at her waist. "What I told the monk about Lindston Priory was a lie. When you so adamantly refused his mention of rites, I had a feeling you intended to bury Maelen there."

Tears filled Mathilda's eyes. "Yes. Thank you."

A short time later, a man knocked at the door to deliver the burial shroud. Word of Maelen's death had spread beyond Whitsby Village. Many of the peasants her mother had cared for in a tiny village not far from here were gathered outside the house, weeping softly.

Mathilda recognized Milicent Wolford. The child on her hip was alive today thanks to her mother's healing hand. The same for Amos Bradbury, who stood near Milicent. Her mother had cleared his lungs and brought him from his deathbed. Their sorrow gave Mathilda strength.

A small horse-drawn cart came up the field and stopped near the side of the cottage. Mathilda turned just as Fulk slid off the horse. His fair hair was mussed and curled at the ends that hung over his broad shoulders. His eyes were red-rimmed, and his face pinched tight as if he was fighting to control his emotions. The crowd parted for him. Eyes were carefully averted as he approached Mathilda. He roughly cleared his throat.

"I am sorry about your mother," he said in a rough, strained voice. "She was a good woman."

Tears spilled from Mathilda's eyes. She nodded, words refusing to form. The horse whickered, drawing Mathilda's attention.

"Fulk, would you do my mother the honor of transporting her body to her final resting place."

Fulk looked stunned. He shook himself and nodded. "I would be honored."

Mathilda led him inside. Annora stood near her mother's body, tears pooling in her eyes as Katherine ran her hand soothingly over her shoulder. Ramona and the rest of the girls were huddled near the window, watching solemnly.

Fulk stepped further into the room, and his eyes landed on her mother's lifeless body. His face twisted, and he let out an anguished cry. Leticia quickly closed the cottage door, giving him privacy from the onlookers outside. His grief was a knife to Mathilda's heart. Tears streamed down her cheeks. She reached out, gingerly, and placed her palm on Fulk's arm. He seemed startled by her touch, but he covered Mathilda's hand with his own, squeezing it.

Philippa gently cleared her throat. "We must be on our way before dark sets in," she said, brushing her tears away.

Fulk lifted Maelen into his arms, cradling her to his chest. Katherine opened the cottage door for him, and everyone followed him. Philippa's driver had returned. A few others from the peasant village had also gathered; some carried shovels. Philippa ushered Ramona, Mathilda, and Regina to her carriage while Fulk laid

Maelen in the cart. Annora and Katherine climbed in after he had her settled. Leticia and the other girls opted to walk.

Once Fulk was mounted on his horse, Philippa urged Eldrid to start out ahead of him.

Mathilda had never ridden in a carriage. She had only been on a cart once. A thick, green damask curtain covered the side windows. Philippa slid the one on her side back, and Mathilda reached to pull hers aside. She watched Whitsby Village, and its waving inhabitants grow smaller until they disappeared in the distance. The matching damask-patterned cushion she sat on was comfortable enough, but the jostling set Mathilda's teeth on edge as they rolled over hardened ruts, bumping her and Ramona against the wall. Philippa and Regina seemed not to notice.

The track veered away from the intended destination, and Mathilda requested Philippa to halt the procession at the sight of a sprawling yew, Mathilda's landmark for the way to the cottage. With no track wide enough for the carriage, they would have to make the rest of the journey on foot.

Stepping off the carriage, Mathilda noticed the line of mourners from the peasant village. She had not realized they had followed. Tears welled in her eyes at the sight of them.

Once Fulk held her mother secure in his arms, Mathilda set off on the path, stopping only to allow him moments to rest until they finally reached the clearing where her mother's hidden cottage stood. Fear rushed through her. When she came here with her mother, a lifetime ago it seemed, the cottage had been veiled. Now she saw it clearly. Why?

Leticia came to stand beside her. "You can see the cottage," she whispered; not a question. She calmly smoothed the end of her long braid as she gazed ahead, unbothered.

Mathilda turned to her, panicked. "Why is it visible?"

"It is not," Leticia assured her. "Only we can see it. Upon your mother's death, the cottage fell to your care as the new Guardian, enabling you to see it beneath the veil."

Mathilda sighed with relief and instructed those who brought shovels to break ground underneath the old elm tree.

She watched them, numb in her grief, as they toiled to remove the earth until there was finally enough room for Fulk to lay her mother's body in the ground. Her feet ached, and her stomach groaned with hunger, discomforts that reminded Mathilda of her aliveness—stark, compared to the still, lifelessness of her mother's shrouded form being covered with dirt. Her eyes moved to the other peasants lingering along the edge of the wood. Their work-worn clothing and thin forms distracted her from her grief.

One of the gravediggers wiped his hands on his soiled tunic. He glanced back at the mound of dirt, a question lingering in his dark, weary eyes, as he looked between Mathilda and Philippa, as if torn whether formality should default him to address his question to the highborn. He bowed to Philippa, choosing formality. "Might we speak a prayer over the body, lady?"

"Of course." Philippa bowed her head and clasped her hands.

Mathilda followed suit. She barely heard any of the words spoken. Her eyes kept lifting to the dark mound that had swallowed her mother. She was grateful for the "amen" that pulled her attention from the grave.

Fulk lingered by the mound to say a final goodbye. He turned abruptly to Mathilda, anger blazing in his tear-filled eyes, and said, "Know that if the bailiff doesn't bring your father to justice, I will." The welling tears spilled over the rims of his eyes, and he dashed them away.

Mathilda didn't know what to say. She understood his anger, the grief he felt. He cast one last look at the grave before disappearing through the trees.

The folk from the tiny peasant village crowded around Mathilda with looks of sadness and concern. She heard a rattle in Amos Bradbury's chest as he spoke his condolences, and realized he was getting on in years. She became acutely aware that it would now be her responsibility to look after them. Her pity for them caused a strength in her to take root. She would not be at her father's whim. Her fear of him had died with her mother. She would continue on here, carrying out her mother's work.

As the last of the peasants disappeared through the forest to return to their homes, Mathilda noticed dusk settling over the clearing. The birds had long since begun their evening songs and were already growing silent. Leticia placed her hand on Mathilda's arm and pressed it gently.

"We must ready your mother for her journey to the Goddess. Would you lead us inside so we may prepare ourselves for the rites?"

"Of course," Mathilda replied, her voice thick with emotion.

Mathilda gasped when she stepped into the cottage. A strange tingling washed over her skin as if she walked through cobwebs. A presence took up the space of the room, and she choked on a sob. Her mother was here. There was no mistaking her essence.

"Maelen is with us, child," Annora confirmed, running a soothing hand over Mathilda's back.

Mathilda nodded and smiled through her tears.

Leticia took a basket down from the hook and took the scissors from the ledge. "Ramona, you and the girls go clip some yew for a head wreath. Not you, Mathilda." She clipped a stem of chamomile and brought it to Mathilda's lips. "Open."

Mathilda chewed obediently.

"Good girl. It will soothe you."

Katherine crushed hyssop with the pestle, and when she finished, she gestured for Mathilda to come closer. Dipping her first two fingers in the bowl, she smeared the paste in an arc across Mathilda's forehead, and in the old tongue her mother often spoke, Katherine said, "Open the mind so the Voice will speak." She kissed Mathilda's cheek, then rested her palm against it.

"May your mother's spirit guide you from the other side."

Tears welled in Mathilda's eyes, and she squeezed them shut, taking a breath to calm herself.

"We have finished the yew crown, Mother," Ramona said.

"Ah, Good. Place it in my basket." Leticia clipped a sprig of hyssop and dropped it in with the wreath while Philippa placed a clipping of rosemary in Mathilda's hair.

"Rosemary," she said, smiling through tear-filled eyes at Mathilda. "For remembrance."

The cool night air was charged with energy as they stepped outside, heading toward the elm. The chamomile had dulled the sharp edge of Mathilda's emotions until she felt she could at least bear them.

Maelen's sisters stretched forth their hands, and Mathilda's eyes widened as the mound of dirt was pushed aside, revealing her mother's silk-shrouded form. Katherine bent, her rich brown hair tumbling over her shoulder as she reached into the hole. She swept it back and pulled open the burial shroud. Leticia placed the yew crown on Maelen's head, and Annora took the hyssop sprig and laid it over Maelen's lips. They each kissed her forehead before stepping back.

"Come, Mathilda," Leticia said. "Speak the words upon your heart."

Mathilda nodded and stepped closer. A gasp stole her voice as she looked at her mother's body. The last time Mathilda had seen her, she was pale and gray. Now, her form was vibrant. It looked as though she were merely sleeping and not... Mathilda refused to say the word. Not even in her mind. The tears that had been pooling in her eyes spilled down her cheeks. She dropped to her knees and took her mother's hand.

"How will I go on without you? Who will guide me now? I am lost without you." Fear and guilt tore at her chest, and Mathilda's sobs turned to a wail. "I am so sorry, Mother. I was not a good daughter in the end. Because of me, you are dead. If only I had listened to you."

She felt a hand on her shoulder and started up. Leticia knelt beside her and brushed Mathilda's hair away from her face, wiping her tears, a motherly gesture that Mathilda desperately needed. Leticia's expression was sympathetic, and the wisdom in her eyes captured Mathilda's attention.

"Child, you are not the cause of your mother's death. Aelle killed her, and he will pay for what he did." Her tone was hard and promising, then her face softened again, and her voice was full of tenderness. "You must bury this guilt with your mother. It is too heavy a burden to carry. Close your eyes. Do you feel your mother's presence?"

Mathilda's damp lashes fanned across her cheeks as she focused on her mother's spirit.

"What do you sense?" Leticia asked.

Warmth spread through Mathilda's chest, and she laughed despite her grief. "Love. I feel her love."

"Yes. Your mother loved you more than anything, and she will always be with you. You are not alone, child."

Mathilda smiled weakly and pressed her mother's hand to her lips. "I love you and will never forget your words. Guide my path when the darkness comes, and the choices are difficult to make on my own. Lend me your strength when I feel I can't carry on. Show me signs when I am too blind to see."

She released her mother's hand and placed it atop the other one, resting below her breasts. She kissed her forehead and stood, feeling strength now. Ramona and the others moved close to Mathilda, comforting her as their mothers replaced the shroud and formed a circle by the grave. Their voices came clear and strong, and Mathilda felt the power in their words.

"Loving Mother, Goddess of our beloved sister, Maelen: Guide her soul across the veil and into your loving arms. Let her join those who came before, sharing in their wisdom, and place her soul as a light upon the sky as a reminder that she is always with us."

A bright light enveloped the grave, and Mathilda had to shield her eyes. When it faded, the women lowered their arms. The dirt that had been removed slid into the hole, mounding over the top.

"What will you do, Mathilda?" Annora asked.

Mathilda glanced around the clearing. She took a deep inhale and released it, then she raised her arms over her head, and the veil that hid her mother's cottage lifted.

"I will live here in my mother's cottage. I will not conceal myself in it. The veil will be lifted for as long as I remain here."

"What if your father comes for you?" Ramona asked.

"He will not. I sensed it the night he murdered my mother and so callously walked out. My father is a smart man. He will not return near here, knowing that he brazenly committed murder. Besides, I know his hatred of me and his fear of the Goddess in me. No, he is finished with my line."

"Shall we collect your belongings, then?" Philippa asked.

"I would like my mother's loom. Nothing else. My mother is the only thing of value to me, and I have her here with me," Mathilda said, looking toward the fresh mound of dirt.

Philippa nodded. "I will have it loaded and brought here."

"Let us help you get settled in," Annora suggested.

"No, thank you. I wish to be alone." She hated to turn away their kindness, but the day's events had wrung her out, and she wanted time to process her emotions.

"Very well, we will come to you on the morrow. Good night, Mathilda," Leticia said, placing a kiss on her forehead.

"Good night." Going inside, Mathilda lit all the candles with a lift of the hand. She leaned against the door, noticing the room for the first time today. Everything looked as she remembered. The vials for potions sat neatly along the window ledge. A few herbs were drying beside the mortar and pestle, waiting for their time to be used.

Over by the table, Mathilda noticed the quill and parchment right where her mother had left them the day she wrote the letter. She picked up the quill and held it to her breast. A fat tear dropped down onto the parchment with a loud plip. She placed the quill back on the table and went into her mother's small sleeping chamber. A blanket that she must have made lay on the bed.

Mathilda vaguely remembered it from her childhood. As she pulled off her tunic, she realized this room looked familiar, as if she had dreamed it long ago. She placed her tunic across the back of a chair and crawled into bed.

Tiny beads and shells hung from the ceiling above her, stirring a distant memory. Her mother must have brought her here as a child. As sleep claimed her, she wondered what else was concealed in her memory from this place.

4

———————

irdsong rose like a chorus across the clearing as a gentle light pushed the darkness from the room. Mathilda slowly stirred, and an awful heaviness settled in her heart. When she opened her eyes, the pain of her mother's death came rushing back, shattering the respite from grief that she'd had during sleep. A sharp, sudden ache in her stomach reminded Mathilda that she had not eaten yesterday. She wished she had thought to at least bring some food from her former home. She would have to find a way to build up her larder soon.

Pulling on her tunic, Mathilda fetched one of the baskets from the ceiling hook in the main room and went outside to see what she could forage. Her eyes fell on the mound of fresh dirt as she approached the old elm. Her breath quickened, and the rekindled pain of loss brought tears to her eyes. Mathilda dashed them away with the heel of her hand, releasing a shaky breath. Her mother was watching over her now. Mathilda did not want to cause her any sadness in the afterlife.

"Good morning, Mother," Mathilda greeted her as she passed. "I trust you slept well in the arms of the Goddess."

She cleared her throat, trying to control her emotions. It was easier to imagine her mother enjoying her new life than to contend with her absence from this one.

Deeper in the wood, Mathilda noticed a patch of sorrel and bent to pluck the young leaves. As she stood, a strange, melodic chime of laughter echoed through the trees. It seemed to come from every direction at once. She remained still for a moment, listening. A flash of red through the distant trees caught her eye.

"Is someone there?" Mathilda called.

There was no response. Whatever she had seen had gone.

When she returned to the clearing, Mathilda saw Regina, Philippa, Annora, and Isobel coming through the wood behind the cottage, all of them carrying baskets. Philippa shone like the sun in her yellow gown and gold embellishments, and compared to the others in their simpler dresses, she looked like a queen.

The girls waved when they saw Mathilda, and she waited by the stone wall at the edge of the cottage to greet them as Annora led their little procession closer. She was a tall woman. She would have made an imposing ruler with her height and her dark, penetrating eyes, Mathilda mused, recalling her regal heritage.

"Good morning, child," Annora said, kissing Mathilda in greeting. "We've brought food and supplies for you."

"Yes." Philippa looked Mathilda up and down as if expecting her to be thinner already. "You missed supper yesterday. You must be famished."

Mathilda's empty stomach groaned at the thought of food. She smiled gratefully at the women. "How kind of you. I am hungry. I just returned from foraging," she added, looking at the heap of greens in her basket, now wilted and unappealing to her.

"You save those for another time," Annora said, noticing Mathilda's frown of distaste. Come. Let us get inside."

At the table in the main room, Mathilda's guests removed the linens covering their baskets and pulled out the contents. They had brought jars filled with brown lentils and barley, greens, onions, and leeks. There were tarts wrapped in waxcloth, berries, a salt-cured quail, and two rabbits. Mathilda gazed at these items that filled the table, and gratitude flooded her heart.

Annora gave her a large green ceramic jar, heavy with salt. "This should last you a while and leave you plenty for curing meats."

"We brought some dresses that should fit you, too," Regina added. She opened a large sack and pulled them out. One was a practical tunic in blue-gray linen with a matching belt; two were more fitted linen kirtles in yellow and dark green. The fourth was a fine, pale-blue kirtle, its neck, sleeves, and hem embellished with white and yellow flowers. The belt had the same floral pattern. Mathilda ran her fingers over the threads of the flowers and lifted her teary gaze to Regina.

A beaming smile lit up Regina's face. "I thought you might enjoy it for feast days."

"Thank you, Regina. They're lovely."

"And these are for you as well," Isobel said, opening her sack. "Pattens to wear over your shoes on rainy days. Mother and I bought them at the market on our way here." She brushed the ringlets of curls from her face that had escaped her long, thick braid and placed the protective wooden overshoes beside the dresses.

Mathilda wiped away the tear that rolled down her cheek. "I cannot thank you enough for all this. My mother's lessons in weaving are instilled in my brain. Once I sell some things, I promise to repay you all."

"Nonsense," Philippa replied, waving her hand and dismissing Mathilda's offer. "You are the daughter of our beloved sister. She would want us to take care of you, as she would have done for any of our daughters."

Mathilda's tears ran freely, and she didn't trust herself to speak. She nodded in response.

"Oh, my dear girl," Annora soothed. Her expression turned soft and motherly as she came around the table and embraced Mathilda.

"I know this is difficult for you, but we will help you through your time of grief."

Mathilda welcomed her comfort. She buried her face into Annora's shoulder. "I don't know what I'll do without her."

"You are strong, like Maelen," Annora said, pulling back to gaze at Mathilda. She smoothed a hand over Mathilda's hair and smiled. "You have kindness and a heart full of love, just as she did. Many will help you in this time of sorrow."

"We will all do what we can for you, Mathilda," Philippa added. "Whatever you need, ask it of us, and it is yours. Now, dry your eyes and eat this," she said, handing one of the tarts to Mathilda.

Mathilda unwrapped the waxen cover to reveal the tart and took a bite, savoring the saffron-herbed cheese on her tongue. "Thank you. It is a comfort to have all of you here. It keeps my mind from being idle."

"Good." Annora smiled. "Finish that, and then we'll help you put the supplies in your larder."

While she ate, Isobel peered into Mathilda's basket of wilted herbs. "The next time you forage, cast a spell to keep whatever you find fresh. Just imagine it staying how it looked when you first plucked it and send your magic out into whatever it is you want to keep fresh. Mother and I do this often."

"I will do that. Thank you."

When she finished, Mathilda went to collect the items on the table. "Were any of you in the eastern wood this morning? That is where I had gone to forage."

"No, we came west," Annora replied. "Why do you ask?"

"I heard a woman laughing when I was foraging." Mathilda's hands stilled around the jar of lentils as she recalled the strange laughter. "I could not tell where she was. Her voice seemed to be the wind, coming from everywhere."

Concern flashed in Annora's eyes. "Did you see anything?"

"Only a glimpse of red, too far away to tell what it was."

Philippa laughed. "It was probably some village woman in a secret lover's tryst."

"Maybe." Mathilda frowned. Her intuition nagged at her that it was something more troubling.

Philippa's eyes were serious now. "What are you thinking?"

Mathilda's thoughts turned back to her time in the wood. "I don't know. I sensed something along the wind that was not quite right. It was the way the laughter felt, how it somehow surrounded me. I can't explain it really, but it left me uneasy."

"Perhaps you should raise the veil back up, Mathilda," Annora urged. Regina and Isobel nodded in agreement. "Especially since your father has turned to darkness."

"I will *not* cower to him," Mathilda said. "He will not have a hold over me in any way."

From the doorway, someone spoke. "Good day, Sisters."

The sudden greeting startled Mathilda. She turned and saw Katherine and Katrina. They also arrived bearing baskets. Mathilda greeted them and invited them inside.

Katherine's dark-blue tunic swished around her ankles as she carried her basket over to the table.

"I see you are well on your way to having a stocked larder," she said, looking pleased at the items spread over the table. "This will also help. We have brought mushroom and onion tarts and spices for your cookery. Plenty for your pottage." Her wooden bracelets clacked together as she pulled the items from the basket.

"I am truly blessed. Thank you, Katherine. You too, Katrina." Mathilda noticed Katrina looked well. The olive-colored tunic she wore brought out the green in her eyes and added brightness to her cheeks, a vast improvement to how pale and wan she looked the previous day, no doubt brought on by Mathilda's behavior. Guilt suddenly ate at her.

"I fear I treated you dreadfully yesterday. Can you forgive me?"

Katrina reached out to hug her. "Of course, I forgive you. You'd just lost your mother."

Mathilda looked around at all the women in the room. She had lost the person she loved most in the world, and it had ripped a gaping hole in her heart, but these women were slowly stitching it back together again, and she felt space in her heart opening for them —a sisterly love she had not known before, as she looked toward the girls, and she was, in a way, a daughter again to their mothers. Mathilda squeezed Katrina's hand. "Thank you. All of you."

"Can we help you put these away?" Katrina asked, gesturing to the table and its contents.

"Yes. We were about to start this task before you arrived."

The girls made quick work of putting the dresses away and sorting and shelving the lentils and spices, while their mothers made room for the rest of the items.

A loud crash came from outside the cottage, as they were finishing, startling everyone. Mathilda nearly dropped the jar of salt in her hands. Everyone quickly set down what they held and rushed outside.

Beyond the door was an overturned pushcart. One of the two wheels had come off and had rolled past the cart and stopped against the stone wall. A shovel and hoe lay to the side of the cart, a mattock beside them with the handle pointing upright. A multitude of seedling pots lay on their sides, and Ramona was gathering them up.

The back of her dark-gray tunic had a swath of mud indicating she had fallen—more than once, by the look of it. As Leticia turned to heave the large cart upright, Mathilda noticed a gaping tear in the hem of her tunic. It dragged beneath her heels as she moved to pick up another pot. Ramona straightened when she saw everyone gathered in the doorway. She brushed aside a section of her hair that had escaped her braid, leaving a dark swipe of dirt across her cheek.

"Leticia?" Philippa said, aghast. "What goes on here?"

Leticia straightened with a loud huff. Her mud-streaked apron hung loosely and had twisted around her side. She had dirt smudges on her face and hands, and her hair stood out in disarray with bits of leaves in the strands.

"It seems I cannot push a cart through the forest. This is the second time I have overturned this wretched thing." She kicked the wooden wheel, then cried out in pain.

A giggle bubbled up in Mathilda's throat as she looked at Ramona and her mother's disheveled appearances, and the cart leaning heavily on its side with its missing wheel. Before she knew it, she was laughing out loud. Isobel and Katrina giggled, prompting Regina and their mothers to join in. Leticia took in the scattered mess and gave a loud cackle.

Mathilda's laughter built until her stomach ached and she doubled over, tears streaming down her face, gasping for air through her hysterics. But her joy quickly turned into sorrow. Her mother should be here. She would have thoroughly enjoyed this wildly outlandish moment with her sisters. Before Mathilda knew it, she was sobbing. Her knees gave way, and she crumpled to the ground.

As soon as she could, she caught her breath. "I am sorry." She wiped her raw eyes on her sleeve. "I did not mean to darken the moment."

Leticia came around the cart and crouched. She cupped Mathilda's face with her hands, and Mathilda sensed she was thinking the same thing about her mother. Leticia's eyes, full of empathy and grief, conveyed the words she seemed unable to speak.

"Come see what I've brought," Leticia gently said, helping Mathilda up. On their way to the cart, she bent to pick up a bottle of wine that had fallen out and handed it to Mathilda after brushing off the dirt.

The rest of the items Ramona had hastily placed back in the cart were a cluttered mess. There were shovels and digging tools—the handles sticking out in all directions, and various seeds and sprouts in pots. There was a woad-dyed wool blanket that someone had refolded, but missed the leaf caught on the side.

"What is all this, Sister?" Annora asked.

"We are going to start Mathilda a proper garden. I could not sleep last night for worrying about the child starving to death."

Annora threw up her hands, sending the silver bracelets on her left arm jangling down to her elbow. "Oh, good heavens, Leticia. You knew we were coming this morning to look after her. She wasn't going to starve in one night."

Leticia sniffed, ignoring the bite in her sister's words. "Be that as it may. Come along, ladies, we have work to do, and the day is nearly wasted. That includes you as well, Philippa. You are not above working."

Philippa scoffed. "I have never claimed to be above hard work," she said haughtily. "And I take offense to your remark." The hem of her fine, silk gown kicked up over the tops of her slippers as she stalked over and yanked a shovel from the cart with a pale, delicate hand.

Ramona caught Mathilda's eye and flashed a tiny grin. Mathilda couldn't help smiling back.

By sundown, Mathilda was exhausted. The garden her mother had once kept beyond the side of the cottage had hardened from disuse, with weeds thriving where plants once grew. Now, thanks to good weeding and a fresh turn of the soil, onions, leeks, and cabbage filled the left side of the garden; beets, parsnips, and radishes, in the middle; and beans, on the right. Her back ached, and the shovel's rough handle had raised blisters on her palms, but it was worth it. The great mother would nurture the seedlings until the turning of the wheel brought about harvest time.

Mathilda and the other girls gathered the tools and set them against the wall. Their clothes were all sweat-stained and filthy, and as she looked from them to their mothers, who were standing near the garden, looking over their hard work, her heart swelled with gratitude for their selfless care that had gotten her through the past two days.

"Oh, my dress! Look at me," Philippa moaned.

Mathilda's gaze turned to Philippa. The bright-yellow gown she had arrived in was streaked in dirt from knee to hem, and dirty hand-prints marred both sides of her hips where she had wiped her hands throughout the day. Her shoes were a disgrace. There was no trace of yellow left on them now. Mathilda tried not to giggle as she noticed Philippa's hair. Stray pieces had pulled from the coiled braids at the sides of her head, and dirt was caked through the pale strands where she had tried to smooth them from her face.

"Oh, woe, woe. The princess has soiled her dress!" Leticia mimed a swoon, wrist to forehead. "I am certain you said earlier that work was not beneath you."

Philippa glared at Leticia. She reached down at her feet, picked something up, and flung it.

Mathilda heard her own gasp echoed from the others as the clod of mud slid down the side of Leticia's face. Regina's fingers flew to her lips, and Ramona gaped in shock at her mother.

"You will pay dearly for that," Leticia said through clenched teeth.

Mathilda shared a nervous glance with Katrina. The rest of the girls and their mothers looked on in stunned silence. Leticia took a pot of dirt and lunged toward Philippa with it, but at a slight flick of Philippa's wrist, Leticia's feet flew out from under her, sending her crashing to the ground on her bottom. "Oh, you... You *devil!*"

Philippa barked a laugh. "I have been called worse."

Leticia's jaw clenched so hard that Mathilda was sure she had cracked a tooth. Her eyes narrowed as she watched Philippa laugh. She flicked her wrist, returning the favor, and Philippa landed hard on the ground beside her.

"How *dare* you!" Philippa shrieked.

"Sisters!" Katherine shouted over their banter. "Have you taken leave of your senses? You should be ashamed." She gazed at the two women like a disapproving mother.

The clearing fell silent, save for the crickets humming in the deepening twilight.

The indignation that had hardened Leticia's features melted

away. She wiped the mud from her face and eyed Philippa. "I am sorry, Sister. If your dress wasn't a mess before, I'm afraid it is now."

Philippa's chin lifted, a practiced habit that looked ridiculous in her current bedraggled state, but she caught herself. A slow grin spread over her face. She seemed almost girlish and carefree. Mathilda felt she was seeing Philippa for the first time.

"I am sorry, too." Philippa lifted a muddied section of her hair and let it drop. "Look at us." She gave a melodic, natural laugh, instead of her usual practiced one. "What would Maelen say?"

Leticia pushed to her feet and reached out her hand to help Philippa up. "She would have doubled over with laughter at the sight of us," Leticia replied, looking wistfully toward the grave. "How I wish she were here to laugh at us."

The women's sad gazes turned toward the mound beneath the elm. Mathilda's gaze followed. She felt Isobel's hand clasp hers, and she gave a squeeze of thanks for steadying her emotions as the women joined them at the wall.

Regina scoffed as she eyed her mother. "Very uncivilized."

"Yes, Daughter, entirely uncivilized." Philippa winked, and Regina's mouth dropped open in surprise. "Please bring the soap that I brought for Mathilda. It appears we all need it."

Behind the cottage, a stream trickled peacefully below the slope, feeding the upper part of a small pond Mathilda had discovered on her way to forage earlier. As she led everyone toward it, she felt a weariness that made her long for her bed.

Isobel stepped alongside Mathilda when she reached the edge of the pond. She gazed at the water with an unreadable expression. "It's bound to be cold."

"Yes," Mathilda answered, watching the stream merge into the pond. She could imagine how cold the water would feel with no sun to warm her.

"You girls hurry and undress to your skins," Leticia said. "After you bathe, your clothing will need to be scrubbed." She bent to pick up a broken limb. "We'll build a fire to stave off the chill while you bathe." She used her foot to break the limb and tossed it on the ground near the water's edge, then went to gather more kindling.

Annora, Katherine, and Philippa found several large pieces of wood beyond the trees. They piled them with the limb Leticia had already placed, and Katherine stretched her palm toward the stack. A plume of smoke billowed up as a flame caught on the wood.

Katrina was the first to undress. She picked up the soap and rushed past everyone, jumping in. She gasped at the cold and quickly worked a lather over her face. The water rippled around her bare shoulders, cast in shades of indigo and orange as it caught the night shadows and light from the fire.

Mathilda peeked at the other girls. If they were uncomfortable undressing in front of one another, they didn't show it. She was grateful for the deepening twilight as she let her tunic drop. She felt terribly exposed standing in nothing but her skin for all to see.

Isobel and Ramona's naked forms darted past. "You may as well get it over with," Ramona called over her shoulder before sloshing into the water.

"She's right," Regina said, removing her dress. She had already let her hair out of its braid, and it tumbled in a heap over her shoulders as she bent to remove her shoes. She straightened and caught Mathilda's hand, and before Mathilda could dig in her heels, Regina had pulled her in.

Mathilda shrieked from the chill bite of the stream. She heard Katrina laugh behind her as she walked out far enough for the water to give her enough modesty until it was her turn with the soap.

"You'll get used to it," Katrina said.

"Quick! Give me the soap," Regina urged. "I am freezing."

Ramona passed it over. Regina started a lather in her hair and gave it to Mathilda to use.

Mathilda noticed the women along the bank as she and the girls passed the soap around. Their light conversation carried across the water as they leisurely undressed, their movements slow and graceful. None of them showed a hint of discomfort over their nakedness, and as they stepped into the water, the chill failed to disturb them. These women had a certain grace about them—a light, something indescribable that Mathilda recognized. She had seen it in her mother, too. She averted her eyes and put her attention on bathing before the tears could come.

"Your mother used to come out here in the dead of winter," Katherine said suddenly, looking at Mathilda. She ran the cake of soap languidly up her arm, the ends of her long hair fanning across the water like brown sea grass. She made the act of bathing a ritual, the way she took her time running the soap over her body in slow, purposeful motions.

"Maelen would strip bare and plunge in this water no matter the weather," Katherine continued. "The five of us came here often," she said, looking across her shoulder toward her sisters. They smiled fondly at the memory.

"Yes. When we were younger and times were less dangerous for us witches to gather," Leticia said, taking the soap. "Though I never could stand the frigid water like Maelen."

A smile touched Mathilda's lips at the thought of her mother braving the pond in the dark months. "The cold never did bother Mother."

"No," Katherine agreed. Her eyes turned far away as if she were recalling a memory, and Mathilda wished she knew everything these women knew of her mother.

They finished bathing and used the last of the soap to wash their dresses.

"I will bring you more soap, Mathilda," Philippa said once they had finished and stepped out of the water. She carried her dress over toward the fire and shook it out. "Everyone, stand near me."

Mathilda moved in closer with the others, a pool of water gathering around her feet from her dripping tunic. Philippa quickly reached out as if to grab something. Mathilda felt her tunic tug; it suddenly felt lighter. Philippa flicked her wrist, and an arc of water pulled from each dress and splashed over the fire. A thick plume of smoke rose, and an angry hiss came as the fire winked out. It happened so fast that Mathilda could only gape in surprise.

"There was no time to dry them," Philippa said in explanation. "It is late, and we still must eat."

They quickly dressed and trudged up the slope to the cottage. Darkness shrouded the inside, swallowing the objects in the room that Mathilda had yet to familiarize herself with. She smelled nettle as she stepped through the doorway. Glancing up, she saw the shadowy silhouette of a sprig of nettle hanging over the door. She had not noticed it before. Her mother must have hung it to ward off harmful spirits.

Mathilda moved carefully through the darkness as she eased around the table toward the hearth. She lit a fire, and the room seemed to come alive as the light grew brighter, chasing the darkness into the corners. Shadows from the dancing flames rippled across the stone, making the walls look as if they were breathing. Mathilda smiled. It was a comforting thought imagining the cottage as something sentient.

The women moved around the room now that there was light to see by.

"Do you mind if we help ourselves to your larder?" Katherine asked. "I thought we might put on some lentils."

"Of course," Mathilda said. "Take anything you'd like. I will help you prepare the meal."

"No," Katherine said, holding up a hand and smiling warmly at Mathilda. "You and the girls sit down and rest. Let my sisters and me cook for you."

Mathilda didn't know what to say. She was not used to being doted upon to such extremes. She nodded gratefully to the women and sat at the table with their daughters. As she scooted her chair up beside Ramona, she realized there were exactly five chairs at the table. The sixth one rested by the hearth. She imagined her mother sitting here once with her sisters, and her eyes fell on the girls sitting near her. Isobel and Ramona were talking amongst themselves, their voices soft and tired, while Katrina braided Regina's hair. Would they gather here with her someday?

As the hearth flames burned lower and the soup had finished cooking, the girls gathered on the floor near the fire, allowing their mothers to sit at the table.

"We had a productive day," Leticia remarked. She spooned some broth into her mouth and swallowed. "I am pleased you can now care for yourself, Mathilda."

"Thank you, Leticia. I don't know what I would have done without you—without all of you."

"We will ensure you have food until harvest time," Annora promised. "In the meantime, do what you can with your herbs and weaving for trade in the village."

"I will."

As Mathilda finished her soup, she looked around the room and recalled the first time her mother had brought her here. She had felt almost enthralled by the cottage then. She had felt the magic her mother had imbued into this place. Even now, it settled around her like an enchantment, and she wondered if a part of her mother's magic would always belong here or if it would fade with time. Her thoughts turned to her father then. It felt as if a blackened storm cloud had passed over her mind, choking out any light or joy.

"What is the matter?" Ramona asked. "You look troubled?"

Her comment drew everyone's focus.

Mathilda stood and placed her bowl on a ledge. She turned toward the women who sat at the table, looking at her with concern.

"What's going to happen to my father? It is for the four of you to decide, isn't it?" She unconsciously picked at the edge of her cuticle, letting her hands drop by her sides when she realized what she was doing.

"It is for the Goddess to decide," Philippa corrected, leaning back in her chair. Her expression suddenly looked troubled. All the women did. Mathilda wondered what had suddenly shaken them.

"Do not worry about this matter," Leticia said, her tone

comforting and motherly. "This is a matter between the Goddess and us. She will show us the way when the time is right. For now, you settle into your new life, and should you have any worries, give them to the Goddess. She will shelter you, Mathilda. Now, let us clean up and leave you to get your rest."

As everyone got up to clear away the mess from dinner, Mathilda couldn't help but feel a sense of unease settle over her. The way these powerful Guardians had looked when she asked about her father... Something had worried them. Leticia had quickly tried to dismiss it, but Mathilda felt it in her gut; something terrible was coming.

5

____

The morning sun streamed through the little window over the table, highlighting dust motes drifting lazily in the rays. It had been three weeks since Maelen's death. Mathilda's emptiness and grief had lost their sharp edges, replaced by a dull ache that sometimes overtook her when she least expected it. She had kept outside mostly, weeding the garden and spending time in nature, where she gained most of her peace. The first week had been the hardest, but day by day, she found she could bear it.

Gazing at the dust motes, Mathilda suddenly had a mind for cleaning. She took the rush mats outside for a beating and sprinkled them with fleabane and lavender. They were threadbare in places, but she didn't know if she could come up with the materials to make new ones. Sighing, she slid the mats back into place and went into the bedroom to change the linen.

Something under the edge of the bed caught her eye as she removed the mattress. One of the stones on the floor was darker and did not sit flush with the others around it. It shifted when Mathilda pushed her foot against it. Curious, she lifted it.

Hiding beneath, in a shallow hole dug into the earth, was an ornate wooden box with intricate carvings and symbols along its edges. Mathilda laid the stone aside, carefully pulled the box from its hiding place, and placed it on the bed. It was surprisingly heavy for its small size. Mathilda raised the lid and gasped. Gold and silver coins filled it to the brim—so many that, without a lid to corral them, a few spilled over the edge.

Her mother had never mentioned anything about the box, let alone that they had so much wealth. A small rolled parchment, tied with a scrap of green ribbon, lay atop the coins. Mathilda removed the ribbon and unrolled the parchment to see her mother's flowing script.

My dear child, if you are reading this, I am no longer with the living. I planned to tell you about this box upon your eighteenth birthday. I have kept its existence secret for fear that your father would find it before you could protect it.

The box is enchanted. For every coin that you spend, one will replace it. It is imperative that you do not use this money for anything other than dire situations. If you draw attention to your spending, you will be found out for the witch that you are and burned, so take care of what you use it for. You must continue our line.

Remember those who cannot care for themselves. Your lessons in weaving and blending herbs for healing tonics will come in handy to earn a living to help them. Never forget what I have taught you and remain the kind young woman you are meant to be. You have been the greatest joy of my life. No mother could be prouder of her child than I am of you.

Your loving mother,
Maelen

Tears streamed down Mathilda's face as she hugged the letter to her chest. The bitter sting of her mother's absence renewed. She allowed herself a brief moment of misery, wiped her tears away, tucked the letter back in the box, and returned it to its hiding place. Replacing the stone, Mathilda closed her eyes, summoned her magic, and set an intention: Anyone whose eyes landed upon the matching stones would see nothing out of the ordinary. How they'd survived many winters without going hungry was now clear. Maelen had been clever in selling her wares in the village and tending to the poor. No one had suspected anything.

AT MIDDAY, Mathilda sat down to eat a mushroom tart. She longed to do something creative that would lift her spirits. She looked toward the window, and an idea came to her. She pictured a simple woolen tapestry to keep out the winter chill. Perhaps it would be dyed blue and have a floral pattern. She wrote a short letter and set out for the druid tree.

The day was warm, with gathering clouds slowly blocking out a brilliant azure sky. Mathilda crossed the clearing and took a small foot path that was nearly hidden and followed it through the trees. It would take her less than half the time to reach the druid tree now than it did when she lived in the village, something she was grateful for.

The wood was quieter than usual as Mathilda approached the old tree. There was no birdsong or creatures rustling through vegetation. *Odd.* She scanned her surroundings carefully before dropping her letter into the hollow and whispering Philippa's name.

The odd stillness seemed to follow Mathilda on her return walk.

She kept keen eyes and sharp ears on her surroundings. The broad path eventually branched off to a less-traveled one, and Mathilda felt better knowing she was nearly back to the safety of the cottage.

A twig snapped somewhere away in the trees. Mathilda spun around. In the distance, she made out the figure of a woman, wearing a white dress and having the most startling shade of red hair Mathilda had ever seen. She was too far to make out any other features. Mathilda raised her hand to wave, but stopped as the woman's gaze sent a chill down her spine. They stared at each other for several moments before Mathilda turned away and hastened home.

When she reached the cottage door, Mathilda turned and scanned the trees, still a bit shaken from the woman's strange energy. Seeing nothing, she closed the door and set about preparing a stew for supper. It had been several days since she'd had a visitor. Leticia and Ramona had dropped by to check on her and left more supplies. Leticia promised she and her sisters would not smother Mathilda so much in the coming weeks, and, although Mathilda enjoyed being alone, she wished for their soothing presence after what she had just encountered in the wood.

That night as she readied for sleep, Mathilda heard the owl's call cut through the steady pattering of rain. Donning her shoes, she wrapped her cloak around her nightdress and set out into the rain. The clearing was dark and quiet. She felt a prickle of unease as she remembered her encounter with the strange woman. Not sensing the woman's energy, Mathilda let the unease drop away.

A large brown owl swept from a towering oak by the forest's edge, carrying a rolled parchment in its talons. Swooping over her, it released the roll, apparently enchanted to stay dry despite the rain, before disappearing into the darkness. Mathilda caught the scroll and scurried back home. After lighting a candle, she read the message.

Mathilda,

I received your letter. I will send my servant to

meet you by the well in Whitsby Village at midday tomorrow. I think you will be pleased with the quality. There is no need to pay him. Thank you for the offer.

Philippa

Mathilda smiled and went to her bed. Tomorrow, she would begin weaving the tapestry.

~

THE SUN WAS NEARLY OVERHEAD when the buildings of Upper Whitsby came into sight. As the trees thinned toward the village outskirts, Mathilda saw her old home. It looked abandoned. The door gaped open like an empty mouth. Mathilda peered inside; she saw the place had been pillaged, most likely by their neighbors. The table and chairs were gone, along with all the cooking utensils that had hung over the hearth. Her father's chest and all his potion bottles had also disappeared, although he likely had sent someone to fetch those. By the look of dirt and piled leaves gathered in the doorway, her father hadn't returned since the day he... Mathilda cut the thought short. It hurt too much to linger there. She backed away from the door and forced herself onward.

Making her way to the center of the village, Mathilda noticed many guarded glances cast her way. Whether they were looks of guilt over clearing out her old home, or the uncomfortable glances one sometimes got after a loved one had passed, she could not say.

A large square stood at the heart of the village. Merchant vendor stalls with canopies over their tables ringed the perimeter. They sold foods, pottery, textiles, leather, and other goods. Folks crowded around, trading or browsing wares. At the bustling square's center was the well. Several women waited by its stone base to fill their buckets. Philippa's servant had yet to arrive. Feeling somehow exposed, Mathilda stood off to the side, tucked against a building, out of sight but keeping her eyes on the well.

Just then, the Angelus bell rang: three strikes from the large church bell with a deep, sonorous tone that lingered in the space between strikes. A hush settled over the square as the villagers either paused to lower their heads or knelt for prayer before the next three tolls came. Remembering what her mother had taught her—to show reverence, blend in, and to remember the love, compassion, and inclusiveness in Christ's teachings despite the fear in the message that was often spread to them—Mathilda fell to her knees. The haunting pauses between the bell-strikes settled over her with unease, and she lifted her eyes to the large, rough-hewn stone church opposite her hiding place, and the graveyard that would have taken her mother's body had Philippa not lied. Its shadow cast long across the square, stopping short of where she knelt, a clear reminder that she was apart, that she was different.

As the bells stopped and the villagers returned to what they had been doing before prayer, Mathilda saw a man working his way through the crowd. As he drew closer, she noticed his green tunic and brown hose were crafted from quality wool. His coat and leather shoes were also clean. He seemed well-fed and clean-looking. This must be Philippa's servant. He stopped by the well, looking around, and she moved forward to meet him.

"You are Mathilda?" There was a keen intelligence behind his eyes as he waited for her to answer.

"I am," she replied, noticing that he was near Philippa's age.

"I am Thomas," he said, raising his voice to be heard above the rattle of a passing cart. "My mistress bade me to deliver something to your care. It is heavy, and I am to drive you as far as the track allows."

Mathilda was surprised. The wool she requested for one small tapestry couldn't weigh that much. "Surely I can manage on my own."

The man shook his head. "I assure you, the cart is needed."

Mathilda heard a hint of Francien dialect like she sometimes caught in Philippa's speech, piquing her curiosity. "How long have you served with Philippa?"

He smiled fondly, as if recalling a memory. "I grew up in the de Buade household with Lady Philippa. My mother served hers. The lady and I played together as children."

Mathilda wondered how Philippa and Regina kept their identities as witches hidden beneath so many servants living under their roofs. They must be quite adept at being discreet.

There were more stares as Mathilda followed Thomas toward the cart hitched just beyond the church. A few merchants that she and her mother knew well enough gazed at her with open curiosity. Thomas and Mathilda passed a woman in a green kirtle, a dirty apron tied around her plump middle, whom Mathilda vaguely recognized. The woman's eyes flashed with sympathy, then with surprise as she looked from Mathilda to Thomas.

Mathilda thought, *What were these people thinking? If only Ramona were here, no one could have any secrets.*

The horse whickered softly when Thomas approached. He gave an affectionate rub to the mare's head and helped Mathilda climb into the back of the wooden cart. She noticed a pushcart secured to the end slats and a footed chest tied to the back, behind the driver's seat, and wondered why Philippa would transport the goods she'd requested in such an expensive container.

Once she was settled, Thomas flicked the reins that started the horse into motion. Mathilda braced herself against the side of the cart, grateful to get away from the village.

When they reached the curve where the track veered, and the old, sprawling yew came into view, she bade Thomas to halt and allow her to dismount. He urged the horse as far into the wood as the cart would fit before stopping, then helped Mathilda out.

"Thank you," she said, relieved to be done with the bumpy transport. She glanced at the chest, feeling awkward. She wouldn't be able to carry it on her own. She cleared her throat. "I, um..."

"Allow me." Thomas climbed onto the cart to untie the chest.

Mathilda watched him remove the bindings that secured it to the cart, still curious as to why Philippa didn't send the textiles in a traveling chest. He pulled the large hand cart from the back and tied the chest onto it.

"Is your house far?" Thomas asked.

"Not too far."

When they reached the cottage, Thomas removed the bindings on the chest. "Where would you like me to place it?"

"I can take out what I need here. No need for you to carry this heavy thing inside just for me to unload it."

Thomas smiled. "Lady Philippa wishes for you to keep the chest."

Mathilda didn't know what to say. "Tell her I am grateful," she finally said, turning to lead him inside.

Thomas helped situate the chest along a wall in the main room.

"Can I offer you food or drink?" Mathilda asked when he finished.

"Thank you, but I had best be on my way." He lowered his head in farewell, and after Mathilda closed the door behind him, she rushed to open the lid on the chest.

Philippa had sent much more; Mathilda saw fine linens dyed in beautiful shades of blues, yellows, and greens. There we also silk ribbons. She ran her fingers across them, pulling out a brilliant blue one. It had a lovely sheen in the light.

Mathilda drew out the skeins of wool and separated them by color, placing them on the table. She imagined a blue tapestry. White yarrow flowers and leaves would decorate it. After she completed it, she would start on another tapestry or something else she could sell. She set aside a pale-green linen thread for herself. It would make a lovely new kirtle.

For the tapestry, Mathilda measured out the blue wool, grateful for the task that would bring cheer to the cottage and keep her warmer in the winter. Her thoughts turned to her mother and the dresses they last made for the Beltane festival. They had always done the weaving together. It would be a difficult task by herself, but she could manage.

She worked through the afternoon and well into the night, preparing the loom: looping and pulling the threads, making sure the tension was correct, pausing only long enough for a quick meal of greens. When her fingers ached, and her eyes drooped, she finally stopped.

Surveying her work, Mathilda groaned. It was much less progress than she thought. She had not set half the thread. Abandoning the loom, she readied herself for bed. Her eyes were heavy, and her thoughts few as she lay down. Giving up on her task was frustrating, but she would start fresh tomorrow.

Mathilda had a strong urge to rise and write a letter to Ramona for help, but her body was too weary, and sleep overtook her.

A KNOCK CAME at the door not long after dawn. Mathilda swiped the breadcrumbs from her morning meal off the table, wondering who could be here so early. She cracked the door open and peered outside.

Ramona stood on the stoop. Her dark eyes lit up with a mischievous grin. "Are you going to invite me in or leave me standing out here?"

Mathilda laughed. She could not believe her luck. "Of course. I didn't expect to see you." She opened the door fully. "Come inside. I was just about to write a letter to you."

"Oh? What about?"

"I want to weave a tapestry for the window. Would you mind helping me?"

"Not at all," Ramona replied. She removed her cloak and set it across a chair.

Mathilda offered Ramona something to eat, which was declined. Mathilda wondered why her friend had appeared.

"I sensed you needed my help last night, and here I am."

Mathilda gave a silent thanks to the Goddess.

"Where did you come by all of this wool?" Ramona asked, looking at the array of colors.

Mathilda smiled. "I wrote a letter to Philippa asking her to buy some wool from her. She kindly sent much more than I requested, along with a chest to store it in. As you can see, I have already begun. With your help, I will soon have my tapestry."

By midmorning, their hands were stiff, and Ramona complained of aches in her shoulders.

"My arms seem to have forgotten how strenuous this is," Mathilda remarked, pulling the heddle rod forward so she could pass the weft through the shed. "My mother used to work for many hours and never complained. I suppose her love of weaving eased the task. We've been at it for hours and haven't even gotten halfway through."

"We *could* give it over to magic," Ramona suggested.

Mathilda looked at the loom. Her magic tingled in her palms, pulled by the temptation to give in and use her gift.

"No!" she said firmly. "I want to have the satisfaction of doing this myself."

Ramona shot Mathilda a look that suggested that she had lost her wits. She sighed heavily. "Very well."

Mathilda took the wooden weaving sword and passed Ramona the shuttle. "I'll work the beater this time." She placed it between the shed and beat up the thread with the sword's edge, pushing them up tight.

They stopped at midday to eat a meat pie. Mathilda's arms and shoulders ached so that even the plates seemed too heavy to lift. After sharing a cup of wine, they returned to the loom.

Mathilda sat with a groan. Gazing at the loom, she gave a deep sigh."Very well," she relented. "I'll use magic. But just this once—and only because I already did some of the weaving myself."

Ramona's lips twitched.

Mathilda's magic sparked with anticipation as she pictured the shuttle weaving through the threads and the image of how she wanted the finished tapestry to look. She passed the shuttle through the threads as Ramona slid the beater up. Letting go, they watched as the weaving began on its own. The lines moved quicker than the blink of an eye, meshing the colors in with what they had already made. The tapestry was completed in a matter of minutes, leaving Mathilda astonished.

"I... I did not expect that to go so quickly." She tried to pull her thoughts together. "And I'm very disappointed that I gave up so quickly," she added firmly, taking the scissors. "You must not breathe a word of this to the others. I do not wish for them to know that I gave up so easily."

"I will not tell a soul," Ramona vowed.

"The next time, I will do it *all* myself," Mathilda muttered. She cut the tapestry free of the loom, one thread at a time, knotting each one.

"Of course you will," Ramona said. She had a grin on her face that suggested she found it humorous that Mathilda had used magic to finish the weaving.

Looking at her new tapestry, Mathilda's disappointment eased. She couldn't help smiling when she spread it out on the table. The white yarrow flowers and their delicate leaves in the center of the weaving looked exactly as she had imagined.

"It is beautiful," Ramona said, running her fingers over the threads of the flowers. "No one would guess you used magic to finish it." She flashed a grin at Mathilda.

"I will let you get away with teasing me, Sister. Only because you speak the truth. It is beautiful."

Ramona giggled. "I'd better take my leave. Mother will be expecting me."

"Thank you for coming to help. I have missed you. I thought I needed solitude, but I was wrong. Promise you will come again soon."

"I will. Good day, Mathilda."

6

———

By the end of May, Mathilda had completed the kirtle from the green linen Philippa had sent. The days spent at the loom, weaving the threads into the fabric she needed, and then hand sewing the pieces together to form her dress, were far more satisfying than when she had used magic to complete the tapestry.

On a clear morning with a lavender sky so vibrant she couldn't contain her itch to be outdoors, Mathilda slipped on the kirtle, tore a chunk of bread off a day-old loaf, and grabbed a basket. She hurried into the forest, eating the bread along the way. Through the distant trees, a molten light seared the horizon, and she shivered with anticipation.

Mathilda had discovered the forest had a certain energy in the early dawn, an aliveness that renewed her spirit. She set out first thing each day, eager to feel that energy through the soles of her bare feet.

Ambling along the familiar footpath, she came to a densely overgrown area where the birds were silent. A strangely familiar energy surrounded the place like fog shrouding water. Mathilda put up her guard, trying to discern what she sensed.

Somewhere in the distance, a woman began to hum. Mathilda couldn't tell what direction it came from: It seemed to come from everywhere. The air suddenly became heavy and thick, almost stifling, like breathing in hot steam.

"Hello?" Mathilda called.

The humming stopped, but Mathilda could still sense the presence.

"I know you are there," she called firmly, the authority in her voice showing her lack of fear.

Farther through the trees, a figure moved onto the path. Mathilda saw the strange red-haired woman she had seen once before. Her flame-colored hair stood out like a beacon in the dense woodland. Now that she knew who she had sensed, Mathilda began to recognize the odd energy this woman had from before, making it easier to recognize in the future, and something told Mathilda she *would* need to recognize it. The hem of the woman's dark-green dress skimmed the path as if she were floating. Mathilda tightened her posture, standing guarded and somewhat apprehensive as the woman stopped before her.

In her nearness, her hair was even more startling against her pale skin. Mathilda realized she and the woman were close in age, or they seemed to be, if the woman's face revealed her true age. Something about her unsettled Mathilda. Trying to read her was like trying to see through a wall.

"Good morning," the woman said. Her voice had a musical quality, rich yet light.

"Good morning," Mathilda replied, her tone clipped in her defensiveness. "I have seen you before."

"Yes."

"Who are you?" Mathilda almost winced. Her mother would not approve of her rudeness, but the bite in her words came with a will of their own. If this stranger was offended, she didn't show it. She looked amused instead.

"My name is Cassandra. And you are Mathilda."

Mathilda didn't like the stranger knowing this simple fact about her.

Cassandra's lips twitched as if she knew a secret. Her eyes, a mix of green and pale brown, held Mathilda's. Her gaze dropped, sweeping over the rest of Mathilda's features, over her dress, and back up again, as if comparing herself. Mathilda also took the opportunity to study Cassandra. Her dress, clearly fine once, was well-worn. She could see from the stitching and the weaving that great care had been taken with the making of it. Mathilda dragged her eyes back up to meet Cassandra's.

"How do you know my name?" she said smoothly.

Cassandra smiled. "Because you are my half sister. Aelle, my father, is also your father."

She spoke in a calm, authoritative tone, her gaze unsettling, as if it reached unfathomable depths. Mathilda felt the shock of the words to her core. So, it was true. Aelle did have a child with Gundred. She prayed that her features did not show the shock and betrayal she felt. Mathilda had all but discounted the rumors, but seeing Cassandra only confirmed it. She had Aelle's cruel features. Though she did not have his dark eyes, they still had the same hardness; her mouth had the same smirk.

"You are wondering if I am like our father," Cassandra said, surprising Mathilda again.

It seemed Cassandra inherited more than Aelle's looks. His power also flowed in her veins, allowing her to read Mathilda like a book. She would have to be careful.

"And are you?" Mathilda challenged.

"It depends," Cassandra said coolly. "I have not had the need to be cruel. What about you, Sister? How far does your cruelty go?"

Mathilda's lips curled in disgust. "I can assure you, I am *nothing* like Aelle." She sensed that Cassandra was after something. For a moment, her composure slipped. "What do you want?"

"Fear not, Mathilda. I want nothing from you. I am only curious. Do you also have our father's power?"

So, she could not completely read Mathilda after all. *Good.* "What has that to do with you?" Mathilda asked, neither confirming nor denying.

"Nothing. As I said before, I am merely curious."

"Well, I am not curious, so if you will excuse me, I will be on my way." Mathilda smiled politely, despite her rudeness, before she turned to go.

"Good day, Sister," Cassandra called. "I will see you again."

With her mood now ruined, Mathilda abandoned her morning walk. She fumed as she took the path toward home. Cassandra had spoken soft words, but Mathilda sensed an underlying malice in her nature. She would not open herself to Cassandra. Sister or not, she knew without a doubt that Cassandra was not to be trusted.

The uneasiness Mathilda had carried on her walk home fell away when she reached the edge of the wood where the cottage stood. Golden rays of sunlight streamed through the trees, bathing the clearing in an ethereal light. Dew glistened on the grass and clung to the hem of Mathilda's dress as she crossed the glade. Near the door, a thumping sound caught her attention. Turning, she saw a young hare trying to get past her magical barrier into the garden. She bent over and picked it up by the scruff of its neck.

"I am sorry, little one, but I cannot let you in. Your full belly will mean a hungry one for me come harvest time." She plucked some clover from the edge of the garden and let the hare free. It quickly nibbled on the greens and hopped away.

Mathilda went inside and set about making a tart with the wild garlic she had found before her run-in with Cassandra. Her mind relentlessly churned over their meeting. Why had Cassandra suddenly sought her out? Had their father put her up to it? She almost considered veiling the cottage, but it was likely Cassandra already knew of its existence since she so easily found Mathilda before.

Sometime after the sun slipped past its peak, Mathilda, sitting at the loom, heard the jingle of a harness. Philippa and Regina had come to call.

Thomas nodded to Mathilda as he reached to open the carriage door. Regina stepped out. Her smile was like the sun breaking through a gloomy sky.

"You look beautiful, Mathilda," she said, wrapping Mathilda in a warm hug.

Mathilda hugged her back. The last of the morning's uneasiness faded. "Thank you. How were you able to get the carriage here?"

"I had Thomas scout the wood recently for an alternate route. There is a way just north of here," Philippa said, stepping down from the carriage. She smoothed out her skirts and eyed Mathilda. "Is your dress made from the linen I sent?"

"It is," Mathilda replied, smiling proudly.

Philippa admired the dress's cut and fit. "Your mother taught you well. Are you working on anything at the moment?"

"I started a tapestry. I hope to sell it if it pleases me."

"Very good. What say you to coming with us to the village? It's market day, and I heard some new silks have arrived. I would very much like to see the dyes. You have a keen eye for quality, Mathilda. I could use your opinion."

Mathilda was flattered. "Very well."

With a nod from Philippa, Thomas opened the carriage's door and helped the women get in.

Whitsby buzzed with trade when they arrived at the village square. They left Thomas to stay with the horses in front of the church and crossed over into the thick of the market. Many of the upper class perused the wares with servants standing at the ready. Mathilda wondered if she appeared to be Philippa's servant. She hoped that anyone who knew her assumed that she was. The last thing she wanted was having to answer questions as to where she had been since she left.

They passed under the awning of a merchant stand.

Regina suddenly gasped. "Mother, look at these hairpins. May I have them?"

Mathilda turned at her comment. In front of the merchant were several gold pins on the table. Two were inlaid with pearls, and one had a sapphire surrounded by filigree. They were beautiful.

"Not this time, Daughter," Philippa replied. "Remember, we are here to look at the silks."

Regina cast one last longing look at the pins before moving on to look at the rest of the wares. Mathilda noticed Philippa nod to the merchant, followed by an inconspicuous drop of coins in his hand. She took the pins and tucked them into her purse.

"I want her to have the pins," Philippa said, turning to Mathilda, "But I do not always give the child everything she asks for on demand. I will save them for a special occasion."

"That is kind of you, Philippa. Regina will be delighted."

They caught up to Regina and passed by the food stands, heading toward the end of the square.

The silk merchant had drawn a curious crowd. Folks leaving the alehouse lingered outside the door flap, trying to catch a glimpse of what was inside, but at the sight of Philippa, most dispersed as she approached.

Several chests filled the space, and Mathilda wondered what they held. Having only ever seen silk in Philippa's clothing, her imagination was limited in conjuring any ideas. She walked alongside Regina as they followed Philippa to the far end of the space where the mercer stood. He wore a richly dyed tunic, the deep shade of an emerald, and Mathilda couldn't help but wish she had threads in the same color. His pointed bycocket hat sported a large brown pheasant feather sticking out of its fold. Anticipation flashed in his large tawny eyes as he watched them approach.

When they reached the table, Mathilda noticed a wooden rod attached to the side of it. Ribbons of indigo, yellow, and red hung from the rod, and a few brocade mantles lay stretched across the table beneath them.

The mercer's eager eyes fell on Philippa. "Is there anything the lady wishes to see?"

"I will let you know," Philippa politely answered. She turned to Mathilda. "What do you think?"

Mathilda ran her fingers along the green brocade, gazing wonderingly at the pattern. "I have no experience with silks, but it seems a fine quality."

A breeze carried through the pavilion, flicking the red silk ribbons. Mathilda grimaced as she thought of Cassandra's brilliant hair.

"You do not like the red?" Philippa asked.

"No," Mathilda said quickly, "I like it well enough." She hated letting thoughts of her half sister ruin her contentment.

Philippa's brows lifted, and her expression demanded more. "Then why that look?"

Mathilda sighed. "Oh, very well, I'll tell you." She walked away from the mercer, with Philippa and Regina following, and stopped near a chest when she felt she was far enough away to not be heard. "It appears that the rumors of another child by Aelle are true. Her name is Cassandra, and she has been watching me for some time. I only just met her this morning." Mathilda looked toward the table at the red flapping ribbons. "This silk reminds me of the color of her hair."

"Oh, Mathilda, how unpleasant that must have been for you," Regina said.

Philippa turned, and Mathilda realized the mercer was watching them. "I will take the indigo and yellow ribbons. Two each," Philippa said, setting him to task. She turned back to Mathilda and whispered, "What makes you think she's been watching you?"

"I've felt her presence for some time. Once, I saw a glimpse of red through the forest, then another time, in the distance, I saw her."

"What did she speak of? What was her nature?" Philippa asked urgently.

Mathilda reflected. "She told me Aelle was her father. I sensed something unsettling in her. I don't know what exactly, but it felt wrong. She wanted to know if I had power."

"What did you answer?"

"I merely said that was none of her concern and left her."

Philippa frowned. "Be careful, Mathilda. It is rather odd that she sought you out now after everything that has transpired. Do not reveal anything to her."

"I won't."

Philipa nodded and returned to the table to pay the mercer.

A wave of fatigue suddenly washed over Mathilda. She stepped outside and braced against a cart full of ale barrels. The driver looked across his shoulder and sneered at her. Mathilda released her hand from the wooden slat, and the man clicked his horse into motion once the crowd dispersed, moving closer to the ale house.

Regina put a hand on her arm. "Are you ill?"

Mathilda tried to brush the feeling away. "I'm fine. I think I must be tired from sitting at the loom so long today."

"We should get you back."

Philippa stepped out from the pavilion to join them. She held a small cloth-wrapped bundled with the silk ribbons. Her eyes suddenly narrowed as she looked toward the alehouse. "Mathilda, who is that *knave* staring at you? He smiles as if he knows what you look like beneath your chemise."

Mathilda followed Philippa's gaze. There, in the shadows of the alehouse, Duncan stood, bearing a broad grin. He caught her eye and winked. She blushed and quickly looked away.

"Mathilda!" Philippa scolded. "Do you know that scoundrel?"

"I met him at the Beltane festival. He fancies me, nothing more."

"I certainly hope not. Come, girls. We take our leave now." Philippa shot a look of disdain toward Duncan and ushered Mathilda and Regina ahead of her like a protective mother. The walk back to the church was not far, but it felt like leagues to Mathilda. The sun's heat made her fatigue worse. She was glad to climb into the carriage with the knowledge that she was heading home.

"Are you well, child?" Philippa asked.

Mathilda answered. "I have been at the loom for too long, sometimes well into the night. I'm afraid I have not eaten properly in my eagerness to weave."

"Is your larder still supplied?" Philippa asked, looking concerned.

"It is. I will try not to spend so long weaving in the coming days and eat properly."

"Make sure you do," Philippa said. "You must take care of yourself."

The sun had passed midday when the carriage stopped in front of the cottage. Mathilda thanked Philippa and Regina as she disembarked. Once inside, she went into the larder and poured a cup of water from the pitcher she had filled earlier at the stream. She suddenly broke into a cold sweat, nearly overcome with weakness. Alarmed, she rushed outside to stop Philippa, but the carriage was already out of sight.

A calmness washed over her as she remembered her mother had always treated her fevers with yarrow, so she took a small basket and headed toward the pond where the yarrow grew plentifully. Her legs grew heavy going down the slope, and walking became a burden. She collapsed onto the grass.

A surge of panic rushed through Mathilda. Rolling onto her side, she plucked several bunches of yarrow and put them in her basket before lying back again. *You have the yarrow. Just get to the cottage.* After a few moments, she rolled over onto her knees and fought against the weakness to stand. She trudged up the small hill away from the pond, gripping her basket tightly to keep from dropping it. Each step felt as if someone was strapping heavier and heavier iron weights to her ankles. She struggled for breath. Near the top of the incline, Mathilda collapsed again. She closed her eyes. *Just for a moment...*

~

"HERE, DRINK THIS," her mother's voice urged.

"Mother? Am I dead?"

"No. You have a fever. You must drink this now."

Mathilda felt a cup touch her lips. The liquid felt warm going down her throat.

"Now, rest, Mathilda."

"Mother, please do not leave me again."

"Hush now, just rest."

WHEN SHE WOKE, Mathilda found herself tucked into her bed. Disoriented, she thought she heard someone moving around in the other room. She remembered talking to her mother, but that could not be true. Her mother was dead. She felt dead, too, for that matter. Her head throbbed, and her whole body felt wrung out. She pulled the cover back and tried to ease out of bed.

A woman's voice called from the other room. "I would not do that, Mathilda."

Mathilda didn't recognize the voice. Alarmed, she tried to push herself up against the bedstead, but her muscles wouldn't obey. Footsteps approached the doorway. A shock of red hair was the first thing she saw. *Cassandra.*

"What are you doing here?" Mathilda snapped.

Cassandra's eyebrows rose. "That is not the gratitude I expected for caring for you."

Mathilda flinched as though Cassandra had slapped her. "*You* took care of me?"

"I found you on the ground, out of your senses with fever," she said cooly. "Someone had to tend to you, or you would be amongst the dead by now." She picked at the edge of her sleeve, looking suddenly insecure.

Mathilda noticed the fabric of her gray tunic had worn thin at the elbows. She wondered what kind of life Cassandra had and suddenly felt guilty for speaking so harshly to her.

"Thank you," Mathilda said with meaning.

Cassandra looked up. Surprise flashed in her eyes at Mathilda's change of demeanor. She gave a slight nod. "Are you hungry?"

"Yes," Mathilda replied, becoming aware of the gnawing ache in her stomach. She caught the scents of onion and sage and looked questioningly at Cassandra.

"I've made a stew for supper. I hope you don't mind; I helped myself to your larder."

Mathilda didn't know how she felt. Intruded upon, grateful... uneasy. She kept her mind guarded. "What day is it?" she asked.

"Saturday."

Mathilda's forehead furrowed with worry. "You've been here three days?"

"Yes."

Mathilda wondered what secrets Cassandra had learned while she was under the grip of the fever.

Cassandra sniffed lightly and shook her head. "Do not worry, Sister; your secrets are still guarded. I did try, you know. You are stronger than I expected."

"Why do you say that?" Mathilda asked, growing angry. "Why does my power interest you so?"

"Because, dear sister, I, too, lost my mother to our father's rage. In the weeks since her death, Father has grown even more unstable. There might come a time when I need you to help me stand against him."

Mathilda froze. The night of her mother's death came flooding back. Could it be true? Would Aelle kill his mistress? There was no sadness or regret in Cassandra's words. Mathilda studied her, weighing the truth of what she had said.

"Oh, here, you mistrusting fool." Cassandra sat on the bed and held out her hands, palms up.

As soon as Mathilda touched Cassandra's hands, the vision flooded her mind.

A woman with hair the color of pitch stood before Aelle. She clenched the sides of her brown kirtle in her fists. Though she was a full head shorter than he, her presence was still commanding. Her green eyes glared defiantly. Gundred. Mathilda somehow knew this was Aelle's mistress. The familiarity in how the two beheld each other suggested it.

"You do nothing you say you will do," Gundred said, her voice as biting as a stinging wasp. "When will you help me in my endeavors? You are becoming obsessed, Aelle. I grow tired of your promises."

"Speak to me with that sharp tongue once more, and you will regret it." His voice was scathing, and Mathilda shuddered at the sound of it.

Gundred took a step forward, her fists on her hips. "I grow tired of your promises," she repeated, as if carving each word in stone.

Aelle struck her swiftly, with a force that spun Gundred around, knocking her to the floor. Hatred poured from her eyes. She spat the blood from her mouth and got to her feet, then lunged for Aelle. Her nails drew blood across his cheek, but that was the last wound she would inflict. His hands encircled her delicate neck and squeezed.

Mathilda gasped, yanking her hands from Cassandra's.

"The vision isn't my own," Cassandra said, matter-of-fact. "It's Father's. I delved into his mind to find out what happened."

"Where were you when he did this terrible thing?" Mathilda asked, trembling from the shock of witnessing Gundred's murder, from seeing her father's rage once again.

Cassandra's eyes were distant. She gazed somewhere far beyond the walls.

"I took my leave after their shouting started. I grew weary of it all, so I went to Father's outbuilding. I waited long after they had grown quiet in case they argued again. When I returned, I smelled smoke. I expected to find Mother by the cooking pot. Instead, Father had her dead body thrown into a raging fire outside our home. Her limbs had already blackened when I came around the side of the house and discovered the fire."

Mathilda was numb from the horror she had seen in the vision. She could only imagine what Cassandra must have felt. "I am sorry for you, Cassandra."

"But you still do not trust me."

"Perhaps in time."

"I should check on the stew." Cassandra got up from the bed and swept out of the room.

Mathilda wondered at Cassandra's cool indifference to her mother's death. Perhaps she dealt with loss that way. Time would only reveal her true self.

Cassandra returned with a bowl of stew. "Here you are. I should take my leave. The fever has left you, and I think you are safe to be alone now."

Mathilda took the bowl gratefully. "Will you not have some stew before you go?"

Cassandra paused, looking conflicted. "Very well. After all, I did cook it, did I not?"

"Help me out of bed, and I will eat with you at the table."

Mathilda balanced on Cassandra's arm to pull herself upright. Once she was on her feet, she drew away. "I think I can manage from here."

At the table, Mathilda watched Cassandra sip at the broth. She was quite pretty, Mathilda realized, now that some of the strangeness had ebbed. Her features were delicate, giving her an impish appearance, but it was her hair that made her so striking. Such a vibrant shade of red that Mathilda had never seen before. It tumbled over Cassandra's shoulders and down her sides with a wildness, as if it preferred to be untamed. Mathilda found it fascinating.

"What was your mother like?" Cassandra asked.

A gentle smile touched Mathilda's lips. "My mother was the most beautiful soul I ever knew. She was full of love and kindness, laughter, and forgiveness. She cared for everyone she met. Everyone who knew her loved her. I miss her very much." She absently stirred her stew. "What about your mother? What was she like?"

"Mother was a power-hungry wretch," Cassandra said with disgust. "All she cared about was how she could become more powerful. She wanted people to tremble before her." Cassandra threw her hands up, shaking them in mock fear. "I despised her. Father was the only kind soul in our house, but my mother corrupted him. He loved me deeply." Her face softened at the memory. "So you see, Sister, you had your mother's love, and I had our father's."

Mathilda's mind reeled. She had never imagined her father could love anyone other than himself. Spooning some broth, Mathilda wondered what it must have been like for Cassandra to have Gundred as a mother. No wonder she didn't grieve her death.

"Where is our father?" she asked, almost wishing she hadn't.

"Why at home, of course. Where else would he be?" Cassandra looked at Mathilda as if she had taken leave of her wits.

Mathilda paused, considering. "I don't know. I guess I thought he might have left for distant lands after what he did to our mothers. The bailiff is looking for him."

"The bailiff is wasting his time," Cassandra shot back.

Mathilda wondered what she meant, but did not ask. She was tired of Aelle and his cruelty. Let fate bring him to his due punishment.

The fire burned low, and nighttime shadows descended over the room. Mathilda finished the rest of her broth, feeling tired again.

"I should be going now," Cassandra said, rising. "I'm glad you are feeling yourself once more."

Mathilda looked up at her, surprised. "Are you not concerned with traveling on foot in the dark?"

Cassandra's head lifted. Her eyes were cold and hard. "There are things far more frightening than darkness." Her gaze shifted toward the window and the nighttime awaiting her. "No, I do not fear it. I embrace it."

A foreboding arose in the back of Mathilda's mind as she watched

Cassandra move toward the door. Careful not to reveal her unease, she smiled.

"Thank you, Cassandra. I do appreciate that you took care of me. Perhaps we will meet again."

"I am certain. Good evening, Sister."

Mathilda stood long after the door had closed, still hearing the word that seemed to devour her with sharp teeth: *sister.*

As she readied for bed, Mathilda's thoughts were troubled. Cassandra's presence still clung to the walls of the cottage like an unwanted spirit. She already longed for the dawn and its soothing comfort. She climbed into bed, realizing how much had changed—how much *she* had changed. Tomorrow would mark the last day of May and her eighteenth birthday. Gone were the carefree days of her girlhood. She cried herself to sleep over the loss of them.

THE WIND ENCIRCLED THE COTTAGE, almost lovingly. It rose, higher, whispering through the wood, twisting left at the Three Paths. It continued past Whitsby Village and farther still until it reached a tall stone house beyond a clearing, where it suddenly died.

Cassandra settled into bed, wondering what secrets Mathilda kept hidden. Her sister's powers were far stronger than she had anticipated. Even in sickness, she somehow kept her mind closed. In time, perhaps Mathilda would come to trust her. Every day, her father seemed to grow harder as he worked toward some hidden goal she could not fathom. His presence no longer held comfort. It carried agitation and, worst still, a danger that frightened her. She could not help but feel she would need her sister's help. With what, she could not say.

A ruckus from outside distracted Cassandra's thoughts. Something must have gone wrong with one of her father's spells. She sighed, wondering what had happened this time. Another noise followed, sounding like a scream. Alarmed, she rose from her bed and went to investigate.

Light streamed from between the wooden door of the small stone outbuilding her father used for practicing his magic. Cassandra walked silently toward it.

"Father?" she called.

His reply came quickly and harshly. "Go to bed, Daughter."

A woman's voice, high and desperate, called out, "Help me!" In the same moment, Cassandra heard glass shattering on the floor and banging noises as if two people were locked in a struggle.

Cassandra's heart raced. Something was terribly wrong. She could feel the imminent danger from outside the building. She rushed ahead and peered through a crack in the door. She could make out her father's dark hair and broad back as he bent over a table. Cassandra couldn't see what was on it. Suddenly, his hand lifted in the air, and she saw the flash of a knife blade. The knife came down, and a woman's arm fell limp over the side of the table.

Cassandra stumbled back, slamming a hand over her mouth to stifle her scream. She turned and ran back into the house, blinded by tears. *Why, Father? What have you done?* Closing the door, she sagged against it, gulping in deep breaths between her sobs. "It wasn't real, it wasn't real...." She dug the heels of her palms into her eyes, repeating the words in her mind, but the image of the woman's pale, limp arm cut through the lie. Another sob ripped from her throat, and she dashed up the steps to her bed, praying that sleep would claim her and erase the terrible image from her mind.

After some time, she heard her father come into the house. His footsteps paused by her door. She pretended to sleep as he opened it and stepped into her room. Cassandra sensed him lingering by her bed, and she kept her breathing slow and steady despite her fear.

"Sleep, Daughter. Before long, I will give you a life like none before us has ever known."

His footsteps retreated, and the door closed. Cassandra let out her breath. What did he mean? She tried to sleep, but sleep eluded her until dawn.

7

Mathilda was on her knees in her garden, pulling stubborn weeds, when she heard Regina's voice behind her. "There you are."

Mathilda got to her feet, wiping her hands on her apron. She turned to see her friend, who stood with her arms crossed over her breasts, wearing a dress the palest shade of red that would have been most becoming on her were it not for the scowl on her face. A little distance behind her, holding a small sack, was Eldrid.

He lingered behind her with a look of casual grace, but Mathilda had the impression he was more than adept at defending Regina if need be. It wasn't just his size and the sword that hung from his belt, but also the way he carried himself. Something predatory about his stance said he would readily pounce. But, Mathilda thought, Regina could surely defend herself. She was a witch, after all.

"Good day to you, Regina." Mathilda eyed Eldrid with a questioning look. He hovered oddly close to her.

Regina's scowl deepened. "Mother insisted that *he* come with me, although I'm sure I don't know why. She outright refused to let Thomas accompany me, even though she knows how skilled I am in defensive magic." Regina huffed dramatically. She tossed her head, and the sun glinted off the golden caul that held her hair. "Your garden looks well-tended," she added, finally noticing the crops.

"It is," Mathilda agreed, looking at its progress. The beans had climbed nearly half the length of the wooden stakes. The leeks had shot up taller, and the cabbage was filling out nicely. "I'm enjoying the work. What brings you here this morning?"

Regina finally relaxed enough to unfold her arms. "I've come to remind you that it is only two weeks until the summer solstice."

"Yes," Mathilda agreed, looking questioningly at her friend.

Regina held out an imperious hand to Eldrid, who gave her the sack he held. Mathilda could have sworn he swallowed a grin. "My mother had this made for you," Regina told Mathilda. "Here, open it."

Mathilda reached for the sack, but noticed her still-dirty hands. "You had better do it."

"You and your mother made our dresses for Beltane." Regina opened the sack and drew out a pale-yellow tunic with delicate white elderflowers embroidered around the neckline. "Mother and I wanted to return the gesture for the summer solstice celebrations."

Mathilda smiled. Her hands itched to take hold of the dress. "Regina, it is beautiful. Thank you. Will you come inside for a visit?"

"No. Mother made me promise I would come straight home." Regina disappeared inside the cottage long enough to deposit the dress. "I will see you again at the solstice festivities," she said when she came outside again.

"Thank you. Please tell Philippa I am grateful."

"I will. Goodbye, Mathilda. Come along, Eldrid," Regina added in a sour voice.

Mathilda took off her dirty apron and cleaned her hands. From inside the cottage, she took the soap and a clean chemise and set out for the pond. Stripping out of her dirty tunic, she waded into the water with it, scrubbing it clean first, then herself.

As she stepped out of the water, she felt a presence. It was not

Cassandra she sensed. Mathilda had made a point to learn her energy. This was someone else. She quickly pulled the clean chemise over her head and collected her belongings.

She walked up the bank toward the cottage, alert, taking note of her surroundings. Something made a shuffling noise behind her. She whirled around, heart racing.

"Greetings, Mathilda," Duncan said, grinning.

Mathilda was immediately aware of how the thin chemise did nothing to hide her figure. "What are *you* doing here?" To her embarrassment, it came out as a shriek. She yanked her dripping dress against herself, mortified.

"Ah, the lady is modest in the extreme," he teased.

"*Of course,* I am modest! You should not be here. How did you find me?"

"I followed your finely dressed friend and her servant. She should be more careful to mind who is trailing behind her. I dare say she needs a better guard than that delicate flower she brought along."

"You fiend! What do you want?" Mathilda glared, outraged at his rambling and his intrusiveness. How could he not see that she was mortified standing before him in nothing but her underclothes?

"Peace, Mathilda. I will be polite." His tone was subdued, but the edges of his lips still turned up. "Run along inside and get dressed. I wish to speak with you."

Mathilda bolted inside, grateful to have the privacy to collect herself. How dare he show up here like this? No decent man would approach a half-dressed woman. *Did he see her bathing?* She nearly died at the thought of him seeing her naked, and yet a tiny part of her hoped that he had.

Her cheeks flooded with heat at that line of thinking. Mathilda covered her face with her hands, embarrassed at herself. Maybe he hadn't seen her until after she had put the chemise on. With that somewhat comforting thought, she pulled on a light-gray tunic and took her wet one out to drape along the wall just past the door to dry, but Duncan was leaning against the stones, blocking her way.

"Will you be so kind as to step aside, so that I may place my dress to dry?"

He stayed where he was against the wall, smiling at her. She hadn't noticed before what a lovely smile he had. A tiny laugh line showed along the right side of his mouth, drawing her attention. Her fingertips twitched with an impulse to trace it. This startled her. What was it about this man that made her act so wantonly?

She forced herself to speak coldly. "I will ask you again: Please remove yourself from my wall."

He arched a brow, and mischief danced in his eyes. "Will you turn your witchcraft on me if I don't?"

Mathilda gave him a flat look. "I am greatly tempted, but no. I will not waste it on you."

Duncan barked a laugh and stepped aside. It was the same deep laugh she remembered from the last time they'd met. Concealing her grin, Mathilda spread her dress over the stone wall and turned to him.

"Will you come inside then?"

"I will," he said, the mirth still in his voice.

In the main room, she drew out a chair for him at the table, suddenly feeling uneasy. "Would you care for anything to eat? A drink, perhaps?"

"No. Sit down, Mathilda." No laughter in his voice now.

"Very well." Mathilda smoothed her dress, willing her hands not to tremble, and sat down across from him. "What would you like to speak about?"

"You are aware of the growing animosity between your country and mine?"

This topic was not what she expected. "I am."

"Your *king*," he said, curling his lip at the word, "has too many arrows pointed north. It is getting harder to cross over into Northumberland unnoticed. My English kin have warned me not to be deceived by talks of a treaty, so I plan to stay in England until the solstice. Then I will return home." His voice suddenly softened. "I would very much like it if you would return to Scotland with me as my wife." His eyes held hope, and something else. Fear. He worried she would say no.

Mathilda felt as if the floor fell away. She knew she should speak, but her tongue felt leaden. She was stunned and quickly becoming overwhelmed as her emotions besieged her senses.

"You don't have to answer me now," Duncan said softly. "I will be here 'til the solstice festivities."

Mathilda's gaze dropped to her hands resting in her lap. Duncan reached for them. She was sure he could feel her racing pulse as he rubbed his thumbs across her wrists. She looked up, and her breath hitched at the intensity of his gaze and the emotions swimming in the depths of his amber eyes. They consumed her.

"I think we are well-matched, Mathilda. You have kindness and spirit, and I cannot take my thoughts from you." He moved his hand to her cheek, resting his palm against her skin. She flushed at the heat in his gaze. He leaned closer, brushing his lips against her temple.

Mathilda's breath came quick and uneven. "Duncan, I—"

He cut off her words with his mouth. His hands cupped her face, fingers brushing along the back of her neck as his lips moved against hers. Mathilda could not stop herself from melting against him or keep her fingers from winding in his hair. As his mouth trailed down her neck, a wildfire tore through her, and for a moment, Mathilda felt as if she could belong to him. The thought terrified her, and she quickly pulled away. His gaze held hers. It was all she could do to cling to the shred of stability she had left.

"You should go," she whispered.

He took in a deep breath, dropping his gaze to collect himself. "Aye." He stood and made his way toward the door, then turned. "Consider my offer, Mathilda. I will make a good husband. I will care for you until we are old and gray." His gaze was intent and full of longing. "I will see you again."

She longed to rush into him, to feel the heat of him against her and the crush of his lips on hers once again, but she knew if she did, she might not ever let go. "Good day, Duncan."

Mathilda closed the door behind him and leaned against it. Her chest rose and fell quickly as her thoughts ran wild. She darted to the table and took out the parchment, ink well, and quill, and began to write with a shaking hand.

I must speak with you. Come alone.

Mathilda

She rolled the parchment and hurried off through the woods. When she reached the druid tree, she whispered Ramona's name over it and placed it in the hollow.

Returning to the cottage, Mathilda could think only of Duncan. She unconsciously touched her fingers to her lips as she thought of their kiss. He made her feel alive. He was handsome, strong... more than capable of taking care of her. But did she *want* someone taking care of her? She certainly did not need caring for. If only Ramona could be here now.

That night, no response came. Mathilda drifted asleep, wondering why Ramona did not send a reply.

A POUNDING at the door woke her. Mathilda thought she was dreaming at first, but then someone called her name. Her room was still dark; not even a hint of gray dawn light streaked the horizon. She got out of bed, lit a candle, and hurried to the door.

"Ramona? What are you doing here so early? It's not yet dawn." Mathilda noticed her hair had been braided in haste, and a flush of color tinted her cheeks as if she had run the whole way.

"Mother sent me." Ramona stepped inside and set her lantern on the table. She looked worried. "Something has happened. She said her sisters needed her and that I was to come here until she fetches me."

Mathilda felt suddenly uneasy. "That's odd." She tried to think. "Give me a moment to dress." In the bedroom, she quickly pulled a tunic over her chemise and ran a comb through her hair. Leticia's sisters needed her? And Ramona was to stay here? What could it mean?

"I am glad you are here. I sent a note yesterday," Mathilda said, rejoining Ramona. She stretched out her hand and lit two additional candles to give them more light, then went to get the bread from the larder. She brought it out to the table, along with the knife and two plates.

"Yes, I know," Ramona answered. "My mother retrieved it. She would not let me go out alone last night to send you a response." She pulled a chair and sat at the table across from Mathilda, looking unsettled. "I don't understand it. She has never restricted my comings and goings."

Mathilda cut off a chunk of bread and placed it before Ramona. "Just yesterday, Regina came by with Eldrid. He carried a sword and was hovering close to her. She said her mother made him come along with her instead of Thomas. What could the elder coven be keeping from us?"

"Well, I know my mother will tell me nothing until she wishes to, but I'm sure we will find out soon enough," Ramona said. "What did you wish to speak to me about?"

Mathilda felt herself blush. She swiped the crumbs from the table into her palm and dumped them on her plate, collecting herself. "Duncan. He came here to see me yesterday."

Ramona looked completely scandalized. "Oh! Mathilda, how did he find you?"

"He followed Regina here from the village."

Ramona frowned. "What did he want?"

"He... Duncan asked me to be his wife." She dropped her gaze to her lap, twisting one end of her belt around her finger. "He told me that he plans to return to Scotland after the solstice, and he wants me to go with him." She made herself meet Ramona's eyes.

Ramona's mouth fell open. "What did you tell him?"

"I didn't answer. He told me to think on it and let him know by the solstice festivities."

Ramona seemed to struggle with her thoughts. Her voice was soft when she finally spoke. "What will you do?"

Mathilda leaned back against her chair with a heavy sigh. "I don't know. I never imagined I would marry, but Duncan makes me feel things I have never felt." She remembered the softness of his lips and the feel of his touch. She couldn't stop the fond grin that tugged at her lips. "A warmth fills my heart when he's near—or whenever I think of him at all. I wish my mother were here. She would help me see the way."

Ramona softly sighed. "He does seem besotted with you, and I think he would strive to be a good husband. He has integrity. I saw it in him, but Scotland?"

A knock came at the door, interrupting their conversation.

"Please say nothing of this, Ramona."

"I won't speak of it. I promise."

Regina and Katrina were waiting on the stoop. Regina's strong-looking servant, Eldrid, lingered nearby. And just like the last time, he wore a sword.

"Good morning, Mathilda," Regina said. "May we come in?" The tightness in her voice matched her features. At Mathilda's wave, she stepped inside. "Ah, Ramona. Obviously, our mothers are up to something." She glanced over her shoulder at Eldrid with an odd look as Katrina followed her into the cottage.

"Did Leticia say anything to you regarding this early morning outing?"

"No," Ramona replied. "My mother woke me well before dawn and told me to come here as quickly as I could, and to stay until further notice."

"Good morning," Isobel said from the doorway. She looked baffled. "My mother sent me here. What is going on?"

"We do not know," Mathilda replied, growing more uneasy. "Please join us." She closed the door behind Isobel and busied herself with blowing out the candles individually to calm herself. The gray, overcast light now coming through the windows was enough.

"There will be an explanation later," Regina added. From the set of her chin, Mathilda felt sure she'd extract that explanation from Philippa by any means necessary.

"I have bread already on the table," Mathilda said. "Please make yourselves comfortable while I get more plates." She went to the larder and brought them out, then fetched cups and the pitcher of water. "What shall we do with ourselves?" she said, pulling her chair up to join everyone.

"We'll catch up." Katrina smiled. "Since you're the one I haven't seen in the longest time, Mathilda, you start. What have you been doing with yourself?"

Ramona shot Mathilda a wide-eyed glance. Mathilda quickly blocked the thought of Duncan from her mind.

"Well," she said, "I was very sick for a few days. My half sister, Cassandra, found me unconscious and nursed me back to health."

"Your *sister!*" Katrina sputtered.

"Half, but yes," Mathilda said. "The rumors are true. Aelle has another child."

"What is she like?" Regina asked, leaning forward.

"I don't entirely know. Cassandra keeps herself guarded. She did tell me that Aelle killed her mother, too. He choked the life out of her, just as he did with my mother, only with his hands."

Isobel flinched with shock. "How horrible."

"Indeed." Mathilda ran her fingers across the rim of her cup, thinking of the moment Cassandra had shown her the vision. She met Isobel's eyes. "Cassandra despised her mother, and she did not seem to grieve her death. But I was astonished to learn that my father adores Cassandra." Mathilda realized the sting of this realization no longer bothered her. "Perhaps he sees something in her that he lacked in me," she added.

"Oh, Mathilda." Katrina's eyes were warm with sympathy. "I am sorry."

"Thank you, but I have come to accept it, and it no longer hurts so much," Mathilda said. "Now, enough about me. What of you, Katrina?"

"Not a single thing has happened to me. Mother and I have assisted with three births, one of which was a cow. The rest of our days have been spent tending our garden. The only excitement I've had is the dress Regina dropped off. That, and having to wake before dawn to come here. Regina." Katrina turned to her, who sat on Mathilda's other side. "It is your turn. What adventures have you been on since we last saw one another?"

Regina waved a world-weary hand. Her rings glimmered in the growing light coming in through the window. "Oh, besides having to be trailed by my father's man, there were two more offers for my hand in marriage."

"Regina!" Katrina exclaimed. "That *is* a bit of excitement!"

"My father refused both offers, of course. Mother made him." She surprised Mathilda with her matter-of-fact tone, but then her voice softened and became accepting. "I suppose she was right to do so. None of them is like me. Like... us," she said, dropping her gaze.

"Don't worry, Regina," Ramona comforted. "One day, you will find someone like you or at least someone who accepts you as you are. Your father is a fine example."

Mathilda's heart lurched as she thought of Duncan and his acceptance of her. She dashed him from her mind as she turned her attention back to Regina.

Regina met Ramona's eyes. "Perhaps so, but in the meantime, no one understands why my father has refused so many marriage offers. Some were fine prospects, high-ranking and titled. I've heard whispers at court that something must be wrong with me."

Ramona started to speak, but Isobel interrupted her. "Quiet, I hear voices."

Mathilda's heart raced as she cracked the door and peered out. "Your mothers are returning. They do not appear pleased." She opened the door fully. "Good morning," she greeted the women.

"Good morning, Mathilda," Annora replied. "I am sorry we disrupted your day by sending our daughters upon you so early, but it was necessary, I assure you."

The women filed into the cottage, all of them looking grave and weary. A pit of dread settled in Mathilda's stomach as she wondered what they had to say. She offered them food and drink, but they refused.

Annora removed her spice-colored veil covering her thickly braided hair and placed it on the back of a chair. There were lines in her dark skin that made her look bone-weary. She said, "Listen to me: A child went missing two weeks ago. A girl, aged fourteen." Her eyes found Mathilda's, and there was a heaviness in her gaze that spoke volumes. Mathilda already knew her next words.

"Your father is behind her disappearance, Mathilda." She said this as gently as possible, but it didn't help.

A wave of sickness washed over Mathilda. She leaned against the wall to stay on her feet. "Before my mother died, she said Aelle murdered a twelve-year-old girl. The girl's spirit visited her, but they were interrupted, and Mother never found out why she was killed."

She heard Ramona's gasp from beside her and swallowed hard with shame and terror. *How could her father murder so easily?*

"Your mother sent word to us about that," Annora said. "We have been trying to find out what your father's been about all this time, but it has been difficult without Maelen. We need all five of us to be at full strength. It has not been easy masking ourselves from Aelle without her. Philippa had a vision of the second girl he killed. She could not speak because, in life, Aelle cut out her tongue."

Mathilda clasped her hand over her mouth in horror.

Philippa moved toward the window. Silver streaks stood out in her perfectly arranged hair. "I asked the girl to write the name of her murderer on parchment," she said. "She showed me your father's name, written in her own blood."

Mathilda's heart felt as if it would burst. Her breaths came quickly now, and she tried to calm herself and listen to the women.

"We cast a spell to find your father," Leticia said. "And the Goddess sent a crow to lead the way. We found out he has a house about half a morning's walk past Whitsby Village. We went to the border of Aelle's property, but no further. He has a protection spell cast over the place. We could not pass." Her dark, intent eyes found Mathilda's face. "Child, I know that at the Beltane feast, your mother told you that you would be instructed in our ways. Those teachings were delayed by Maelen's death, and we allowed you time to grieve. The time for grieving has ended. We need you, and all of you, to fully understand who we are and what we do. It can no longer wait."

Mathilda gave a nod, not trusting herself to speak now.

Leticia turned toward the door. "Let us go out to our sister's grave."

Mathilda, numb with shock over what her father had done, followed everyone outside. When she approached the grave, sadness closed over her. Her mother should have been here to teach Mathilda everything she needed to know.

"Take our hands, girls," Leticia instructed. "Encircle the grave."

Mathilda reached out and took Annora's and Ramona's hands.

"Be warned, it comes at once," Philippa said. "We have no time to prepare you for your journey ahead."

As the elders began to chant in the old tongue, Mathilda wondered what Philippa meant by "it comes at once." In the next moment, the earth shuddered under her, and her body rocked as if she had taken a blow. Images and visions flooded her mind. Suddenly, Mathilda knew ancient spells she had never heard of before, and potions she had never seen. Years of controlled practice over the elements became known. She was flooded with exhilaration.

But something else followed. Whispered voices from another

realm hissed instructions for harnessing the dark in her magic. Mathilda felt she was lost in an evil fog. A presence spoke to her in a demented voice that made her shake with fear. It told her how to use her magic in a darker way, how to spell objects to obtain her goals. She no longer felt like she was at her mother's grave, safe with the other women. She felt lost in a nightmare and completely alone. Fear gripped her heart, and she fought back a scream.

A tiny ball of light appeared in the distance, growing larger as it drew close to Mathilda. Its presence soothed her. She watched, mesmerized, as it took form, and realized with a start that the glowing figure was her mother.

"Mother, where am I?"

She smiled and touched Mathilda's cheek. "My beautiful child, you are safe. You are in a spell. You are learning all the ways of our magic that I told you about. This darkness you sense is what you must defend all of nature against. You must accept the teachings of this knowledge to know how to defeat it. Your father will test the balance of all we have ever known. You *must* find a way to cut him down before all is lost."

"But how? What will he do?"

The light that was her mother began to fade. Panic rose in Mathilda's chest at the thought of losing her again. "Mother, please don't go! I need you. Please tell me how to stop Father." Mathilda reached for her mother, but her hand went through her.

"You will know what to do." Her mother's voice was assuring. "Your coven will help you. You will preserve them, and they will protect you."

Preserve? "But I need you." Mathilda's words came out fragile and as thin as a moth's wings. Tears flooded her eyes. "Mother, *please* stay."

Her mother's voice became distant. "As stars above, as air between, as earth below, your soul shall keep."

"What does that mean? Mother?"

The light was gone. Her mother's soothing presence was also

gone. In its place was a crushing emptiness. A void filled with nothingness. Another voice came loud but distant. *"Wake."*

Mathilda opened her eyes. Her cheeks were wet with tears. The elder coven was standing over her. She glanced over her shoulder and saw that her sisters were still on the ground, locked in the spell.

Annora knelt beside her. "Tell us, child. What did you learn?"

Mathilda pushed herself up on her elbows. "I saw my mother." It was hard to speak steadily, but the urgency in Annora's voice told Mathilda she must try to relate exactly what she'd seen. "Mother told me that Father would test the balance of all we've ever known, and that I must find a way to cut him down. She said some other things I did not understand."

Leticia frowned. "Tell us everything our sister said, child. Leave nothing out."

Mathilda nodded. She got to her feet, joining the women.

"Mother said I will preserve my coven, and they will protect me. Before she faded away, I heard her say, 'As stars above, as air between, as earth below, your soul shall keep.' What does it mean?"

Leticia looked perplexed. "I know not. We will meditate on it, see if we can find clarity." She returned her gaze, still more piercing, to Mathilda's face. "Before we wake our girls, you must listen. The Goddess favors you most and has granted you great power. You will be responsible for your coven; their welfare will be in your charge. Do not do any reckless thing to jeopardize them or the line. There is a spell that you must learn for the guarantee of future Guardians that come after you. I will put it in your mind, as well as in the minds of your sisters, shortly. It is imperative that all of you give birth within the same year."

Mathilda felt suddenly overwhelmed. It must have shown, because Katherine gently patted her arm.

"The first time each of you lies with a man, his seed will spill into you, but your belly will not swell just yet. The seed will lie in wait until the spell is spoken for it to take root in your womb. Only after each of you has been with a man should you all recite the spell as one.

The future line depends on the five of you completing the spell together. I will put the spell in your mind now."

Mathilda knew her cheeks were red. She felt the heat of embarrassment as these women gazed at her while Leticia spoke of a thing most women never said out loud. She swallowed her discomfort, however, understanding this was her legacy.

Leticia placed her fingers on Mathilda's temples. Her unspoken words filled Mathilda's mind. "It is done. When the time comes, you will know the words to use. Now, one final thing. Our time as Guardians is almost over."

"What do you mean, over?" Mathilda asked warily.

"I was given a vision last week," Leticia said. Her voice was clear and steady. "We are to die soon, my sisters and I."

Mathilda stared numbly. Her mother's death replayed in her mind, and now these women who had become mothers to her would also die? She suddenly burst into tears. She felt arms encircling her and soothing sounds as she sobbed into her hands.

"Mathilda, you are so strong," Annora soothed. "You can bear this. I know you can."

"And you must," Leticia said gently. "Your sisters will need your strength."

Leticia was right. Mathilda wiped her face. "Do they know?" she asked, looking toward the ground where the girls still lay as if sleeping.

Tears threatened to build in Leticia's eyes, but she willed them away.

"Our daughters know nothing of this. Upon our deaths, they are to come to you. You must comfort them and guide them. They will no longer live in the homes of their childhood. They will go where you go. Henceforth, Mathilda Longhurst, you will think of yourself as one unit with your coven. The Guardians that protect all."

Mathilda's throat constricted. The sting of tears pricked her eyes again, but she was too numb to cry more. Leticia turned and faced the others. "Wake," she whispered.

Mathilda watched her sisters slowly stir, overwhelmed with the sorrow she felt for their coming loss. As if sensing her distress, Leticia gently squeezed Mathilda's shoulder, then moved toward her daughter.

"How do you feel?" Leticia asked Ramona.

Ramona got slowly to her feet, as if testing whether her legs would hold her up. "Other than the pain in my head, I am fine."

"That was very odd indeed," Regina said, rubbing her temples.

"How often do we have to use dark magic?" Ramona asked.

"As often as necessary and only when dire," Leticia replied. "You will know exactly what to do when the time comes. Do not fret, Daughter."

Katrina asked, "May I try something, Mother?"

"You may," Katherine replied.

Katrina stretched forth her hands, and the skies blackened. When she waved her arm, the clouds quickly rolled away.

"Do not ever let anyone see you use your magic," Katherine said urgently. "You could burn because of it. Do you understand, girls?"

"Yes," they answered together, all except Mathilda, who could not find her voice.

"Good. Now we shall take our leave," Leticia said. "Mathilda, we will meet you at the Three Paths on the solstice at Terce, to travel to the solstice festivities." Her look at Mathilda was long and full of meaning.

Mathilda nodded. "Good day," she answered in a voice thick with emotion. "Thank you all."

Ramona turned back and spoke directly into Mathilda's mind. *I will keep your secret.*

Thank you, Mathilda silently replied. She had almost forgotten that she had told Ramona of Duncan's proposal.

She watched with great sadness as her mother's coven disappeared through the trees. Maelen would soon be reunited with them.

THAT NIGHT, as Mathilda lay in bed, her thoughts were with Duncan. His offer of marriage tugged at her heart. She imagined lying in his arms as the years wore on, happy and content. She heard their laughter that would come so easily. However, given what Leticia had told her today, Mathilda knew she could not go to Scotland with him. Her sisters would need her. She fell asleep with a heavy heart and her mother's odd words in her mind.

As stars above, as air between, as earth below, your soul shall keep.

8

The solstice finally arrived, like an old friend bringing fond memories. With the first light of dawn, Mathilda was well into the wood, collecting greenery and flowers to weave for a crown. Already, the heat was rising, and she knew there would be an evening storm. She saw some sweet violet and gently plucked a few purple sprigs, adding them to the poppies already collected in her basket.

Mathilda loved the solstice celebrations: the feasting and bonfires, the stories that followed, but her heart ached fiercely over the ominous death prediction Leticia had made. How could she even think of celebrating with the knowledge that her sisters were about to lose their mothers? She placed fern fronds in her basket, knowing she must play the part and not give away the sad secret she held.

On her way home, Mathilda came upon the tiny clearing where she had first met Cassandra. It had been weeks since she had seen her, and Mathilda wondered what kept her away. Perhaps she was staying close to home to keep an eye on their wicked father.

Entering the cottage, where the stone walls held the night's coolness, Mathilda placed her basket on the table and set about making a crown. Thoughts of Duncan invaded her mind as she worked, no matter how many times she distracted herself. She could not allow her heart's pull toward him to continue. It would only hurt more in the end. Mathilda forced her attention back to her task, focusing on the colors instead. The violets would be a lovely contrast to the yellow dress Regina had given her to wear. Her fingers moved deftly as she wove the remaining flowers and greenery into the wreath. She finished quickly, tying off the end, then went to bathe.

The sun was nearly halfway through the trees when Mathilda finished dressing. She collected the food she had set aside for herself in the larder and headed out into the wood. Along the path, she came across some merry village folk also making their way to the stone circle at Keswick for the festivities. Mathilda waved to them, wishing her heart felt as light as theirs.

Up ahead loomed the old druid tree. Sunlight filtered through the branches, and leaf shadows danced along the ground of the Three Paths. Leticia and Ramona stood waiting, baskets in hand.

"Good day, Mathilda," Leticia said. "You look lovely. Yellow suits you."

"Thank you." Mathilda offered what she hoped was a bright smile to Ramona. She carefully kept her thoughts only on the festivities. She didn't think Ramona would peek into her mind, but she had to try to lock away all her sad thoughts.

"Let's be on our way," Leticia said, adjusting her basket. "It is a long journey."

Mathilda did her best to keep her voice cheery on their long walk to the stone circle. The woodland opened to grazing pastures, and sheep dotted the landscape. Soon, rolling hills in the distance came into view. They finally reached their destination: a huge flat clearing where stones of varying sizes and shapes sat like strange sentinels.

The sun had climbed nearly to midday, and Mathilda was glad for the diversion. Groups of people trickled out of the surrounding wood, making their way toward the giant stones in solemn admiration. Mathilda saw Regina and Philippa standing by the grove with the others and headed over to greet them.

"You all look beautiful," Regina said proudly.

"Thank you," Isobel replied. "As do you."

A sudden hush came over the clearing. Mathilda looked around to see what the whispers were about.

"The Old One is here," Katrina said, pointing.

Mathilda followed Katrina's gaze to the edge of the wood. The grizzled old Druid moved slowly toward the clearing. He seemed to be as ancient as the stones themselves. Once, he seemed larger than life. His long, silver hair hung limply about shoulders that now slumped, and he leaned heavily on a walking stick.

"Come," Regina urged. "There are so many people here. I want to walk around and see everyone."

"You girls, don't go far," Annora called after them. "The Old One will start the ceremony soon."

Mathilda followed her sisters around the stones. Everywhere, people sat on the ground, basking in the sun's rays. Others stood about in conversation, gauging the position of the sun. More still came from the wood. Mathilda peered through the crowd, looking for Duncan. The thought of seeing him again sent a wave of mixed emotions coursing through her.

Ramona fell back and let the others go on. She pulled Mathilda to the side. "You seek Duncan?" she asked.

"Yes." Mathilda felt her heart racing. "He will want my answer."

"What *is* your answer?"

Mathilda dropped her gaze. "I cannot be his wife. Not after what my father has done. I must be here." She could not tell Ramona the full truth, not yet.

Ramona nodded. "I shall find him for you, then." She closed her eyes momentarily, and Mathilda knew she was seeking Duncan's mind. "He is there, Mathilda," she pointed. "By the woodline."

Mathilda saw him standing by a massive yew at the far end of the clearing, away from the crowd, eyes fixed on her.

"Oh, Ramona. He has seen me. I don't know if I can face him. What shall I do?"

"Go to him. You cannot put it off now."

Mathilda looked over her shoulder. No one was watching her, so she darted toward Duncan. When she reached him, he pulled her into the dense cover of trees.

He took in her looks, and his eyes glowed with admiration. "You are beautiful."

His compliment made her giddy. She blushed and turned away, but he tipped her chin toward him and kissed her, gently at first, but it quickly gave way to passion. She met his urgency with her own blazing passion and was disappointed when he pulled away and took her hand, leading her deeper into the wood.

"Where are we going?" she asked, breathless.

"I want to be alone with you. It's too distracting here."

She walked with him in silence, her heart heavy as she thought of what she must say. He led her through the wood and stopped beneath an ancient, gnarled oak. He looked into her face, studying her with those penetrating eyes. Sadness flashed within their amber depths, and he sighed heavily. Settling on the ground, one knee bent, the other stretched, he reached out to her.

Mathilda took his hand and nestled in beside him. Duncan's sadness told her he already knew her response. It should have been a relief that she didn't have to tell him her answer, but it felt too much like despair to her. He pulled her against him and held her in a resolved silence.

She rested her head against his chest, content for a while until the breeze disturbed the ribbons of her crown, fluttering them across her nose. She removed it and laid it on the ground. Duncan's silence seemed to last too long. It spoke loudly, unnerving her. "What are you thinking?" she asked.

"I am fighting against myself, Mathilda." His gaze moved somewhere beyond the distant trees. "I know you will refuse my offer of marriage. And yet, I cannot let you go. Not without knowing you."

He turned to her then. What she saw in his eyes overwhelmed her. No man had ever looked at her the way he was looking at her now; she had never imagined anything like this. An all-consuming hunger burned in his eyes as he raised his hand to her face, cupping her cheek. His thumb brushed along her lower lip, searing her with his touch. Mathilda closed her eyes and leaned into his hand. His lips touched hers, and her eyes fluttered open. He kissed her again, gently, as his gaze remained locked with hers. The kiss gave way to something more, something unexplainable, burning and inextinguishable.

Mathilda did not protest when Duncan removed her dress, untying the sash at the back and lifting the fabric over her head. His mouth sent fire along her skin as he trailed kisses from her collarbone to her naval. His clothes were next to go, discarded in a pile along with her dress. She became aware of the feel of the grass and hardened earth beneath her skin as he settled over her.

"Do you want me to stop?" he asked.

Mathilda shook her head, too enraptured for words. Duncan kissed her lips again and paused, his gaze searing right through to her soul. The sun broke free from a cloud then. Rays of light streaked through the trees over his bare shoulders, bathing them in golden light.

"Are you sure?" he asked softly.

"Don't stop," she whispered.

His thigh shifted against hers. Suddenly, she felt a brief pain as he entered her. He was still for a moment, and the discomfort passed. Before long, he moved again, only there was no pain. She had never known such feelings could exist. She gasped into his shoulder, relishing this new bliss as time ceased to exist. He began to quicken his movements, groaning as he suddenly went stiff and collapsed over her. Mathilda remembered what Leticia had said to her. A man's seed would spill into her. She now understood what Leticia meant.

"Are you all right?" Duncan asked.

"Yes, I am." She whispered a laugh. She was more than all right. She felt like a goddess.

He raised himself onto his forearms, gazing down at her, and smoothed her cheek with the back of his fingers.

"I am not sorry," he said. "If I must part from you, I would take a part of you with me."

"Duncan—"

"Do not speak of it. Just let me love you."

He began to move inside her again. Mathilda wished she could tell him the answer that he sought. Being with him this way was like nothing she had ever imagined. She felt his love and loved him back with everything she had to give. They lay in each other's arms as the sun drew high, blissfully unaware of the world.

CASSANDRA STALKED along the edge of the wood surrounding her house. Frustration mounted as she thought of her father's refusal to let her go to the standing stones to celebrate the solstice. He had left shortly after dawn, promising her he would return with a gift. She looked up, shielding her eyes. The sun would soon peak. Anger raged again at the thought of missing the festivities. She picked up a stone and flung it, screaming as it took flight.

As she circled the grounds again, she saw her father emerge from the wood. She gasped in horror at the sight. He walked with a long strap of leather in his hand. Attached to that leather were five young girls, she guessed between the ages of twelve and fifteen. They were all gagged and blindfolded, their hands bound to the leather strap that her father held tightly in his grip. A few of the girls stumbled as he dragged them along behind him. Cassandra heard their muffled cries through the cloths in their mouths.

"Father, what is this?" Her voice shook. "Who are these girls? Why have you brought them here?"

"I told you, Daughter. I have a gift for you." His eyes danced with the promise. Happiness had transformed his features. Gone were the menacing glares and anger that always flared in his eyes. She had not seen him this happy in years. But she saw something that unnerved her. Instability.

"Hurry, we must prepare before the peak of the solstice," he said, looking excitedly at her.

Cassandra tried to think. Whatever he was planning, could she stop it? He had once loved her. "I do not understand," she said, trying to keep her voice calm. "Prepare for what?"

"For our new life. Come, Daughter. Stand before me."

A shadow of something dark and ominous hovered over him. In a flash, it was gone, leaving her nearly choking on her fear. She knew better than to disobey him, and what he was capable of should she try. Whatever power he drew from was beyond her knowing and not to be trifled with. Her legs went weak as tremors shook her. She felt terror for the girls who trembled and cried. Their fear rolled over her in waves.

Her father removed the satchel from his shoulder, took out a bowl, and pulled the knife from his belt. "Give me your hand."

Cassandra gaped at him, shaking with fear.

"*Now!* We have little time."

She stretched out her trembling hand and cried out in pain as her father sliced across her palm with the knife. He caught her blood in the bowl and pressed the tip of the blade into his palm next, adding his blood to hers. Placing the bowl at her feet, he went over to the line of girls. Cassandra saw that they had all stopped struggling and stood like statues, staring skyward, waiting. He must have enchanted them, she thought.

Then he lifted the knife. The blade flared in the sunlight and slashed across the throat of the first girl in line. Cassandra screamed in horror. Her legs gave way, and she fell to the ground. Her father moved to the next girl. The knife flashed again, and again, the blood arcing out into the sun, until the last girl lay slumped at his feet.

Cassandra's screams sounded mad in her own ears. She screamed until her throat was raw. Then reason crept in. *Run!* She willed strength to her legs and scrambled to her feet, but her father's shout rooted her where she was.

"*Stay where you are!* Do not move."

She froze, gasping for breath, choking back her sobs. She dared not anger him. He would let nothing get in his way, not even her. She saw that now. As the blood flowed from his victims, he caught a little of it in the bowl from each girl and joined Cassandra, centering the bowl on the ground between them. She shuddered at his unnaturally brilliant smile. His eyes gleamed with feverish intensity as he took her hands in his. She recoiled from his touch.

"I give you immortality, Daughter. I finally found a way. We will live on together through the ages, and nothing will stop us. Our power will be the strongest in the land."

Cassandra could not understand. Only a madman would speak such things. Only a madman would murder innocents.

The blood in the bowl began to boil and bubble up over the edge. Cassandra felt herself being lifted away from the ground. Her father rose with her, and his grip tightened around her hands.

All at once, her vision went gray. Her veins began to burn as her blood pulsed and bubbled excruciatingly through each one. An agonized scream ripped from her throat as the spell took over.

In her mind's eye, she could see her father. His hectic smile suddenly turned sour. Something was wrong. He began to chant furiously, words Cassandra could barely hear, much less recognize.

Then, loud and clear, she heard, "*No!* I will not be robbed of this!"

Her eyes were still closed, Cassandra was sure, but now her inner vision showed something black and shadowy streaking out from her father's body. *His soul.* Cassandra knew it was somehow being pulled from him.

"*No!* You will not take this from me."

Cassandra knew not whom he shouted to, nor could she break the spell. Suddenly, her father's hands let go of hers. She felt his hot palms on her hair.

"Take it." His voice was harsh and desperate. "Take my powers. You will have all of my gifts."

Cassandra heard nothing else. She fell to the ground, unconscious.

~

AT THE STANDING STONES, as the sun climbed higher, Leticia found herself in a vision. In it, many souls cried out at once, and she fought for clarity through the thick fog that enveloped her mind.

She felt a hand on her shoulder. "Sister." Annora's voice was full of urgency.

Leticia found she could see. Her sisters stood outside the grove. All of them looked fraught with alarm. She realized the noise from the crowd sounded distant now. She glanced around, gaining her bearings. The people had all gathered within the circle as the ceremony was about to begin.

"We all shared the same vision," Katherine acknowledged. She looked deeply alarmed. Leticia had never seen her so disturbed.

"Let us go into the sacred grove," Annora suggested. "We will get more clarity there."

Leticia sensed she would not make it out of the grove. She glanced over her shoulder and saw her daughter, the love of her heart, standing with the other girls a short distance from the stones. How she longed to run to her and pull her into a final embrace, but she knew she could not. She had a duty to the Goddess above all else. "Ramona," Leticia called, getting her attention. "Go and find Mathilda. All of you need to stay with her now. She will know what to do from here."

Leticia watched the confusion play across Ramona's face. Her mouth opened to speak, but Leticia could not bear to have her find out what was about to happen. She cut off any questions before they could come.

"We must go now. Know that we love you." She drank in her

daughter's face, the shape of it, her dark, beautiful eyes, now full of worry. She forced herself to smile and realized her sisters were also imprinting their final moments, smiling despite their tear-filled eyes. "Hurry, Daughter," Leticia said.

Ramona looked on in confusion as her mother and the other elder witches left the group around the standing stones. The other girls seemed just as disturbed as she was by their mothers' actions. Fear pricked at her insides, but she remembered the urgency in her mother's words. She shook herself from her frozen state and led her sisters just inside the circle. "Stay here, all of you. I will fetch Mathilda."

~

IN THE SACRED GROVE, Leticia held out her palms. "Let us join hands, Sisters."

A powerful energy coursed over her as the solstice sun reached its zenith. Waves of light, only visible to her and the women beside her, swirled over the entire area around them, weaving through the stones in varying patterns. Suddenly, a vision of Aelle slammed into Leticia's mind. She heard her sisters' gasps, felt Katherine and Philippa's grip tighten on her hands, and knew they all shared the vision. Before Aelle stood five young girls. What he did next nearly sent Leticia to her knees as she watched him take their innocent lives. A sharp stab of fear pierced her heart as she heard Aelle promise Cassandra immortality.

"We cannot stop this," Katherine said. "We are not powerful enough as four."

Something unspoken transpired between the women. Duty, an understanding that these precious breaths were of their final moments. A lifetime of love in their shared sisterhood shone through their tears.

Leticia sniffed and pulled herself together. "Focus all of your energy on Aelle. He *must* not gain immortality. Cassandra will be left in our daughters' hands. They will deal with her in their own time. Now hurry; his spell is taking hold."

Philippa smiled. "This is it, Sisters. We will soon join Maelen."

They began to chant in unison. Louder, they continued. Leticia sent the full strength of her magic through their circle, binding it with her sisters' in a surge of pure, white light that streaked beyond their plane. She saw Aelle the moment their power encircled him; she felt his rage and the surge of his filthy magic as he lashed out through the unseen connection.

Her sisters' power had reached its peak, and Leticia knew it was time to let go. She saw the flow of their magic like patterns in a weave. It wrapped around Aelle, tightening. Then the flow pulled, drawing out his blackened soul. As their magic took hold of his life force, Leticia pictured the final stitch of a weave and tied it off, releasing the last of her energy to the Goddess. A familiar presence stood before the women, with burnished hair and a bright smile. Maelen. A brilliant light exploded across the grove, and as the sun passed its zenith, they all slumped over at once.

MATHILDA HAD JUST DRIFTED to sleep when a twig snapped behind her.

"Mathilda!" Ramona's voice was taut with disbelief. "Get dressed. You must come with me at once."

Mathilda burned with mortification. She jerked upright, covering her breast with her arms as she looked around for her dress. It lay in a heap beside Duncan. She reached across him and pulled it to herself, yanking it over her head, then got to her feet and smoothed it down, feeling the heat of shame across her cheeks. Duncan sat watching her in mild amusement as she struggled, completely comfortable in his own nakedness.

Ramona kept her back to them as they finished dressing.

Mathilda caught up her flower crown and turned to Duncan. His head was bent as he worked to tighten his belt. Her breath hitched as the realization came that she would not see him again. A crippling wave of regret and longing washed over her, nearly breaking her. He looked up then, and their eyes met. She saw the glaze of tears form in his eyes and the same crushing loss that she felt shadowed their amber depths. He cleared his throat roughly and ran his hand across his eyes. When his gaze landed on her again, the strength that she so admired in him had returned. He wore a look of resigned acceptance.

"I must go," Mathilda said to him. "I am truly sorry I cannot be your wife."

Duncan took a step toward her. His expression was a mix of love and loss as he cupped the back of her head and pulled her into his arms. "Goodbye, Mathilda," he softly said. He kissed her one last time before she turned away, full of the love they could no longer share.

"Goodbye, Duncan." She let Ramona quickly pull her away.

"Mathilda! How *could* you?" Ramona scolded once they were away from Duncan. "What if someone had seen you out here in the open? Any of the elders could have searched you out and easily found you if they had wanted to."

Mathilda's response came harsher than she intended. "I will not apologize, Ramona." Losing Duncan made her tongue sharp, so she decided to keep silent.

After a few moments, Ramona shot a glance at her. "Something has happened," she said, dropping the subject. "Right before the sun peaked, my mother and her sisters told us to find you and suddenly left us. I told Regina and the others to wait at the stones, but we must go to them until our mothers return."

Ramona's words hit Mathilda hard. This was the moment she had been dreading; the moment Leticia had warned her about. Being with Duncan had temporarily lifted the burden, but now it came crashing back down on her. Mathilda felt sick. She knew they would not be coming back.

She and Ramona never reached the stones. As they came to the edge of the wood, they heard wailing in the sacred grove. Ramona sped up. Mathilda made herself follow, dreading what they would find.

Mathilda was not prepared for the scene awaiting her. All the women lay on the ground as if they had dropped where they stood. Regina was slumped over Philippa, wailing and shaking her repeatedly, as if trying to wake her mother from a deep sleep. Isobel smoothed her hands over Annora's face in a quieter grief. Katrina sobbed and spoke the words of a healing spell over Katherine.

"Mother!" Ramona shrieked. She ran across the clearing and dropped to her knees beside Leticia. Tears streamed from her eyes. "What happened?" she demanded of the other girls.

Regina snapped from her grief. She smoothed Philippa's hair away from her face and turned to Ramona. "We do not know," she sobbed. "From where we stood, we saw them through the trees, holding hands in the grove. We thought perhaps they were holding their own sacred solstice ritual, but then they collapsed."

Her sisters' grief nearly overwhelmed Mathilda. Their loss was too familiar. Before she could comfort them, she felt strongly drawn to Leticia, as if she called to Mathilda. She knelt beside Ramona and touched Leticia's hand. An image of Cassandra flashed in her mind. She nearly stumbled back as a feeling of dread washed over her.

"What is it?" Ramona asked, wiping her tears away.

"I don't know what happened to your mothers," Mathilda began. "But it has something to do with Cassandra, possibly my father, too. They were fighting an evil that cost them their lives." She looked at the women, and a realization hit her. Whatever darkness they had fought against was left for their daughters and her to fight.

Her gaze swept over her sisters and their grief-stricken faces and the lost looks they shared, and she suddenly found she couldn't speak for the rising panic and grief rising in her chest. She recalled the words Leticia had spoken, urging her to be strong in the wake of their deaths, and found the words she needed to relay. "Let us lay your mothers in the earth. They would want it this way."

Her sisters nodded their agreement, staring numbly.

"Let us join hands, then," Mathilda said. "Mother Goddess, take the bodies of your devoted daughters into your loving embrace, and guide their souls on their journey in the afterlife."

The grove trembled. The earth split and rolled back. Massive roots stretched above ground like gnarled fingers and wrapped themselves gently, even lovingly, around the elder Guardians before drawing them into the soil. Mathilda watched with deep sadness as these powerful women disappeared with the roots below ground, and the earth repaired itself until the grove appeared undisturbed once more.

Katrina sniffed beside her, drawing Mathilda's attention. She dreaded what she had to say next, but she promised the women she would take care of their daughters.

"I must tell you all something," Mathilda said, breaking the heavy silence. "Your mothers spoke privately to me before this day. They knew of their own deaths beforehand and told me as much."

Isobel began to sob again. "Why then did you not tell us? We could have said goodbye."

Tears stung Mathilda's eyes, and she took a calming breath. "They forbade me from speaking of it to any of you. I gave my word."

Anger flared in Katrina's eyes.

"They made me promise," Mathilda said. The words broke off on a sob, and she tried to collect herself. "I did not want to keep this from you," she managed. "It has been the heaviest burden I have ever carried, and my heart has broken every day holding this secret."

Katrina's eyes softened. She nodded and dropped her gaze.

"There's more," Mathilda added gently. "Your mothers instructed me to watch over you all. Per their wishes, you will no longer remain in your houses. You are to come live with me."

"We are all on our own." Regina stared at the ground that had closed over her mother. A tear trailed down her cheek, lingering at her chin before it fell onto the earth.

"I am so sorry for your losses." Mathilda wiped away the fresh tears that sprang to her eyes. "Let us get away from this place. I will take you back to my cottage. Then I must find my sister and get to the bottom of this."

Mathilda helped her sisters gather up the baskets. They heard singing from within the stone circle as they stepped out of the grove. The celebration suddenly felt wrong given the magnitude of what just happened, and Mathilda couldn't wait to be away from it.

As they left the clearing, Mathilda glanced over her shoulder. She knew Duncan had gone, taking all her hopes of a carefree life with him.

9

At the cottage, Mathilda did all she could to make her sisters comfortable. As she stood in the larder, she realized with a start that she didn't have much prepared to serve them. She gathered what she could; some bread, cheese, a few vegetable tarts, and the wine, and set everything out on the table where everyone sat looking tired and so lost that it hurt Mathilda to the core.

"I'm sorry I don't have a proper meal prepared. Once I find my sister and return home, I promise I will make something suitable for you to eat." She glanced toward her bedroom and winced. She would have to get sleeping arrangements set up too. "Make use of my bed or anything else for your comfort while I am away. There are some extra blankets in the chest in the bedchamber."

Katrina looked up. She looked almost ill with her pale face, and red-rimmed eyes. "Thank you, Mathilda. We will be all right."

Mathilda reluctantly left them alone to grieve. She paused at the edge of the wood, where the tiny footpath from the cottage twisted away through the trees. Closing her eyes, Mathilda brought a clear image of Cassandra into her mind. She bent and touched her fingertips to the ground to make her intentions known to the Goddess.

After a few moments, Mathilda felt the pull to start walking and knew that she would find her blood-sister.

"Mathilda, wait," Ramona called.

"Yes?"

"I want to come with you."

Mathilda hesitated. "I don't think that is a good idea. You just lost your mother. You should stay with the others and comfort one another."

"No. I must get out for some air. Besides, the others are lying down, and I am too restless for that."

"Very well. But I warn you, I do not know what we will discover when we find my sister."

"I care not. My heart has died today. Nothing can hurt me now." Any joy that had ever graced Ramona's features was lost to her now. Her expression was one of dazed numbness.

Mathilda reached out and took Ramona's hand, squeezing it lightly before she released it and took the path.

"Where are we going?" Ramona asked.

"I cannot say. I have asked to be guided to Cassandra. We will know when we arrive."

They walked side by side down the quiet path. Ramona made no sound, but Mathilda noticed tears streaming down her face. Her heart ached for her sister.

"I am truly sorry, Ramona." Mathilda's voice cracked. She stopped walking and forced strength into her words as she turned to Ramona. "Although it seems impossible now, I promise your pain will get better. Every day gets easier. Eventually, the hole in your heart will heal a bit."

Ramona nodded. She wiped her eyes, and when she looked up, Mathilda saw strength in her gaze. "I know you speak the truth, for you went through the very same thing. I accept your comfort."

Mathilda smiled and started walking again. The woodland had thickened, and they had to mind the sharp thorns from the blackthorn thickets. They took a deer path up a small incline until it leveled out, and the trees were spaced farther apart. After a time, Mathilda felt Ramona studying her. "What is it?" she asked.

"Why did you give yourself to Duncan? Was it because of what my mother told you about the next line of Guardians?"

Mathilda's heart twisted at hearing Duncan's name. She smiled despite the pain.

"No. I gave myself to Duncan because I love him. I could not bear the thought of him leaving. I wanted to feel his love before we went our separate ways. Now, I will have the ultimate part of him once his child is born."

Ramona's face was open and curious. "Are you certain you love him?"

"I am. I think I knew it the first time our eyes met, even though I tried to push him out of my heart." There was so little to smile about, but Mathilda felt herself doing so again at the memory of that first encounter with Duncan.

Mathilda's magic tugged her attention toward her left. Through the trees, she saw a massive clearing surrounded by dense woodland.

"There," she said, pointing to the house in the distance. "That is the place."

They stepped out of the wood and Mathilda noticed a track that led south through the trees. The large house situated at the far end of the clearing was made of stone and was tall, likely housing an upper floor with sleeping chambers. Her eyes trailed higher where the peg tiles caught her attention. That's when she saw Cassandra. Standing on the roof, the wind whipped her hair wildly around her darkly clad form. The wrongness of the situation hit Mathilda all the way across the clearing.

"What is she doing up there?" Ramona asked.

"I don't know. You had better stay back." An urgency pulled Mathilda faster toward the house. She heard Cassandra's sobs as she drew closer.

"Sister," she called. "What has happened? Why are you up there?"

"There is no use," Cassandra wailed. "I tried; there is no use."

"What do you mean?"

"Nothing works. I have tried everything."

Alarm shot through Mathilda. "Cassandra, are you well?"

Cassandra barked a mirthless laugh. "Am I well? I will never be well again." Before Mathilda could say another word, Cassandra walked to the edge of the roof as easily as she would have crossed a room and flung herself down.

Mathilda heard the scream rip from her own throat. Cassandra's crumpled body lay nestled in the grass. Mathilda rushed to her and dropped to her knees. She gasped as she brushed aside the fiery hair covering her sister's face. Cassandra's neck was twisted in an ugly position, and a trickle of blood ran from her nose, trailing over the bow of her lip. Her eyes, glazed and unblinking, looked nearly yellow as the light caught the mix of green and brown tones in them. Her face still held its stricken expression even after death.

"Oh, Cassandra, why?"

Ramona scrambled over to Mathilda's side. Mathilda saw her own horror mirrored in her face.

"Why did she do this?" Her voice had an edge of hysteria.

"I do not know." Mathilda cleared her throat, trying to steady the building emotions that pricked at tears in her eyes.

Suddenly, Cassandra's body jerked. Her broken neck healed itself, moving back into its rightful position as the blood drew back up into her nose. Mathilda couldn't find her voice or move a muscle. In the next instant, Cassandra sat up, looking momentarily dazed.

Mathilda pushed away so quickly she fell backward. "H-how is this possible?"

"Father," Cassandra spat. "That is how it is possible," she said, rubbing her neck. "Because of him, I cannot die."

Mathilda got to her feet. What she felt went beyond horror, and it terrified her. "Cassandra, you must explain this to me at once."

"Our father learned an immortality spell," she said, rising to her feet. "It took the death of five innocent girls today to accomplish his feat." Anger flashed across her face as she shook out her skirt and met Mathilda's eyes. "It was supposed to have given us both immortality, but something happened that I cannot explain. While he was at the peak of his spell, Father fought with someone in his mind. They stopped him from gaining immortality."

Like a pattern on a weave coming together, Mathilda's thoughts flashed to the stone circle and the elders who'd lost their lives, but she blocked them from her mind quickly before Cassandra could read her mind.

"He is dead, Mathilda. Our father is dead."

Mathilda's chest tightened. Though she had not had any happy memories of her father since her childhood, the tears still came. She blinked them away, allowing the numbness along the edges of her mind to take over.

"And now I cannot die," Cassandra said, her voice breaking. "I did not want this," she sobbed.

Mathilda's eyes flashed briefly toward Ramona's as she wrapped her arm around Cassandra.

"I am sorry, Sister," she said, while Cassandra's words echoed like a drumbeat in her head. *Our father is dead.* She could not grieve for Aelle, not for a moment. "I do not know what to do to help you."

Cassandra's response was a mix of anger and despair. "You cannot help me. I have cut my throat, tried to drown myself, and then the jump from the roof... I am doomed to eternity in this wretched life, with no one by my side to comfort me."

Even through this unspeakable wrongness—the immortality, the uncertainty of what would happen now, Mathilda was moved by her sister's words.

"You have me, Cassandra. You have me to comfort you."

Cassandra rested her head on Mathilda's shoulder. "What am I going to do?"

"Let us get you inside. You should rest after your ordeal." Mathilda helped Cassandra inside the spacious home. She blinked with surprise. Though in need of a good cleaning, the house and its furnishings looked as though they should belong to a wealthy merchant, not a mistress and her daughter. A large oak table sat in the center of the room. Ramona pulled out a chair.

"Here. Sit," Mathilda urged. "Ramona and I will get you something to eat. Where is your larder?"

Cassandra lowered herself into the chair. Her dress trailed on the wooden floorboards, which, Mathilda couldn't help noticing, looked none too clean. "Through there," Cassandra said, pointing absently. "The larder's through there."

As she turned, Mathilda's eyes trailed up to the wooden beams that stretched across the high ceiling. A narrow upper-level overlook ran along the walls that she assumed housed sleeping chambers behind the oaken doors. Her father must have used whatever resources he had left to build this place. Two windows in the lower level let in enough light to help her see to the back of the house without the aid of candles.

The state of the larder came as no surprise. Dust settled in the corners and on the shelves. The prepping table had remnants of dried flour caked to it. She and Ramona searched through the clutter for anything already made but found nothing. Mathilda saw some mushrooms and leeks in a basket that she could use for a quick meal, but the table would need a good cleaning first.

"We will make tarts for her," Mathilda said, "but we'll need to clean up first." Then she glanced at Ramona and spoke directly into her mind. *Guard your mind well from my sister. We must hurry so we can get back to the others and warn them of this abhorrent feat.*

Ramona nodded and began clearing the mess from the table.

While Ramona was cleaning, Mathilda took bread and wine out to her sister. Cassandra stared blankly ahead, seeming not to notice when Mathilda set the food down on the table.

"Ramona and I will make tarts for you. Here is some bread in case you are hungry," Mathilda said, sliding it closer. "Is there anything else you need, Cassandra?"

Cassandra stared at the back wall for so long, Mathilda wondered if she'd heard her question.

"No. I just want to be alone," she answered, sounding weary. "I am going to lie down." Her eyes were haunted as she rose from her chair and drifted slowly toward the stairs like a wraith.

Mathilda watched her go with growing unease.

"Rest well, Cassandra. I will come back to check on you as soon as I can."

On the way home, Mathilda and Ramona walked in troubled silence. The sun dipped below the horizon, and the birds began their evening songs, unnoticed by the two women.

"Have you ever heard of such a spell?" Ramona eventually said.

"No, I have not." Mathilda frowned. "My mother spoke of other witches who desired immortality, but according to her, none had ever accomplished such an unnatural feat. Now I know what my father was working on all these months."

"Poor Cassandra. What will become of her?"

"I don't know." Cassandra's immortality frightened Mathilda. Especially having sensed so much darkness in her. She lifted her gaze from the path to Ramona's troubled face. "We will try to do what we can to ease her despair. Let us hope she is not unkind. To have that kind of power over death is very dangerous in the wrong hands."

"You do not trust her." Ramona's tone suggested she felt the same.

"No," Mathilda said. "She was kind to me, but I feel sure we must tread carefully in her company. Especially now. Who knows what she is capable of. She can easily get into the minds of others, as you can. Remember that, Ramona. Keep yourself guarded."

Twilight had settled over the forest when they arrived at the cottage, and a low rumble of thunder sounded in the distance. Isobel stood by the cooking pot, Katrina sliced bread, and Regina set the table. The aroma of stew permeated the air, and candlelight flickered around the room as the evening shadows crept in. Their silence was one of shared grief, and Mathilda recognized how they went about their tasks, doing their best to distract themselves from their pain.

"How are all of you doing?" Mathilda asked as she closed the door behind Ramona.

"We are bearing our grief as best as we can," Katrina replied. She placed the knife by the bread and glanced around as if searching for something else to busy her hands with.

Mathilda nodded in understanding. "I'm so sorry. It is nearly unbearable to lose a mother. I am just now able to speak of mine without difficulty. I understand what you are going through. We will get through this together." She pulled up her sleeves and followed Ramona into the larder to clean their hands.

"I hope you don't mind that we helped ourselves to your larder," Isobel said, wiping her hands on the apron she had tied around her waist. "We thought since we were here, the least we could do was cook supper."

Mathilda smiled. "Thank you, kindly. It smells wonderful. Go and sit. I will fill your bowls."

"What of your sister?" Regina asked when Mathilda joined them at the table. "Did she have anything to do with our mothers' deaths?" She had an angry glint in her eyes as she gazed expectantly at Mathilda.

"No. It was of their own doing in fighting against my father." The blackened burden of his deed weighed heavily on Mathilda. Ramona caught her eye and nodded, urging her to relay the news. "I'm afraid I have something dreadful to tell all of you," Mathilda described what she and Ramona had seen, how Cassandra had thrown herself from the roof and come back to life. When she finished, a stunned silence hung over the room.

"How can that be?" Regina asked. The horror etched on her face was mirrored in the faces around the table as everyone looked to Mathilda for answers.

"My father. He discovered a way to obtain immortality, but at a significant cost." She took a drink from her cup, but the wine tasted bitter on her tongue. "He murdered five young girls today for his sick desire for power."

"Oh, great Goddess." Isobel's words whooshed out, breathless and stunned. "Those poor girls."

Mathilda felt Isobel's shock as her own. She continued. "His spell was meant to grant both himself and Cassandra immortality, but your mothers learned of his plan. In their attempt to stop him, they lost their lives. My father is also dead from their spell."

"Why did your sister throw herself from the roof then?" Regina asked, leaning forward in her chair.

"Cassandra did not want any part of my father's plan. She is distraught. She had already attempted several times to take her life before we arrived, unsuccessfully, of course. We will closely watch to see how she deals with her new power. Let us hope she is not like my father, or this may be our life's work, keeping her in check." Mathilda suddenly pictured Aelle, his sudden rages, and his cruelty as she absently stirred her stew, her appetite lacking. "Tomorrow, we will go to Whitsby for supplies," she said, her thoughts taking a turn. It seemed strange to think of anything so normal as housekeeping.

"Not I," Regina said. "I will go to my father's house. I must tell him of Mother."

"Of course," Mathilda replied. "You will return here, will you not?" She felt a spike of alarm as she considered that Regina might not obey her mother's wishes to stay here in the cottage.

"Yes."

Katrina sighed with relief. "I thought for a moment you would leave us."

"No. I only wish to retrieve some things from my home and comfort my father."

"I will accompany you," Isobel said.

"No, thank you. I must go alone."

Mathilda looked up in surprise. The distance was too great for someone unaccustomed to walking, not to mention the dangers for a woman traveling alone. "Are you sure, Regina? It's a long journey. One of us should accompany you."

Regina suddenly looked lost and insecure as she seemed to grapple with the idea of going alone. Her chin lifted, and the steely glint was back in her eye. "Thank you, but I must be alone for a time. I will hire a cart from Whitsby for the journey."

Mathilda still worried about the danger, but she remembered her own experience after her mother died. "I understand." She sipped a bit of broth, grateful for the warmth. In spite of so much more urgent business, she found her thoughts drifting back to the solstice. To Duncan's body against hers, and his warmth filling her.

Regina seemed to hear her. "Are you thinking about the man you were with at the celebration?"

Isobel and Katrina suddenly leaned forward, looking expectantly at Mathilda.

Mathilda swallowed roughly. She took a long drink of wine before speaking. "I spoke greetings to several men. Which one are you referring to?"

Regina shot her a flat look. "Do not pretend with me, Sister. I am no fool." The corners of her lips edged up despite her tone.

Mathilda sighed. "No, you are not. His name is Duncan. I met him at the Beltane festival. He asked me to be his wife."

Regina gasped. "You let him have his way with you. That is why you were in the wood so long."

Heat rose to Mathilda's cheeks. "I did not *let* him have his way. We love one another. It was mutual affection."

Katrina looked worried. "Are you going to marry him?"

Mathilda's gaze dropped to her lap. She smoothed her skirt as a distraction from the stinging tears. She took a breath, willing them away. "No. It is out of the question. Duncan has gone back to his homeland, and I am needed here."

"Well then, I am deeply saddened for you, Mathilda." Regina's tone was more angry than sad. "To find someone who truly loves you and accepts you as you are, and then lose them suddenly from your life, it must be difficult."

Mathilda knew the bite in Regina's tone was out of her own longing to find love, yet the sting of her words nearly brought tears.

"You have his seed in your womb then," Katrina said, matter-of-fact, snapping Mathilda out of the moment. "That leaves us four to accomplish our goal."

Mathilda shifted in her chair. "There is no need to rush," she said, sounding motherly. "Nothing is pressing us to continue the line so soon."

"What was it like?" Isobel asked. "Being with a man, I mean." Her large, expressive eyes held a mix of curiosity and innocence.

Mathilda flushed at the memory. "It was... uncomfortable at first. But then, once the discomfort passed, it was beautiful."

Regina's mouth twisted. "Such a loss," she repeated.

A crushing sadness tore at Mathilda's heart as she recalled the blaze of devotion in Duncan's eyes as he seared his love into her skin with his lips. "I do not wish to speak of this any longer." The words came out harsher than she meant. "Will you excuse me?"

Choking on a sob, she rushed outside to the rainwater barrel, quickly dipped the cup, and took a long drink. The barrier she had put up around her emotions finally gave way. She braced her hands on the edge of the barrel, and her body shook under the weight of all the day's events as they crashed down on her. Tears streamed down her face.

She heard the door to the cottage open and quickly swiped her hands across her cheeks. She had to be strong for the others. Their loss was much greater than hers.

"It is all right to cry over Duncan," Ramona said. "You love him."

A blue-blackened sky stretched above with a rim of orange on the horizon—a beautiful close to a horrific day. Mathilda looked at her steadfast friend. Even in the shadows, Ramona's compassion shone.

Mathilda let out a sob. "I am sorry, Ramona. I don't mean to cry. The loss you have endured today is far greater. Forgive me."

"There's no need to apologize. We all have suffered today." She reached out and took Mathilda's hand, squeezing it. "Tomorrow will be the first day to start over. We will survive this together, as you said."

Mathilda found she could smile. She pressed Ramona's hand. "You are a good friend, Ramona. I'm glad you are here with me."

Ramona returned the smile. "Come on. We should try to get some sleep."

"Yes. We don't know what tomorrow will bring."

10

___

Mathilda woke a little after dawn, later than usual. She eased out of bed, careful not to disturb Ramona, who slept on the floor beside her. She pulled on her tunic and crept out of her room. The others were asleep in front of the hearth, and Mathilda moved quietly around them. On the table, she found a note with her name on it.

Mathilda,

I have gone to my father's house. Wait for my return before you go to the village. I shall be back with you by midday.

Regina

MATHILDA FROWNED, tucking the letter away. Regina must have slipped out sometime in the night. It worried Mathilda to think of

Regina traveling alone, though she reminded herself that Regina could certainly use magic to protect herself, if she had to.

The gray tones of dawn had already bloomed into rose-hued clouds streaking across the brightening sky when Mathilda stepped outside. Mist hung in the air from the night's storms, dampening her hair, and the sound of water dripping from the trees pattered across the forest floor.

Thoughts of Duncan crept into her mind. He would be safe in a rugged land with his kin by now. She remembered his smile, the laugh line at his mouth. Would he find happiness soon? Would he forget about her now that he was gone? A sick pit formed in Mathilda's stomach as she imagined him with another woman, forging his life with her.

She forcibly shook off the thoughts and focused on her walk. It felt good being alone with nature. Everything here was far from sadness. It was pure and peaceful, giving her a sense of renewal. She ventured a little farther until she came to an ancient beech. A massive hole at its base beckoned to her. Mathilda smiled with anticipation as she crouched and stepped inside. Cool, damp air enveloped her senses, and she closed her eyes, breathing in bark and desiccated leaves. The earth was smooth and compacted, likely from an animal bedding down, and Mathilda settled on the ground with a contented sigh. After a time, she got to her feet and left the dark haven.

On her way back to the cottage, she wondered if the others were awake. Now that her sisters were staying with her, she would need to arrange better sleeping quarters for them. Mathilda knew she would have to take some money from the secret chest to meet their basic needs until they could make a more permanent arrangement. With that thought, she smiled. Having them beneath her roof comforted her.

Mathilda slipped her pattens off outside the door and went inside. Katrina had just set bread and berries on the table for Ramona and Isobel.

"Good morning, Sisters." Mathilda leaned against the wall and removed her shoes.

"Have you been walking?" Katrina asked. "Your hair is all damp."

"Yes." Mathilda lifted a section from her shoulder and let it drop. "The forest is wonderful at dawn. Perhaps you all will join me tomorrow. I feel new each time I go out there."

"Where is Regina," Ramona asked.

"She set out before dawn to visit her father. Her note said she'll be back by midday."

"She doesn't want a longer visit with him?" Katrina asked. She ripped off a piece of her bread and bit into it as she sat down with the others.

Mathilda shrugged. "Apparently not. I am sure she has her reasons." She took off her damp cloak and draped it on the back of a chair. "I am going to look in on Cassandra. I wanted to see how you were all faring this morning before I go."

Ramona said, "Would you mind if I come with you? After what I witnessed yesterday, I am also worried for her."

"You may come," Mathilda said.

"Be careful," Isobel said with meaning as she looked up from her bowl.

AN ODD SORT of stillness hung about Cassandra's house. Mathilda felt uneasy. She rapped on the door and waited. "Cassandra? It's Mathilda. I've come to see you."

There was no answer. "Maybe she's gone out," Ramona suggested.

"No. She is here," Mathilda said, feeling the strange tug of Cassandra's darkened energy. "I feel her presence. Come, let's look for her."

They walked around the back of the house. Strange sounds came from the stone outbuilding, and Mathilda quickened her pace toward it.

Ramona shivered. "I do not like the feel of this place."

"Nor do I. Stay close."

Mathilda didn't bother to knock this time. She pushed open the outbuilding's door and stepped in.

She wasn't prepared for what she saw. Dead birds littered the floor in heaps; tits, finches—most of them were unidentifiable due to the dark stains to their tiny bodies. A crow with its throat cut lay at Mathilda's feet. Blood covered nearly everything. She swallowed against the bile that gnawed at her insides.

Cassandra was standing over a long wooden table beneath the window on the back wall, holding down a struggling crow. Mathilda saw that its surface, too, was streaked with crimson. Cassandra turned to face her, and Mathilda nearly choked when she saw the splatters of blood dotting her face and dripping from the ends of her hair and the knife in her hand. There was a dark stain down the front of her dress, and Mathilda forced her eyes from the sight of it.

"What are you doing, Sister?" Mathilda asked carefully. Cassandra must have gone mad, and she dared not agitate her further.

"I am practicing my new power. What does it look like I am doing?" She spoke clear and sure, not like someone who was mad. Though there was a determined gleam in her eyes that Mathilda recognized. She had seen that same look in her father.

Mathilda raised an eyebrow. "Killing these poor creatures is part of your practice?" Her careful tone slipped, but she couldn't help it.

"I am not killing them. Well, not permanently. Watch."

Cassandra stabbed the crow and flung it to the floor. Ramona clamped a hand over her mouth and rushed outside. Mathilda heard her retching.

Cassandra scoffed. "Stupid girl." She uttered a spell that Mathilda did not recognize, except for the filth that that it left surrounding the room. She had sensed this kind of magic the night

Aelle killed her mother. All at once, the dead birds on the floor went into a flurry of motion. They spread their wings and flew out of the building in a cloud. "See," Cassandra said. "I gave them life. No harm done."

A dark foreboding slammed into Mathilda's mind. "But why would you kill them only to revive them?"

Cassandra shrugged, averting her eyes from Mathilda's gaze. "Why are you here, Sister?"

Mathilda fought the anger and repulsiveness from her mind, recalling the purpose of her visit. "I wanted to check on you. Yesterday you were quite upset. Would you like us to cook dinner for you?"

"No. I will manage on my own."

Mathilda was relieved. Cassandra's deed had left her shaken. She needed to get out of this place and its vile energy that seemed to hold her down. "Very well. We will take our leave. If you need anything, you know where to find me."

"Good day, Mathilda," Cassandra said curtly. She turned her back and gazed at the bloodied table.

Mathilda studied her for a moment. She felt her sister's struggle, her need to reach out but some obstinate will keeping her from doing so. Beneath the wickedness of Cassandra's actions that Mathilda sensed, was a rush of feelings: regret, hopelessness, and something much darker. As soon as she tried to pick it apart, a wall slammed up in her mind as her sister collected herself. "Good day, Cassandra," she finally said.

Outside, she went around the house, where she found Ramona leaning against the wall. Her face was starkly pale against the dark-gray kirtle she wore. Her braid hung over her shoulder with the tie of her ribbon slipping. "Are you all right?" Mathilda asked, tightening the tie for her.

"I am now. What is wrong with your sister? She showed no remorse at all when she killed those birds."

"No." Mathilda glanced over her shoulder as they started across the clearing for home. "I'm afraid for her. She made it quite clear that she wanted nothing from me, and I fear to intrude upon her now would only anger her. After what happened today, she needs to be watched, but I will stay away for some time. She might come back to her senses."

"I do not think that she will," Ramona said solemnly. "I sensed great malice in your sister."

"As did I," Mathilda said." She shuddered at the memory of the bloodied birds, at the lack of emotion and unnatural ease of how Cassandra brutally killed them. "I fear what she may do next."

WHEN MATHILDA and Ramona arrived at the cottage, they found a lively commotion in progress. Several carts were lined up outside the door, one with a horse standing dangerously close to her mother's foxglove, as men unloaded large traveling chests from the backs of them. Regina herself stood beside the cottage door. She wore a richly dyed woad gown with a wide golden band at the hem. A floral pattern of intricate stitching ran down the front of her dress, disappearing into the belt tied at her waist. She looked as regal as her mother ever had, while she issued orders like the high lady of a manor.

Mathilda made it to her side. "Regina, what is all this?"

"I wanted to do my part in helping us get on," she stated as if it were obvious. "These were my mother's servants. Now they are mine."

Mathilda looked on, speechless. "May I speak privately with you?"

"Certainly."

They went around the side of the cottage, away from listening ears.

"Regina, I know you mean well, but we have no room for all this.

We barely have room for sleeping arrangements as it is, and now you bring servants? Where will they sleep?"

Regina waved her off. "Don't worry. I've thought everything through. These men will sleep in the carts—hear me out," she added when Mathilda opened her mouth to protest. "With all of us here in your cottage, it will be hard at first. They are here to help us get on until I can secure a maid—and I am working on that. If Father would relent..." Her voice trailed off, but the uncertainty only lasted an instant. "Most of them are laborers," she went on, as briskly as before. "They will build anything you wish, another cottage, storage buildings, make this cottage larger..."

Alarm shot through Mathilda. "No! This cottage must remain *exactly* as my mother designed it. I do not mind if we add another house, but my cottage is off-limits. Is that understood?"

"Quite," Regina said in a small voice. Her proud posture shrank. She seemed more like a wilted flower now.

Mathilda saw tears pooling in her sister's eyes and was immediately remorseful. "I'm sorry, Regina. I know you mean to help." She should have realized Regina needed to take on projects to handle her grief. "I was only afraid, for a moment, that something would change this place—and my mother's memory." She shook her head, feeling silly. Nothing could change her mother's memory. "If you are happy having all this, then I will grow to love it, too."

Regina smiled and wiped her tears. "Thank you. And I promise no hand will touch this cottage."

Mathilda gestured toward the servants, who were still swarming around the yard. "Do you trust them? Could they betray us?"

"No. These servants swore an oath to my mother to keep our nature a secret. Besides, they are spellbound. They will become mute if they even try to utter a word about what we are."

"I see." Though she didn't like the idea of magic used this way, Mathilda understood why Philippa chose to bind her servants' tongues. "How did your father take the news of your mother?"

Grief shadowed Regina's eyes before they glazed as if some

memory played out in her mind. "Not very well, I'm afraid, but he said very little. Father and I do not like to show our feelings. I bid my farewell to give him privacy to grieve alone. After a fortnight, he plans to tell the court that Mother caught fever and died while visiting distant relatives. That will give him time to compose himself, and we will hold a memorial service then."

Regina's practicality startled Mathilda. "I see."

A sheen of tears flashed in Regina's eyes which she promptly blinked away. "Let us make sure the supplies are unloaded properly."

Mathilda watched in amusement as Regina went back to her lady-of-the-manor role. The thought of having strange men tending to her made Mathilda uncomfortable, but if it distracted Regina from her mother's death, then she would accept these changes. It would be a good distraction for the others as well. Mathilda was thinking about how much busier the cottage would feel in the coming days, when she realized she could hear sounds of clucking and scratching.

"Chickens!" The scurrying birds, with feathers that looked as soft as black silk, dotted the ground, darting between her feet, pecking their way around the edge of the cottage. Mathilda stepped around them. "Regina, where will we keep them? They will be picked off by foxes or hawks."

"No, they will not. We will cast a protection spell around the border of the property. They will be fine."

Mathilda had to admit Regina was thorough. "You *have* thought of everything."

"Yes. I said that already." Her demure smile turned to one of satisfaction.

Katrina joined them. Though her dull, brown kirtle was a stark comparison to Regina's extravagance, she was no less lovely. The excitement that was etched on her face lent her a look of radiance.

"This is wonderful," Katrina gushed. "I have never seen so much finery. And *servants*! We will not have to work so hard around the property now."

Mathilda smiled at Katrina's enthusiasm. Maybe things would be all right after all.

By suppertime, beef and barley stew filled the cooking pot by Mathilda's own hand. There was warm bread and fresh ale and Mathilda was pleased to see Regina had brought wine from her father's house. She had grown to enjoy the taste since trying the bottle Leticia had left for her.

"I must say, Regina, it is nice having the men help with the heavy chores to free us up," Mathilda admitted. "Thank you for everything. I hope I was not too harsh on you earlier."

"No. You were right to protect your mother's home," she said, stabbing a piece of meat with her knife. "I would have done the same thing. I hope you will not mind all of the extra commotion around here in the coming months. I am used to such goings-on, so for me, it will be like home."

"Good. I want you to feel at home."

Somehow, the servants had found the time between Regina's orders to prepare rough covers for the carts by nightfall. They had also pushed the small writing table in the main room out of the way and prepared bedding for Regina, Isobel, and Katrina. Ramona had opted to place her own bedding on the bedchamber floor next to Mathilda.

Thankfully, the noise had subsided. Mathilda lay in her bed, restless. She felt guilty that her sisters slept on the floor, but at least their provisions were better improved now that Regina had taken the situation to hand. She hoped the new cottage would be completed before the cold season so that everyone could be more comfortable.

The sound of Ramona's even breathing soothed Mathilda. Before long, she, too, found sleep, though it was troubled with a dream.

Mathilda saw her soul hovering above her body against her will. She tried to reach out to the others, but her sisters were lost to her. She struggled wildly to get back inside her body, but no matter how much she fought, she could not reach it.

Mathilda woke with a jerk to a still-darkened room. She crept outside, using her magic to light a flame on the cresset lamp as she made her way through the dark to her mother's grave. Crickets hummed in the otherwise stillness, comforting her as she settled beside the mound.

"Hello, Mother," Mathilda said softly. "I come to get clarity. I had a disturbing dream that I fear is a vision of what will come." She told her mother about the terrible loneliness she had felt as her soul struggled outside her body, and ended with a long sigh "I can't help but wonder if I am going to die."

She wove her fingers through the new grass growing atop the mound and pictured her mother's face. "How I wish you were here to help me interpret this strange vision." For whatever slight comfort it could give, she laid both hands on her mother's grave, as close as she could get to her. She closed her eyes and breathed in the essence of her surroundings—its heady earthen scent and stillness. A soft breeze rustled through the elm's canopy above her like a hush.

Suddenly, in her mind's eye, she saw four quartz crystals sparkling and shiny. At first, she saw only the stones themselves. Then, in another image, the stones adorned her sister's foreheads. Her sisters spoke to her without their voices but in various locations.

The vision ended, and Mathilda opened her eyes. "Thank you, Mother." She had no doubt Maelen had sent her the message. "That gives me peace for tonight."

She kissed her fingers and touched them to the grave. Collecting the lamp, she went back to her bed.

In the morning, after eating a porridge Katrina had prepared, Mathilda took out her mother's box of magical stones from the small chest in the corner of her bedchamber. She rummaged through, noticing the various textures and hues of blues, greens and browns of each stone—all of them smaller than her palm. The light caught in one nearly the size of an egg but longer and with flatter edges. Mathilda pulled it out, recognizing it from her vision. She held the large quartz up to the light. Its rough, milky surface faded to smooth, clear edges on one end that cast sparkles around the room.

"What do you have there?" Ramona asked from the open doorway.

"Quartz." Mathilda cupped the stone in her palm and told Ramona about her dream "I was so frightened when I woke, I went out to my mother's grave for clarity. She sent me a vision."

Ramona's expression was troubled. She stepped into the room and sat on the bed. "What did the vision show?"

Mathilda said, "You, Regina, Katrina, and Isobel were all in different places. Upon your foreheads, each of you wore a crystal like this one. You all spoke to me in my mind, but your mouths did not open. I could hear you all, the same way you and I can speak into each other's minds when we are near one another.

"I remembered," Mathilda said, "that my mother had the very same crystal in her box of stones. This one. I plan to break it into five parts, polish them, and fashion them into necklaces. Then, we can spell them to communicate with each other no matter where we are."

"That is very wise," Ramona said. "After everything that's happened recently, we may find these useful."

Mathilda knew the stones would also mask their use of magic, which could well be important. "Come, let us tell the others and start with this task."

After Mathilda relayed her dream, she took the stone outside to the wall and with a borrowed chisel and hammer from the men, she chipped five pieces off while her sisters stood around her, watching with interest.

"Now what?" Isobel asked when Mathilda passed her piece of quartz.

"Let us polish them against the rougher stones of the wall," Mathilda said. She lifted her piece of quartz, feeling the edges with her fingers. "I will fetch us some water and cloths before we begin."

The sun had passed midmorning by the time they finished

smoothing and cleaning the stones. Mathilda led everyone inside to complete the final task.

In her bedchamber, she pulled back the rush mat, revealing the etched circle on the floor.

"Let us cast our magic into these stones," Mathilda said. She sat, crossing her legs, and placed her quartz piece on the floor. Her sisters joined her, settling down with the soft rustle of fabric of their skirts as they laid their stones in front of themselves.

"Close your eyes," Mathilda said. "See your quartz in your mind, and your magic encircling it." Mathilda imagined the stone she had chipped for herself and saw the white light of her energy swirling around it. "Now, open your eyes, touch a finger to your quartz, and repeat after me: 'When the lips close, the mind shall speak.'"

Mathilda's eyes were fixed on her stone as her sisters' voices echoed the words. When they finished, she gently rested the tip of her index finger against the top of her crystal. A black dot began to form, turning red at the edges like fire eating through parchment. She lifted her finger and watched as her magic seemed to burn hole into the stone. A brilliant light enveloped it before disappearing.

Regina turned her head toward Mathilda; a look of intent still etched on her face. "Do you think it worked?"

"There is only one way to find out," Mathilda said, taking her crystal and getting to her feet. She pulled the mat back in place on the floor and took the leather cords she had cut earlier and passed them to her sisters. "Attach these to your stones for a necklace and let us go out into the wood and separate."

Mathilda drew her own necklace over her head. "Once we are well into the wood, I will ask you all a question individually, and you will respond only in your mind, then we will meet back here." She led everyone outside and with a quick nod to her sisters, she cut across the clearing ahead of them and into the wood.

Mathilda walked until she came to the clearing where she first met Cassandra. *Regina, can you hear me?*

Yes, I can. Regina's voice came clear in Mathilda's mind, closer than if Regina was standing by her side. Mathilda smiled. It worked. She repeated her question to the rest of her sisters with success. With a sigh of relief, Mathilda started walking again.

"What are you doing, Sister?"

Mathilda jumped at the voice. She tucked her necklace beneath her chemise before turning. "Cassandra. What are you doing here?" Her sister had color in her cheeks and a brightness in her eyes. The emerald tone of her dress complemented her coloring. Cassandra had taken care with her appearance. Her hair, clean and brushed to a shine, tumbled around her shoulders. She clasped her hands at her waist and started walking toward Mathilda.

"I found myself with nothing better to do, and I thought I would come to see what you were about."

"I was just taking a walk," Mathilda replied, her gaze sweeping across the forest.

Cassandra fell into place beside her. "You are getting a late start, are you not?" She glanced up at the sun directly overhead.

Mathilda carefully focused on Ramona while keeping her mind closed to Cassandra, a task she found easy. *I happened across Cassandra. I will open my mind to you. I am not sure what she wants. I may need you.*

Ramona's reply came quickly. *I will listen in until I know all is well.*

"I was not feeling well when I woke," Mathilda lied. "I am recovered now. What have you been about since I last saw you?"

"Oh, a little of this, a little of that," Cassandra said. The smile that edged her lips looked like one of anticipation. "Walk with me, dear, sweet sister."

Mathilda's brows lifted at her sister's suspicious, saccharine tone. She studied Cassandra as she took a small deer path that ran alongside her path home. Cassandra seemed more herself, but a wild sort of energy thrummed around her, contradicting the calmness of her countenance.

"How are you getting along with your...?" Mathilda trailed off, loath to speak about her sister's immortality.

"I am getting along just fine. In fact, I would like to have you join me in three nights for supper. You will be my guest of honor."

Cassandra did seem improved, but something stirred beneath her words, a taint that somehow bled through them. Mathilda wanted to root it out. "I suppose I could join you, only why are you honoring me?"

Cassandra stopped walking and turned innocent, even hurt, eyes on Mathilda's face. "Can I not honor my sister?"

Mathilda was careful to mask her suspicion. "You can."

"Then you'll come?"

"Yes."

There it was again: that wild, uncontrolled energy that flared around Cassandra like a dark aura. Mathilda didn't like the feeling it gave. She felt uneasy accepting her offer, but something inside pushed her to sort out what was behind Cassandra's motives.

A broad smile crept over Cassandra's face. Mathilda recognized the smile from the one that Gundred wore in the vision Cassandra had once shared. It was chilling, yet beautiful. "Excellent. Good day, Mathilda, until we meet again."

Mathilda bid her sister farewell and walked quickly back to the cottage, feeling uneasy. Ramona was waiting for her when she came to the clearing.

"Did our sisters return from the wood?" Mathilda asked, worried.

"They are inside."

Mathilda nodded. "What did you hear?"

"Everything." Ramona stepped closer. "Are you actually planning to attend Cassandra's supper?"

"Yes. I am curious to see what my sister is about. She was too cheerful, falsely so."

"Did she seem well?"

"Outwardly, yes, though something felt off. I hope this supper will show me the depth of her intentions."

Ramona grasped her arm. "Mathilda, no." Her eyes were wide and pleading. "I saw for myself what your sister is capable of. Do not go."

Mathilda ran her fingers over the crystal necklace. "I won't be alone," she said. "I'm pleased we put these crystals to use today."

11

"I cannot believe you are going through with this," Regina muttered. She shook her head, yet again, and reached for the comb on the table.

"Regina, I will be perfectly safe." Mathilda sat still as Regina combed her hair, drawing it out in long golden waves. "Do not worry for me."

"This is not wise, Mathilda. I do not trust Cassandra."

Mathilda didn't want to admit it, but her sisters' worries gnawed at her. Katrina and Isobel said little, but Regina had no qualms about voicing her own firm, insistent concerns.

"I do not trust her either," Mathilda said, "That is why I must go."

Regina deftly wove a section of Mathilda's hair into a braid and coiled it over her ear, looking to make sure it matched the coil on Mathilda's left side before pinning it securely. "For my peace of mind, will you *please* let a servant take you by cart? I do not like you traveling on foot in the dark. Especially going to see *her*."

"Regina, I have linked our crystals. If anything goes wrong, you will know it. Besides, I will not inconvenience the servants for your fear of my walking. Those carts are their sleep shelters."

Regina sniffed daintily. She ran the comb through the hair that she had left loose at the back of Mathilda's head one final time before placing the comb on the table. "Very well. I do not like it, though."

Mathilda stood and smoothed out the skirt of her simple blue kirtle. She pulled the material at her waist up over her belt to shorten the length so as not to dirty the hem during the long walk.

Isobel sat by the hearth, sewing by the firelight as Mathilda stepped out of the bedchamber; Katrina sat to her right, gazing at the flames with a worried expression. She gazed at Mathilda, and her unspoken words were heavy in the silence.

"Be careful, Sister," Isobel said in a hushed, somber voice.

Mathilda smiled, despite her unease. She took the lamp from the table. "I'll be back soon," she said, giving a nod—partly for her own encouragement.

Outside, she found Ramona waiting by the cottage door, her face set and resolved. Her dark eyes were full of concern.

"We will focus all of our energy on you," she said. "All you have to do is ask us to come. I will lead the way to fetch you."

"Thank you, Ramona." Mathilda forced a smile. "I must be off. The sun is nearly gone." The walk to the Three Paths was peaceful in the dimming light, but night came quickly in the forest. An indigo sky soon stretched over the canopies above with the first stars flashing. Mathilda used her magic to light the lamp as she took the path that ran left of the druid tree. The lamplight cut out a soft glow through the darkened wood. A beetle scurried across the path, and Mathilda was careful not to step on it as she walked amongst the shadowed silhouettes of trees that surrounded her like familiar friends. The light caught in the eyes of a deer up ahead. Sensing no danger from her, it moved slowly into the shadows of the trees.

By the time she reached Cassandra's home, it had grown fully dark, and the peacefulness from the forest was replaced by a biting unease. Candlelight glowed from inside the dwelling, surrounding the edges of the windows in warm, golden hues. Raucous laughter carried outside. Mathilda frowned, wondering who else had been invited. She stilled her nerves with a long inhale and knocked.

Finally, the door swung open. "Ah, Mathilda. Do come in." Cassandra wore a dress of such dark green that at first glance, it appeared black.

Mathilda stepped warily into the house. Three people she had never seen before already sat at the table: two men and a heavily bosomed woman, drinking and making merry. The portly man closest to the door took indecent liberties with the woman, groping her breast. She slapped his face hard with a resounding crack. He pulled the woman from her chair onto his lap, undeterred, and kissed her. Mathilda was astonished that she did not protest.

"My sister has arrived," Cassandra announced over the noise.

No one regarded Mathilda with much interest save for the other man slumped at the opposite side of the table, who briefly glanced up but turned his attention back to his ale. Mathilda's unease grew. This night, these people: All of it felt wrong.

"I know. You are uncomfortable," Cassandra said. She took Mathilda's arm and led her toward the table with a smile that seemed genuine. "Come. I will pour some wine for you. You will relax soon enough."

"Who are these people?" Mathilda asked. She pulled her arm free from her sister's hold and noticed the lone man tip his cup to his mouth, spilling it over the sides of the rim. She watched with disgust as it ran down his neck and into the collar of his dingy yellow tunic.

"Just a few new friends. I will introduce you."

Cassandra poured the wine into a pewter chalice and gave it to Mathilda. "Please, I insist." She gestured for Mathilda to sit at the head of the table.

Mathilda reluctantly sat, smoothing her skirt as she cast a glance down the table. It was surprisingly elaborate. A crisp white linen stretched across it, with a wide, double blue band and birds and flowers embroidered between the banding. The chalices were elaborate with floral etchings that matched the handle of the knife by Mathilda's hand.

"Here is John Abbott," Cassandra said, drawing Mathilda's attention. She pointed to the man hovering over his ale. "That is Stewart Bidwell, and the woman on his lap is Isolde Fitton. Everyone, this is my sister, Mathilda."

Isolde pushed herself off of Stewart with an unsteady drunken waver. "Pleased to make your acquaintance," she droned. The neckline of her tunic was scandalously low, and when she bent in a low bow toward Mathilda, a hint of her ample cleavage peeked out. Stewart gave her a hearty slap across her backside, and she squealed, tumbling into her own chair.

Cassandra briskly clapped her hands, drawing Mathilda's eyes away from Isolde. Four servants rushed into the room with trays laden with food and laid them on the table.

"You hired servants?" Mathilda asked.

Cassandra's brows lifted, and she shot an amused look toward Mathilda. "Goodness, no, I have no money. I enchanted them. They will do what I say until I tire of their hovering."

Mathilda gaped, repelled by the audacity. "Do you think that is wise, Cassandra? What if they tell someone about you?"

A serving man near Mathilda uncovered a lid from a large platter, revealing a roast pig surrounded by an array of vegetables. Farther down the table, the other servants ladled soup into bowls. Mathilda frowned. How had her sister paid for this luxurious meal and the adornments of the table? She decided she did not want to know, as it was surely from duplicitous means.

"They will not. It is part of the spell. They have no idea they are under my control. It is as if they are sleeping."

"You," Isolde said to a servant. "Bring me more wine."

The man reached for the bottle and headed her way.

"Put the bottle back on the table, Reginald," Cassandra ordered. "Remember, Isolde, this is my home. I give the orders."

Isolde sulked. "I was only havin' a bit o' fun."

"Stupid girl," Cassandra muttered. She picked up her chalice and raised it, turning her gaze to Mathilda. "I drink to your health, Sister. You brought me back from the brink, and I owe you a debt of gratitude."

Mathilda felt her brows lift. She didn't want her sister beholden to her. "I think we are even. You did care for me when I was ill."

Cassandra gave her a smile that felt oily. Nothing about this night felt right, and Mathilda wasn't about to chance poisoned wine. She waited until Cassandra sipped first before she raised the chalice to her lips. As the wine touched her tongue, the four servants closed in on the table. Each of them caught up a knife. Before Mathilda could lower the chalice, each servant had slashed his own throat open.

Mathilda gasped, choking on her wine. The four servants crumpled to the floor. In the same moment, Cassandra began to chant low and harshly. Unfamiliar words poured from her lips as her eyes remained locked on Mathilda.

Mathilda felt her muscles go rigid. The chalice fell from her hand as her body began to burn. A molten fire blazed through her veins, agonizingly slowly, and a scream ripped from her throat. Something dark crept inside her, like a stain upon her soul.

Her vision went gray. She felt herself rising out of her chair, as if her soul had been cut loose from her body. The sounds from the background disappeared, save for Cassandra's voice. Mathilda did not know what was happening. She no longer felt as if she belonged to herself, as if she was somehow outside her body. A crippling sense of panic rose as she fought to focus and get back. Mathilda thought of Ramona's face before everything went black.

Mathilda twitched, feeling a strange pulse in her body. There was no sound, no light. How long had it been like this? Suddenly, the light came, faintly gray behind her closed eyes. Sound washed over her, garbled at first, but then clear.

Mathilda slowly came to, remembering. She pushed herself to her feet, stumbling from dizziness. "What did you do?" she shrieked.

"I returned the favor, of course," Cassandra said, smiling. She stood near Mathilda, looking pleased with herself. "Welcome to your new life of immortality, Sister."

Rage poured through Mathilda. She held out her hands, and a force of energy she had never experienced came rushing into and through her. The blast sent Cassandra out of her chair, flying backward into the wall.

Cassandra picked herself up off the floor. A shocked expression was on her face. Mathilda sent out another blast of energy, this time pinning her against the wall.

"How *dare* you do this to me! The very thing that you had forced upon you—your life torn upside down, now bestowed upon *me*?"

"Is that any way to show gratitude?" Cassandra asked, her voice strained. She had the audacity to look hurt.

"*Gratitude!*" Mathilda raged. "Do you think I *want* this? What is wrong with you?"

Cassandra looked over at the table. Mathilda followed her gaze. Isolde, John, and Stewart were slumped over, dead.

"What happened to them?" Mathilda demanded.

Cassandra shrugged. "Something went wrong, obviously. The spell's power must have been too much for them."

Mathilda was shocked at her indifference. "Do not *ever* come to me again. You are no longer my sister; you are no longer welcome at my home. You disgust me."

Cassandra's face held a mix of hurt and anger as Mathilda turned to leave.

"You will not abandon me, Sister." Her voice caught between a threat and a plea.

Mathilda flung open the door so violently that it struck the wall. The cool night air rushed over her like an embrace.

"*You need me!*" Cassandra screamed from behind her. "You will see, you need me...."

Mathilda had forgotten her lamp. She ran, stumbling over the unfamiliar landscape, blinded by tears. Another fit of rage tore through her, and she screamed. One of her coils had come loose and hung at her cheek, and she roughly pulled it free from the pins, yanking some of her hair out in the process. The violation she had suffered was overwhelming. Her rage gave way to deep, racking sobs, and she stumbled, losing her balance. An arm grasped around hers, and Mathilda screamed in fright, pulling violently away from whoever held her.

"Mathilda. It's me, Ramona."

"Oh, Ramona..." Mathilda collapsed on the ground at her feet. "What am I going to do?"

Ramona crouched beside her, gathering Mathilda in her arms. "I am so sorry. We tried to stop it. We remembered how our mothers stopped Aelle and spared Cassandra. We stopped the two men and the woman from gaining immortality, and we spared you."

Mathilda took a shuddering breath. "That is why they are dead then. I am glad."

Someone else rushed up through the dark. "Oh, thank goodness." Mathilda recognized Regina's voice. "You were *supposed* to lead the way, Ramona, not abandon us." Regina dropped down on Mathilda's other side. "Mathilda, Sister, are you all right?"

"No." She looked up as Isobel and Katrina caught up to them, heaving from breathlessness, and she sobbed again. Ramona and Isobel hooked their arms around Mathilda's and pulled her up.

The full moon shone brightly upon the forest floor, and they walked slowly and silently along the path toward the Three Paths. After a time, the druid tree loomed ahead. Moonlight streamed through its wide branches, and long shadows stretched across the paths.

Isobel broke the heavy silence. "Cassandra is quite powerful. We thought we'd never break her spell."

A bitterness rose in Mathilda as she thought of Cassandra. Her sister was now her enemy. If only she had realized this sooner.

Back inside the cottage, Ramona and Katrina helped Mathilda undress and settle into bed. Isobel brought in a mug. "Drink this," she said. "It's a sleeping draught."

Mathilda downed it quickly. "I am glad you are all here with me." She shuddered, imagining what it would be like if she were alone after what had happened.

"We will do all we can for you, Sister." Isobel took the empty mug away and kissed Mathilda's cheek.

Ramona pushed the door nearly closed behind the others and got into her makeshift bed. "Mathilda?"

Mathilda gazed numbly into the darkness, at the shells swaying overhead in the moonlight, almost hating to shatter the silence.

"Yes."

"How do you feel, truly?"

Mathilda tried to think of how to answer. "Not at all myself," she finally said.

"You gained a great deal of some strange magic tonight. I felt it through our bond. It was frightening."

"Yes. I believe some of Cassandra's—my father's powers transferred to me. Whether by intent or accident, I know not."

"I am sorry we were not there sooner. We could not break the circle until we completed the spell over those horrible people your sister invited to dinner."

"I know. Ramona?"

"Yes?"

"Thank you." The horror of what had happened still clung to Mathilda as exhaustion finally pulled her into the relief of sleep. She began to dream.

She was walking in the wood behind her childhood home and found herself at the place where she had healed the bird with the broken wing. As she sat down upon a fallen tree, heavy with the new burden she carried, she sensed she was not alone. The familiar presence she felt was comforting.

"Hello, Mother. Cassandra must have killed me, then, if you are here." She smiled with the relief that she would no longer have to bear her immortality and could finally be with her mother again.

A brilliant white light haloed her mother's vibrant form, and she smiled as she sat alongside Mathilda.

"No, my daughter, you are not dead. I called you here to the realm of Spirit to comfort you. I knew this terrible deed would happen, but I was forbidden to tell you until now. I could only warn you."

"As stars above, as air between..." Mathilda recalled.

"As earth below, your soul shall keep," her mother finished. "You are hurt and angry. I know you are, but you must not let this anger consume you. You must keep to the goodness of your heart." She took Mathilda's hand in hers, and though Mathilda could not feel her touch, she felt the warmth and comfort of her love. "You have an enormous responsibility upon you now. The one who calls herself your sister is spoiled. Her soul is rotted, and she is of no good. You *must* keep the balance. It will be upon you and your coven to do this."

"I will do all I can," Mathilda said, meeting her mother's gaze. "It will not be easy to let go of my anger, but for you, I promise to try."

"I know you will. Immortality may seem a burden now, but one day, you will find yourself in a life of happiness. Fear not; I have seen it." Her smile was one of promise. "Now, I must go. You sleep, child. I will no longer return to you. Your destiny has been fulfilled. My love and blessings upon you always, dear Mathilda."

A jolt of alarm shot through Mathilda. She consoled herself with the knowledge that she had seen her mother more than once in the spirit world, a blessing most never had with their loved ones.

"Thank you for your guidance. You were all that I could hope for in a mother, and I am proud to be your daughter."

"I know you are, and I am so proud of you." She cupped her hand to Mathilda's face. "I love you, my daughter. Fare thee well, and may the Goddess always keep you in her favor and shelter you in her hand."

Mathilda eased out of the spirit realm and into a peaceful sleep.

~

Sunlight filled the room with a harsh light. The morning birdsong that usually surrounded the cottage now came from deep in the wood, indicating the lateness of the day. Mathilda sighed. She hated sleeping past dawn. As she sat up in bed, the night's events came rushing to mind, tingling at the back of her eyes, turning her thoughts dark. She dashed away a tear and took a deep breath, remembering her promise to her mother. With one long exhale, she let go of the rage building inside her. Her mother's love gave her strength, and even though she said she would no longer return, Mathilda felt a deep peace. She quickly dressed, frustrated that she was getting a late start on the day, and went outside to find everyone.

Isobel, Regina, and Katrina were working in the garden. "Good morning, Mathilda." Isobel dropped a handful of weeds into a bucket by her feet. Her gaze mingled apprehension and relief. "How did you sleep?"

"Quite soundly," Mathilda replied. "Your potion worked a bit *too* well." She shielded her eyes and gauged the sun's position. "Just as I feared, midmorning and a wasted day."

She felt Katrina's eyes on her, searching and concerned, and quickly looked away. Her sisters were still grieving for their mothers, and she wouldn't add to their burdens.

"Mathilda," Katrina began gingerly.

"I am fine," Mathilda said quickly. From the corner of her eye, she saw Ramona come around the cottage with a basket and slip inside the cottage. "What is Ramona about?"

Katrina shrugged. "She told us earlier to stay out here until she comes for us."

Before Mathilda could think what that meant, the noise of a pickaxe drew her attention across the clearing.

"The workers are making good progress," she said. They were digging the foundation for the second cottage and had already removed enough ground, roughly half the size of her own cottage.

"Yes, they are." Regina got to her feet, dusting her hands on her apron. "My father is sending more stones today. He promised to send more laborers, too."

"That is very generous of him," Mathilda said. "You must miss him very much."

Her eyes fell to the distant trees, the same westerly direction they always turned when she recalled her father. "I do. But my mother discussed at length with Father and me how important it is for the five of us to stay together. I understand now, and he does too. Besides, I won't be married off for the benefit of the treasury. I can never marry. It would put the coven in danger." The disappointment on her face revealed the lie in her determined voice. "But I must fulfill my promise to my mother to continue the line. That will be hard to accomplish with no husband."

Before Mathilda could think of anything to say to her, Regina cleared her throat. "How are you feeling? I am sorry I did not ask straightaway. I felt it would be wrong to bombard you with questions."

Mathilda didn't want to talk about it, but it might be best to get it out of the way now. "I feel odd. Something inside me is not quite right, but I believe it's due to the shock. I may never get over the violation of what Cassandra did."

Regina nodded. "I understand. What she did was abominable. I am sure it will take quite some time to adjust to... to your immortality," she said delicately. "But, I like to think you had an enhancement. It will do little good for anyone to strike at you now, which, for a Guardian, is a great advantage."

Mathilda hadn't considered that possibility. She felt a thin sprout of hope. "Perhaps."

"I did not mean to eavesdrop," Katrina said, dropping a large cabbage into the basket by her feet as she straightened. "But Regina is right, your sister cannot harm you. Also, it's clear that Cassandra is quite unstable. Who knows what she may do now. I think we must secure the future line of Guardians, as soon as we can." She blushed, realizing what she had suggested.

Mathilda considered the idea. Nothing in her heart urged that they should move toward this goal so soon. "I understand your fears, Katrina, but we needn't rush into it. We have over five months to complete the spell." She suddenly thought of Duncan and wondered what he would think of her now after everything that had come to pass. "If it happens sooner, so be it. If you can find true happiness, pursue that first." She fell in beside her sisters by the edge of the garden and began plucking weeds, content in the silence of their companionship.

Around midday, Ramona burst out of the cottage. "Sisters," she called. "Come inside. I have a surprise."

Isobel's eyes lit up. "Oh, I do love surprises." Mathilda couldn't help smiling as she and the others made their way inside.

Ramona met them at the door, grinning in delight. She gestured toward the table. There in the middle, on a plate, Mathilda saw a small cake. A glaze of honey coated the top, and a ring of bright calendula flowers encircled it.

"Happy birthday, Regina," said Ramona.

Mathilda turned toward Regina. Regina's expression was one of surprised endearment. Mathilda felt a burst of sisterly love as she watched her move toward the table.

"Oh, how kind. How did you know it was my birthday?"

"I overheard the servants speaking of it. This honey cake was my mother's recipe," Ramona said proudly. "I hope you like it."

"I love honey cake. Thank you."

"Happy birthday, Sister." Mathilda kissed Regina's cheek. "I wish I had known before now. I would have helped prepare a special supper."

"I have everything I need right here," Regina said. Her smile reached out to all her sisters.

Mathilda saw Katrina brush something away from her cheek.

"Oh, now you've made me cry." Katrina held out her arms to draw everyone into a hug. "I love all of you."

12

Mathilda threw some grain along the edge of the hedgerow. As it scattered, several hens rushed out, pecking wildly. Katrina mostly took on the task of feeding the hens, but it was her day to look in on one of the peasant families. Several children had come down with a feverish illness that had confined them to their beds, and her healing talents were needed. Mathilda was glad the families her mother had once tended had embraced her and her sisters as their new caretakers. Her thoughts turned to Isobel. She had gone with Katrina to sell some tapestries in the village, and Mathilda hoped she would fetch a good price so they could have the coin to put back for when they needed to buy supplies.

She took the emptied bucket over to the nail on the wall at the side of the cottage and saw Regina in the garden. Regina had been pulling beets. Mathilda saw the full basket, and as she went over, she noticed dirt smudges on Regina's face. She dared not comment on that, lest she wound her sister's vanity. The long apron covering her dress and her simple, tight braid made Regina look as common as Mathilda.

"Katrina will be back soon," Mathilda said, hiding the amusement that edged her lips. "We had better clean ourselves."

"Yes," Regina agreed. "I will fetch the soap and a bucket and meet you at the pond."

As they left the garden, a bloodcurdling scream split the silence. Regina dropped the basket in shock. Beets tumbled onto the grass. Ramona flew out of the cottage, ash-faced. "What was that?"

The scream had come from the wood, in the direction of the path that led to the village. "Katrina!" Mathilda gasped. She ran toward the trees with her sisters close on her heels.

"There," Regina said as they shot across the clearing. "I see her."

Katrina rushed down the path toward them, her skirts fisted in both hands. A basket was clamped in the crook of her right arm, which bounced against her side as she ran. The linen veil she had neatly wrapped her hair in that morning had slipped and hung from the back of her neck like a flapping pennant. The terror on her face was chilling. "Mathilda! Something is out there."

Mathilda glanced around the wood, her heart pounding wildly. She saw nothing giving chase and let out a heavy, relieved sigh. "Calm down. You must slow your breathing. Tell us what happened."

Katrina sucked in a deep breath and let it out in a rush. "I was almost home when I heard a noise behind me. I turned and saw something in the shadows. I thought at first someone had followed me from the village, but then I saw it move. It was not human, not entirely."

A chill slithered down Mathilda's spine. Her gaze flew again to the shadows of the trees beyond the clearing. "What do you mean, 'not entirely'?" Mathilda asked.

"I don't know how to explain it." Katrina's hands twisted in her skirt. "At first glance, I saw a man standing by the trees in the distance, but then he changed. When I blinked, there was no man, only... something else."

"What did you see, Sister? Tell us," Regina urged.

"I don't know," Katrina sobbed. "A fearful beast."

Mathilda noticed Ramona looking intently at her. *What is it?*

I got into her mind, Ramona said. *What she saw was a man, but he changed into something else. A bear or wolf. I could not tell.*

Mathilda tried to make sense of this frightening possibility as she turned her gaze back to Katrina's shaking form. Motion at the treeline made everyone jump. Isobel stepped into the clearing, looking content as though she'd had a pleasant walk through the forest.

"Oh, thank goodness," Regina gasped.

Isobel looked surprised to see them all so frightened. "What has happened?"

"Did you see anything strange in the wood on your walk home?" Mathilda asked.

Isobel turned warily toward the wood. "No, why?"

"Katrina saw something she cannot explain," Mathilda replied. "She saw a man who changed into a beast." Katrina looked so pale that Mathilda took her arm to steady her.

"Let us get you inside and calmed," she soothed.

Inside, Katrina sank into the chair Mathilda pulled out for her. Ramona placed a chalice of wine in her hands, and everyone stood over her while she took a long drink. Her hitched breathing finally calmed after a few moments.

Mathilda suddenly noticed something. "Where is your necklace, Sister?"

Katrina flushed. "I forgot to put it on this morning."

Mathilda bit back her scolding words. "Did you sense anything strange before you saw the creature?"

Katrina rested the chalice against her lap, gazing into the liquid with a furrowed brow. "No. Nothing. I gave the Dawson children their remedy and set off straight for home. I saw nothing. I heard nothing." She paused, her forehead furrowing. "The wood was oddly quiet now that I think on it."

"What happened when you saw the man?" Mathilda asked.

"I heard a rustling, popping sound like branches snapping. I turned and saw the man only for a second. Then I saw the beast in his place." Katrina shuddered and gulped the rest of the wine.

"Mathilda, do you think this is the work of Cassandra?" Ramona asked.

The worry Mathilda felt was mirrored in her sisters' faces as they turned to look at her, their brows furrowed and their eyes troubled.

"I don't know," Mathilda said. "But from now on, we will travel in pairs, never alone. Keep your wits about you—and wear your pendants anytime you are out of doors. Who knows what Cassandra's twisted mind might conjure next."

LATER THAT NIGHT, Mathilda lay in bed. Crickets chirped outside the cottage, and darkness had long settled in. Mathilda gazed into the blackness of the room, lost in her thoughts.

"Ramona," she whispered. "Are you awake?"

Ramona answered immediately from her pallet on the floor. "Yes."

"I want to see what Katrina saw. Would you come up here?"

Mathilda sat up, leaning against the headboard. She heard rustling and felt the bed move as Ramona sat down.

"Here, take my hands," Ramona said.

A flash of a vision came as soon as Mathilda's hands touched hers.

For the briefest moment, a man stood behind a tree. His form suddenly blurred. A black shape, indistinct, now took his place, obscured in the shadows of the dense brush.

Mathilda let go of Ramona's hands with a frustrated sigh.

"I couldn't tell what it was either. But it was human, at least at first. That much is certain." Mathilda paused, trying to think what to do. "Will you go out into the wood with me at dawn? I would like to see what I can find."

Ramona agreed. She lay back down on her pallet and was soon

asleep, to judge from her quiet breathing, but Mathilda couldn't close her eyes for a long time.

She was awake again before first light, the cottage still and quiet around her. Best to slip out before all her sisters woke up. Mathilda woke Ramona, and they dressed quickly and quietly and headed out without disturbing the others.

A thin fog hung over the clearing like a veil into another realm. The first hint of color stained the sky the palest shade of violet, casting the fog in wavering hues of gray with the lightest touch of blue. A blackbird suddenly struck up a cheerful song, prompting a chorus of birdsong through the woodland.

"I see why you like to come out here this early. It is beautiful."

"Yes," Mathilda agreed. The beauty of her surroundings tugged a contented smile to her lips. She tipped her head toward the trees. Her eyes closed, and she drew in a long, replenishing breath. "My mind gains much peace in these early hours."

Ramona drew in a long breath as her eyes filled with wonder at the stretch of pink clouds above the clearing. "It feels as if the energy of nature is soaking into my body. Would you mind if I start my mornings with you out here?"

"I think it's good for all of us to start our mornings out here together," Mathilda said, starting across the dew-dampened clearing. "We could use a little clarity, especially after what happened with Katrina."

They crossed into the wood and took the same path Katrina had walked until it veered left toward the little peasant village. Mathilda felt uneasy as she looked ahead.

"This must be where Katrina saw the creature. The energy here feels wrong."

Mathilda approached a blackthorn thicket up ahead. The unripe sloes hung in abundance, and she made a mental note to return here later in the season to gather them.

Ramona reached out and plucked something caught in the thorns. "You were right. This is the place," she said. She held up a tuft of black fur. "I believe our sister might have encountered a wolf."

Mathilda reached for the fur and frowned at the residue of familiar dark magic still lingering on it. "It certainly looks like it could be from a wolf. I can feel my sister's magic on it. Let us take it back to the cottage. I will see what Cassandra has done." She placed the fur in the pocket of her apron and took the path home.

The sky had brightened when they stepped out of the wood, and the airy pink clouds from earlier had gathered into themselves, now gray and looming as they stretched above the clearing.

"Where have you two been so early?" Regina asked. She set a pitcher in the center of the table by the eggs Isobel had just placed there. "We thought we would have to eat without you."

"To the wood," Mathilda replied, removing her shoes. "We wanted to see if we could find any clues about what Katrina saw."

Katrina stepped out of the larder with a plate of cheese and berries. "And did you?" she asked, brushing away the wisps of hair that had worked out of her braid.

Mathilda pulled the fur from her pocket and held it up in the light of the dancing hearth flames. "Let us quickly eat. We have work to do."

After their meal, Mathilda led everyone into the bedchamber. Ramona rolled up her pallet and rested it in the corner, while Mathilda pulled back the mat, revealing the magic circle. "Everyone, join me on the floor."

She placed a candle in the center of the circle. "Fire." At her command, the flame rose, and she tossed the fur into it and joined hands with her sisters. They closed their eyes as Mathilda began the incantation.

"We, your faithful Guardians, stand in need of your help. Great Mother, we beseech that you grant us sight and understanding in what we seek."

"Hear us, Great Mother," they all said.

The flame on the candle shot up toward the ceiling. The floor shook, and a clay pot fell off the table, breaking their concentration. The candle went out. An eerie silence filled the room.

"What happened?" Katrina asked. "My vision was cut short."

"Cassandra blocked us out," Mathilda said, sighing in frustration. "I saw her face as my vision winked out."

Ramona turned to Katrina. "Before we were cut off, what did you see in your vision?"

"I saw the same thing as I encountered yesterday. Nothing more. What about you?"

"I saw a man walking through the wood from the village," Ramona answered. "His appearance was but a shadow. That is all."

"I saw a chalice full of blood, bubbling and boiling over its rim," Regina added.

"And I saw three figures of men," Isobel said. "They each stood tall but became great beasts upon four legs."

"I saw bones cracking and shifting," Mathilda said. "Then, creatures like wolves, only bigger, ran through the wood. There was a shadow of a human willing them. That is when I saw Cassandra. She knows what we are about and casts us out from discovering what she is planning." Mathilda watched the smoke from the extinguished candle snake upward. An uneasiness settled around her body, leaving her unsettled. "We must guard our minds, Sisters. From here on, we will go to the wood each morning at dawn. The Goddess will grant each of you the peace and wisdom you need to be strong of mind. We cannot allow Cassandra to penetrate our thoughts. She is watching us, and I can't tell why."

Her sisters' gazes felt heavy, their worry palpable.

A thought suddenly appeared in Mathilda's mind. "Perhaps I was too hasty in cutting her out of my life. I wonder if it would be best to put on the pretense of goodwill, pretend to be amiable, and keep her in our close watch?"

A look of fear crossed Katrina's face. "I don't think that is a wise decision," she chided. "You don't know what I felt yesterday, Sister.

The evil radiating from that *thing* is not something I want to invite into my life."

Mathilda made a decision. "I understand," she said. "And that is why I will do this alone. I will go and see Cassandra, but I will not put any of you in her reach. Until I learn what she is about, you will all stay here as one, linked to me." She got to her feet, prompting her sisters to join her, and took the candle, setting it on the table. Mathilda knew, too, that the sooner she went to see Cassandra, the better. As little as she wanted to go, there was no time like the present. "I'll take my leave of you now," she said.

Regina scoffed in disbelief. Her eyes shot daggers, and she opened her mouth to say something, but Ramona beat her to it.

"No," Ramona protested. "You mustn't go alone. Look what Cassandra did to you the last time you paid her a visit."

"Yes, but like her, I am immortal. What more can she do to me? Rest assured, if there is trouble, I will reach out to you."

"Sister, perhaps you should wait and see what she does next," Isobel insisted. She spoke calmly, but Mathilda saw the worry in her eyes and how her hands bunched anxiously at her skirt.

"There is no time for that," Mathilda said as she replaced the rush mat over the circle. "Cassandra is busy with something, and I must know what it is. No good can come of it if we wait."

She took off her apron and laid it over a chair in the main room. Her sisters hovered close, words no longer coming from their lips as fear, or acceptance had sealed them shut for now. She saw that they all wore their pendants and gave a quick nod before heading out.

"Be careful, Mathilda," Ramona said as she turned to go.

As Mathilda made her way through the wood, she came across an owl perched on a low branch. Owls had always fascinated her, with their quiet intelligence and vibrant energy. They carried purpose to their actions, even in stillness. This one felt wrong. Too watchful of her with a slothful energy. "Reveal," she commanded.

Immediately, the atmosphere surrounding the owl rippled. The creature began to swirl, wings, eyes, and beak swimming together. In the next heartbeat, a woman fell from the tree, naked and stunned. About the same age as Mathilda, her dark hair was a mess around her shocked, pale features, with twigs and bits of leaves in the strands where she had fallen. She gazed up at Mathilda, her dark eyes wide with fear.

Cassandra's magic was present in this shifter, and Mathilda fought the contempt building on her tongue. She took a breath and met the woman's gaze. "Do not be afraid. I mean you no harm. Who sent you?"

The woman stared dumbly at her, easing backward on her elbows.

"No matter," Mathilda went on. "I already know. Would you care to walk with me to your mistress's house? I, too, am headed there."

The woman scrambled to her feet and darted away into the wood, heedless of branches and thorns underfoot and against her bare skin.

Mathilda's lips edged up. "Very well," she said to herself. She knew the woman wouldn't accompany her, but she couldn't help herself when she'd asked. When she reached Cassandra's house, the door was standing ajar.

"Come in, Sister," Cassandra called from somewhere inside.

Mathilda carefully guarded her mind by picturing a thick, impenetrable fog set to keep her thoughts shrouded as she entered the house.

"What are you doing here?" Cassandra asked. "As I recall, you said you wanted nothing more to do with me."

"I did. At the time, I meant it," Mathilda replied. The room was dark compared to the brightness of the day, and it took her eyes a moment to adjust. She finally noticed Cassandra standing by the back wall, arms crossed over her breasts with a guarded expression. She wore a dress of deep-blue fabric. Her hair tumbled wildly down her shoulders, nearly reaching her waist.

Cassandra scoffed as she moved away from the wall. "And now you expect me to believe you come back with forgiveness in your heart and a changed mind?"

Mathilda schooled her features against the anger pricking at her insides. "I know you sent that creature, whatever it was, after Katrina. And you had the owl watching us. What happened to her, by the way? Has she made her way back here yet?"

"She returned just before you arrived, covered with scrapes and bleeding," Cassandra spoke as lightly as if she were discussing the weather. "The woman is useless. I sent her away."

Her sister's callousness had Mathilda biting her tongue. She realized her jaw was clenched, and she released an exhale through her nose as she met Cassandra's challenging gaze.

Minding her tone, Mathilda said, "I've decided that I would rather make peace with you than see your malice toward me heaped upon my sisters. They are innocent in our dealings."

Cassandra's eyes turned hard as she regarded Mathilda. She grasped the back of the chair, looming over it, and she glared at Mathilda. "You expect me to believe that? After the five of you tried to get past my masking spell? Exactly how does that show making peace?"

Mathilda had anticipated her sister's mistrust, so the venom in her tone did not rile Mathilda. She moved toward the table, resting her hands over the back of a chair, letting her sister see the honesty in her eyes. "You are right. We did try to find out who sent that creature. We travel through the wood, and none of us wants to put ourselves in peril. Now that I know it was you, I want a truce. I will no longer hold anger in my heart toward you. If it will keep my sisters safe, then it is worth rebuilding a relationship with you."

A flash of bitterness showed on Cassandra's face. "You hold your new *sisters* dearer to you than your own flesh and blood?"

"I trust them with my life. You took my life."

"I *gave* you life," Cassandra spat. She pushed away from the chair, shaking her head. "You ran off before I could even explain the possibilities. We have vast powers, now, you and I. There's no limit to what we could do together."

Mathilda sensed the taint of her sister's magic and the darkness that shadowed the back of her eyes, which seemed so wrong. She lifted her chin, challenging Cassandra. "I only want to do good. To do things beneficial to the earth and humankind. Is that what you have in mind? Because if so, then yes, I will happily work with you."

Cassandra could not hold their gaze. A strange look passed over her features as she turned away, and for a moment, Mathilda could have sworn she saw regret and disappointment on her face.

Mathilda pressed on, hoping to pull forth any goodness that was still in her sister. "Look, I came here to mend what is broken between us. It is difficult for me, as I am sure it is for you. But let us try. For the sake of those who do not deserve to be caught up in our feuding."

"Very well, Sister." Cassandra's tone was placating. She pulled out a chair and sank down in it. "If you truly are honest about wanting to rebuild our bond, then time will reveal your secrets. I will know if you are playing me foul."

"I agree," Mathilda said. "Time does have a way of bringing things about." She gazed at her sister, content for now at their resolution. "I will leave you to your day, but before I go, will you tell me what you sent after Katrina and why?"

Cassandra rolled her eyes and sighed dramatically. "Oh, fine. I see there is no putting you off." She leaned forward, clasping her hands before her on the table. "And to prove my goodwill, I will be truthful in my answer."

Mathilda perked up, eager to hear what she might say.

"After you left here that day the way you did, I found that I could no longer trust you. I knew you were angry, and I feared you would retaliate in some way." Her hands clenched harder as if it was difficult for her to relay such truths. "I needed to protect myself, so I have a few loyal ones who look after me now—three men who I met in a tavern, and Alys, the woman you saw earlier. I change them into beasts to spy upon those who are against me. I sent one of my men in the guise of a wolf to follow Katrina. Can you blame me? Had you thought of it, you would have done the same."

Mathilda wondered what their relationship would have been had

Cassandra not chosen the path of darkness. "Very clever," she said, softly. "However, I am not against you. I never was, really. I was hurt and angry, but I am past that now." She went toward the door, turning briefly before leaving. Her sister sat proudly with her chin lifted. There was no softness to lend to her harsh features and stiff form. Defiance flared in her eyes as she watched Mathilda.

Mathilda sighed sadly. "Thank you for your honesty."

"Do not play me for a fool, Mathilda," Cassandra called, stopping her. "I will allow this sudden desire of yours to mend things over. But until you prove yourself true, I will be on my guard."

It was then that Mathilda realized Cassandra would never trust her, no matter what she did, and yet she felt the same. "Very well. Good day, Cassandra."

MATHILDA CLOSED the cottage door and leaned against the wall with a sigh. Her sisters sat around the table looking as tired as she felt.

"Well?" Regina said, rising delicately from her chair. She smoothed her dress, a practiced habit that came across as ladylike and serene, but the fierceness in her eyes belied it. She said, "Do you believe Cassandra will uphold her end of a truce?"

"Perhaps. Cassandra is wary of our motives." Mathilda sat down at the table with her sisters, feeling as though a heavy yolk was over her shoulders. The encounter with Cassandra had left her weary. Regina poured some water for her, and she took the cup gratefully, bringing it to her lips for a long drink. "We must try to seem more trusting. Oh, and I encountered another shifter on my way. A woman in the guise of an owl. I cast a Reveal, and she fell from the tree. I must say, she was rather shocked when she hit the ground. And naked too!" Mathilda giggled as she recalled the memory." You would think Cassandra could have chosen a creature more common for the light of day."

"What did you do next?" Isobel asked.

"I invited her to walk with me to her mistress's house. Naturally, she ran off."

"I would think so," Regina said dryly. "Naked, running through the woods? I'm sure she had a fine time of it."

Katrina brought them back to the main subject. "Why did Cassandra send that creature after me?"

Mathilda clasped her fingers around her cup, loath to speak of her sister again.

"She was afraid I would retaliate after what she did to me. My sister now has a few 'loyal followers,' as she put it, looking out for her. She's been using them to watch us—seeing through their eyes—to ensure we weren't planning to come after her."

"She has been watching us," Isobel said disgustedly.

"Yes. Cassandra will undoubtedly continue to watch to ensure she can trust me—and she wants to trust me; I could sense it. So it seems now, Sisters, we wait and see if she will be satisfied knowing we are not going to retaliate," Mathilda said with resolve. "We must be vigilant and wear the crystals at all times. They will block her attempts to read our minds. Cassandra is an unsettled, restless soul. Eventually, we will have to do something about her."

Dread settled into the pit of her stomach as Mathilda gazed into her cup, imagining she and her sisters going up against someone as dangerous as Cassandra.

13

A chilly wind swayed the crimson maples surrounding the clearing. It tore through the beeches that had already flushed out their deep golden hues, leaving them shivering in the gusts with shriveled leaves dropping much earlier than previous Octobers. The servants claimed a harsh winter was coming. Mathilda had felt inklings of something along the wind to support their belief. Fortunately, she mused, the garden had filled her larder with a fine yield to see her through the winter. She watched the workers coming and going from the small wooden shelter Regina had suggested they build to give the men a roof over their heads during the winter. It would be used for storage once the men finished their work.

She added another log to the fire and glanced around the silent room, already feeling the loss of her sisters' company. The door opened, and Ramona darted in with a scattering of leaves dancing around her ankles.

"This wind…" she fussed. "Our sisters are fortunate to have their cottage completed just in time for the cold, dark months." She took off her cloak and laid it over a chair. "They are eager to sleep under their new roof tonight now that they have the cottage set up to their liking."

Mathilda smiled at her friend. "They certainly are. Thank you for staying on with me. I have gotten used to our bedside chats."

"Are you sure adding the second bed will not distress you?" Ramona asked, stretching her hands toward the hearth for warmth. "It has taken up most of the extra space in your bedchamber."

"No. Not at all. I am glad we could finally afford one. Now I won't have to lean over whenever I want to talk to you," Mathilda teased.

At the sound of an approaching cart, they both turned toward the window. Mathilda shook her head. "Regina must have sent for more supplies. I don't know where she thinks she will fit anything else. The place must be stuffed to the rafters by now."

"We had better help the men unload the cart before Regina works them to their deaths," Ramona said, pulling on her cloak again. "Our sister certainly seems determined to have the place as fine as any castle." She stepped outside the door and held it firm against the wind for Mathilda.

Mathilda slipped on her cloak and stepped outside. She was surprised to see a carriage pulled up alongside the farm cart that now stood in the yard. She turned toward Ramona and grinned. "Regina does have a taste for luxury. Are you sure you would not be more comfortable with her in the other cottage?"

"I am happy where I am. I do not need finery."

Regina, dismounting from the carriage, heard her. "That is too bad," she said, as Thomas helped her step down. "Because this is mostly for you and Mathilda." She pulled her fur-lined cloak tight as a gust of wind tore through the clearing.

Mathilda couldn't hide her surprise. Regina saw it at once. "Do not give me that look, Mathilda Longhurst. You have been like a mother to us all. You took us in, bore our suffering as your own, gave up your solitude, and I want to do something for you in return."

Regina motioned toward the carriage. Mathilda saw two women, both well into their middle years, step down. They wore matching gray kirtles beneath their cloaks, and full aprons covering their dresses.

"This is my maid, Hilda," Regina said, putting her hand on the thinner woman's arm. "Father finally relented and let her come to live with me."

The woman had the palest blue eyes Mathilda had ever seen. They seemed almost clear. Hilda nodded in greeting, and Mathilda smiled in return. The other woman, plump and motherly, approached. Wisps of gray hair peeked out from her cap, and she reached to tuck them in place as she drew closer.

"And this is Gertrude," Regina said, smiling fondly. "She is also from my father's house and knows our ways," she said with meaning. Mathilda understood. Gertrude knew about Regina's magic. "She is loyal," Regina said. "Gertrude is now your servant, Mathilda. She has her own bedding and will be at your whim."

Mathilda gave a start. She knew how much this moment meant to Regina, and she nearly had to bite her tongue to keep from protesting.

"Also," Regina continued, "my father has allowed me to keep the laborers until they can complete a small stable. Now that these horses belong to us, they should be housed properly. Father insisted—if that is permissible," she hastily added.

Mathilda looked at the two mares and shook her head. "Very well, Regina. You have brought me around to your way of living thus far. I do not think a small stable will be a problem. You may proceed if it makes you happy."

"It does." Regina didn't trouble to hide her satisfied smile. She turned to the cart where Thomas stood awaiting instruction. "Thomas, please help Gertrude and Hilda carry the gifts into Mathilda's house."

Mathilda felt she should offer to help them, but Regina pulled open the cottage door. "Mathilda, Ramona, come inside."

After a few moments, Thomas entered with a small chest. Hilda and Gertrude followed him, carrying another chest between the two of them. They set the chests down in front of the hearth.

"Regina, what is all of this?" Ramona asked.

"You will see," Regina said. She bent to open the lid of the chest the women had carried in and pulled out new bed linens and a bundle of other clothes, including a fine, crisp-white table linen. Mathilda wondered how she would keep it looking pristine.

Gertrude and Hilda began to unpack plates and bowls from the chest Thomas had carried in. They were made from a green ceramic that Mathilda immediately loved. Hilda took out cutlery next, and then Gertrude set something on the table that made Mathilda catch her breath.

"Glass!" Mathilda rushed to the table and picked up one of the beakers. She had only seen glassware once at market. These were much finer. They were a smoky, clear color and had lines engraved into them, with bubble-like rounds that stuck out for better gripping. Mathilda watched Ramona run her fingers over one of them in admiration.

"Regina, I don't know what to say." Mathilda set the cup she held down on the table with the others. "A simple 'thank you' seems lacking."

Regina smiled. "Say you love them."

"I do love them."

Thomas had stepped outside during the unloading and returned with yet another chest.

"There's more?" Ramona said.

Regina opened the lid of the new chest. "These are for you and Mathilda." Her voice turned reverent. "They belonged to my mother." She pulled out a beautiful gown in a pale-green silk and a second gown in deep blue.

"Oh, Regina, how will we ever wear them?" Ramona ran her fingers across the blue fabric. "They are too fine for us."

"Who will see you in them?" Regina's eyes gleamed with a dare. "As long as you don't wear them in public, I don't see why you shouldn't enjoy them." She bent to pull out more clothes. "I have more practical dresses for you, too. These kirtles were mine, but I no longer wear them. Gertrude can alter them if needed."

Mathilda looked over the gifts, the spread of fine fabrics, beautiful cutlery, and glassware, with awe. "Regina, this is too much."

Regina waved that away. "Nonsense. After everything you've done, you deserve the very best. Now, I had better get the rest of the things into my cottage before darkness sets in." She turned, her skirts swishing around her ankles, and made for the door.

Tears filled Mathilda's eyes as she watched her sister cross the room. "Regina?"

"Yes, Mathilda?"

"I want you to know you have helped heal the hole in my heart. I never thought I would get over the death of my mother. You are very dear to me. Your fervor for life is a joy. Thank you for everything."

Regina gave a gracious nod. "You are welcome, Sister. You know I would do anything for you. For all of you." She came back to kiss Mathilda's cheek, then Ramona's. "I have a celebratory supper planned for our first night in the cottage. I want you both to join us."

"Of course we will," Mathilda said. When the door closed behind Regina and Hilda, she turned to Ramona, "Well, shall we put these fine things away?"

Gertrude answered first. "Oh, no, mistress!" She sounded scandalized. "I shall do it."

Ramona did her best to hide her grin, but Mathilda saw it. She sighed.

"Thank you, Gertrude. I see I shall slowly be consumed by this way of living. Come, Ramona. Let us talk of Samhain."

"How do I look?" Ramona asked as she twirled around in Philippa's blue dress. She patted her braid that Gertrude had pinned into a wide coil at the base of her head.

"You look lovely," Mathilda said. "Blue suits you." She admired her own hair, which Gertrude had braided and woven through with a pale-green ribbon. "Gertrude certainly knows how to arrange hair most tastefully, does she not?"

Ramona twirled again, with girlish delight. "Yes. I think she will prove most useful."

Mathilda had to agree. Gertrude had done more work in one afternoon than Mathilda ever could. "I don't know," she said, "if Regina knows what a jewel she has given up."

Ramona winked. "Let us keep the secret between us then."

Gertrude stepped into the bedchamber. "I have your cloaks, mistresses. The air has a terrible bite tonight, and you will need these."

"Thank you, Gertrude." Mathilda drew her cloak over the green silk gown she dared to wear. "It could be quite late before we return. Do not wait up for us. Ramona and I can manage on our own."

The two girls crossed the clearing in a giddy excitement, lifting their skirts to avoid dirtying the hems. Regina's cottage was made of stone, like Mathilda's, but larger in size. The windows were Mathilda's favorite feature of the exterior with their deep-set jambs and double arches. A plume of smoke rose from the chimney, looking white in the waxing moonlight.

Mathilda knocked at Regina's door. The lively conversations of her sisters carried outside. It warmed her heart to know that they were finally settled in and enjoying their new home. Katrina swung it open, beaming. She wore a deep-yellow kirtle and a matching ribbon in her coiled braids. Mathilda had never seen her so happy. Isobel stood behind her, wearing a new russet-colored dress. Her hair was intricately woven and looped at the sides of her head.

"You both look beautiful," Mathilda said.

"Thank you." Katrina ushered them eagerly inside. "Look at how perfect everything is."

Mathilda stepped into the inviting warmth of the cottage. A fire crackled in the hearth, and candlelight danced everywhere she looked, flooding the room with golden and amber hues. A gold silk table linen adorned the large dining table in the center of the room, its threads shimmering beneath the light. The finest silver plates, cutlery, and chalices Mathilda had ever seen were laid out, waiting. She noticed Hilda bustling around the separate hearth in the kitchen at the back of the cottage.

"Regina, this is lovely—*you* are lovely," Mathilda said, taking in her sister's gown. It was a shade of blue so pale it looked nearly silver, the perfect complement to Regina's fair coloring.

Regina thanked her. "Welcome, Sisters. Please sit."

Mathilda took a seat beside Ramona. Regina sat at the end of the table to Mathilda's left, and Katrina and Isobel sat opposite Mathilda.

Hilda brought out the wine and filled each of their chalices. Mathilda thanked her and turned to Regina. "Gertrude is wonderful," she said. "Thank you for sending her to us."

A look of smug satisfaction flashed over Regina's face before she schooled her expression. "I am glad. She was my mother's favorite. Hilda was my father's favorite, which is why it took so long for him to let her go. She has been dear to me since I was a child." Mathilda saw Hilda smile fondly as she slipped out of the room.

Ramona said, "Mathilda and I were talking of Samhain earlier. We would like to visit our mothers' graves and then pay our final respects to Maelen upon our return."

"That would be wonderful," Isobel said. "I am looking forward to communing with them."

"Yes," Mathilda said sadly. She ran her fingers over the rim of her chalice as she thought of the last time her mother had visited her in her dreams.

"What is it, Mathilda?" Regina asked.

"My mother came to me many weeks ago in a vision. She told me now that my destiny has been fulfilled, she will no longer commune with me."

"Oh, I am sorry." Isobel reached across the table and took Mathilda's hand.

Mathilda made herself meet her sister's eyes. "Do not be sorry. It was a happy goodbye."

"We will prepare a special plate for her that night regardless," Regina said.

"Thank you."

Hilda returned with a cabbage stew for everyone. Mathilda watched her move around the table, serving with a practiced hand. She wondered if Hilda needed help, but she didn't dare ask and offend the woman.

"The creamed fish will be ready shortly, my lady," Hilda said to Regina before leaving them to their stew.

Katrina said, "Isobel and I are adding the finishing touches on the tapestry we wove. I think it will fetch a good price."

Mathilda tasted her stew. It was rich and delicious. "Let us hope," she said. "Ramona and I are nearly finished with the Smithsons' tunics. With so many villagers coming to us at the market for more clothing, we are well on our way. We can provide for the peasants all winter with the profit. Especially if your tapestry sells."

"That is happy news," Katrina said. "I will drink to that."

After supper, Mathilda and Ramona said their goodbyes and returned to their cottage. Gertrude waited dutifully by the hearth as they entered. She had built up the fire for the night; the popping and cracking of the logs rang in the room. Gertrude rose from the chair to take their cloaks. "Did you have a nice supper with Mistress Regina?"

"We did." Mathilda couldn't stifle a yawn. "You didn't have to wait up for us."

"I don't mind, mistress. Come. I will get you both settled into your beds."

As tired as she was, Mathilda couldn't be more grateful for having Gertrude's help getting out of the bulky gown, and as she unwound the ribbon from Mathilda's braid, she decided this was a luxury she wouldn't take for granted.

∼

THE FOLLOWING morning was crisp and bright. A frost had covered everything overnight, and the grass shimmered in the sunlight. Mathilda and Ramona pulled their furs around themselves and headed over to meet the others for their daily outing.

Hilda opened the door to Mathilda's knock. "Good morning, Hilda," Mathilda said. "Is your mistress awake?"

"She is."

"I am almost ready," Regina called from inside.

Katrina and Isobel stepped outside, both disheveled-looking, with bruised-looking shadows beneath their eyes. Instead of furs, they had thrown blankets around their slumped shoulders. Ramona shot a surprised glance at Mathilda but wisely kept her opinion of their appearance to herself.

"We were too weary this morning to do more than put on a tunic and reach for the bedding," Katrina offered as an explanation.

"I told you not to drink so much wine," Isobel scolded. "You are fortunate indeed that Regina has a bathing tub, or you would have had an icy plunge in the pond last night when you woke the whole household with your retching."

Katrina glared daggers. "Isobel, if Mathilda or Ramona wanted to know what happened last night, they would have asked. Kindly keep your comments to yourself."

"I would," Isobel said, "but I would like our sisters to know that I didn't partake of wine. I am only miserable because *you* kept us all awake."

"Well, well," Ramona said. "I do believe we left just in time last evening."

"I think you are right, Sister," Mathilda replied. "You are in dire need of quiet contemplation, Katrina."

"I know," she said, sounding pitiful.

Regina stepped outside, wrapped tightly in her furs. She, too, had dark shadows under her eyes, but at least she had taken the time to properly dress and braid her hair. "Well, what are we waiting for?" she asked, as if *they* had delayed her.

Once they were in the wood, Mathilda took off her shoes. The others followed suit.

"Oh!" Katrina gasped. "My feet are nearly numb."

Isobel smirked. "Good. Perhaps it will help you recover from your miserable condition."

Katrina looked outraged. "I already said I am sorry I woke everyone!" At her outburst, a flock of blackbirds exploded from a thicket, making everyone jump.

"Isobel, Katrina," Mathilda scolded. "This is supposed to be a peaceful moment. Do not spoil it with your bickering. Now, take my hands, and let us begin."

As they obeyed, calmness descended. A vibration of energy pulsated between the women, alive and tangible. It warmed the ground beneath their feet and melted away the frost, leaving a dampened circle of earth enclosing them. A crisp breeze blew among them, whirling some dried leaves into a lively dance. The leaves swirled overhead, contained in the magic surrounding the women.

"Look at that!" Isobel exclaimed. "How wonderful!"

"Our magic is strong," Mathilda said. "The earth is responding to us." She looked up, watching as the leaves twirled out of the circle and flew skyward. Smiling, she settled in for her meditation.

A PALE SUN climbed toward midday. A thin covering of clouds kept any tangible warmth at bay. Mathilda finished filling a basket with provisions of bread, parsnips, and leeks for Cassandra. The food gifts would show her goodwill and give her an excuse to make sure her sister was holding up her end of the bargain by staying out of trouble.

Ramona was pulling on her boots and cloak. Mathilda said, "I know your feelings toward my sister, Ramona. You do not have to come along."

"I want to go. The walk will do me good."

"Make sure to clear your mind along the way. I do not wish to set her off."

An uncomfortable energy hung in the air as they stepped out from the trees into the clearing surrounding Cassandra's house. As they approached the door, a low growl came from behind them. Mathilda was not surprised. She turned around. The creature before them had golden eyes and fur as black as night. A shifter in the form of a massive wolf. It seemed Mathilda's sister still did not trust her.

Mathilda sighed. "I am not here to harm your mistress. I brought provisions." She opened the basket. "See?"

In a swirling streak, the wolf returned to human form. The man stood naked before them. His hair was as black as the fur he previously had in animal form, and his skin was bronzed from days spent in the sun. Ramona gasped and turned away.

The man's dark, piercing eyes bored into Mathilda. She sensed something odd in him that she couldn't pinpoint, a strange energy that was somehow also familiar. Alarming. She stood firm as he walked to the door, never dropping her gaze. He pushed it open and motioned for them to enter.

The house was in shambles. The table itself was a disgrace. Two chairs lay overturned beneath it, one of them broken. The linens were stained deep purple in several places from the overturned chalices, left untouched. Mathilda's eyes moved with disgust to the flies that buzzed and crawled across the food remnants on the plates from the previous night's supper. How could her sister live in such filth? It outraged her that Cassandra cared so little about anything.

Ramona turned away, coughing and covering her face with her hands. Mathilda rounded on the shape-shifter. "Where is your mistress?"

The man went into a room off to the side. Mathilda heard him speaking in hushed tones and heard Cassandra groan. A few moments later, Cassandra emerged from the room. Her crimson hair was unbound and strewn wildly about her head, falling to her waist in a tangled mess. It looked as if it hadn't seen a comb in days. She wore only a chemise. Mathilda was nearly scandalized at the sheerness of it and how Cassandra had barely had it pulled up for modesty.

"Did I wake you?" Mathilda asked, trying to keep the bite out of her voice.

"Yes." Cassandra squinted in the dim light. "No matter," she slurred. "What time of day is it?"

She was still drunk. Mathilda swallowed her disgust. "Past midday."

"Well, that is earlier than usual. Marcus, fetch me a drink," Cassandra commanded. "And put something on. Have you no shame?"

Marcus left the room and returned a moment later, still naked, but carrying a chalice.

Cassandra took a long gulp. A deep-red trickle ran down her chin, and she wiped it with the heel of her hand. "What brings the two of you to my *humble* home?"

Mathilda ignored her sarcasm. "I brought provisions from our harvest."

Cassandra flicked her hand. Marcus took the basket from Mathilda and unpacked it onto the table. "Thank you, Sister," Cassandra said, sounding sincere at least. "I am..." She suddenly broke off and glared across the room. "What is that look upon your face, Ramona? Do I sense disdain?"

Mathilda felt the outrage coming from Ramona; it echoed her own. When Ramona spoke, though, her voice was mild. "No, I was merely wondering what you have been doing with yourself to keep abed at this late hour."

"If you must know," Cassandra sneered, "I spend my nights making merry. What else do I have to do?"

Ramona pinned her with a firm gaze. Before Mathilda could silently warn Ramona to hold her tongue, she said, "There are many peasants who would benefit from your company. Surely you can find the time for them?"

Cassandra's face contorted and flushed a deep red. "*Do not* come into my home and tell me how to spend my time. Is that understood? I only tolerate you because of my sister. Perhaps it is best that you do not speak when in my company." Her hand clenched into a fist. "Otherwise, I might be forced to do something about you."

Mathilda saw the dangerous look in Ramona's eyes. "Cassandra," she intervened, "what do you have planned for Samhain? Surely you have some dead loved one you plan to visit?"

"No. I do not. I will spend it making merry and enjoying myself." Cassandra smiled at Marcus. He still hadn't obeyed her order to dress, and Mathilda could not help noticing that Cassandra didn't seem to mind at all.

Mathilda cleared her throat. "We had better be off." She felt Ramona's frustration simmering dangerously in the air. "I hope you enjoy the provisions," she added, picking up the basket from the table where Marcus had left it.

Cassandra eyed Mathilda's new kirtle. She folded her arms. "I see that you are well taken care of, Sister. How *is* life at your little cottage, now that servants and plenty of provisions are heaped at your door?"

Mathilda ignored the bait. "Life is wonderful, as it always has been. We are busy with our weaving; we sell what we make. Perhaps you have a talent that you could benefit from?"

Cassandra snorted. "My talents are not for sale."

Marcus barked a laugh at the comment.

Mathilda had had enough. "I will leave you be. Take care of yourself, Cassandra."

As the door closed behind her and Ramona, Mathilda heard her sister's chime of laughter. The cold, clear air outside came as a relief.

"Your sister is a most *vile* creature," Ramona snapped as they crossed the clearing, heading toward the wood.

"She certainly wears down one's patience," Mathilda agreed. For now, Cassandra seemed only able to wallow in her misery at what Aelle had done to her. Soon, though, she was likely to lash out, when and how Mathilda couldn't guess. "If she has any good left in her soul," Mathilda said, "I can only hope her connection to us will keep it alive."

Ramona's expression was stony. "I am sorry, Mathilda, but I think that is impossible. She is too far gone."

"I fear you are right, but I must hold out for goodness. Without it is chaos."

14

athilda sat by the window, oblivious to the bustling activity coming from both cottages as her sisters and the servants prepared for Samhain. She had been helping Gertrude peel vegetables before the woman shooed her away to finish the rest herself, giving Mathilda a much-needed moment alone. The thick brown wool blanket Mathilda had draped over her lap staved off the chill lingering around the window as she gazed past her reflection into the deepening twilight, lost in her thoughts.

Ramona came up, wiping her hands on her apron. "What troubles you, Sister?" The apple she had just cut lay on a plate, its black-starred center reminding Mathilda of the circle of life and the veil to the spirit world that was now at its thinnest.

The dull sadness that Mathilda had kept tucked in a corner of her mind all day flared again, and she sighed wistfully. "I was just thinking of my mother. Of all our mothers."

A look of pity swept over Ramona's features. She reached for Mathilda's hand. "I feel terribly guilty that we plan to commune with our mothers whilst you cannot."

Mathilda mustered a smile for her friend. "Do not be sorry,

Ramona. I am happy that you got this opportunity. I have had many visits from my mother. I know she is at peace." Mathilda squeezed Ramona's fingers gently before releasing her hand and rising from the chair. "I look forward to seeing Leticia, Katherine, Annora, and Philippa. They were so kind to me after my mother died. I grew to love them very much."

"Thank you," Ramona said. Laughter from the men out in the clearing carried inside, drawing her attention. "You know, I overheard the laborers talking of mischief-making tonight. Are you going to allow it?"

"Oh, let them make merry." Mathilda laid the blanket over the back of the chair. "It will do us all some good to hear their laughter this night. As long as their jests are in good nature, I say we join in."

"Mistress," Gertrude said, from the hearth where she stirred a pot, "the stew is ready. Would you care to approve its flavor?"

Gertrude's eyes were bright with anticipation. Mathilda saw a dark stain on the front of her apron where she had spilled some broth, likely sampling it. She couldn't have noticed the spill yet, Mathilda thought; Gertrude was so fastidious she would have promptly changed her apron. She was a hard worker, but she had a gentle face, enhanced by the few strands of silvery hair escaping from her simple white cap. Mathilda had grown quite fond of her.

Ramona drew her cloak on. "I'm going to look in on the others," she said.

"I'll join you shortly." Mathilda dipped the spoon in the cooking pot and blew gently before tasting. "This is wonderful, Gertrude. What gives it such a delicious flavor?"

Gertrude swelled with pride. "Fennel and ale. It was my mother's own recipe. It goes back many generations." Tentatively, she added, "I thought you and the other mistresses might like to leave some by your mothers' graves."

"That is kind, Gertrude," Mathilda said. "I would like that very much." She reached for her own cloak. "I am going to see if Hilda needs anything. I shan't be long."

The evening air was crisp. The commotion from the men, now inside their shelter, carried outside, but Mathilda instinctively found the stillness. She inhaled deeply, feeling the evening's peace in her soul.

A slight rustling came from the edge of the wood, sending a tingle of warning down her spine. A shadowy silhouette slowly moved out from the cover of the trees. Mathilda tensed, her magic crackling beneath her skin as she anticipated one of Cassandra's shifters. Her tenseness gave way to surprise as the figure approached. She saw that he was a monk by his coarse linen tunic and the wooden cross that hung from a leather cord around his neck. His head remained lowered beneath his hood, and as he approached, she caught a glimpse of a sword's hilt around the back of his belt.

Why did he wear a sword? She reached for her magic, readying herself. Then she heard his voice, gruff and warm and unmistakable.

"Blessings upon you, mistress."

Duncan! Mathilda flew to him. His powerful arms wrapped around her, and he swept her off her feet, swinging her through the air as if she weighed no more than a stalk of grain. She showered him with kisses.

When he set her on her feet, reality and worry closed back in. "Duncan, why are you here? It is dangerous."

"I have missed you, Mathilda. I had to come."

She drew back, looking him over. "Why are you dressed like that, for goodness' sake? You frightened me."

His eyes sparkled with the mischief she loved. "How else was I to travel across the border?"

She lowered his cowl and wove her fingers through the waves of his dark hair. It had grown longer since the last time she saw him. "Take off that ridiculous disguise. You look disturbing."

Duncan's brows rose. "You try to get me out of my clothes so soon, woman?" His grin disappeared, and along with it, the teasing in his eyes, leaving only desire so strong that Mathilda caught her breath.

He caught her about the waist and pulled her against him. His kiss was tender at first, but as Mathilda kissed him back, desperate hunger flared between them. He groaned against her lips, twining his fingers in the hair at the nape of her neck, guiding her back toward her cottage with his lips pressed against hers.

Mathilda was vaguely aware of giggling coming from Regina's cottage before she came up against the door of her own. She felt it swing open behind her and heard a disapproving gasp. Gertrude.

Duncan raised his head long enough to command, "Leave us."

Gertrude stood in the doorway, frowning, as if she would protect Mathilda's virtue with her own body.

Mathilda caught her breath. "It's all right, Gertrude," she managed. "Please go help the others."

Gertrude stalked out the door, shaking her head and mumbling something about "the audacity of men."

Mathilda smiled archly up at Duncan. "You offended my servant. You should apologize before you leave."

"Later. First, I must attend to you," he said, kicking the door shut with his boot.

MATHILDA'S HEART STILL RACED, even as her breathing slowed. The seashells hanging above the bed swayed gently, and Duncan gazed up at them. His chest still rose sharply, catching Mathilda's eye in the dim candlelight. She laid a hand over his heart; its rhythmic pounding was an assurance. He was here, blessedly alive. She shifted herself to where her head rested on his chest and placed a reverent kiss over his heart.

"You do not know how I have missed you, lass," he said against her hair.

"Lass," indeed. The endearment made Mathilda smile. She ran her fingers over his arm, savoring the line of his muscles. She marveled at how the simplicity of touch felt as strong as any magic she had used.

He turned his head toward her, eyes sparkling.

"What is it?" she asked.

"I was just thinking," he said, "of the eve of Beltane where I met the most beautiful woman I have ever beheld." His eyes were serious now, full of warmth. "In my mind, you'll always be that golden-haired lass."

That night felt like a lifetime ago. Mathilda felt wistful, remembering the sweetness of it.

"You have made some changes here since I last saw you," Duncan remarked.

"Not I." Mathilda drew the blankets up over them both against the chill in the room. "It was Regina's doing," she said. She told him briefly about what had happened since he had last seen her: how her sisters had lost their mothers on the solstice, how the five of them now lived together, and how Regina had brought them so many good things. "Her father has been generous," Mathilda added, "giving us so much from his own property." She smiled. "Of course, Regina usually gets her way."

Duncan rolled onto his side to face her. "And what of your own mother? I remember seeing you with her at Beltane." He propped himself up on his elbow and reached for a lock of her hair, wrapping it around his fingers.

Mathilda's bliss leached away as the image of mounded grave dirt came to mind. She couldn't keep the numbness from her voice as she replied. "She is dead. My father killed her."

Duncan's eyes darkened with anger. "What was his fate?"

"He died shortly after. His own spell turned badly."

Duncan let go of the coil of hair he had been holding and kissed her temple. "I am sorry, Mathilda. Truly."

His tenderness nearly brought tears to her eyes. "Thank you. But I have found happiness with my sisters. My life is no longer sad."

He studied her face closely, seeming to notice something new.

"You look different," he mused. "I don't know how to describe it. There is a certain... vibrancy about you."

Mathilda tried to keep her expression neutral. "Is there?" She didn't want him to ask too many questions. She knew her looks had changed, subtly but clearly, ever since Cassandra's spell had taken over. Millennia of secrets descended through each line of Guardians, stilled her tongue out of habit from telling Duncan of her immortality.

"You are not with child, are you?" he asked, brushing his knuckles over the swell of her breasts.

Another topic she wished to avoid. In truth, she did carry Duncan's child. It lay in her womb, patiently awaiting its time to grow. "Even a man would know I would have a growing belly by now."

His teasing smile broadened. "Then it must be the love we made that has painted the bloom on your cheeks."

Mathilda laughed. "Perhaps."

He traced his thumb over her lower lip, nipping at it before kissing her. As Mathilda kissed him back, the clang of spoon against pot in the main room broke into the peace. Gertrude must have come back, and now she was announcing the fact, none too subtly.

Duncan groaned in frustration. "Your servant did not heed my command. You should whip her."

Mathilda's mouth fell open. Surely, he wasn't that kind of man. "I would never do such a thing. She has gone to much trouble preparing a stew for our dead loved ones. We are taking it to them this night." No sooner had she said this than she heard Ramona's soft voice in the main room; likely, she was collecting the portion they would take on their journey.

"Peace, my love." He kissed her again, tenderly. "I meant it in jest. Would you mind if I came along?"

My love. She smiled at his words, wondering if he realized he had uttered them. "No." She drew back the covers and rose from the bed. "I would be glad of your company."

~

MATHILDA WORE a cloak over her dress, both dark, to shroud her on her journey and fit her for the occasion. Duncan retrieved his horse from where he had left it grazing beyond the treeline and helped her up in the saddle, then settled in behind her. The others had already left for the stone circle some time ago. Mathilda had heard them depart while she and Duncan were abed.

"I am sorry I delayed you from traveling with your sisters," he said, taking the reins. "This will not be nearly as comfortable for you as the cart would have been."

"Maybe not," she said. "But it is faster."

"That it is." He pulled Mathilda close, flicked the reins, and the horse set off into the woods. Once they were off the rugged path and onto the more traveled one, Duncan loosened his grip on Mathilda. "Are you comfortable?" he asked.

"Yes." In truth, Mathilda was reveling. She had never expected to have Duncan here with her, his body pressed against her own. His nearness sent a shiver through her, and she blushed at the memory of their earlier passion in her bed. Thankfully, he could not see her, or he would immediately know her mind.

"What do you plan to do once you reach the circle?" Duncan asked, drawing her from her passionate thoughts.

"We will commune with our loved ones. The veil to the other side is at its thinnest tonight, allowing us access to speak to them." She turned her head enough to see him and added, half-teasing, "Are you sure you can witness such a thing?"

Duncan's jaw tightened, and a haunted look passed over his face. "You would not want to know the things I have witnessed. A little necromancy is nothing compared to the horrors I have seen."

Mathilda sat quietly, pondering his words. She could only imagine what he'd seen in battle. Did he have comfort from the clan he led or merely the burden of responsibility? "Duncan?"

"Aye?"

"Are you happy in your homeland?"

A silence, long enough for her to listen to the horse's hooves against the cold ground and the rustle of some small night creature in the underbrush. Then Duncan answered, "Enough. I have my kin and childhood home. It keeps me content." His tone carried the weight of his circumstances. It was a resigned contentment she recognized in the life she found herself in without him. "What about you? Are you happy?"

"Enough," Mathilda echoed.

A horse whickered in the distance, and she gazed beyond the trees, sensing Ramona's familiar presence first.

"My sisters are just ahead."

"How do you know this?"

"I have my ways."

Duncan laughed. "I find you a most interesting woman, Mathilda Longhurst."

Sure enough, the cart came into view up ahead. Mathilda recognized the lanky driver, Peter, as one of the workers. Ramona sat in the back. The hanging lanterns cast a soft glow on her face.

"Greetings, Sisters," Mathilda called as they caught up to them.

Katrina whispered something to Isobel and giggled wildly as Isobel blushed.

"I *can* hear you two, if you will recall," Mathilda scolded. As she and Duncan drew up alongside the cart, she fixed Katrina with a look as she spoke to them in their minds. *Please keep your comments about my lovemaking to yourself, Katrina. Isobel need not know your thoughts.*

"Are you not going to properly introduce us?" Regina asked, her tone teasing. She sat with her back against the slats, looking as though she were seated on a chair of velvet and not in the back of a rough cart bouncing over hardened ruts. The lantern light caught the gleam in her eye as she faced Mathilda.

"Duncan, these are my sisters," Mathilda said proudly. She named them for him one at a time.

He bowed slightly to the women.

"Duncan?" Regina said in her formal, lady-of-the-manor tone. "When do you plan to leave your country and marry Mathilda?"

"Regina!" Mathilda nearly shrieked. "Do not interfere in this matter." *Or I may not forgive you next time,* she silently added. Duncan could not surrender his responsibility any more than she could abandon hers. That knowledge stung bitterly.

Regina managed to look contrite *and* determined. "My apologies, Sister. I only have your well-being at heart."

"I have tried," Duncan responded. "She will not have me." His words were jesting, but his eyes, resting on Mathilda's face, were full of unspoken regret and deep loss. She knew his pain. It had hollowed out her heart for months since they parted. Tears pricked her eyes, and she turned away before they could fall.

"Can we just drive on in silence?" Mathilda barked. Kindlier, she added, "Please?"

"As you wish," Regina said. Peter glanced over his shoulder, and she gave a nod. He flicked the reins, swaying the lanterns hanging at the back as the horses picked up the pace.

The duration of the journey was spent in long stretches of silence. Any conversation quickly died away in the solemnity of the occasion. When they finally arrived at the stone circle, Duncan halted the horse beside the cart and helped Mathilda down. His hands lingered at her hips longer than necessary.

"Thank you," she said. "Are you sure you wish to join us?"

"Yes. I would not want to miss such an event." He led his horse to the nearby oak and wrapped the reins around a low limb.

Mathilda canted her head. "Are you mocking me?"

"Certainly not. I am curious. I heard of such goings-on from my grandmother when she walked amongst the living."

"What was her name?"

"Agnes Blàr. She was a devotee of the Goddess, like you."

Mathilda heard the warmth in his voice. "You speak fondly of her."

"Yes, she was very dear to me."

"Then you should witness." She took a lantern and followed her sisters into the grove, setting it on the ground at the place where the elder coven had fallen. The air had grown significantly colder since they had first set out, and their breath clouded as they moved closer.

Duncan settled in against some rocks, a mix of curiosity and apprehension crossing his face as he watched them prepare.

Ramona laid the sack of food on the ground, and Mathilda took out the other gifts of food Gertrude and Hilda had prepared: a thick coffyn filled with the stew, some bread, cheese, and apples, and passed them out to her sisters to place upon their mothers' resting site. She noticed that Isobel struggled to keep her emotions in check. Her lower lip trembled as she reached for the bread in Mathilda's hand.

"There is no shame in tears, Sister," Mathilda comforted. "It has been long since we last stood on this sacred ground, but the wound is as fresh in our hearts as though it were yesterday. Let us join hands and call the spirits of your mothers. Isobel, you may start if you wish."

Sniffling, Isobel nodded and took in a deep breath. "I call you forth, Mother. Let your spirit come to me on this hallowed night."

Regina was to Isobel's left. Though her features were carefully composed, her voice trembled with emotion. "I call you forth, Philippa de Buade, my beautiful mother. Let your spirit come to me on this hallowed night."

"Katherine, my mother, I call forth your spirit on this hallowed night," Katrina said, the words rushing out as though her emotions might overwhelm her.

Ramona followed. Her voice was soft and solemn as she spoke. "I call forth the spirit of Leticia, my dear mother. Let your spirit come to me on this hallowed night."

Mathilda closed her eyes and cleared her mind of all intrusive thoughts. "Agnes Blàr, I invite your spirit into our circle on this hallowed night. You may speak through me."

The wind began to pick up. The hood of Mathilda's cloak blew back from her head as she was swept up in a vision. In her mind's eye, she saw an old woman coming toward her. The woman was stooped and slow with age, but nonetheless, Mathilda sensed her strength. She wore a patterned cloth around her slender shoulders, which she pulled up over her head to shield her face from the wind. The light from the lanterns cast golden hues across her body. Mathilda felt her confusion as to why she was called from the spirit realm by a stranger.

As Agnes drew close, a look of delight spread over her finely wrinkled features. She pointed, and Mathilda could see Duncan through her eyes. As Agnes spoke, Mathilda's mouth gave the words. She watched Duncan's intense gaze turn to surprise before she lost sense of herself to this woman.

"Duncan, my lovely lad. I never thought I would set eyes upon you again. Och, I see you look at the young woman in disbelief." She shook her head, leveling Duncan with a firm look. "Her words are not her own, and I shall prove it. That scar on your left arm was given to you in your twelfth year. Your father took you into the wood to hunt for a hare. A boar rushed through the thicket and caught you off guard. You slew the beast, but not before its tusk tore into you. You gave me that tusk in your declaration to always look after me." A look of shock registered across Duncan's face. "There, I see that you believe. Now, listen closely. The woman you love will bear a child. That child will not be for you. She will belong to the Goddess. Do not attempt to take the babe or interfere in its upbringing. It is forbidden. Do you understand, lad?"

"Aye," Duncan replied, dumbfounded.

"Good. Your mother sends her love. She is very proud of the man you have become. Take care of yourself, Duncan. War is coming. You must keep to the Highlands until after the next Lughnasadh has passed. Remember this."

The woman turned away and walked back into the shadows. Mathilda came back to herself as the vision left her. Her sisters sat wide-eyed, and Duncan stared intently at her, his expression shaken. She smiled reassuringly.

"Mathilda?" he asked. "Is it you?"

"I am here, Duncan. I saw your grandmother. What did she speak of?"

His eyes went wide. "You don't remember?"

"No, I was merely a vessel for her to use, completely unaware. Tell me, please. What did she say?"

Duncan dropped his gaze. "She gave me a warning. She said war is coming, and I am to keep to the Highlands until the passing of the next Lughnasadh."

His words landed heavily in Mathilda's gut. It was a dire warning. For a spirit to be so specific, there must be a terrible consequence if not heeded. One that she did not dare give over to her mind lest it run wild with endless possibilities and interpretations.

"I see. Remember your grandmother's words, Duncan. The dead cannot entirely reveal the things that are to pass. Their warnings should be heeded. Was that all she said?"

Regina's eyes flashed to Duncan. "Can I tell you what my mother said?"

Duncan's shoulders dropped with relief. Mathilda wondered what had caused his unease. "Of course, Sister," she said. "I am sorry. Tell me of your mother."

A look of excitement lit Regina's face. "She said I was to linger by the Three Paths in three days' time when the sun is at its peak. I will certainly do so."

Katrina said, "My mother told me my future lies where the bells ring out." Her brows knit. "Though that makes little sense to me."

"Katrina," Isobel said, "my mother told me to gather the yarrow and cast a spell to make it fresh again for you."

Katrina started in wonder at Isobel's revelation. Mathilda did, too. She wondered what they would need the yarrow for. She turned to Ramona, eager to hear what Leticia had said.

"Ramona dear, you look pale." She felt a tug of unease as she took in her sister's haunted expression. "What did you learn?"

Ramona seemed to pull herself out of some dark place. Her eyes found Mathilda's, wide and filled with fear. "My mother told me that my greatest joy would come from tragedy."

A chill ran down Mathilda's spine. She watched her sisters' eagerness fade upon hearing Ramona's words. Frantic thoughts swirled in her mind: tragedy? What tragedy? Had Ramona not already suffered enough? She tried to draw on wisdom rather than fear.

"Remember," she said gently, "whenever that time comes, we are here for you. Whatever is to pass, we will help you."

Katrina reached across and took Ramona's hand. "Mathilda is right. We will all help you. No matter what."

Ramona nodded. "I know." She got to her feet and gave a tiny smile that did not reach her eyes. "We must get back. Gertrude is keeping the food warm for Maelen."

Mathilda watched with a heavy heart as Ramona reached for the empty sack and started back toward the cart. Mathilda took up the lantern, and Duncan joined her as they followed the others away. Their magic still lingered around the grove like invisible fingers, brushing their cloaks as they exited the sacred trees.

As they traveled home, Duncan's gaze was fixed ahead in the darkness as if he could see something Mathilda could not. The cart's wheels ahead of them made the only sound in the stillness of the wood.

"What weighs upon your heart, Duncan?"

She felt his chest expand against her back as he inhaled deeply. "I did not tell you everything from the vision. It took me off my guard, and I needed to ponder upon it."

"Tell me what you learned."

He let out a heavy sigh, ruffling Mathilda's hair. "My grandmother told me that you would bear my child. A daughter. I am not to be a part of her life. She said the child would belong to the Goddess. What is the meaning of her words?"

Mathilda felt his burden as her own. What she would give to be a family with him—to tell him everything. "I cannot speak of its meaning. Trust me when I say that it is not just my secret to tell. There are many things you do not know, and others involved that must be protected." Duncan's hand rested on his thigh, and Mathilda covered it with her own. "If there is indeed a child from our union, I will send word to you. That much, I promise."

Duncan was silent. After a moment, he hugged Mathilda close. "You are going to bear my child. I like the thought of it." He slipped his hand over Mathilda's belly, letting it linger.

She smiled and leaned into him. If only she could be a part of his world.

It was still dark when Mathilda woke to the sound of rustling. Duncan was already up and dressed. "What are you doing?" she asked. "It is not yet dawn."

"I must go. It would not be wise to tarry when I have the darkness to shield me."

Mathilda lit a candle and watched him pull on the monk's tunic. He draped the cross over his head and sat down to strap on his boots. She studied him in the candlelight. His broad shoulders flexed as he bent, muscles visible beneath the layers of clothing, undoubtedly built from years of practice with the sword. His dark hair swept across his upper back, the rich tones highlighted in the flickering light as he reached for his other boot. He was most pleasing to look upon, but what she felt for Duncan went beyond what his outer appearance sparked. Her heart ached sorely at the thought of him leaving.

He leaned over and kissed her gently. "I love you, Mathilda. I know I have not known you long to profess such a thing, but I do. Fiercely. The moment I set eyes upon you, I felt it in my heart at once. I will have my English kin come to you. If a child is in your womb, they will get word to me."

Mathilda fought to hide her feelings as she got out of bed and pulled on her tunic. She knew he would be expecting a confirmation of her pregnancy after his grandmother's vision.

"What are you thinking?" he asked. There was a softness to his voice that nearly undid her stoicism.

"I was thinking..." she broke off, fighting the tears. "I was thinking that I have enjoyed your company. I am going to miss you, Duncan."

He cupped her cheek, resting his forehead against hers. "We will meet again." His eyes intently held the conviction as they met hers. "I will find a way." He placed his hand against her belly. "You take care of yourself and the bairn. If it is a girl, name her Charlotte, after my mother."

He leaned in and kissed her again, and as he did, dread slammed into Mathilda's heart. She knew with absolute certainty this would be the last time she would ever see him. Her throat tightened, and she pushed away the building anguish as he straightened and reached for his sword. She would not send him off knowing this dreadful premonition.

Mathilda walked with Duncan to the door, the feeling of dread growing ever stronger. She pulled it open for him. The grass was covered with a heavy layer of frost, and a light rain had begun to fall since they woke. He lingered there, tracing her face with his eyes, then kissed her deeply. He pulled away with a regretful effort and turned to go. She watched him cross the clearing, a whirlwind of emotions gripping her heart, but as he reached the wood, something inside her broke.

"Duncan," she called.

He turned, and Mathilda ran to him, tears streaming down her cheeks. She flung her arms around his neck and kissed him with everything she had to give.

"I love you, Duncan Ferguson. I will hold you in my heart for all of my days upon this earth. Take care of yourself for me. For your child."

"I will. And you do the same."

They gazed fiercely at one another, neither willing to depart as the cold rain washed over them. Mathilda raised her hand to brush away a rain-beaded tendril of hair that had fallen over his eye.

"Goodbye, Duncan," she said, summoning the will.

He kissed her one last time and disappeared into the darkness of the wood.

A knot settled in Mathilda's stomach as she watched him go. She ran back into the cottage, unbothered by the frost that numbed her feet, and flung herself onto the bed, sobbing until she fell asleep.

MATHILDA FELT a nudge at her shoulder, and she jerked awake. Ramona stood by the bed. Her long braid hung over her shoulder, and a look of worry shadowed her dark eyes.

"I am sorry," Ramona said. "I did not mean to startle you. I wanted to check on you since it is late. Are you well?"

"No," Mathilda wiped the tear that escaped her eye. "Duncan will not return. I sensed it before he left."

"Are you certain? Perhaps it was just the sorrow of his leaving."

"No. I've learned the difference between a feeling and a foretelling. Duncan is to die soon. I felt it deeply." A sob worked its way out of Mathilda's throat.

Ramona sat down and wrapped her arms around Mathilda. "I am sorry. Truly."

Mathilda sniffed and wiped her nose. "He also knows about the child. His grandmother told him I would bear him a daughter."

"I know. We all heard it," Ramona admitted.

Mathilda lowered her gaze to her hands. "He will be expecting word about the pregnancy soon. I could not tell him about us, about how I could control when his child would be born. I do not know what to do."

"I do," Ramona said calmly. "I had a dream last night. Or a vision. I saw all of us with our bellies swollen with child. It was a sign. We must do our part now to continue the line of succession, Mathilda."

Mathilda met her eyes. "I fear you are right. But none of you has been swept away by the love of a man. I do not know how you can go through the deed not having that."

Ramona took Mathilda's hand. "Sister, leave our fates to us. Love is not needed to bear a child."

Mathilda felt helpless. Her sisters should not be mere vessels for men's desire. "I know this, and yet I want you to find happiness as I did."

For the first time, Ramona smiled. "Who is to say that we will not? For the moment, our line must continue, and we must proceed with the spell. I care not for love. Only to honor our responsibility."

Mathilda knew she was right. They had to uphold their duty first. She remembered Ramona's vision last night, and again that word *tragedy* haunted her, but she said, "Very well. I will not interfere."

15

—————

egina smiled brightly and took Mathilda's arm in her own. "You look terrible." She adjusted her fur more tightly around her shoulders, eyeing Mathilda questioningly.

"Good day to you, too, Sister," Mathilda said, smiling in return.

The sun glinted through the trees, though it provided no warmth. Mathilda was grateful to Regina for convincing her to get out of bed and enjoy a walk after her visit from Ramona.

"How are you, Mathilda, really?"

"I have an ache in my heart that wants to tear me apart, but I have you and the others, and so it will pass."

Regina regarded her thoughtfully. "Ramona told me that we are to find mates soon."

"Yes, Duncan knows that I am with child. He will expect word. I want to give him the good news of a child soon."

Just through the trees up ahead, Isobel was collecting kindling and putting it in a large basket. She looked up at their approach. Her nose and cheeks were flushed pink from the cold. Bits of wood chips were snagged on the fur she wore.

"Where is Katrina?" Mathilda asked. "I thought she was helping you."

"She said she wanted to look in on some sick children in the peasant village." Isobel dropped the wood she was holding into the pile she had made and dusted off her hands.

Mathilda frowned. "She went alone?"

"No, Ramona followed along at a distance to keep watch since Katrina refused her company."

"Remind me to have a talk with Katrina," Mathilda said. "She should know better after what happened the last time she went off alone." She turned her gaze toward the distant trees. "Walk with us, Isobel. I am in need of distraction from my thoughts."

Deeper in the wood, a mob of crows cawed angrily. Mathilda glanced up as a hawk wheeled overhead, dipping away with the current, leading the pursuing mob further along. A welcome silence settled in, but was broken by a sudden thrashing. A massive stag startled them all as it staggered through the brush across from them. An arrow protruded through its side. A runnel of blood ran from the wound, staining the smooth brown hair. The stag let out a haunting bellow that rang through the trees.

"Mathilda!" Regina gasped. "That poor creature. We must do something."

Mathilda didn't hesitate. When she took a step forward, the stag stamped on the ground and gave a warning snort.

"Careful, Sister," Isobel warned.

Mathilda gazed into the creature's eyes, projecting a soothing magic toward it. She inched her way closer until she was standing before the stag, close enough to feel its warm breath, and lifted her arm as slowly as possible, speaking soft words until it calmed. Then, daring to close the distance, she rested her hand on its nose, feeling the hard bony shape of its skull beneath her fingers. She reached into the depths of her mind, finding her life's essence, and poured all the connectedness she felt into the deer. The same familiar energy swirled in the depths of its large, black eyes, and a bond of trust was formed.

In the distance, hounds barked, echoing through the forest.

"Quickly, Sisters," Mathilda said. "Make haste. Isobel, you pull the arrow out. Regina, use your magic to heal the wound. I will comfort him."

Isobel's eyes widened. "How about *you* pull out the arrow, and I comfort him?"

"Isobel!" Regina scolded. "He is in pain, and the hunters will be here soon."

"Very well." Isobel stepped warily toward the creature and took hold of the arrow. She grunted. "It will not budge."

Regina sighed. "Oh, here. Let me." She gripped the arrow and pulled hard. "It *is* stuck. Where are Ramona and Katrina when you need them?"

The hounds' barking drew closer.

"Both of you, place your hands on his wound," Mathilda said. "Focus. See the arrow sliding out."

Mathilda honed her power on the arrow as they touched the wound, lending them her strength as she soothed the stag. Slowly, it glided out and dropped to the ground. The blood stopped flowing as the wound healed.

"Now run, my friend. Run," Mathilda urged.

As the stag bounded out of the tiny glade and disappeared, Mathilda quickly said a masking spell to hide herself and her sisters. The hounds were upon them in the instant they vanished. The hounds howled and sniffed all around the invisible circle. One of the dogs ventured over to sniff out where the stag had stood.

Isobel's eyes darted to Mathilda. *Sister, they will pick up the scent of the stag if you do not do something.*

I will confuse their minds before their masters arrive. Mathilda closed her eyes and concentrated. She placed the scent of the stag in the air in the opposite direction, then fixed her gaze on the dogs. They whined and turned in circles, unsure where to go. She blew out a puff of air, and one of the dogs caught the scent. Turning, it sounded a loud bay, prompting its companions to pursue.

Somewhere behind the knoll, she heard men shouting. Gradually, their voices faded as they made off after the hounds.

"It is safe now," Mathilda said. "Let us get back."

Isobel squeezed Mathilda's arm. "Well done, Sister."

They saw Katrina coming through the wood along their way. The cheerful melody she hummed carried along the wind. They stopped and allowed her to catch up.

"Katrina, what is that in your hair?" Isobel asked. "And your dress is all wrinkled. Where have you been?"

Katrina blushed furiously and smoothed out her tunic.

"Katrina," Mathilda urged. "What were you about?"

Katrina raised her head, meeting their eyes, and swallowed hard. "My mother told me my future lies where the bells ring." If Mathilda didn't know better, she would have thought Katrina sounded embarrassed. "I had a dream last night about the priory at Lindston," Katrina went on. "Their bells ring daily, so I went to see what would happen." Another flush of crimson stained her cheeks.

"For goodness' sake, Katrina, tell us now," Regina scolded impatiently.

"Very well." Katrina squared her shoulders and lifted her chin. "I encountered a monk walking through the wood. I might have enchanted him to lie with me."

Isobel gasped.

Mathilda felt scandalized. Of course, she and her sisters were all meant to lie with men, and soon, but like this? "Sister," she said, "surely you did not. They have strict rules on celibacy. You made him break his vow." Though she didn't necessarily agree with such strict rules, Mathilda understood the importance of honoring beliefs.

Katrina's face fell. "I know!" she wailed. "And I feel horrible over it, but I wanted to choose someone pure of heart." She met Mathilda's eyes, frightened but eager. "I have heard tell that the men of Lindston Priory are indeed pure in heart. Do you judge me harshly?"

Mathilda softened her expression. "Oh, Katrina. I do not. But where is Ramona? Did she not accompany you on your return?"

Katrina shook her head, confused. "She did not accompany me at all."

Fear stabbed at Mathilda. A sudden instinct pulled her off the path. "Come, Sisters. I fear Ramona has fallen into trouble."

They tore between the trees, breaths clouding the air as their lungs heaved. Mathilda stopped abruptly near the outskirts of the peasant village. *Where are you, Sister? I can sense your presence.*

"Here. I am here," Ramona weakly called.

They found her lying on the ground beneath a hazel thicket. Her dress was torn and muddy, pulled roughly up around her waist. Mathilda saw a trickle of blood on the inside of her bare leg. As she ran forward, Ramona struggled to sit up, her eyes full of tears.

"Oh, Ramona." A sob ripped from Mathilda's throat. She dropped to her knees and pulled her sister into her arms.

"He... he caught me off guard. I tried to fight him... tried to use my magic to free myself, but he was a witch. He bound my hands with unseen ropes. My body was frozen. He hurt *me...*" Ramona wailed.

Mathilda felt numb. Her mind reeled. *A witch did this? How could he do such terrible violence to one of his own kind?*

Through her own tears, Katrina said, "If this was done with magic, we cannot fully heal her here. Not without our sacred totems and herbs."

"The yarrow," Isobel said. "My mother told me to gather the yarrow and keep it fresh. We must get her to the cottage at once. I will make a poultice to stop her bleeding."

"Let us say a spell to ease her pain and slow the bleeding at least," Regina suggested.

They placed their hands over Ramona and sent their magic into her.

"It is done," Mathilda said. "We must hasten. The spell will only hold for a short time."

When they came to the cottage, Katrina flung open the door, and Mathilda helped Ramona inside. Gertrude gasped as she took in the sight.

"Gertrude, please ready Ramona's bed at once," Mathilda said, rousing the woman into action. "Then fetch me a bucket of water and clean cloths. Isobel, you get the yarrow prepared for Katrina."

When Ramona was settled, Mathilda took her mother's sacred ritual knife and a jar of salt from the chest at the bottom of the bed. Gertrude returned with the bucket of water and cloths, and Isobel followed her with the poultice.

"Leave us, Gertrude," Mathilda said. She turned to Ramona. "How are you feeling?"

"The pain is back," Ramona said, gritting her teeth.

"We are going to take care of you. Try to relax if you can." Mathilda carefully poured the salt around Ramona's bed, then put the tip of her mother's knife into the edge of the salt ring. It made a hissing sound where the blade had touched.

"Take my hands, Sisters," Mathilda said. "Focus the flow of your magic into this circle." She closed her eyes and took a calming breath. "To the powers that be: We humbly ask that you allow this sacred salt to absorb our sister's pain. Remove the foul remnants of magic left in her body, and bind the man who did this to her. Make her whole once more and ease her memory of the horrors from the evil done upon her."

"To the powers that be: So mote it be, so mote it be, so mote it be," they all said together.

The entire salt circle hissed as their magic took effect. Ramona gasped sharply, as if she had gulped a lungful of air in a moment of intense pain. Her back bent, arching away from the bed. She stayed frozen in that awful arch for several moments, her eyes wide and her face anguished, before suddenly going limp.

Mathilda sighed with relief. "It is done. Regina, quickly collect the salt back in the jar."

On the bed, Ramona lay with her eyes closed, exhausted.

Mathilda brushed her sister's hair away from her sweat-dampened face. "The worst is over," she told Ramona gently. "I will clean the blood from you while Katrina works her magic to complete the healing." She heard Katrina sob. "Katrina? What is it?"

Tears streamed down Katrina's face. "This is all my fault. Had I not gone alone into the wood, Ramona would never have met with this fate."

Ramona opened her eyes. "Do not weep for me, Katrina," she said. Her voice was drained but steady. "These things had to pass. My mother's prophecy just became clear. 'My greatest joy will come from tragedy.' I shall bear a child. It is what I set out to do, and now it is done."

Katrina rushed to the bed and collapsed to her knees with a sob. "I love you, Ramona, and I am truly sorry this happened to you."

Tears shone in Ramona's eyes as she nodded and reached for Katrina's hand.

"Here is the salt," Mathilda said. Regina replaced the lid on the jar. "We will place it beneath your bed. Whoever did this to you will be powerless for a fortnight. Remove the salt when it yellows and bury it. You will have power over the vile man, and he can never harm you again."

Mathilda lingered after everyone left. She sat on the edge of Ramona's bed, keeping her own emotions in check. She recalled Ramona's acceptance from the prophecy foretold by Leticia, and marveled at her sister's strength. It made her angry that Ramona had to suffer to fulfill her destiny. "How are you feeling?"

"The pain is gone," Ramona answered weakly.

"I meant your spirit."

Ramona's gaze was far away, and she looked as if she were caught between crying and screaming away her pent-up anger and fear. "I am weary, and I am angry. I cannot shake the memory of being bound against my will. Not to mention what he took from me. My sense of safety—of being able to protect myself with my magic, my trust... It shall be hard to recover from such evil, but I know I will with time."

Rage scorched Mathilda's insides. She forced herself to breathe, quieting the feelings. "Will you tell me how it happened?"

Ramona nodded reluctantly. "I followed Katrina toward the priory. I saw what took place between her and the monk, so I headed back to the path to allow her some privacy. I knew she meant to stop at the peasant village on her return home, so I went there to wait for her." Ramona paused, her eyes haunted as she looked through Mathilda, recalling the memory. When she spoke again, her voice was soft and trembling. "He found me just before I reached the outskirts. I never even heard him approach. Just the feel of his hand clamping around my mouth. And his smell. I'll never forget it. It was like that of an animal." A tear streaked down her cheek, and she swallowed. "He pulled me into the cover of the scrub, and then he..." Her voice shook, and she broke off with a jagged breath as she struggled to control herself.

"I was so surprised, I did not even think to use magic at first. I just fought him. When I finally came to my senses and reached for my power, he must have sensed it, and that is when he bound my hands and stiffened my body. I could not even see his face." She hesitated, gazing warily at Mathilda.

"What happened then?"

Ramona didn't want to say it. Mathilda could see that much, but her sister finished, "He shifted to animal form when he left me."

The rage was back. It roared uncontrolled until Mathilda's body shook with it. "I should have known Cassandra had something to do with this," she said through gritted teeth.

"Mathilda, it is done. I will soon bear a child, which is all that matters. Do not let this fester in you. I surely will not."

Mathilda shook her head in awe. "You are beyond wise, Ramona. I am proud to call you sister."

Ramona's face transformed then. A look of peace settled over her as the anguish and tenseness released. Her body softened against her pillows, and she smiled. "Thank you for what you did for me today."

"You are welcome. Here, let me pull the covers tight for you. I will go and let you rest."

Mathilda waited until well after dark before slipping back into her room, careful not to disturb Ramona. She eased into her bed, recalling the day's events. She had not been able to sense Ramona's danger because of the power of the witch who raped her. She knew of only one person who could have exerted such power.

Mathilda's breathing quickened with her rage. She wanted to rip the man's head from his neck and throw it at Cassandra's feet. It took a force of will to shove the feelings aside. Ramona did not need her behaving like a vengeful terror, but eventually, she *would* deal with Cassandra. Until then, she would need to tread carefully until each of her sisters could give birth.

Just as Mathilda drifted into sleep, an owl called, sharp and clear, jolting her fully awake. She listened for the second call. When it came, she quietly got up and slipped out of the room. Gertrude lay before the fire in the main room, snoring softly on her pallet. Mathilda stepped quietly past her and went outside to wait by the door.

A branch shook on the tallest oak across the clearing. Mathilda watched as the owl swooped across to her, carrying a rolled parchment in its talons. It dropped the roll into her hands and flew away over the cottage.

Mathilda unfolded the letter and said, "Illumine." The words glowed on the page from her magic.

> I must speak to you. Meet me at dawn in the clearing where we first met.
>
> Your sister,
> Cassandra

Mathilda squeezed her hand shut, crumpling the letter into a ball. Her teeth clenched so tightly she could hear them grind, and the rage she had held in check now flowed through her in a torrent. A blue-white flame sparked in her hand. In a moment, the letter had burned to char. The blackened pieces caught the wind and drifted away across the clearing. Mathilda stood there a moment longer, gaining control, before returning to bed.

DAWN CAME TOO SOON. Mathilda had slept very little, and the thought of having to face Cassandra only made her temper fouler as she tramped through the wood. Thankfully, she had left Ramona sleeping soundly. Rest would aid the healing process.

When she came to the clearing, Cassandra was already there, pacing briskly in a circle. The hem of her scarlet dress that she brazenly wore, regardless of the laws prohibiting the color for commoners, swirled around her ankles.

She stopped when she saw Mathilda. "There you are. How is Ramona?"

Mathilda couldn't tell whether her concern was real or feigned, and didn't care. "You *were* behind her attack, then." She did not bother to hide her anger.

Cassandra looked startled. "*No*, I was not. I am sorry for what happened to Ramona. Truly. It was Marcus. I found out last night. He bragged of his deed in a drunken stupor. After that, he was suddenly made powerless. I assumed it was you who cast the binding spell over him?"

Mathilda nodded as she recalled the binding spell she and her sisters cast at Ramona's bedside after the attack.

A look of distaste passed over Cassandra's face. "The vile man. What he did to Ramona was the last straw. That is why I sent for you. I have a bit of a problem on my hands. It seems the fools I granted immortality to are proving less than worthy—"

"*You made them immortal?*"

At Mathilda's cry, everything in the forest went silent. Her magic pulsed in her veins. Her body shook with the effort to keep from unleashing all of it at her sister.

Cassandra flinched, eyes widening at the outburst. "Calm yourself, Sister. I will explain everything."

Cassandra's soft voice seemed ridiculous in Mathilda's ears compared to her previous outburst. She glared at her sister. *Calm herself?* She barely held to reason by a shred as it was, without being told what to do. Something Cassandra said stood out. It was Marcus who attacked Ramona. Mathilda remembered she had sensed something in him the first time they met. She was glad to hear her spell had bound the vile man. She took a breath, regaining control of her senses. "Very well. Continue."

Cassandra visibly relaxed. "I became very drunk one night with a few new friends I invited to supper. I had been lonely, and I was feeling generous that night, so I decided to make them immortal. They were very grateful upon hearing of my plan, naturally. But right before casting the spell, I realized I wanted none as powerful as me, so I created a loophole. They can die, Mathilda, but it must be by your hand and the four others you trust so dearly."

Mathilda shook her head, stupefied. "Why do you tell me this? You give me power over your creations."

"I trust you more than them," Cassandra reluctantly admitted. "Marcus has raped a multitude of girls from the village. One was quite young. I was disgusted when I found out. Then there is Alys. That stupid girl forgets her place. She seduced the two other men in my trust, and now I question their loyalty to me. I see the error of it all, and I want them stopped."

Mathilda gave a bitter scoff. "What have the other men and Alys done besides offending your vanity?"

"They are murdering villagers over the slightest upset or for sport. Alys drives them on in her twisted sense of amusement. Word is quickly spreading of something unnatural in the wood. It is only a matter of time before the church steps in and sends out a hunting party—and I do not mean for game. Our hides will be bound to a stake if they find us out, Mathilda. Imagine their horror when we don't die. As amusing as I find that thought, I don't think your sisters will be laughing should they be found out. You *must* stop them."

Mathilda shuddered at the thought of her sisters bound to a stake. "And if I agree to this, what then?" she asked sharply. "Will you create more immortals once you are bored or addled by drink?"

"I will not," Cassandra said solemnly. The truth of her promise was plain upon her face. "Just get rid of these fools before they ruin all for us."

Mathilda thought of the villagers she and her sisters had cured with their "remedies." She imagined how they might view her if they became suspicious. She glared at Cassandra, furious that she had put Mathilda and her sisters in this mess. "Very well. I will talk to my sisters on this matter and send word if we agree to help."

There was an air of assurance to Cassandra that said she knew she had the upper hand. "Do not tarry long. You must cast your spell when the moon waxes full."

"That is but four days!" Mathilda needed to prepare. It would take time to consider the best route to destroy the four immortals and protect her sisters, too.

"I will arrange everything," Casandra assured her. "You and your sisters only need to agree on the location I choose and be willing to spill a drop of blood. Oh—and I will need you to reverse your binding spell on Marcus."

"Absolutely not," Mathilda said. "Not after what he did to Ramona."

"You must, or I will not be able to lead him to his destruction. I will make Marcus believe I found a loophole around the binding. He will go where I tell him without question if he thinks I returned his magic. He will be in my favor."

Mathilda held Cassandra's imploring gaze, weighing her words. "This had better not be a trick."

"I assure you it is not." Her sister's face was open, her eyes firm on Mathilda's, and seemingly honest from what she could tell.

Mathilda shook her head, angry at herself, but unable to abandon Cassandra to whatever her foul magic might cause.

"I will need a lock of hair from each person before the time comes," she said.

Cassandra understood that for the consent it was. A look of relief spread over her face. "You will have them. I will get word to you after I plan with Marcus and agree upon a secure site. It will have to be far from any village."

Mathilda turned on her heel and left the clearing without another word. At the cottage, she found Gertrude emptying Ramona's chamber pot.

"How is she this morning?" Mathilda asked.

"Well enough, mistress. 'Tis good to see her in better spirits after..." She broke off, unable to finish.

"All will be well, Gertrude." Mathilda patted the woman's arm, hiding her own turmoil as well as she could.

Inside the cottage, Ramona sat up in bed, propped against several pillows. She had more color in her cheeks today. Her sisters had already helped her dress.

Mathilda made her voice cheerful. "Good morning, Sister. You look well."

Ramona smiled. "Thank you. "I feel better. Did you go for your meditation?"

"No." Pushing past reluctance—Ramona would hate to hear this —Mathilda told the truth. "I met with Cassandra."

Ramona's eyes turned hard. "Why would you do that?"

The bitterness and anger Mathilda felt gave her words an edge. "She sent word to me late last night to meet her at dawn. It seems she has created a mess for us all. Thanks to my sister's stupidity, three men and a woman who have been with her recently are immortal. She needs our help putting them down."

"Why should I help her?" Ramona demanded.

"I know. I am loath to help Cassandra, too." Mathilda paused, feeling pain in her heart over what she had to say next. "Ramona, I discovered it was Marcus who violated you. Cassandra also told me he had raped several girls from the village recently, and that the other three in her company are murdering innocents for sport. We cannot allow such a thing. You know this."

Ramona's jaw tightened. The thoughts she turned in her mind played across her eyes in anguished emotion. She blinked away her tears. "You are right. What must we do?"

Mathilda took a steadying breath. "We must ready ourselves to destroy them all on the coming full moon. Cassandra will send word to us when a plan is ready."

At dinner time, everyone gathered around the table in Mathilda's cottage. She told them all about her agreement with Cassandra as soon as Gertrude had left them to go eat with Hilda.

Regina was the first to break the silence that followed. "Do you trust her?" Her fierce gaze demanded truth.

Mathilda had thought long and hard about this. "I do."

"Why?" Regina demanded.

Mathilda laid out her reasoning. "My sister wants to be all-powerful. She doesn't wish for anyone to compete with her." Her immortal servants surely were competition.

Regina shook her head. "But will that not set us up as her next competition?"

"That's true," Isobel put in. "What then?"

"Yes," Katrina said. Her face was pale in the firelight. "Won't Cassandra want to be rid of us, too?"

Mathilda understood their concerns. Her sister had made no secret of her dislike of them. She sighed. "I don't know. We must first destroy these vile creations before they can cause any more harm." Mathilda took a breath, calming herself. Too much was at stake to let her frustration and fear take charge. "For now," she said, "we are all to stay out of the village or anywhere near it until we have resolved this. People fear what they do not understand, and they are growing worried about what lies in the wood."

"What about the peasants?" Isobel asked. "Who will look after them?"

"Leave that to me," Mathilda answered. "I will see they are cared for."

"And what about Regina?" Katrina said. "Tomorrow is the day foretold by her mother to be at the Three Paths. What will she do?"

"Why, be there at midday, of course," Regina said matter-of-factly.

"But the danger," Isobel insisted.

"We *cannot* ignore the foretelling," Mathilda said. "Katrina, you and Isobel shall accompany her. There is power in three."

THAT NIGHT, Mathilda awoke to Ramona crying in her sleep. Her heart broke for her sister. She whispered a soothing spell into her hands and blew the words away with a puff of air. As the spell took hold, Ramona quieted and fell into a deep sleep.

Mathilda lay awake thinking of Marcus and what he had done to her beloved sister. Mathilda had never relished the thought of taking a life, but it would be a pleasure to do away with him.

16

"Hilda, please help me undress," Regina called breathlessly, rushing through the door after her morning outing with her sisters. Her chilled fingers worked furiously at unwinding her braids.

Katrina came in behind Isobel and closed the door. "Why are you changing your dress?" Katrina asked. "You just put it on."

Before Regina could answer, Hilda stepped into the doorway of the bedchamber. "I have your bath ready, my lady. I will help you undress."

"Thank you, Hilda. And mistress will do. Remember, I no longer hold my station." Regina turned to Katrina. "And to answer your question, Sister, I want to look my best for whatever awaits me at the Three Paths."

Katrina suddenly looked thoughtful. She drew off her woolen mittens slowly and laid them aside with her cloak. "What do you think will happen at the Three Paths? What if it is something horrible?"

Regina ran her fingers through her unbound hair and tossed it over her shoulder. "With everything that has happened," she said, "I understand your fears, Katrina. I do. But it is not danger that awaits. There would have been a warning along with the vision. It has to be something wonderful."

"*Mistress,* I suggest you hasten," Hilda said. "Destiny does not tarry. Not even for you." She gave Regina a pointed look before she turned on her heel.

Regina submitted, smiling fondly. "Yes, Hilda." She had never allowed anyone to order her about so rudely, but Hilda had been in Regina's life for so long that she was like a kindly grandmother. And though Regina secretly found her cheekiness endearing, she did like to put on airs just to rile the woman.

WHEN REGINA finally swept out of the bedchamber, wearing a fine surcoat over a lavish gown, she couldn't help but notice how Isobel's brows arched. Momentarily self-conscious, she raised a hand to the golden caul encrusted with delicate pearls that covered her hair and drew a deep breath. She was about to encounter her destiny. There was nothing wrong with looking her best.

"Sister," Isobel said delicately, "perhaps you might be... *too* over-dressed." Katrina got up from lacing her boots, and Isobel took her seat, reaching for her own boots. She pinned her dark eyes on Regina. "After all, you *are* going into the wood, not to court. What if we are set upon by robbers?"

Regina went to the door and lifted her foot for Hilda to slip a patten over her shoe. "Isobel, if a robber sets upon us, then that is *his* misfortune."

Hilda flicked an amused glance up at her mistress and shook her head. "I pity the robber who happens across you. He'd certainly have his hands full." Ignoring the implied remark that she was difficult, Regina lifted her other foot for the second patten and turned to her sisters. "If anyone should question us, I am headed to the priory for confession."

"Confession!" Hilda muttered. "I pity the priest."

Regina did her best to ignore that, too. "You two are my servants," she told her sisters.

Katrina scoffed. "Servants!"

"Look at me, Katrina." Regina spread her arms, displaying her finery. "Dressed this way, I have to play the lady. If you and Isobel are my serving-women, that is the most befitting story I can muster."

"Fine," Katrina said sourly. She narrowed her eyes. "But do not dare to give me orders, or it shall be *your* misfortune."

Hilda barked a laugh, prompting a scowl from Regina.

THE WOOD SURROUNDING the Three Paths was still, save for a crow cawing in the distance. A thin layer of pale-gray clouds covered the sky, and a chilly breeze swept up a scattering of dead leaves across the women's feet. They had not encountered a single soul along their way, for which Regina was thankful. She did look a spectacle, dressed as she was.

"What now?" Katrina asked, cautiously looking around.

"We wait," Regina replied. "If we sense anything odd, we will mask ourselves."

"Why not do it now?" Isobel suggested. She briskly rubbed her hands together, glancing warily through the trees. "I do not like being in the open, knowing Cassandra's wretched creatures could be anywhere."

"Look," Katrina said, pointing. "The sun is at its peak."

Regina shielded her eyes and glanced up at the muted light coming through the clouds. Her anticipation abruptly died as a low growl came from behind them. *Slowly turn around,* she thought to her sisters, thankful they all wore their necklaces to communicate this way.

Two unnaturally massive wolves barred the path behind the women. The wolves growled again, baring sharp teeth. At the same time, a third wolf approached from behind the druid tree. This one was even more terrifying. Its coat was black as ink, its muzzle longer than a man's forearm. It snapped its jaws. Saliva dripped from its red tongue.

Regina swallowed her fear and sprang into action. *Quickly, Sisters! Take my hands.*

The three joined hands. Instantly, all of them vanished from view.

Follow me into the scrub, Regina said.

But before they could take cover, the wolves had encircled them.

Regina, they see us! Isobel said.

Regina's anger swelled. How dare these shifters attempt to attack her and her sisters? *You are right. Make ready to defend yourselves.*

"Reveal!" Regina shouted.

A blurring motion surrounded the wolves as Regina's magic forced them into their human forms. She and her sisters quickly hurled a blast of magic, rocking the men backward.

"Isobel, you and Katrina focus all your energy on creating a barrier. I will continue the assault."

The man who had been the black wolf lunged toward them, but Regina sent him tumbling back into the druid tree with a powerful surge of energy as the other two men attempted to get through the barrier. Just then, they all heard an approaching rider galloping through the wood. Isobel waved her arm, winking herself and her sisters out of view. Regina watched with frustration as Cassandra's men quickly returned to wolf form and disappeared through the forest.

Regina stamped her foot. She had wanted to finish off those fiends once and for all. "Well, damn it all to hell!"

Isobel gasped. "Sister! Don't talk so!"

Regina would have answered, but the rider they heard tore along the main path and abruptly halted his horse at the intersection of the Three Paths. The beast snorted and pawed at the ground, as if in protest at lingering here amidst remnants of foul magic from the shifters.

An overwhelming sense of rightness settled over Regina. It felt as if the whole world had aligned and placed her here in this specific moment. She was awestruck by the stranger. He was most pleasing to look upon. He had large, expressive eyes, a strong jawline, and, blessedly, a straight nose. His hair was pale, like hers, and he had a look of kindness about him. He was not richly dressed, but he was no peasant either. He was clean and well-groomed. He wore a well-made cloak of dark wool, gloves, and boots of smooth leather. Who was he?

At her thought, the man turned, fixing his vivid blue eyes directly on her. She gasped.

Quiet, Sister, Katrina scolded.

Can he see us? Isobel asked, panicked.

Regina did not answer. She dared not move. She kept her eyes locked on the man as her heart beat wildly. Finally, he turned away and urged his horse forward. Regina stared after him until he disappeared beyond the distant trees.

Katrina let out a shaky breath. "Regina, he was staring right at you. Do you think he saw us?"

Regina's voice shook as she answered. "I don't know. I could not read him." She smoothed her trembling hands over her skirts. "He may have sensed our energy. Many humans are sensitive to it but rarely understand what they sense. Perhaps that is why he lingered."

"Let us get away from this place," Isobel urged. "I have had quite enough for one day."

When they reached the clearing, they went to Mathilda's cottage first, eager to tell her and Ramona what had happened. Hilda and Gertrude paused their mending as Regina swept through the door. Mathilda and Ramona looked as if they were about to settle down at the table. They looked up expectantly at Regina.

Gertrude chuckled. "Now, mistress Regina, that is a look I have seen before."

"Yes," Hilda agreed. "She wore that same face when she broke the chain of her mother's favorite sapphire necklace."

Mathilda frowned. "You look troubled, Regina. What occurred at the Three Paths?"

Regina sighed and slumped, unladylike, into a chair. "Would you like me to start with the wolves or the stranger?"

Mathilda's brows lifted in surprise. She pulled out a chair and sat. "The wolves," she said flatly.

"Three wolves tried to attack us," Regina began. "Shifters. We defended ourselves, but a rider came along, and the wolves ran off." The memory of what happened chilled her.

"And the stranger?" Mathilda asked. She looked troubled at learning of the attack, yet eager to hear more of the story.

"That is complicated," Regina recalled their time in the wood. "Isobel masked us, but the man looked right at me. I could have sworn he saw me. He sat on his horse, studying me, or so it seemed. I do not know if he saw or sensed me, and I could not read him. That is what troubles me most."

Mathilda seemed to ponder this. "It was your destiny to be in his path today," she said matter-of-factly. "I am certain you will meet the stranger again."

"Perhaps," Regina said. She dared not get her hopes up again. Disappointment was a bitter companion.

"As for Cassandra's wolves," Mathilda said, "We will soon deal with them." She sank against the back of her chair with a satisfied smile. "On a lighter note, Ramona and I found a way to get supplies to the peasants without endangering any of the servants. Watch." She waved her hand across herself. The air shimmered around her, blurring her features, and suddenly she wore Gertrude's face.

Katrina squeaked. "Oh! How wonderful. I never considered altering our appearances."

Mathilda returned to her true form. "Use any form you like as long as it is someone Cassandra or her men will not recognize."

"Do we change our appearances to ourselves while visiting the peasants?" Isobel asked.

"No. I think it's best we stay in whatever form we take when we leave here. We can say—well, we can say that *we* sent us," Mathilda said, laughing.

"I like it," Regina said. "It sounds like an exciting adventure." A flicker of disappointment nagged at Regina as she looked down at her gown. All the trouble she had gone through, and for only a fleeting moment with her supposed destiny. She put her smile back on and met Mathilda's gaze.

Mathilda smiled back at her. "Good. Then decide who you would like to be, and tomorrow we shall pay a visit to the peasant village."

A COLD WIND tore through the clearing, whipping the cover on the cart. Two men loading the supplies secured the corner quickly before it could lift off the frame.

"Will it hold, Elliot?" Regina asked her driver.

"Aye, mistress, 'tis secure."

"Let us be on our way, then."

Mathilda climbed into the cart and helped Ramona settle in with Isobel and Katrina following them over the sides. Thankfully, they all wore borrowed men's clothing, making it much more manageable to clamber over the wooden slats.

"Here are some blankets, mistress, to keep you warm on the journey." Gertrude reached over the side of the cart to hand Mathilda a stack of thick woolen blankets.

"Thank you," Mathilda said. "We shall need these today." She tucked one around hers and Ramona's legs and passed the rest to Isobel. "Well, Sisters, are you ready?"

"We are," Katrina said eagerly. Her fingers twitched against her tawny-colored hose, which were much too big for her.

They each waved an arm over themselves, changing into their preferred person.

Katrina burst into laughter. "Regina, who are you supposed to be?"

"I remembered the blacksmith's father from when I was a child. He had a crooked nose, and I always wanted to straighten it, but Mother forbade it, so now I shall." Regina pulled her nose straight with a satisfied grin. It made a crackling sound, and Isobel groaned as if she would be sick.

"Well, I see the rest of us chose from the laborers, except you, Isobel," Mathilda said.

"I know who she is," Katrina said archly. "She is Robert, the son of Master Bainard, the stonemason. He came to do repairs once when his father was ill. I think he made an impression on our dear sister."

Isobel blushed. "I overturned a basket, and he helped me gather everything up. He was very kind to me."

"You are keen on him," Katrina teased.

"Leave her be," Regina scolded, sensing Isobel's discomfort. She wrapped her legs in her blanket and called over her shoulder, "We are ready, Elliott."

The cart abruptly lurched forward, and they proceeded through the wood. Blessedly, they met no shifters or trouble of any kind on their journey.

Per Regina's instructions, Elliott halted the cart in the cover of trees on the outskirts of the village. He pulled open the covering, and Regina watched the others rise to jump out. Ramona and Mathilda climbed over the sides. Isobel followed them. The sound of her boots thumped against the hard ground as she landed with ease.

Somewhere behind the cart, a goat bleated. A man leading the animal by a long rope emerged. He glanced at the women-turned-men with an odd look as he passed by them.

"Regina, dear," Mathilda whispered. "If you are waiting for Elliott to help you down, remember, you are a man."

Regina's eyes widened as she realized her predicament. She had never climbed out of anything on her own and was unsure how to go about it with dignity.

Katrina sighed. "It is not that hard. Watch me." She lifted her leg over the side and placed her foot on the wheel, then the other, and jumped evenly to the ground. "See, it is not so difficult. Think of your feet landing soundly, and you will be fine."

Several curious villagers had gathered to watch them. Realizing she had no choice, Regina put her right leg over to the ledge and tried to get her balance. As she swung her left leg over, she lost her footing and fell, landing on her bottom.

Katrina laughed. Rage swept over Regina. Never had she been so humiliated. Before she could think, she caught up a stone and flung it at Katrina, grazing her hip.

Katrina's lips flattened into a thin, angry line. "Why, you—"

"Enough!" Mathilda shouted. "Remember why we are here. Control yourselves. Be vigilant."

Regina felt heat flood her cheeks as she stood, struggling for composure. Without a word, she dusted herself off and helped the others unload the supplies.

The visits were as uneventful as the journey had been. The women went to Amos Bradbury's house first, since his dwelling was the closest to the wood. He graciously accepted their supplies without suspecting who they were beneath their disguises. They encountered no trouble or suspicion at any of the other houses. Even so, Regina was glad when they finished at the last house. Maintaining her role as a servant, and a man no less, was more difficult than she had imagined.

When they had returned to the cart, Regina climbed up onto the ledge and swung her leg over, successfully this time. As she reached to close the covering, she froze. The stranger she had met at the Three Paths was preparing his horse to leave the village. How had she missed him? Regina watched as he rubbed the horse's nose and spoke soft words. His kindness to the beast moved her.

He suddenly looked up and met her gaze. She gasped, feeling a sense of recognition in his eyes, and yanked the cover closed. Safely hidden behind it, Regina wondered why she had been so quick to get out of sight. It wasn't as if the stranger had seen her in her true form, though it certainly felt as if he had.

When all of her sisters had settled in the cart, Elliot turned them toward home. "That went well," Ramona said.

"Yes," Mathilda agreed. "We will need to buy more materials for our weaving soon. Perhaps we can try another outing in disguise."

"Regina," Isobel said, "you have not spoken since we took our leave. Has something happened?"

Regina gazed up at Isobel. She had not realized she was so lost in her thoughts. "I saw the stranger who came across us at the Three Paths. He was in the village."

"That is auspicious to see him twice so soon," Katrina said.

Regina couldn't keep the sadness from her voice as she answered, "It seems it is our destiny to meet."

Katrina raised an eyebrow. "He is quite handsome—more than handsome. I would imagine you would be happy at the thought of meeting him."

Regina shook her head. "I do not dare get my hopes up because he would never marry someone like me. We are witches, Katrina. I do not need to remind you what happens to our kind when we are discovered."

"I was not suggesting you marry the man," Katrina replied dryly. "I was thinking more along the lines of a secret tryst."

Isobel tried to stifle a giggle without success.

Regina found she could smile at her sister. "I am sorry for speaking harshly, Katrina. Sometimes, I still dream of being someone's wife. I saw my mother and father together, in mutual understanding, and before committing my life to the four of you, I always held fast to the hope that it would someday happen to me."

"We must make great sacrifices to protect one another," Mathilda said sympathetically. "And I hope you will find happiness with our coven through the years. I know it is not the same as having love and passion with a partner, but it does fill the void sometimes."

Regina slipped her arm around Mathilda. "You are very wise, Sister. I hope I did not stir up old wounds in you. I am happy, truly."

~

THAT EVENING, Mathilda and Ramona supped at Regina's cottage. As they took their leave, an owl called. Mathilda turned just as it flew from a bough and dropped a small pouch into her hands before flying off.

"What could that be?" Ramona asked.

Mathilda peered into the pouch, and dread came like a knife to her heart.

"Cassandra sent the locks of hair I requested. There is also a letter." She untied the red ribbon around the parchment and unrolled it to read aloud:

Be at Carwyn's Field in two days. I have convinced my immortal fools to arrive when the full moon peaks. I should warn you: They are under the impression that they are to kill all of you. My apologies, but that was the only incentive to get them there. They are rather bloodthirsty for your heads. I do hope you are ready.

A heavy silence settled between the women as they gazed at the letter.

"What are we going to do?" Ramona asked in a shaky voice.

"I have a plan. Let us sleep for now. Tomorrow, we will prepare."

~

THE EARLY MORNING air was bitterly cold. Snow had fallen sometime before dawn, and the ground was beginning to lose all traces of green. Wrapped in her fur, Mathilda knelt beside her mother's grave and placed her hands over the mound, taking in the energy surrounding the site. Her fingers felt the cold bite, and her knees had numbed, but she pushed away her discomfort and closed her eyes.

"Mother," she said quietly, "I come to you with a heavy heart. We are to go against Cassandra's immortal creations, and I worry for my sisters. They are strong, but they can die." Tears stung Mathilda's eyes. How could she face life without them? She drew in a breath. "Cassandra's followers know my sisters are vulnerable, and I am certain they will attack them first. I know you can no longer come to me, but please, Mother, *please* send us your strength and beg of your sisters to aid their daughters. I will give an offering to the Goddess, but can you ask that she watch over us and protect us? Coming from you, the Goddess might hasten to help our cause."

Mathilda stretched prostrate over the grave for several moments before rising. Though she couldn't feel her mother's presence, Mathilda held on to the hope that she still heard her plea. The snow fell heavily now, and as she returned to the cottage, she was welcomed by the large fire Gertrude had built up. Mathilda smiled gratefully at the woman and draped her fur over a nearby chair to dry.

Ramona stood by the bedchamber door, winding her hair into a braid. "You are all wet," she said.

"I went to spend time with my mother. The snow is beautiful."

"The first snow..." Ramona said nostalgically. "Mother and I always loved the first snow. We would run and make merry through it." She tied a blue ribbon at the end of her braid and tossed it over her shoulder.

Mathilda's heart suddenly felt light. "That is a wonderful idea. I will wake the others, and we shall all make merry. Gertrude, keep up the fire. Ramona and I are going into the snow."

Gertrude shook her head. "As you wish, mistress, but you will catch a terrible chill."

"Mathilda, this is the first time I have seen you truly smile in a month," Ramona said. "It makes my heart happy."

"Mine too. Come on."

They ran across the clearing to the other cottage. Mathilda bent outside the door, scooped up some snow, and packed it into her hands.

"Quickly, open the door."

Ramona pushed it open and raised a finger to her lips, silencing Hilda as Mathilda crept into her sisters' bedchamber. She broke off a chunk of snow and shoved it down Katrina's chemise. She immediately woke up shrieking. Isobel raised herself up on her elbows, groggy and confused. Mathilda quickly dumped the snow down the neck of her chemise and darted away. Their shrieks woke Regina, but the snow had melted by then. Mathilda looked down at her red, cold fingers and rushed to Regina's bed.

Regina clutched her covers tightly around herself. "Do not even *think* of it," she warned.

Mathilda giggled as she wrested the covers away and plunged her cold hands down the back of Regina's chemise. Regina screamed and bolted from the bed, looking as if she would do Mathilda harm.

"That was very wicked of you, Sister," Katrina scolded. Her petulant expression made her look like a little girl.

Mathilda laughed. "Yes. And I enjoyed every minute of it. Dress quickly, everyone, and come outside. The first snow has fallen. Come, Ramona." Mathilda darted past a beaming Hilda and went outside to compact more snow. "You do the same, Ramona. We will bombard our sisters when they come outside."

Ramona gaped at her. "Mathilda Longhurst, you *are* wicked."

"It seems I am," Mathilda said, packing more snow.

The cottage door suddenly flew open, slamming against the wall, and a blast of magic sent Mathilda and Ramona careening backward.

"Now!" Regina shouted.

Katrina and Isobel took the packed snow for themselves and started hurling it at Mathilda and Ramona while Regina made more for them to throw. Mathilda screamed and scrambled to make her own, but the snow pelted them too quickly.

A pile of snow smashed against Ramona's head, and Mathilda laughed. "Sister, we need a truce," Mathilda said. "We are outnumbered."

Ramona wiped the slush from her eyes. "Agreed," she said, out of breath.

"We surrender," Mathilda shouted.

Regina's smile was triumphant, and she looked like a queen as she gazed down at Ramona and Mathilda. "Sisters, we have bested our enemies."

Mathilda smiled fondly at her and got to her feet. "Come, Gertrude has a roaring fire awaiting us." She shook the snow from herself and led them all inside her cottage.

Gertrude clucked at the sight of them, but Mathilda noticed the smile lingering on her lips. "'Twill be a wonder if no one falls ill after this," she said, helping Mathilda strip out of her soggy clothes.

"Indeed." Hilda stepped into the cottage with a blast of cold air and an armload of clothes for the others. "You would think they would have outgrown such childish games by now."

Hilda's fine features and scolding tone made her seem rather queenly, and Mathilda giggled as she pictured how she must often have reprimanded Regina with that same look.

"Careful, Hilda," Regina replied. "Or I shall haul *you* out into the snow for a taste of defeat."

Hilda merely shook her head and proceeded to undress her mistress.

"The cider is ready," Gertrude announced.

"Oh, thank you, Gertrude," Katrina said through chattering teeth.

The sisters gathered around the fire, cups in hand, and wrapped themselves in blankets. Mathilda sighed contentedly. "I do not know about the rest of you, but I thoroughly enjoyed this first snowfall. I needed the distraction, for there is something I must tell you."

She pulled her blanket tighter around herself, hating that she must ruin everyone's good spirits. "I received a letter from Cassandra last night. She has convinced her followers to meet us at Carwyn's Field before the moon peaks tomorrow. We will need to prepare for this day for what is to come. My sister has provided me with a lock of hair from each of the ones we will destroy. I will use them to make a spell for our defense."

Isobel's eyes were wide as she listened. "I am frightened, Mathilda. What if we fail?"

"We will not," Mathilda assured. "And I am frightened, too, but the locks of hair have ensured our victory. My spell will link each of you to the one whose hair I give you. As they attempt to attack you, their power will weaken, eventually stripping away as you fight them, and they will be vulnerable to death."

"I want Marcus," Ramona said. "I want to be the one to put him down."

Mathilda saw the fire and determination in her eyes and shook her head. "No, Sister. I will not grant you that request. As much as I desperately want to allow it, vengeance *must* not corrupt your heart. If we do not go into this with pure hearts, we cannot prevail."

Anger and frustration crossed Ramona's features, and she dropped her gaze to the floor.

Mathilda reached out and squeezed her hand. "It breaks my heart to deny you that which you so rightly deserve. If our fates were not such as they are, I would sit by and happily watch you destroy that wretched man."

"I know," Ramona said. "And you are right, but I am worried that he will distract me from my purpose."

Mathilda pondered momentarily on Ramona's words before turning to her sisters. "We will need a gift for the Goddess. Before supper, I shall take a trap into the wood and see what we can capture by dawn. This day we shall spend in quiet contemplation, preparing our minds for our task."

17

By morning, the snow had stopped falling. Only a few stray flakes lingered in the air, drifting aimlessly in their descent to the ground. Mathilda laced her boots and went outside with Ramona to check the trap. The rumbling, hollow crunches of their footsteps in the snow were the only sounds they heard in the wood, save for the quiet pips of a nearby bird. As they approached the wooden box, something inside thumped against the sides. Mathilda lifted it carefully and peered through the hole on top.

"Is it a plump hare?" Ramona asked, her expression hopeful.

"No," Mathilda replied.

"A badger, then?"

"We have a stoat."

"A stoat," Ramona said flatly.

"I had hoped for something larger, but you will have to make do," Mathilda said to the creature peering at her from inside the box. "We'd best get back," she said, glancing at Ramona. "I saw Gertrude with the basket of sloes you foraged, and I would not want to miss out on whatever she is making with them."

Ramona smiled. "Nor would I." She eyed the box Mathilda held. "What will you do with the stoat until we are ready for it?"

"I shall put it into a slumber and take it to the stable. I would not want to have it screeching and disturbing the poor horses."

The cottage was wonderfully warm when they returned, and smelled of woodsmoke mingled with a sweet, fruity scent. Gertrude had made tarts with the sloes and was setting them on plates. She looked up as Mathilda and Ramona came in.

"I saw the two of you coming through the wood. I've been keeping these warm for you."

"Thank you, Gertrude," Mathilda said. "They smell wonderful." She pulled off her boots and set them by the fire to dry, and went to clean her hands. Regina and Katrina came into the cottage as she returned to the table.

"Where is Isobel?" Mathilda asked.

"She is still abed," Regina said. She pulled off her cloak and moved toward the fire to warm her hands. "I tried to rouse her, but she refused to get up,"

"I heard her crying sometime in the night," Katrina added. She sat at the table and took a pinch of tart, placing it in her mouth. "Mm, sloes?"

"Yes," Mathilda replied. "I will go over and check on her." She quickly ate and headed back out into the cold.

Hilda was building up the fire when Mathilda came in. She straightened and wiped her hands on her apron. "Good morning, mistress."

"Good morning. Isobel is still abed?"

Hilda nodded and lowered her voice. "I heard her crying a moment ago. She refused my offer to help her dress."

"You go help Gertrude while I talk to Isobel. We will be along shortly."

Mathilda waited until she was alone before going into the bedchamber. She sat down on the edge of the bed. Isobel was huddled under the covers, sniffling.

"Sister," Mathilda said gently, "what is it?"

Isobel rolled over. Her cheeks were still wet with tears, and her eyes were swollen from crying. "I am afraid," she whispered. "I dreamed of growling and black shadows and light encircling me."

That did not sound like an ordinary dream. The growling had to represent the wolves. The shadows must be the dark magic they wield, but the light... Mathilda smiled as she thought of the Goddess. "You had a vision. Did you see anything else?"

"No, I was so frightened of the growling that I woke." Isobel pushed herself up, leaning against the bed's wooden headboard.

"What did you feel in the vision?" Mathilda asked. Any detail might be important.

Isobel considered this, drying her eyes on the sleeve of her chemise. "I felt fear, but there was also a great strength in me and around me."

"It is all right to be frightened." Mathilda smoothed Isobel's thick black curls away from her face. "But we will prevail," she assured her. "Your vision showed you as much. The five of us together have great strength."

Isobel considered this. "But... something might go wrong." Her dark eyes were full of pleading. "What then? Mathilda, our sisters, and I are not like you. I am not ready to die."

Mathilda had been scared—she still was, only now, after hearing Isobel's vision, she felt confident and less frightened. "The strength you felt in your vision showed you that you will succeed. The light surrounding you was of the Goddess. She will protect you. You must not think otherwise." Isobel smiled weakly and nodded. Mathilda felt a fierce love in her heart as she gazed at her sister. "And I will do everything in my power to protect you and the others. I swear it. Now. Let us get you ready. We must make our preparations for the evening. We have a gift for the Goddess."

Isobel's eyes widened. "A plump hare?"

"No, a young stoat."

Isobel's excitement fell away. "Oh."

Mathilda smiled. "Do not be disappointed. Stoats are resilient creatures, as are we."

~

THE AFTERNOON FADED INTO DUSK, and a purposeful solemnity settled amongst the women. Mathilda sent Gertrude and Hilda to the other cottage so she could prepare for her spell. She plucked a single strand of hair from each of her sisters and went into the bedchamber, pulling back the woven rushes that covered her magic circle. Regina placed a statue of the Goddess on the floor in the center, along with a candle, while Ramona prepared a sage and lavender incense to ward off negative energies. She passed it around to her sisters, each breathing in the aroma. Isobel and Katrina handed out the corded pouches they had made, then settled on the floor with the others.

Mathilda pulled a strand of hair from the locks Cassandra had sent. She placed them in a bowl and added the strands she took from her sisters. Raising the bowl to her lips, she spat, then passed it to her sisters to do the same. When the bowl came back around to her, Mathilda lifted it. "With this hair, link us to our enemies. Keep us true to our task and safe from harm."

Mathilda then took her mother's knife. She made a tiny puncture in her finger, the sacrifice Cassandra required, squeezed a single drop of blood into the bowl, and passed it to her sisters. Once their blood was collected, Mathilda lifted the bowl again. "With this blood, the life-form of your faithful servants, grant us the power to smite those who would do evil against all humanity. May they burn for their malice and never rise again."

Mathilda looked to her sisters, feeling their fear and the strength of their determination. "Take the locks of hair I gave you and dip them into the bowl, then put them into the pouches and place them around your necks against your skin."

Once they had done so, Mathilda felt the power of their magic seal the spell. She let out a relieved breath.

"You must keep these pouches against your skin until after our task is complete, then burn them. Now about our gift..." Mathilda got to her feet and straightened out her skirts. "Let us go to the stable. We are ready."

Dressed in their warmest clothes, the women filed out of the cottage. Mathilda took a sack and put the sleeping stoat inside, and met her sister's eyes with what she hoped was a look of strength. "Let us go to the Three Paths and present this creature."

The air felt unnaturally thin as they made their way deeper into the wood. Not a sound came from any direction. It was as if all life had been sucked out of the forest, and a haunting silence was left in its place. Even Mathilda's lantern seemed loath to shed its light. The darkness swallowed up more than seemed possible.

"Do you feel it?" Isobel rubbed her arms as if chilled. "I sense something strange in the air."

"It is the balance of things gone awry," Mathilda replied. "With each evil and unnatural deed from Cassandra and her creations, there is a price to pay. I have sensed it for some time now."

The Three Paths were finally before them. The druid tree loomed behind the intersection, still as the silence, watching. Waiting.

Mathilda stood at the intersection and opened the sack, drawing out the sleeping stoat.

Her fingers sank into its sleek white fur. Such a beautiful creature. She was loath to take its life, but it was necessary, and the stoat would feel nothing. With a resolved exhale, Mathilda took the knife from her belt, sliced the stoat's throat open with a single, swift motion, and let the blood drip along the ground where the paths met.

She held the stoat's body in her raised hands. "Beloved Goddess, accept this gift from your servants. Grant us protection in our task."

A whisper of a breeze stirred Mathilda's hair. A shimmer, like heat haze, moved over the ground. A single drop of blood rose from the earth, hovered for a moment in the air, and then streaked away into the dark sky.

The Goddess accepted the gift. Mathilda watched as the rest of the stoat's blood, one drop following another, vanished into the night. Mathilda cradled the small, snow-white creature, its fur still warm against her hands. At last, a single drop of blood fell from the sky, landing on the stoat's head before dissolving into its coat.

Mathilda smiled. Now she could return the gift the stoat had given. She lifted one hand and held it over the stoat's heart, sending her healing magic into its body. A golden hue glowed faintly around its limp form, and in a moment, it began to stir. Mathilda lowered the creature to the ground, grateful for the life that was spared.

"Run along," she said gently. "You served your purpose." The stoat scampered out of sight.

"That was kind of you, Sister," Regina said.

"Not I," Mathilda said. "The Goddess is merciful to those who faithfully serve. That is why she left a remnant of life for me to revive." Lifting the lantern, she turned and led them away.

The large clearing of Carwyn's Field lay glittering and undisturbed beneath a thick blanket of snow. Stars twinkled overhead through the trees, and long shadows stretched from the climbing moon. An uncomfortable silence clung to the air like a vengeful spirit refusing to depart.

Mathilda knew her sisters felt as uneasy as she did. She did her best to banish the fear from her heart and smiled reassuringly. "Let us prepare our minds whilst still alone." She reached out, and as they joined hands, a faint glow surrounded their palms, growing brighter and pulsating through their bodies with heat and energy. The snow beneath them quickly melted, leaving a perfect circle vibrating with their magic.

"Do you feel the power in us?" Ramona asked with awe. "It is stronger than before."

"I have felt it growing since we left the Three Paths," Mathilda replied. "It had to, given what we are to do."

Isobel laughed. "It feels amazing."

Just then, a twig snapped in the wood.

"They are coming," Regina said.

Ramona's eyes were wide, searching the darkness. Mathilda cupped her hands and whispered into them. She turned to Ramona, opened her palm, and blew. Her spell swept into Ramona's eyes like dust, clouding her vision.

Ramona gasped in shock. "What did you *do?*"

Mathilda felt deep remorse, but this was the only way she could protect her sister. Ramona's anger could cost her her life.

"I am sorry," she said. "I do not want Marcus to distract you. You will only see blank faces: no eyes, noses, or mouths. Nothing to distinguish him from the others. We must stay focused on our task."

Ramona gritted her teeth in frustration. She turned back toward the trees, a look of steely resolve replacing her anger.

A shadow moved by the edge of the clearing, and resolved itself into the shape of a man. The others came from different directions, surrounding their circle.

"Make ready, Sisters," Regina said. "They are upon us."

Mathilda saw Marcus coming toward Regina and knew that they were linked. The other two men went for Katrina and Isobel, and the woman named Alys came for Ramona. Alys's face twisted into an ugly smile, so certain she was of her victory. As the four lunged toward the circle, they put up their arms, sending out a blast of their filthy magic.

Mathilda watched as her sisters fired back, willing their strength to hold. The opposing energies met with a crackling of light. Her sisters' magic was brilliant white against the dirty hue pushing against it. Mathilda held up her hands and made spiral-like motions in the air. With each gesture, her magic forced an immortal to shift positions with one of her sisters into the pure energy of Mathilda's binding circle. Her sisters quickly wore down the men with their power, continuing their assault and pushing them further into the circle. Alys proved to be the strongest in the lot. She fought Ramona with surprising strength. The hatred in her eyes was unsettling as she was finally worn down and forced into the binding circle with a furious scream of defeat.

As she crossed over the barrier, Mathilda reached toward the sky, gathering the earth's energy. A blue-white ball formed in her hand, growing larger as she concentrated. She flung the ball of light toward the group, engulfing the immortals in white fire. Burned flesh tainted the air as their screams echoed through the clearing until, finally, all was silent.

Ramona yanked the pouch from her neck and threw it into the flames. At once, her sight returned, but Mathilda knew the bodies were now unrecognizable, a mass of black, shriveling forms. The others tossed their pouches into the flames, watching in stunned silence as the charred remains disintegrated into the blaze.

Mathilda placed a hand on Ramona's shoulder. "Are you angry with me, Sister?"

There was an unreadable expression on Ramona's face as she stared at the flames. A knot settled in Mathilda's stomach at the possibility that her sister might not forgive her.

Ramona turned from the fire and met Mathilda's gaze. "No. I wanted to make Marcus suffer, and he did. I am glad I did not get to see him. A terrible anger arose in me, but your spell soon removed it. Thank you."

Mathilda let out a breath. For a moment, she could have wept with relief.

"We did it," Isobel said. Her voice held a mix of disbelief and awe. "Those immortals thought they would win. I could sense their conviction, and I was so afraid at first, but I felt the Goddess and my mother's strength around me, encouraging me. I am glad that it is over."

"They planned to make us suffer," Regina said. "I read Marcus's mind. They did not know our strength." She shook her head and turned back to the flames. "I am not even sure I knew it before tonight."

"I felt your stren—" Mathilda suddenly broke off.

Something unseen slithered into the clearing—a presence, vengeful and familiar.

Guard your minds, Sisters, Mathilda quickly said. *We are not alone.*

A shadow formed along the edge of the field, and Cassandra strode from the shroud of the wood. Her fiery hair made a stark contrast with the black she wore and the white snow. She looked to the flames, her expression unreadable, and then turned to face the women. Her cold eyes fell on each of them before settling on Mathilda.

"Well, I see that you were more than capable of destroying my little pets," she said, assessing the charred remains. Mathilda could feel how hard Cassandra was fighting to keep her feelings guarded, the strength of the magic she had to use to keep her thoughts and emotions from showing. Her mask was slipping, and chaos exuded from her.

"Of course, we were strong enough to help you," Mathilda replied. "Else we would not have agreed to try. Why are you here, Cassandra?"

Her sister's response came lightly, almost cheerfully. "Oh, curiosity. I had planned to assist you should something have gone wrong, but I see now that I greatly underestimated your strength. Well done, Sister."

Mathilda sensed fear in Cassandra and something else. Something far worse. Jealousy. It oozed from her like a stench.

Mathilda realized abruptly how tired she was. Days of worry and fretful sleep had caught up to her. She would no longer participate in whatever twisted game her sister was playing. Ramona and Regina both stepped up beside her, and each took one of her hands. Mathilda was grateful for their strength.

"We finished this for you, Cassandra." Mathilda's voice sounded exhausted in own ears. "And now we are done with all of it. No more. Let this day be a reminder to you of what can happen when you recklessly share your gifts of immortality. Go home. Find happiness and peace." Mathilda pictured the serenity of her cottage and longed to be behind its walls. "You have no need to make more protectors. We are not your enemies."

Cassandra gave a bitter laugh. "You make it sound so wonderful. As easy as that." She began to pace, reminding Mathilda of their father when he was in one of his moods. She stopped abruptly and glared at Mathilda. "Find peace?" she demanded. "Happiness? Do you think I will ever be as happy as you and your little group of sisters? That *is* what you call each other, is it not?"

Mathilda ignored the biting sarcasm. "Those things are not hard to find if you surround yourself with those who love you as you love them. You will find your happiness, Cassandra, if you let go of what you fear."

Cassandra's face contorted in anger. "I fear *nothing*."

A deep sadness settled in Mathilda's heart. Cassandra could not let go of her anger. Mathilda couldn't imagine what it must be like to feel such hatred all the time. She said, "Remember my words: I am not your enemy."

Cassandra glared at each of them in turn, her eyes like chips of ice in her pale face. Then she turned on her heel and stalked away into the darkness.

Mathilda watched her walk out of sight. "We must be more careful of her than ever," she said quietly. "Cassandra finally saw our strength, and she is jealous of our bond and our power. I also sensed great fear in her. She could easily let that fear and jealousy fester. I will try to maintain peace between us, but I do not think it will last."

Regina had moved to the edge of the group, her eyes on the path Cassandra took. "I am certain it will not," she said.

"Let us go home," Ramona said. "I am weary."

"As am I," Mathilda said, turning toward the heap of burned embers one last time, and raising her arms. The ground shook around them and opened up at her will, drawing the charred remains from the bodies and debris into the earth. The snow smoothed, leaving the clearing as if it had never been disturbed.

THE DAYS PASSED, bringing more snow and bitter cold than Mathilda had ever seen in any December before. One morning, she stood just outside her door, gazing longingly toward the wood. It had been over a week since she had gone for her walks or even meditated outdoors. The laborers had been kind enough to clear sections of the snow between the cottages and at least one path to the giant oak toward the edge of the clearing. A muddy swath, which Mathilda had walked too many times, led from the garden to the oak.

The door opened, and Ramona poked her head out. "What are you doing out here in the cold?"

"Contemplating," Mathilda answered. "Yule is nearly upon us, and I tire of being indoors. What say you to a trudge through the wood to collect evergreen boughs?"

"I think we will be soaked to the bone, but I will welcome the wet chill if it means we can escape these walls."

Mathilda told the others and went to dress warmly. Gathering their sacks and tools, they all started on their way.

Farther into the wood, the dense evergreens sheltered the ground. The shallower snow drifts were easier to navigate. Mathilda saw a pop of red holly berries up ahead and smiled.

Isobel saw them too. "Those are lovely." She rubbed her red-chilled nose with her mittens.

"Yes," Mathilda replied. "Help me cut some sprigs. Ramona, you and the others cut some evergreen from the pines."

When she and Isobel were alone, busy with the holly, Mathilda said quietly, "Sister, I cannot help noticing the radiance of your smile. What happy secret are you keeping from me?"

Isobel's cheeks flushed prettily. "I overheard the stonemason talking of his son, Robert. He will be visiting for Yule." She reached to cut another sprig of holly, and Mathilda noticed the tremor of her hand. "I thought this might be my chance to fulfill my duty to ensure the future generation."

Mathilda couldn't help smiling. "Are you certain that is what you want?"

"It is," Isobel said firmly. She held open the sack for Mathilda to drop the holly sprigs into. Content with what they had gathered, the women tied their sacks and turned for home.

A horse snorted in the distance, drawing the women's eyes toward the snow-covered track behind them. A rider approached, easing his horse away from the icy patches.

"'Tis Clovis, my father's steward," Regina said, looking surprised. The women moved toward the edge of the track and waited for him to draw up alongside them. "Good day," said Regina. "What brings you here?"

"My Lady," Clovis greeted her, bowing his head respectfully. "I was coming to see you, to bring word from your father."

"Yes?" Regina said, looking alarmed. "What news?"

"He plans to visit you three days before the solstice. He also wishes to know the progress of your stable before I return home."

Regina smiled. "Father must have a new project in motion and needs his workers to return. Am I correct, Clovis?"

"You know your father well, my lady. He wishes to expand his own stables." A fallen limb lay ahead of them. Clovis guided his horse around it.

"I am happy to report my stable is complete," Regina said. "The workers are planning their return before the Yule celebrations have ended."

Clovis came to a stop. "Very good, my lady. I will tell his lordship." He bowed his head to her. "I bid you all good day."

"Would you like to accompany us to my cottage to rest and eat?" Regina asked. "We are not far."

"Thank you, my lady, but I must return."

Regina nodded. "Safe journey to you, Clovis. Oh, and please tell my father I am pleased to hear of his upcoming visit."

"Very good, my lady. I will relay your message."

The sound of the horse's hooves quickly faded in the snowy wood. "Well," Mathilda said, recovering from her surprise. The lord of the manor was coming to see them. "We had better make haste to the cottages," she said, "and hang our greenery. We'll have much work afterward to prepare for the visit."

18

Regina glanced out the window at the servants bustling between the cottages making the final preparations in merriment for her father, who would arrive later in the day. They had already prepared her bedchamber for her father to use, and carried hers, Isobel's, and Katrina's things over to Mathilda's cottage, where they would stay during his visit.

The snow, at least, had mostly melted, hailing many thanks to the Goddess. The footpaths were clear. This morning, Regina was going out with a small hunting party, consisting of the laborers she had selected earlier. Together, they would go into the wood to search for wild boar.

Hilda and Gertrude both vehemently disapproved of the plan. They had warned Regina in the strongest terms to abandon it, not only because ladies did not lead boar hunts, but more importantly, because if her men found and killed one, they would be poachers. The woods did not belong to Regina. She had no claim to the game in them. Hilda had even refused to help Regina dress this morning, and she had been forced to secure all the layers of her clothing on her own

—an achievement she was pleased to have accomplished without Hilda's help.

The cottage door opened and Hilda came in with another armload of wood. She sized up Regina's dress with a disapproving glare.

"I see you are still set on going, then," she said brusquely. The wood clattered as she dropped it into the basket by the hearth.

"I am," Regina answered defensively.

Hilda planted her fists on her thin waist. "And for the last time, mistress, pray tell, what do you expect will happen if someone catches the men poaching? Your father has spoiled and protected you all your life. These men could hang. Are you willing to sacrifice them?"

Regina had listened to all this before. She felt no less guilty than she had when Hilda first raised the point, but she swept the guilt away. She had been all over the wood since she first came to live with Mathilda, and she had yet to encounter anyone beyond the track or main paths that led to the Three Paths. No one would notice the hunting party. She was determined to have fresh game for her father.

"Katrina is going with me," she said. "We will protect the men at all costs."

Hilda frowned. "And what about you, mistress? These aren't your father's lands. I do not think even your status will protect you if you are caught."

Movement outside the window caught Regina's eye. She saw Katrina hanging a bucket on the wall by Mathilda's cottage. A flurry of chickens pecked at her feet. In only a few moments, it would be time to start the hunt.

"It's improper, addlepated, and dangerous," Hilda went on, her voice rising with each word. "And since you seem determined not to listen to me, perhaps you should consider this: What would your father say?"

Regina stiffened at that. Maybe Hilda was right. But no! She was no longer beneath her father's roof and his care. Regina was determined to show him how well she could get by on her own. And besides, she trusted her magic. She could protect herself and the others.

She pulled her cloak around herself. "I appreciate your concern, Hilda, but you have nothing to worry about. You shall see." She caught up her mittens and swept out the door, closing it in time to cut off her maid's harsh harrumph.

With Hilda's warning still ringing in her ears, Regina walked to the woodline, where she joined Katrina and the group of workers-turned-hunters. Only one in the group had a proper spear; the rest had either axes or daggers. It didn't matter: Regina would use her magic to give the boar a painless death. The weapons were a precaution.

"Remember," Regina told the men, "these are not my father's lands. The punishment is sure to be severe if you are caught poaching. We must stay together so that I can mask us all should we cross paths with anyone."

The men nodded, confident of their mistress's protection.

"You mean *we* will mask them?" Katrina grumbled.

Katrina had been in a foul mood ever since Regina had told her that they would likely be in the wood well past midday before finding their prey.

Far into the wood, Regina had the men settle in an ancient rowan copse, huddling beneath the trees' bare branches. The stillness of the winter wood softly wrapped around them. Regina closed her eyes and smiled contentedly. She had often gone on hunts with her father, and the familiarity of the wait and anticipation excited her.

It was soon clear that Katrina did not feel the same. She began to fidget, pulling at her mittens and sighing softly with boredom. The men cast annoyed glances at her. Regina gave her a gentle, but scolding look, and Katrina stilled her hands with another sigh.

A thick layer of clouds had long swallowed the sun, and the breeze felt chillier without its warmth. The men were intent, watchful, listening for any hint of game. Katrina let out a sigh so jarring it had the effect of a shout. Brows drew in, but no one dared speak to chastise her for fear of frightening off any nearby boar.

Regina glared at her sister. "I cannot help it," Katrina whined. "This bores me. We have been here so long. Can we not just use magic to lure our prey?"

She was being far too loud. Regina whispered through gritted teeth, "We cannot lure the game unless we must. You take the sport out of our little venture, Katrina. I suggest you enjoy your respite whilst you can. Things are about to get lively." Knowing her men needed encouragement—Katrina's sighs had soured their moods—Regina added, "Make ready, my goodmen; you are about to have some excitement."

"And how do you know this, Sister?" Katrina asked, at least in a whisper this time.

"Had you not been consumed by your idleness, you would have noticed the sounds of a boar by now. Your rotten disposition has dulled your magic."

A group of riders skirting the ridge cut off Katrina's indignant retort. *We must not be seen!* The men instantly took cover behind the rowans. Regina and Katrina sprang into action, veiling the group.

The three riders lumbered slowly down the hill and into sight. Regina gasped in relief. "Oh, thank goodness! It is only my father!"

She let go of the veil of magic that hid her men. From her vantage point, she saw that Clovis and Thomas, her mother's old servant, rode with her father. She stood and shook out her skirts, then went over to the track to wait for him.

As she opened her mouth to greet her father, the noise of hoof-beats on the path below reached her. Another rider! "Katrina!" she called out. "Shield the men!"

The new rider rode into sight just as the hunters disappeared, hidden behind Katrina's veil. Regina recognized the newcomer at once. It was the stranger who had eluded her since her first encounter with him at the Three Paths.

He slowed his horse to a stop and looked at their group in mild curiosity. Trying to hide her own surprise, Regina spoke up before her father had a chance to ruin her intentions by ushering her away from this stranger—or worse, dismissing the man. She would not let this stranger leave. At least not without a proper introduction first.

"Good day," she said. Her voice sounded awkward and loud. *This won't do.* She took a steadying breath. "I am Regina Darnley. I have come with my men to meet my father, Lord Darnley, after his long journey. She gestured toward her father, noticing a smudge of dirt on her hand. She discreetly rubbed it against her skirt. "I fear we have interrupted your course. My apologies."

Regina winced. She said she had come with her men, but they were nowhere to be seen, at least not to the stranger. He had made her lose her reason.

For a moment, he made no answer. The cold breeze ruffled his pale, golden hair. Then his eyes flicked to the rowans, and the corner of his lip twitched.

Regina's heart pounded in her ears. His subtleties made her uneasy. Had he seen the men before they were veiled, or worse, had he seen her and Katrina use magic? She tried to read the stranger's mind, but it was like trying to see into a dark, endless chasm. Her worry mounted. She could think of nothing to say.

In the next instant, it no longer mattered. A boar broke from a nearby thicket in a clatter of trampled branches. An open gash on the inside of its left front leg ran with blood, likely driving the animal straight into their path. Before Regina could react, her father's horse neighed in alarm and reared up, throwing its rider to the ground.

Regina's heart lurched with fear. "Father!"

The boar charged toward the fallen man, long yellow fangs bared. Regina could not use her magic in front of this stranger. Her men were still hidden behind Katrina's veil, unable to assist. Impulsively, Regina hiked up her skirts and ran toward the creature, drawing it toward her.

Suddenly, strong hands gripped her from behind. She fell onto the hard earth, wrapped in a man's arms. He pinned her against his body and rolled them both out of the way of the rushing boar. In the next moment, she saw him kneeling and drawing a sword from its scabbard at his waist. The boar was on them, barely a handsbreadth away, and Regina saw the stranger drive his sword into its chest, up to the hilt.

The animal's dying scream pierced the forest. It fell to the ground, its rough coat within reach of Regina's fingertips.

The stranger heaved a sigh. "Well," he said. "That was close."

Regina lay still, trying to catch her breath. The stranger hovered over her, his eyes resting on her face. He likely thought she looked a mess after their ordeal. His expression was hard to read, though he seemed to read her easily enough. There was deep feeling in the way he looked at her, she saw—she hoped she saw—but humor too, a smile that lurked around the corners of his mouth. Her pulse quickened. Overwhelmed by her emotions, she turned her head and realized how close the boar had actually come to them. She could have been killed.

Her breath came in a gasp. "Oh, you brave man." She struggled to her knees, reaching a shaking hand to her hair, as if looks could matter in this moment. "You have done us a great deed this day," she said, trying to steady her voice. "I am eternally grateful to you for saving my father—for saving me."

"It was my honor." He reached out a hand to help her to her feet. She turned then and noticed her father. He stood, chest heaving, sword hanging from his hand, with a look of relief on his face. She rushed to him and kissed his dirt-smudged cheek.

"Are you injured?" she asked.

"Only my pride," he replied, dusting off his fine woolen clothes. "It seems my age has finally caught up to me. Thank goodness we had a hero in our midst." Regina noticed he had more gray in his hair than when she last saw him. It streaked his dull-brown beard, making the lines around his eyes seem more appropriate. He turned to the stranger. "How can I repay your valor, my good man?"

The stranger cleaned his sword against the mossy embankment

before sheathing it. "There is no need to compensate me." Simple words, but the rich timbre of his voice thrilled Regina. "It was an honor to assist you, my lord. I shall be on my way and leave you to visit your daughter." His eyes flicked to Regina's briefly before he turned. *Had she seen regret?*

Regina watched him walk to his horse. In another moment, he would mount up and disappear. Again. An overwhelming desperation came over her. In a rush of panic, she stepped in front of the horse. "Nonsense," she said firmly, rubbing the beast's head and hoping its rider did not see her trembling fingers. "Today, you shall dine with us. After all, it is you we must thank for our feast this evening."

A smile played at the corner of his mouth, the amusement reaching his eyes. Something about seeing that smile again, the way it settled in his eyes with warmth, set Regina's core to fluttering.

"Very well, Lady Darnley. If you insist."

"I do," Regina said, letting her triumph show. Out of the corner of her eye, she caught her father watching her intently. By now, he had to know she was interested in this stranger, but would he approve of him? "Come, Father. I will help you mount up."

"No, Daughter, I am not so old yet," he said as Thomas led over his horse. He swung up easily and turned to his servant. "Lend my daughter your mount, Thomas. It seems she is without a proper means to get home. A state of affairs she seems to enjoy," he added with a frown.

"It is good to stretch the legs, Father. I enjoy walking. Besides, it would not do for me to ride, as Thomas's saddle was not made for a lady."

Katrina had come up to join them. "True," she said. "And Regina, we all know you are the perfect lady."

Regina pretended to ignore that. Her father, mistaking the jab for a compliment, nodded in agreement. "And who is this astute young woman accompanying you?"

"Father, this is Katrina. She is one of the women who lives with me."

"Ah, a pleasure to meet you, my dear."

"Come," Regina said to her sister. "We must hasten home."

The fair stranger gave Regina a questioning gaze, and it occurred to her that she had yet to learn his name. Before she could ask, he spoke.

"Aren't you forgetting something?"

Regina followed his eyes to the boar. She flushed at her oversight.

"My men will be along from their trip to the village at any moment." She glanced toward the rowan copse. "In fact, I think I hear them coming now. On second thought, Katrina, please wait here. Have the men bring our quarry to me upon their return."

Katrina's lips tightened, but she gave a conceding nod.

The man seemed to accept Regina's lie. He led his horse back onto the path behind her father's men.

"What is the name of our brave hero?" her father asked. He turned in his saddle and eyed her and the man, rubbing his beard thoughtfully.

"My apologies, my lord. I am Philip Stevens."

Regina's eyes widened. Tears pooled upon hearing his name, and she turned away before he could see them.

"Are you quite well?" Philip asked. "Have I caused you distress?"

"Forgive me," Regina replied. She cleared her throat from the emotions that had lodged there. "My mother's name was Philippa. She died recently."

A look of genuine sadness crossed Philip's face. "I am sorry for your loss," he replied.

Regina became increasingly vexed as she walked beside Philip. Not only could she not read his mind, but she also could not even pick up on his energy.

When they arrived at the cottages, Thomas took the horses to be stabled and fed.

"It appears your men have arrived with the boar," Philip said.

Regina followed his gaze. "So they have." She walked over to Katrina and softly said, "I am sorry to have left you in the wood. I had no choice."

"I know," Katrina replied. "What did you learn of this stranger? I was unable to read him at all."

Regina glanced over her shoulder and lowered her voice still more. "Nothing, I am afraid. I cannot even read his energy."

Katrina's brows drew in. "That is odd indeed. Perhaps Mathilda can help."

"Perhaps. Now, I must get my father settled."

Regina showed her father, Clovis, and Philip into her cottage while Thomas went to retrieve his baggage. Hilda took their cloaks and went about her work.

Her father glanced around the main room with interest. "You have done a fine job for yourself, Daughter. It is quite comfortable here."

Regina smiled proudly. "Yes, thank you. Father, you, Clovis, and Thomas will have my bedchamber. I have arranged to stay with Mathilda during your visit. Hilda will make up a bed for you, too, Philip." She turned and saw him gazing around the room and wondered what he was thinking. He seemed embarrassed that she had caught him studying the room so intently. His gaze dropped briefly before he met her eyes.

"I am grateful for your hospitality, Lady Darnley."

The servants made quick work of skinning and cleaning the boar, and before long, Hilda and Gertrude had it turning over the spit. While they cooked, Regina had Mathilda's dining table carried into her cottage to arrange for everyone to eat together. As dusk settled in over the clearing, Hilda announced that supper was ready.

"It is a bit crowded here, Sister," Mathilda whispered, looking toward the tables that were pushed together and taking up most of the space around the hearth. "Are you sure you are comfortable with us all here?"

Regina took in the burgundy surcoat over the deep evergreen-colored kirtle Mathilda wore beneath it. She looked beautiful. Regina wondered if her sister knew her own beauty.

"Yes," she said. "I'm sure. I am glad to have my loved ones around me during this joyous time."

Lord Darnley sat at the head of the table, with Mathilda to his right and Philip beside her. Regina sat to her father's left, with Ramona beside her, and glanced approvingly down the table at the silver chalices catching the light from the candles and the evergreen clippings Hilda had laid down the center. A small commotion drew her attention toward Mathilda's table. Isobel and Katrina still stood, arguing oddly about who would sit nearest the door. Clovis, already seated, looked uncomfortable at their heated whispers beside him.

Regina frowned at them. "Isobel, Katrina, do sit."

Hilda and Gertrude brought out the pottage to serve.

"Tell me, Philip, where do you hail from?" her father asked, catching Regina's attention. Philip took a long drink from his chalice before answering. Setting it down, he wiped his napkin over his mouth and turned toward her father.

"I was born in Ipswich. My family died from illness when I was a boy. I went to live with my uncle, who died when I was fourteen. Since then, I have traveled throughout the country, stopping only to find work where I could."

"Are you educated, then?" her father asked.

A muscle twitched near Philip's eye. It was barely noticeable, but Regina had a knack for studying people. It was then that she started to pick up on some of his energy. He was hiding something. She caught Ramona's eye.

Philip is hiding something. Can you read him?

Ramona glanced at him, then met Regina's gaze. *Only a little. He is pure of heart, but there is something important to him that he must keep secret. I suggest you save him from your father's interrogation.*

"Father, let us not intrude upon Philip," Regina said lightly. "He has had a fatiguing day saving us from danger."

"You are right, Daughter. My apologies, Philip."

Philip nodded and glanced at Regina. His eyes were full of gratitude.

"Have you lived here long?" Philip asked, changing the subject.

"Six months," Regina answered. "I could not remain in my father's house after my mother died. It was too painful to be there without her. But I have a happy life here with my sisters."

"Are they... *all* your sisters?" Philip asked, undoubtedly noticing their lack of similar features.

"They are not my blood sisters, but what we lack in familial ties, we more than make up for in our love for one another."

Isobel rose from her table. Regina saw her trying to slip toward the door unnoticed. *What is going on with her tonight?*

"Isobel? Where are you off to?" Regina asked.

She froze, like a rabbit scenting a fox. "I, um..."

"I asked her to go to the stable to check on the men," Mathilda answered.

"Hilda can do it," Regina said.

"No, I want to," Isobel insisted. "I could use a bit of fresh air."

Regina shook her head. She would get to the bottom of Isobel's odd behavior later. "Very well." She picked up her chalice. "So, Father, how long will you be staying with us?"

"Only this night." He looked across the room where Hilda had stood a moment ago. Not seeing her, he reached for the jug of wine and filled his cup. "I am expecting a delivery of two steeds tomorrow, and I must be there to inspect them. Philip, you shall ride out with me on the morn," he added, inviting no argument. "I wish to discuss payment with you for saving my daughter and me from certain death."

Philip looked startled. "I cannot take payment from you, my lord. My honor would not allow it."

"I am afraid I must insist."

Regina shook her head. "Father will not be put off, Philip. You might as well accept whatever he offers and forget about your honor."

Philip leaned back in his chair, looking curious, yet resigned. "Very well. I cannot fight both of you."

Regina hid her smile behind her cup.

After the feast ended, some of the men moved Mathilda's table and chairs back into her cottage. Once the kitchen was cleaned and Regina's father and Clovis settled in her bedchamber, Hilda made up a bed for Philip by the fire in the main room while he went to retrieve his belongings from the stable.

When he returned, he seemed surprised to find Regina still there. Their gazes held for a moment as he lingered by the door.

"I hope you will be comfortable here," Regina said, as a way of hiding her flustered emotions.

He moved further into the room and set his bundle on the floor near the hearth. "I will be. Thank you, Lady Darnley."

Hilda set a candle on the table and moved toward the door, looking expectantly at Regina.

"Well, I will let you get some sleep, then," Regina said, watching him. "Good night, Philip."

His gaze held Regina firmly where she stood. She sensed a deep kindness in him, and it stirred her heart. Flushing, she quickly turned to leave the cottage.

"Lady Darnley?"

Regina stopped in the doorway. "Yes?"

"May I walk with you? I find that I am not yet tired."

Regina's heart suddenly took flight. She smiled brightly. "Certainly. Hilda, you go on ahead. I will be along soon."

Hilda frowned. "Very well, mistress."

"I think your servant disapproves of us walking alone," Philip said, watching Hilda stalk across the clearing.

"You are right. But she'll recover soon enough."

The evening air was crisp, and a slight breeze stirred the remaining leaves on the oaks. Regina walked alongside Philip, trying without luck to read him. It vexed her deeply. It troubled her even more that Ramona could not, and with all the commotion, she had not been able to speak to Mathilda about Philip either.

"You said your surname was Stevens, yes?" she asked, baiting him.

"That's right," he replied.

This time, Regina was focused, and she caught the lie. He was using a false name.

She chose her next words carefully. "Philip, I sense that you are hiding something. Do not be alarmed," she added, when he tensed. "I do not wish you to tell me your secret. I only want you to know that you are safe here should you ever find yourself in need of friends."

Philip's expression softened, and his vivid blue eyes fell on hers. He took a step, closing the space between them. His warmth enveloped her, and Regina froze at his sudden movement. He leaned in, his right hand cupping the back of her head, and placed a feather-light kiss on her forehead.

Regina's breath caught as his lips touched her skin.

"You are a kind soul, Lady Darnley. No one has been kinder. I shall not forget you." He slowly removed his hand and stepped back.

Regina's forehead tingled. It was as if his lips had seared her, marking her in some way. She shivered in response, and he frowned.

"You are cold," he stated, mistaking her shiver. "I will let you go to your sister's hearth. Thank you, my lady."

"Regina," she said, her voice nearly failing her. "Call me Regina, please."

"Sleep well, Regina."

A part of her wanted to reach for Philip and crash her lips against his. He had been so gentle with her; his kiss a whisper of a promise. How had he kept such restraint when the attraction between the two of them was like dry tinder that even the smallest spark would ignite into a roaring blaze? She had to force her feet into motion toward Mathilda's cottage.

Stepping inside, Regina shrugged out of her cloak. Just then, the door opened behind her, and Isobel slipped in. A flush of color tinted her light chestnut skin, and she looked as if she had just emerged from her bed: hair wild, clothes disheveled. A hint of a smile lingered on her lips.

"Where have you been?" Regina asked accusingly. She had a pretty good idea what Isobel had been doing, but jealousy put a bite in her words.

Isobel flashed a look of defiance. "If you must know, I was with Robert, the stonemason's son."

Regina quirked a brow, and Isobel smiled wickedly. Goodnight, Sister," Isobel said, slipping quietly into the bedchamber.

Regina stood, feeling awkward. She caught Gertrude and Hilda's stare from their fireside chairs and flushed. Hilda rose and helped Regina out of her outer layers. Thanks be to the Goddess, the maid kept silent.

As Regina pulled her blanket up around her face, she realized she was the last of her sisters still needing to bed with a man. She thought of Philip. He was not of title or rank, but he was honorable, and she was certain he felt something for her. She certainly felt something for him. That had to count for a suitable choice for a partner, but he was leaving in the morning. With a heavy sigh, she rolled over.

High over the noisy clearing, a family of crows called angrily from their perch in the pines, watching as men moved below them in the gray dawn light.

"Oh, those crows do grate on my senses," Hilda fussed. She wrapped the bread, freshly made, and gave it to Regina.

"Be grateful we have a roosting family, Hilda. Crows are the Watchers of the Wood. They will always tell you when a predator is near."

Hilda gave a contrary humph.

Regina filled two baskets of provisions: one for her father and one for Philip. Satisfied with their contents, she took them outside. Her father stood by the stable, waiting for Thomas to bring his horse. A fond smile touched his lips upon seeing her.

"I thank you, Daughter, for allowing my visit. It was most pleasant."

Regina recalled sitting by the hearth shortly after his arrival. They had spoken briefly about her mother, of fond memories that seemed to heal a part of them. "I am so pleased you came. I hope we won't wait so long until our next visit."

Regina noticed the workers putting the last of their belongings into the carts to take back to the manor. Her father's visit had prompted them to pack up sooner.

"I hope you know," she said, "how grateful I am for the use of your laborers and the supplies you sent. It is kind of you to allow Larson to stay on. The horses will do well in his care."

"I should hope so," he growled. "Larson was my best stableman."

Regina smiled at her father's false gruffness. "Here is a basket of bread and cheese for you and your men. Take care on your journey home." He pressed a kiss on her head and mounted his horse with Thomas's help. Before starting on his way, he gazed at her for several moments, sadness filling his eyes. "You look so like your mother." Then he cleared his throat roughly and turned his horse. "Good day, my dear."

Regina noticed the slight stoop in his shoulders. It hurt to see him getting older. She blinked away the tears in her eyes and went over to Philip, who was saddling his own horse. He looked up and smiled when she approached.

"Here is a basket for your journey," she said, holding it out. "I added an apple for your horse as well." She rubbed her hand over the large chestnut's nose. "He is a gentle soul. What is his name?"

"Amis."

Regina smiled. "Friend."

Philip looked pleased that she knew the word. "Aye."

"I will always remember what you did for me and my father," Regina said, meeting his gaze. "You have my fervent wish for a long and prosperous life ahead." The words felt final, but she said them anyway. After all, Philip had given no indication he would return. The thought of never seeing him again left her feeling disappointed.

A hint of a smile edged at his lips as he gazed intently at her as though he knew her darkest secrets. "I shall call upon you if ever I return to these parts," he said.

"I would like that very much."

"Come, Philip. We ride," her father called.

Philip swung himself into the saddle. "Goodbye, my lady."

She watched as her father and Clovis took to the wood with Thomas following them. The carts with the workers lurched into procession behind them. Philip cast a final glance over his shoulder at her before following them.

"Are you all right, Sister?" Mathilda asked, coming up beside her.

"Yes. I think I shall miss Philip. There was something unique about him."

"My dear, of course, there was. Magic as powerful as his is rare."

Regina stood dumbfounded. "He is a witch?"

"Yes. You did not know?"

"No." Regina couldn't believe she hadn't seen it. "He masked himself well from me. Now it makes sense. Peace of the Goddess! How could I have missed it?"

Mathilda smiled. "Easily enough. Your heart clouded your mind. His mask slipped during your father's interrogation. Otherwise, I might have missed it. It took a great deal of power from Philip to hide his magic from me."

Regina's heart plunged. If only she had known in time! Now it was too late. Philip was gone.

Mathilda was watching her. "Do not worry, Sister," she said gently. "Your Philip will return. Of that, I am also certain."

"How can you know?"

"He is enamored with you. Anyone with eyes could see that."

Warmth flooded Regina's chest. For the first time, she had found someone like her. Someone she would never have to hide her true nature from—but he was gone. Mathilda said he would return, but would it be in time for Regina to fulfill her part in the spell? She had her heart set on Philip, and no one else would do.

~

REGINA'S MIND wandered as Hilda helped her into her gown. Philip's departure had left her consumed with thoughts of the fertility spell. With the end of the year fast approaching, she would need to act soon, but with no sign that he would return, she knew she would have to choose another.

"Mistress, this task would be finished by now if you stood still," Hilda chided. "You have been distracted for the past six days. Am I to assume the handsome young man is the reason for your addled mind?"

Regina lifted her chin. "Perhaps," she admitted.

Hilda bent to smooth out the hem of Regina's skirt. "I am sure he will return," she said, straightening. "He could hardly keep his eyes from you."

If only. At least, with her dress finally complete, Regina was pleased with her reflection. Katrina was sewing in the main room. When Regina looked at her, an idea came to mind. "Katrina, may I speak with you?"

"Of course." Katrina set her sewing on the table and rose. Regina led her outside so they could speak privately.

"What is the matter?" Katrina asked.

Regina swallowed her embarrassment and met her sister's eyes. "I need to find someone suitable to bed with, and I was hoping you would go with me to the priory."

Katrina's eyes widened in surprise. "Can you not choose someone from your father's house?"

"I cannot bed with any of his men," Regina said, scandalized. Her father would surely find out. "No, I must find someone else. You already found someone from the priory to... if you could just..." This was beyond awkward. She cleared her throat. "*Please*, Sister. I am running out of time."

Katrina's features softened. "Very well. I will accompany you. When do you want to go?"

Regina recalled what her mother had told her of the actual mating process. The thought of going through it with a stranger though... *This is your duty.* "Now. If I wait, I am afraid I will lose my nerve."

"If you insist."

"I do." Regina thought of something else. Her sisters surely wouldn't judge her, but... "And Katrina, please do not speak of this to the others. It is a delicate subject." She remembered Mathilda's worry over the monks' vows. "I do not want their questions." She knew she couldn't go through with it if anyone challenged her.

"I will not tell your secret," Katrina promised.

Larson readied the cart. As Regina and Katrina settled themselves in it, Regina said, "If anyone asks, we are looking in on the peasants." Philip's face flashed in her mind as she scooted against the wooden back, but she forced him from her thoughts before she could get emotional. If fate meant for him to be her mate, it would have kept him by her side.

Katrina nodded.

The cart had barely begun to move when Larson abruptly halted the horses with a loud "Whoa." Regina peered out from the cover to see Mathilda standing by her door, waving. Regina's stomach knotted.

"Oh, no," Katrina whispered.

"Where are you off to?" Mathilda asked.

Regina schooled her features to a look of cheerfulness to hide her dismay. "We found ourselves idle and thought we would look in on the peasants."

"Take Isobel with you," Mathilda suggested. "She is feeling quite idle as well."

"I would like that very much," Isobel called from inside the cottage. "I will just get my fur and be along."

Katrina exchanged a look with Regina, an unspoken agreement of what was at stake, now ruined.

Mathilda said, "I will get the new tunic that I made for Mother Downing ready to send with you. Please tell her that I pray daily for her health."

"Very well," Regina said. In her own ears, her voice sounded tight and strained. She could only hope Mathilda wouldn't notice.

"Now what?" Katrina whispered as Mathilda went inside the cottage.

Regina tried to bite down on her disappointment. "We will have to go another time."

Isobel bounded out of the cottage, wrapped in her fur, and settled into the cart. "I'm so glad to go with you. I felt I couldn't bear to look at the walls a moment longer."

Mathilda came out, carrying the tunic. As she reached into the cart, she paused, studying Regina's face. "What troubles you, Sister?"

Regina's throat constricted. She knew she would burst into tears if Mathilda pressed her further. "Why, nothing."

Mathilda studied her for a moment. "Very well. Don't forget to change your appearance."

Regina nodded, and they went on their way. They each chose a face from women they remembered from their childhood, and though the trip started out begrudgingly for Regina, Mother Downing's teary gratitude eased Regina's spirits by the time they left the village. With her mood somewhat improved, she made up her mind she would go to the priory the following day.

Upon her return, Regina sat quietly by the fire, planning her next attempt to get to the priory. Tomorrow morning, she decided, she would tell the others she was going to Whitsby to purchase linen.

In the morning, after a meager breakfast, she and Katrina again got into the cart. Surely, this time they would make it... But again, just as they were underway, Mathilda came out of her cottage.

"Where are you off to, Regina?"

Regina ground her teeth in frustration. "I am going into the village for some linen."

"Very good. I shall go with you. I would like to sell my tapestry."

Regina sighed. She was beginning to think her plan was doomed. She made herself answer as cheerfully as she could. "As you wish."

Mathilda settled herself in the cart. Larson clucked to the horses. As the heavy wheels lurched into motion, Mathilda said, "My, you two are quiet today. What is vexing you?"

Surely, Regina shouldn't tell her. It would only lead to questions. But she couldn't keep the strain out of her voice as she answered, "It's nothing."

Mathilda met Regina's eyes as if she could look straight into her mind. "Sister," she said levelly, "you might as well tell me what has been troubling you and unburden yourself."

Regina sighed heavily. She felt the weight of responsibility pressing upon her to uphold her duty, and though she had resolved to find someone from the priory as a mate, she somehow felt she would be disappointing Mathilda, given her feelings on the matter. "Very well. Time is running out to fulfill my part in the spell." Her throat began to close over. She forced herself to finish, "I was planning to choose someone from the priory as Katrina did." If Mathilda argued with her, Regina was not sure she could bear it. Uninvited tears were pooling in her eyes. But Mathilda laid a kind hand on her arm. "Sister, what is it?"

Regina clenched her fist in her lap, fighting back a sob. "I cannot seem to accept being with any man I can find, when my heart belongs to Philip."

Mathilda's eyes were full of understanding. "You do not need to worry just yet," she said. "There is still time before you must complete your part."

"But I am the only one of us not yet with child. I cannot risk..."

Mathilda interrupted gently. "If your heart desires Philip do not hurry to give yourself to a man you don't love. Be patient a while, dear. Anything is possible."

Though it was not guaranteed she would see Philip in time to complete the spell, Regina felt somewhat comforted by what Mathilda said.

Over the next three days, however, no sign came that Philip would return. Regina paced by the window, watching the sun set on yet another evening. The torment she felt and the duty she was bound to felt heavier than ever. She almost wished she had gone to the priory as planned instead of waiting.

"Calm yourself, Sister," Katrina soothed. "Tomorrow, I will go with you to the priory. We will bewitch a monk, and you can fulfill your part. Do not fret. Everything will be as it should."

When they brought the plan up again with Mathilda, she agreed it was best. "If it will ease your mind," she told Regina, though Regina saw that Mathilda still didn't entirely like it. The following morning, she and Katrina set off with Mathilda's blessing. Regina's heart grew heavier the farther along they lumbered through the wood.

"Do not be so sad," Katrina said. "Philip will return one day, and you can resume where you left off with him. Consider this act a devotion to the Goddess. She will surely reward you for your sacrifice."

Regina managed a smile. "Thank you, Katrina." Maybe her sister was right. Perhaps there would be a reward. "Your presence today is a great comfort to me."

The priory bells rang loudly as Larson stopped the cart along the wooded outskirts of the grange. Dark-clad figures filed through the arched cloister, some branching off into garth. From their vantage, Regina watched the procession unnoticed. She gave a heavy sigh.

"Now what?" she asked.

"We walk," Katrina said. "I have seen a few of the monks feeding the squirrels near the garden wall. Surely, we shall find someone before too long."

With a nervous exhalation, Regina started down the slope behind Katrina.

19

Mathilda looked up from her sewing at the sound of an approaching rider. She peered out the window and gasped. "Gertrude, come quickly."

"What is it, mistress?"

The instant she recognized the rider, Mathilda had put together a plan. It was desperate, but it might work. "Run as fast as you can to Regina's cottage," she told Gertrude. "Find Hilda. Tell her to get into bed and act as if she is gravely ill. I will explain everything later. You must do your part to pretend to look after her. Now go."

To her relief, Gertrude asked no questions. "Yes, mistress."

Mathilda painted on a look of distress as she rushed out to the stable to greet the dismounting rider. "Philip," she called, "I am so glad to find you here. I need your help."

A look of concern swept over his face. "Of course. What can I do?"

Now, to make him believe what she was about to say. Mathilda wrung her hands together in her skirt. "Regina has gone to Lindston Priory to drop off some linens. I went to her cottage just now and found her maid very ill with a sudden fever." Surely Philip would believe that. "I must try to tend to the maid," Mathilda said. "Can you ride quickly to the priory and bring Regina back? If I cannot break Hilda's fever, we might lose her. Regina will be heartbroken."

To her relief, Philip at once swung himself back up on his horse. "Of course, I'll go."

"Do you know the way?"

"Yes. I shall be quick."

"Thank you. Thank you so much."

He dug his heels into the horse's sides. Its hooves tossed up clods of earth as it sped away.

In Regina's cottage, Gertrude and Hilda were all in confusion. "Mistress," Gertrude said, "what on earth is happening?"

"My apologies to you both," Mathilda said, though she couldn't help smiling at how the plan had succeeded so far. "I needed Philip to get to Regina quickly, and this was the only way I could think of to get him there with great speed. We have some time to better prepare you for your sick bed, Hilda, now that Philip has taken his leave."

Hilda giggled, looking for a moment much younger than she was. "I see. I have not done anything like this since I was a girl. I think I shall enjoy this playacting."

"Now," Mathilda said, "to let Regina know she is about to be rescued."

"Mistress." Hilda pointed to the table by the hearth. "They are not wearing them."

Mathilda looked. There lay the crystal necklaces, Regina's and Katrina's, both, left behind. Useless.

Hilda was quick to defend her mistresses. "They were in a terrible rush to leave."

Mathilda sighed heavily. "It is up to fate now. Let us hope Philip can find Regina before it is too late."

~

BEHIND THE IVY-COVERED GARDEN WALL, Regina studied the monk as he sat on the bench, tossing corn and a few tiny seeds. The squirrels and birds flocked to him, unafraid.

"They do not seem to mind him at all, do they?" she asked Katrina.

"No. I think he's perfect for your purpose, Regina. His kindness is obvious, and he has a handsome enough face."

Katrina was right. Though it wasn't what Regina wanted for herself, she felt she could go through with it now that she saw the monk's shining qualities. "So he does. Very well. What shall I do?"

"Pretend that you have some grievous sin upon your heart," Katrina said, "and you must confess immediately, as you are passing through and will not come across another priest or priory for some time. Once he agrees to take you to the priest, you must enchant him to follow you away."

That was, of course, what Katrina herself had done. It would work. "Very well," Regina said. "I shall do it now before I lose my courage." She stepped out from behind the stone wall and let herself in through the gate toward the lone monk.

Katrina pulled her cloak tighter and sat on a stump, watching their exchange. Regina's magic seemed to be working. It appeared the monk was willing to go with her. He stood, and they ambled away from the bench and disappeared over the knoll.

Just then, she heard the sound of thundering hooves behind her from the track that ran parallel to the garden wall. She stood, shielding her eyes from the sun, and recognized the rider in the moment he dismounted. Philip.

Katrina gasped in shock and reflexively stepped back, forgetting the stump behind her. She stumbled. Philip caught her hand.

"Are you all right?" he asked.

His voice was even richer and warmer than she remembered. She had to stop Regina immediately. *Wait, Sister!* she cried in her mind, and realized in the next instant that she had forgotten her pendant again. *Oh, no!* Mathilda was going to nail her hide to the wall, though right now, Katrina had even bigger concerns.

"Where is Lady Darnley?" Philip asked. "I am afraid I have urgent news regarding her maid."

Katrina found her voice. "Her maid?"

"Mathilda sent me to fetch Lady Darnley home right away." He looked concerned, too, Katrina noticed, genuinely anxious. "Her maid has taken very ill."

Katrina understood. Of course, Mathilda had been clever enough to think of a plan. She played along. "Oh, no! Not Hilda." She pointed toward the west side of the monastery, in the opposite direction to the one Regina and the monk had taken. "She went that way."

Katrina hated lying to the man, but Philip must not find Regina in a compromising situation with a monk of all people. As soon as Philip left her, Katrina tore over the knoll after her sister. She arrived on the far side, gasping, clutching at a stitch in her side, to find Regina sitting in the grass beside the monk, looking dejected. Oddly enough, he appeared to be sleeping.

"Did you do it?" Katrina demanded, frantic.

"Not yet, I needed more time to talk myself into it, so I put him in a slumber."

"Oh, thank goodness! Get up, now!" She caught Regina's arm and roughly hauled her to her feet.

"*Katrina!* What is the matter with you?"

"You must come with me quickly. Mathilda sent word that Hilda is ill. She is not, of course, but you must play along." She dragged Regina back up over the knoll.

At the top, Regina yanked her arm free from Katrina's grasp. "Have you lost your senses?" she demanded. "What are you thinking, marching me along like this?"

"Lady Darnley?"

Regina's eyes widened at the familiar voice behind her. Ignoring Katrina's triumphant smile, which she suddenly understood, she turned with her heart thumping wildly.

"Philip, what are you doing here?" Regina asked sweetly.

By the looks of his heaving chest, he had been running. "I've been trying to find you," Philip said. "Your maid," he paused to catch his breath. "She is very ill. I had just arrived at your cottage when Mathilda urged me to fetch you home."

Regina fought to hide her joy. Mathilda and Katrina had saved her just in time. "Sister," she said to Katrina, "can you manage to get home without me?"

Katrina didn't bother to hide her smug look. "Of course. Larson is with the cart still. I will be along shortly."

Philip led Regina back to the garden wall, where he had left his horse, and helped her mount up. Her dress climbed, exposing her legs, but there was no time for ladylike propriety. Hilda was sick, or so Philip believed.

On the ride back to the cottage, Regina became acutely aware of Philip's muscled thighs holding her steady in the saddle. His torso grazed her back, and his arm, appropriately wrapped around her waist, held her gently but firmly. She wondered what his body looked like beneath his clothes. Blushing furiously at her thoughts, she forced herself into the role of distressed mistress.

When Philip halted the horse in the clearing, Regina slid down and rushed into her cottage. Mathilda sat by Hilda's "sickbed." Aware of Philip's presence behind her, Regina did her best to act distraught.

"How is she?" she demanded.

Mathilda kept a straight face, but Regina could have sworn she saw a shadow of a wink. "We managed to bring her fever down while you were gone," she answered. "It may take a little time, but she will recover."

"Oh, that is happy news indeed!" Now, Regina could smile as joyfully as she wanted. "Thank you, Sister!" Mathilda would know what the thanks were really for. Hilda lay back against the pillows, feigning sleep. Regina picked up her hand and kissed it. "I will let her rest. Have Gertrude send for me when she wakes."

Stepping out into the crisp air, Regina knew she was glowing with happiness. Philip was beside her at once. "I am glad your maid will recover."

"I seem to be in your debt once again," she said, looking up into his eyes. "I never would have forgiven myself had anything happened to Hilda while I was gone. She has looked after me since I was a babe. Thank you, Philip."

"Of course, my lady."

The silence between them hummed with unspoken questions. Regina tried to speak lightly. "Are you able to stay on with us? I will help Gertrude prepare sleeping arrangements."

"Alas, I cannot stay."

Deflated, Regina's smile slipped.

"Is there a place where we can talk alone?" Philip asked. "I have much to tell you."

Alone? With pleasure. "Yes. We will go to Mathilda's cottage. Everyone is staying with Hilda, so we will not be disturbed."

Regina pulled two chairs over by the hearth and sat demurely, waiting for him to speak his mind. As he joined her, she wished she had thought to place their chairs closer together.

"Have you been well?" Philip asked. He busied his fingers with his sleeve, seeming uncomfortable.

"Very well. And you?"

He rubbed the back of his neck, suddenly looking embarrassed. "It seems I have allowed myself to come into your father's employ."

Regina's mask of serenity barely concealed her shock.

"That is why he asked me to ride out with him," Philip went on. "Despite my protests, he paid me a large sum, in gratitude for saving you from the boar, and asked me to stay on as a groomsman for a time. I would have come to you sooner, but your father has occupied my days."

He broke off, gazing into the dancing flames of the hearth. "I must say," he added, "I am relieved to be settled in one area for a time. Your father is a good man, so I am content with my situation."

Regina could hardly contain her joy. He was only half a day's ride from her, though she couldn't quite puzzle out why her father had let Larson go—his prized groomsman with a keen eye for horseflesh, to take on Philip in his stead. "I am happy for you," she said.

A knock at the door interrupted their conversation. Regina went to answer it. Mathilda and Gertrude stood on the stoop. Gertrude held a large tray covered with linen.

"I thought you would be pleased to know that Hilda is awake," she said. "She asked me to tell you not to bother yourself over her, for she is being well cared for."

Regina had to stifle a laugh. "I am so glad."

"Gertrude and I have brought supper for you and Philip," Mathilda added. "Make yourselves at home. I will be with Hilda should you need anything."

Regina took the tray. "Thank you both. Come, Philip," Regina said, nudging the door closed. "Let us dine before the food gets cold." She filled two cups with wine and sat down at the table. "How long do you plan to stay on with Father?"

"I am not certain. If it allows me to see more of you, then indefinitely."

Regina nearly dropped her wine. She hid her surprise by taking a long drink.

"I hope you do not mind that I speak plainly," Philip said.

"Not at all." Regina placed her cup on the table and made herself speak just as plainly. "I am relieved to know the depth of your feelings."

Philip reached over and took her fingers in his. He raised them to his lips and grazed a kiss. "I have thought of nothing but you since the day I left here. I felt I would go mad if I did not return..." His eyes closed, dark lashes fanning his cheeks, and he released a contented sigh against her fingers. When he spoke again, his voice turned soft, reverent. "If I could not breathe you in...." He turned her palm up and kissed the inside of her wrist, his gaze smoldering. "If I could not touch you..." He brushed his fingers along her jawline, the touch featherlight and full of promise.

Regina gave a breathy laugh, shivering with anticipation. "Then you should know the feeling is mutual."

The air between them pulsed with desire. Their dinner sat steaming beneath the linen, but neither of them noticed. A new hunger had overtaken them.

Philip leaned in. An electrifying anticipation crackled between them. Regina let out a giddy sigh before his lips claimed hers. An explosion of feelings took over her, frantic and heady. All thoughts of fulfilling the fertility spell were forgotten, replaced with a desperate desire to consume and be consumed.

She stood and pulled Philip toward the bedchamber. He trailed kisses along her jaw as he fumbled to remove her dress, groaning in frustration at the layers of material keeping her body from his. A loud tear of fabric rent the silence.

"My apol—" he began.

Regina cut off his words with a kiss. She drew away and yanked on her dress, tearing a large hole down the front. Philip's eyes widened, and he grinned as she rid herself of the cumbersome garments. The dress pooled at her feet, and his amusement faded, replaced by the heat of his desire.

He lifted her onto the bed and shrugged out of his clothes, his eyes dragging down the length of her body. He slid in next to her and pressed his lips to hers.

Regina gasped as his mouth trailed lower, covering her breast in fire and ice. She gripped his hair, writhing beneath him, a desire beyond comprehension building in her core.

"I cannot bear this torment," she said, eyes wide and pleading. "I feel as if I shall come undone."

"Then you should know the feeling is mutual." His hand slid up her inner thighs, parting them so he could settle between them. "I shall end my Lady's torment."

Regina gripped his shoulders, raising her hips, desperate to sate her need for him. When he finally entered her, slow and deliberate, she felt an instant of pure clarity, knowing that she was supposed to be with him. She had no regrets as his warmth spread inside her. She had the man she had always wished for; now, she would have his child, too.

When his desire was spent, Philip eased his weight from her and kissed her gently. "Are you all right? I did not hurt you, did I?"

"No." She could have laughed at the thought. "I am more than all right." She trailed her fingers over Philip's chest.

He rolled onto his side, propping himself up on his elbow. "When," he said, "were you planning to tell me about yourself?"

Regina thought of the day when Philip happened across her in the wood. She felt he had seen through her cloaking spell, though she hadn't known at the time he was a witch. Now that he was not masking his power, it radiated off him in waves, surprising her with the force of his strength. But he had yet to admit that he held magic, so she would pretend.

"Whatever do you mean?" she asked, innocently.

"I know that you have the powers of the Goddess inside you. I felt it the instant I saw you in the wood with your sisters."

She was right, then. She knew that Philip would not betray her.

"When did you learn of my nature?" he asked, rolling onto his back.

"It was Mathilda who sensed that you were a witch. She pointed it out to me after your first visit here."

They lay in thoughtful silence for a moment. Regina spoke first. "Where is your home, Philip?"

"Nowhere, I am afraid. I am constantly on the move."

"Why is that?" She eased onto her side to see him.

"Memories and habit, I suppose." He sighed heavily, and a haunted look crossed his face. "I am of the Langtree line of witches. My entire family was killed for who they were, betrayed by a neighboring witch accused of cursing a man in our village. The church came for her, and she placed the blame on my family. She cast a spell to bind their magic and watched as they were destroyed. I was in the wood, checking the traps that my sister and I had laid when it happened." He drew in a breath as if what he had to say next might anguish him. Regina took his hand and waited for him to continue. "They were all pulled from our home, tied to the stake, and burned alive. My mother, grandmother, sister, and my younger brother. He had only blessed this earth with his presence for five years. A babe, innocent of his fate. I came home sometime after it had happened to discover my family gone, my home burned to the ground, and everything lost." Tears shimmered in his eyes, and he turned to her with a plea for comfort in the depths of them.

Regina felt a tear slip down her cheek. She wiped it away and laid her hand over his cheek, wishing she could ease his pain.

Philip's gaze turned distant again. "I was fourteen years of age then, and too frightened to remain in my village. I set out for other distant kin, but they refused to take me in after I had to tell them the truth about what had happened to my family. I decided to start anew, beginning with my name. I found work in a village where no one knew me, and I made up a story about my family dying from illness and an uncle who took me in. I found work where I could, never settling for too long out of fear of being discovered. For these past seven years, I've survived by instinct, and by the Goddess's sheltering hand."

Regina remembered the tragedy of the Langtree family. She had been a girl when she and her mother heard the news. It had left them both terribly shaken. "My mother and I said prayers for your souls," she said. "We did not know anyone had survived." She traced her fingers over his heart. "I will thank the Goddess every day for sparing your life."

Philip's eyes were full of warmth at her proclamation. He pulled her close and kissed her, not plundering or desperate, like before, but slowly and reverently. It was the kind of kiss that sought to forget the torturing darkness in the recesses of his mind, and Regina let him lose himself in her.

A CHIME of giggles broke into Regina's consciousness. She tried to shut it out, clinging to blissful sleep, but the sound came again: a pair of voices, rising and falling in laughter.

Regina's eyes peeled open and were immediately assaulted by the bright light of day streaming into the bedroom. As her vision cleared, she saw two forms hovering over her, grins splitting both their faces. She quickly looked to her right. Philip was gone.

Katrina and Isobel giggled again. Mathilda swept into the room. "Can the two of you not find anything better to occupy yourselves with than teasing your sister?" she asked.

Regina raised herself up on her elbows. "Why are you two so giddy?"

"We have a spell to complete," Katrina answered. "Or has your lovemaking addled your brain?"

"If you two do not let me be, I shall addle *your* brains," Regina retorted.

"Gertrude has made spiced porridge," Mathilda said. "Rouse yourself, Regina. We must prepare our bodies; for tonight, we will fulfill our promise to the Goddess."

SHADOWS, lean and spare as bones, stretched along the winter-hardened earth, cast by the skeletal guardian trees towering over the clearing. A waning amber crescent, larger than any moon seen all year, swung low above the swaying giants, shedding its dim light over the five women lying prostrate below.

"Rise, Sisters." Mathilda's calm command broke the reverent silence. "Let us form the circle."

Unperturbed by the cold, the five women stood, joining hands. Mathilda inhaled deeply, recalling the embedded spell placed in her mind. Together, she and her sisters spoke the invocation. "Mother

Goddess, awaken our wombs, nourish the seeds and make them bloom, like fertile fields in summer's heat, bless this beginning and make it keep."

No sooner than they had uttered the words, a violent roar began deep in the forest from the sacred hollows of the Three Paths. The gust tore through the wood and into the clearing, whipping trees and cloaks in a wild frenzy. Mathilda's hair pulled loose of its braid and tangled about her face in a golden cloud.

The power of the Goddess enveloped the circle, a tangible force that flowed like a torrent through her veins. A brilliant light arose from the ground. As it slowly inched up her body, a sudden flutter moved in Mathilda's belly before the light flowed up and out from the crown of her head. A voice like thunder rang between her ears, terrible and wondrous as the light left the circle. The violent wind, barely a whisper now, stirred the remaining leaves on the oaks. They flitted like tattered moths.

"Sister!" Katrina gasped. "Your belly... it is—"

"Swollen," Regina said, taken by a sudden shock.

Mathilda looked down. Her dress was stretched tight across her girth, and a gaping tear rent the seams.

"Perhaps you should also look down, Katrina," she said.

Katrina gasped. "Look at us. All but Regina and Isobel," she said, gazing at their trim figures.

"Their bellies will grow, and they will be the last to give birth," Mathilda said. She turned to Ramona with a smile. "The Goddess spoke to me, Sister. She wanted me to tell you that she has taken pity upon you. She knows your heart yearns for a son. You will deliver a boy, but under these strict conditions: He is to remain in the coven, dedicated to the Goddess and protecting his sisters for all his days upon this earth as Guardian, but his future mate will relinquish her daughter for the sake of the coven, even unto death if need be."

Ramona nodded. Tears welled in her eyes as she turned them skyward. "Thank you," she whispered to the silence.

"We must make an offering of gratitude," Mathilda said. "In the morning, we shall leave a feast at the intersection of the Three Paths. Mayhap it will nourish some weary traveler."

"This might be a little difficult to explain to the servants," Katrina remarked, patting her stomach.

A peal of laughter burst from Mathilda. "Yes, I think you are right. Perhaps we had better cast a spell to alter their memories, then. Make them think we have been in our conditions for some time and be accepting of it."

"That is a good plan," Isobel said. "No need to startle them out of their wits."

THE WEEKS WORE ON. To Mathilda's great relief, no one amongst the servants hinted at anything out of the ordinary regarding their mistresses' sudden pregnancies.

With her back aching from her morning walk, Mathilda settled into her chair with a heavy sigh and smoothed the fabric of her rose-colored tunic. She noticed the spiderwebs of frost disappearing quickly from the windows, chased away by the morning sun.

"Mistress, you must put up your feet," Gertrude said, placing a stool in front of Mathilda's chair.

"Thank you, Gertrude. I think we are to have an early spring."

"'Tis still a week left in February, yet it feels like the bleak midwinter."

"Yes, but I do not think we will see much more of it. I saw signs of new life emerging from the ground."

Gertrude gazed wistfully out the window. "I hope you are right, mistress. I do not think I can bear much more of it."

Mathilda looked up as Ramona shuffled out of the bedchamber. The new chemise she wore with side splits and laces accommodated her swollen middle. Mathilda was glad she had thought to use magic to make them all new clothing to get them through their sudden pregnancies. "How are you, dear?"

"I still have pressure," Ramona said, cradling her middle. "He feels even lower now. This babe is going to come sooner than expected, I am afraid. He is strong and ready to see the world."

"'Tis not wise for you to be on your feet, mistress Ramona," Gertrude clucked.

"Do not fret, Gertrude. I only want a turn about the room before I take to the bed again."

A sharp knock came at the door. Gertrude went to open it.

"Where is she?" an aged voice questioned.

Mathilda stood and made her way over. A stooped woman lingered in the entry. A shawl covered her head and draped around her shoulders, and her wiry gray hair peeked out around the edges of the coarse material.

"Whom do you seek, Mother?" Mathilda asked.

"By the look of your swollen belly, 'tis you that I seek."

Mathilda smiled. "Will you come in and warm yourself by the fire?"

"For a moment. I do not wish to tarry long." As the woman stepped into the room, she set eyes on Ramona. "Must be something in the water," she muttered.

Mathilda swallowed a smile. "I am Mathilda Longhurst. And you are?"

"Margaret Ferguson. Duncan's aunt."

A surge of excitement rushed through Mathilda. "How is he?"

"I would not know. I have not set eyes upon the lad since Samhain. I only just received his letter that you were soon to have his bairn." She paused to loosen her shawl before pinning Mathilda with a glare. "He said you refused his hand in marriage. Is his hand not good enough for the likes of you?"

The words stung. The regret Mathilda carried still hurt, but she smiled despite the older woman's sharp words. "I love Duncan very much."

"Then why have you refused him? The bairn needs his father."

"And I will see that she knows of her father," Mathilda replied.

"Nonsense. 'Twill be a boy. The Ferguson line begets boys."

"I do not doubt you. But *my* line begets daughters."

Margaret sighed in exasperation. "Ach! He said you were a head-strong, defiant lass. But those are fine traits for a wife of Clan Ferguson." Her face softened a bit as she looked at Mathilda. "You'll be needing a heavy hand to handle the men of Scotland."

"Mother Ferguson—"

"Margaret," she insisted.

Mathilda reined in her tumultuous emotions with a deep inhale. "Very well. Margaret, as much as I love your nephew, I cannot marry him. I am needed here. I have a responsibility to my sisters, and I made Duncan aware of my intentions months ago."

The woman grabbed her slipping shawl roughly by its ends and yanked it up over her shoulders. "He said as much. 'Tis a cruel fate that you have thrust upon him," she bit out, turning to Mathilda again. "The lad is sick with love for you. Aye, he hides it well, but I know my nephew. He has not been the same man since he took up with you. You have broken his spirit, and I will not stand for it. 'Tis his wife you shall be."

Tears sprang to Mathilda's eyes. She could no longer hold off the bitterness of longing. Margaret's words had opened the door to the choking desolation Mathilda tried, every hour, to shut away.

From across the room came Ramona. She had been a silent figure until Mathilda's tears fell. Now anger blazed in her eyes.

"My good woman," Ramona said, in a voice like ice. "My sister has made it abundantly clear that she loves your nephew. She never set out to break his spirit, as you claim. You have deeply upset her, and I will not have it. Either you change your manner of speaking, or you are not welcome here."

Ramona suddenly gasped and doubled over. Pain swept over her features as she grasped at her belly. She collapsed against the table with a cry.

"Gertrude!" Mathilda called. "Go fetch the others. Quickly."

Gertrude hurried across the room, scowling at Duncan's aunt. "Yes, mistress." In a flash, she darted through the door, leaving it ajar.

"I will take my leave," Margaret said, looking subdued.

Mathilda pulled herself together. "I am glad you came on Duncan's behalf," she said, as politely as she could. "I am sorry that I have disappointed you. If you kindly tell my stableman where I can find you, I will send word once Duncan's child is born."

Margaret nodded. She cast a contrite glance toward Ramona and pulled her shawl over her head before sweeping out into the cold.

THE SUN SLANTED FURTHER across the floor. Ramona cried out as the pains of labor seized her once again.

"You are doing well, Sister," Mathilda soothed. "It will not be much longer now."

Isobel paced by the foot of the bed. The color had drained from her coppery skin, leaving her with a sickly pallor.

"Isobel, why not take a turn around the clearing?" Mathilda suggested. "Katrina, please go with her."

Regina wiped at Ramona's brow with a cool cloth. "I do not think Isobel would have withstood much more," she said quietly to Mathilda. "It was wise for you to send her away."

Mathilda understood Isobel's worry. She felt it herself as her own delivery drew near.

"I can see the child's head, mistress Ramona," Hilda announced. "Bear down once more."

Ramona gritted her teeth and pushed with all the strength she had left. Hilda quickly pulled the babe out, and Gertrude cut the cord that bound mother to son and nestled him against Ramona's breast.

The urgent, bustling energy in the room shifted as Ramona gazed at her son. Her smile was radiant. Tears filled her eyes as she ran her fingers over the tufts of his dark hair, and she let out a sob. Mathilda wiped her own tears away. Her sister had endured so much. Her heart overflowed with love and gratitude that the Goddess had broken tradition by blessing Ramona with this beautiful boy.

"Oh, Ramona. He is perfect," Mathilda said tearfully.

"What will you call him?" Regina asked.

"Charles," Ramona said weakly. "His name will be Charles."

20

The arrival of March chased away the long winter. Like tiny fairies shaking their dainty heads, the remaining snowdrops that brightened the clearing bobbed, ruffled by a cool breeze. Ramona sat on a blanket with Charles nestled contently beside her. Mathilda smiled at the sleeping babe as she tried to ease herself into a nearby chair. She sighed heavily, shifting to gain some measure of comfort.

"Keep your spirits up," said Ramona. "It will not be long, and you will hold your daughter." Motherhood suited Ramona well. She seemed more content than Mathilda had ever seen her.

"Have you felt any more of the pains?" Isobel asked.

"Yes, but they are not strong," Mathilda replied.

Regina came out of her cottage and sat down alongside Ramona. The small bump of her belly was finally noticeable. She placed a kiss on Charles's head. "He is the sweetest baby," she said, gathering him into her arms.

"Have you sent word to Philip about your condition?" Ramona asked.

"No. I have been meaning to; however, I do not wish for my

father to find out just yet. Perhaps I should send someone directly to fetch Philip."

"I suggest you do it soon; you cannot keep your secret much longer," Katrina added.

THAT NIGHT, Mathilda woke with a sharp pain. With a start, she realized her legs were wet and sticky. She sucked in a gasp to keep from crying out and waking Charles as another pain seized her middle.

"Ramona!" Mathilda whispered.

Ramona rolled over with a jolt. "What is it?"

"My water has broken. I think the babe is coming now! Hurry and fetch Gertrude."

A look of urgency came over Ramona's face as she got out of bed and swept out of the room.

As Gertrude pulled Mathilda's soiled chemise over her head, Regina carefully lifted Charles from the bed and crept out of the room with him.

Mathilda couldn't help but wish her mother were here as another pain racked through her womb. She reached for Ramona's hand for comfort. "I do not know how you endured your birthing, Ramona. You were at it for hours."

"Be grateful she comes quickly for you. I only hope the others are as fortunate."

Katrina stepped into the room. "I brought fresh linens."

"How is Isobel?" Ramona asked.

"She is far better this time than when you were giving birth," Katrina said, setting the linens on the table. "Regina and Charles are distracting her for the moment."

Mathilda cried out once more, and then there was silence in the room. Mathilda watched anxiously as Gertrude quickly rubbed the babe, wiping her mouth. The babe took her first breath and let out a startled cry. Mathilda sobbed, a mix of joy and sorrow as Gertrude wrapped a thick cloth around the babe and nestled her in Mathilda's arms. *Duncan would be so proud. If only he could be here.* She adjusted her daughter to her breast, smoothing her tiny cheek.

"She is beautiful," said Ramona. "And she has Duncan's features."

"He would be so pleased," Mathilda said, running her hand over the tufts of her daughter's dark hair.

"Indeed, he would," Ramona agreed. "Is she to be called Charlotte, then?"

"Yes," Mathilda said, smiling tearfully at her daughter. She prayed that fate would alter the foretelling she had felt about Duncan's impending death.

THREE DAYS LATER, much to Regina's hesitant delight, Philip galloped into the clearing and dismounted. He took note of the babes in Mathilda and Ramona's arms. "It appears there are some new additions since I was last here."

Katrina and Isobel made their way over to the group. Philip's brows drew in as his eyes fell to Katrina's swollen middle. An unreadable expression clouded his features.

"What goes on here?" he asked, turning to Regina.

She took a deep breath. "Would you walk with me, Philip? I need to speak to you alone."

He nodded, following Regina toward her cottage.

"Have you been well?" she asked.

"I have." His tone was clipped, and Regina's heart raced with trepidation. She loved him and wanted to tell him joyfully that he would be a father, but how to begin? If only she could tell him how it came to be that she and her sisters became pregnant together, but her oath of secrecy as a Guardian prevented her from telling him the whole truth.

"How is my father?"

"He is busy with his steeds." His reply was impatient.

"That sounds like Father." Regina ushered Philip into her cottage. She dismissed Hilda, then settled reluctantly into a chair. She could not bring herself to look at Philip. Would he be angry upon her confession? He seemed suspicious enough at the sight of her sisters and the babes.

He did not sit. "What is it?" he asked. "You look dismayed."

She calmed her breathing and raised her eyes to meet his. "I am with child."

Philip stared dumbly, then his face hardened.

"Two of your sisters have given birth, and another is swollen with child, and now you tell me that you are also to bear one. I want to know what is going on here."

His harshness startled her, and she suddenly felt a fear that she could lose him, but she stood firm. "I cannot speak of such things, Philip. Please do not press me further."

His jaw tensed. "The child is mine?"

Regina felt her face flush with anger. "Of course it is. How could you even ask such a thing?"

He paced before the table and paused to look at her. Regina saw hurt and betrayal in his eyes. It crushed her to know she had brought him pain. "I do not know what to think or ask," he said bitterly. "It looks to me that all of you planned these pregnancies. There is no other way to explain it."

Regina could see him puzzling out his thoughts. She was certain he sensed something important was at work here. But then his gaze fell to her stomach, and something flashed in his eyes, hard and dangerous. "Did you use me to gain a child for whatever it is the five of you have planned?"

Regina understood his anger. She tried to sound reasonable in her answer. "You know that I care for you, Philip."

"Yet you do not deny that you used me."

Tears burned in her eyes as she pleaded with him, "I cannot tell you how this came to be. Please believe me when I say that you were not ill-used."

Philip gave a mirthless laugh and moved toward the door.

Regina stared after him in shock. "Where are you going?"

"Back to your father's house," he snapped. "I have work to do."

Regina jumped to her feet and stalked out after him, fuming with anger. "If you leave here in this manner, do *not* return again!"

Philip stiffened but continued his ground-eating gait toward his horse. He mounted and nudged Amis into a gallop without a word or a backward glance.

Regina's anger drained away, leaving her helpless. She crumpled to her knees.

Isobel, who had been hanging linens out to dry, rushed to her side. "Oh, Sister. What happened?"

"He saw your bellies and the babes," Regina said. Every word stabbed at her. "And when I told him I was also to have a child, he accused me of using him."

Isobel's face mirrored the hurt Regina felt. She smoothed her hand over Regina's shoulder in a comforting gesture. "I am sure he will come to his senses after some time has passed. He loves you."

Regina dried her tears. She knew she had hurt Philip by withholding the truth, but instead of believing what she *had* been able to share, he abandoned her. She would choke on her pride before she let him hurt her again. "Obviously not enough," she said.

LONG DAYS STRETCHED into weeks. spring bled into summer. Katrina now held her daughter, and Isobel's belly grew, as did her contentment, but Regina fell deeper in bleakness as her own condition progressed over the passing months. Making it worse was the stabbing reminder of her mother's untimely death that the solstice had brought.

Mathilda understood her struggle. "I know it is hard, Regina, but do not allow your misery to consume you," she said. "It is not healthy for you or the babe. You do not know what the future holds. I am certain Philip will return."

"It has been five months, Mathilda. I have had no word from him."

"Your mind needs peace and rest. Let us go out into the wood to appreciate the season's bounty. It is a beautiful morning, sure to do you some good."

"No. You go on along. I want to lie down."

Mathilda sighed with disappointment. "Very well." She nestled her daughter into the thick linen cloth wrapped tightly around herself and took a small basket before heading out to the wood. She was not very far along when she sensed a presence. She did not need to look away from the berries she picked to know who stood behind her. She tensed despite the calm she tried to project.

"Good day, Sister," Mathilda said, dropping another handful of the berries into her basket. She wiped her stained fingers on a broad leaf and turned. Cassandra looked well. Her usual wild-tumbled hair was neatly braided around her head, and the green dress she wore was most becoming on her.

"Well, well. I set out to call upon you, and here you are." Cassandra spoke lightly, as if their tense encounter at Carwin's field, so many months ago now, had not happened at all. Her eyes dropped questioningly to the bulge against Mathilda's chest. "What do you have in there?" she asked, reaching to open the cloth.

Mathilda backed away from Cassandra, and Charlotte softly cooed at the sudden movement.

A wicked grin spread over Cassandra's face. "It cannot be. My pure and noble sister has been indiscreet with her dalliances." Her chime of laughter echoed through the trees. "There are potions that prevent pregnancy. You of all people should know this."

Mathilda ignored the taunt. "What did you want to see me about?"

Cassandra's leering smile slowly faded as she met Mathilda's gaze. "I came to be in the company of some Norsemen during Yule. I found them handsome enough—and they *were* eager to please—so I spent the past seven months in the Northlands. But alas, I found myself missing my sister, so here I am."

Mathilda highly doubted that. Her sister was back to playing games again, but what could she want so much that she was willing to put aside her pride and bitterness to seek Mathilda out? Perhaps she just loved the taunting and the games.

Cassandra's golden-green eyes intently bored into the bundle in the cloth. "What did you name the child?" she said.

"Her name is Charlotte," Mathilda answered.

"Who is the father?"

"No one you would know."

Cassandra sniffed. "What do your *sisters* say of your shame?"

"They do not see it as a shame," Mathilda said coolly.

"Of course, they do not. The ever-loving little family." Cassandra plucked a leaf and dropped it.

Mathilda had not rested well, and her temper was short. With all the babes now to tend to and their crying bouts during the night, there were fewer hands to help. "Is there anything that you need, Sister? If not, then I must be on my way. It is nearly time to feed Charlotte."

A triumphant sneer spread over Cassandra's face. "No. I have everything I need. Good day, Mathilda."

Cassandra's last comment left Mathilda feeling uneasy on her walk home. She instinctively ran a hand over the sleeping bundle at her breast, eager to relay the news of Cassandra's return to her sisters.

They had all just finished talking it over together, agreeing there was nothing to be done yet but care for their children and wait to see what Cassandra's next move might be, when a rider came into the clearing.

"Who is it, Gertrude?" Mathilda asked.

"I cannot tell," Gertrude said, peering out the window, "but a carriage just came out from the wood behind him."

Isobel opened the door a crack for a better view. Instantly, she closed it again. "It's Philip!"

Regina gasped. "Help me up, quickly. How do I look?"

"You look lovely as always," Mathilda assured.

"I feel like a swollen cow."

"Hush, Sister," Isobel chided.

Gertrude opened the door upon Philip's knock.

Regina's smile fell away.

Philip's expression was stony, and his eyes held no affection. "I come bearing news from your father," he said. "He is gravely ill and has sent me to fetch you to him. I urge you to make haste. I fear there is not much time, and the journey will be tedious in your condition." His eyes dropped to the curve of her dress for an instant before he abruptly averted his gaze. "I will be with the horses while you make ready."

Regina sagged against Mathilda. Gertrude closed the door.

"Oh, Sister," Mathilda said, putting her arms around Regina, "I am truly sorry. Would you like me to accompany you?"

Regina suddenly stilled. A stoic look passed over her face, and Mathilda knew it was a mask to conceal her pain. "No. I must go alone. I could not bear for you to witness my shame in my father's household."

"Surely, they will be kind."

"Mathilda, I am with child and unwed, and now the one person who truly loves me lies dying, and he will think I have disgraced him." Regina broke off with a sob.

"We love you," Isobel said softly.

"Yes," Regina said, wiping her nose. "Yes, you do. I am sorry."

"Come," Mathilda said. "I will help Hilda gather your belongings."

They laid the clothes Regina would need in her trunk. Hilda closed the lid. This is everything, mistress," she said morosely. "It is not right to refuse to let me go with you. You should not travel alone, and in your condition, too."

The thought of traveling alone *was* a risk, but her pride refused to allow anyone to witness her scorn.

"And, my lady," Hilda said, "I could at least advocate for you in your father's house."

Regina managed a smile. She was thankful her servants had been so accepting, especially Hilda. Mathilda's spell had certainly made it easier for them to accept their mistresses' pregnancies in the absence of any husbands.

"No, Hilda. I must go alone. You need to be here to help Gertrude. She would have her hands full with the babes, not to mention having to feed everyone on her own."

"Very well. But I do not like it. Send your father my love."

"I will."

Once Regina was settled into the carriage, Philip nodded to Hadley, her driver. She waved out the window to her sisters as the carriage lurched forward. Philip kept pace with the cart long enough to say a few words to Hadley, and then galloped ahead out of sight. Regina's heart sank.

"I DO NOT like that Regina left on her own," Isobel said, wringing her hands. She stared out the window, looking toward where the carriage had been not long ago. "What if her father passes on? She will have to grieve his death alone, with Philip little or no comfort to her."

"Though it pains my heart to say it, it might be the death of Regina's father that brings Philip back to her," Mathilda said. Charlotte was finished nursing, and Mathilda reached her toward Gertrude. She pulled her chemise closed, laced it tight, and smoothed her kirtle back in place.

Isobel considered this. "Yes, you may be right." She eased into a chair and rested a hand atop her belly.

"You two should be ashamed," Katrina scolded. "Speaking as

though Lord Darnley's death would be a benefit." She tossed the wool she had been winding into the basket at her feet.

"I do *not* think of it as good," Mathilda replied. "I am merely trying to ease Isobel's mind."

Rowan whimpered in her sleep, drawing Katrina's attention to the basket where her daughter lay. Her ire melted as she watched Rowan settle.

"Ah, here comes Larson from his trip to the village," Ramona said, looking up from her needlework.

Mathilda went out to greet him. "What news have you brought for me, Larson?"

The weathered man ran a shaky hand across his face. "Not happy news, I am afraid. The Widow Douglass is dead. Her children have been sent to other relatives."

The news took Mathilda by surprise. "Oh, I am sorry to hear this."

"I could not deliver the meat you sent to the other families, mistress. No one would open the door for me." Mathilda felt a shiver of unease. Something was wrong. "I was able to speak with the old miser who lives on the outskirts of the village. He said something foul is tormenting those who live near the wood, and he claimed the widow died from fright. Their livestock and crops are dying, and he said strange noises come from the wood at night. I can attest to this foulness," Larson said, pausing. A haunted look came over his features, and Mathilda noticed the tremor in his hands again. Dread settled in her stomach. What could have frightened him so badly?

"On my way back through the wood," Larson continued, his voice shaking. "I encountered something I could not explain. I felt at one point as if I were surrounded, as if unseen enemies had gathered about me. There was a dark intent upon the air, mistress. Dark indeed. My horse sensed it as well. I could barely keep him steady. At last, I gave him his head, and as we came down the track at full clip, I saw something in the brush. I cannot say exactly what it was, only that it moved like a beast and had glowing eyes. I worry for Lady Regina out there traveling alone."

Mathilda went numb inside. "Thank you, Larson. Please return the meat to the larder. For now, you and the men keep out of the wood."

"Yes, mistress."

Mathilda rushed into the cottage. "Quickly, Sisters. We must form a circle of protection for Regina at once. She is in danger."

Katrina's face blanched. "What kind of danger?"

"It seems our respite from my sister's wickedness is at an end. Larson encountered a foul creature on his way from the village."

"Then we must go to Regina," Isobel urged. "She will need our assistance."

"There is no time. Besides, Philip's magic is strong. If the two of them combine their powers, they will prevail, but we will project our magic through the crystals to protect them from whatever evil awaits."

REGINA HAD JUST BEGUN to doze off when the carriage halted abruptly. She heard Amis's thundering hooves coming up fast.

"Get into the carriage, Hadley," Philip said sharply. "Do all that you can to protect your mistress."

"Philip, what is it?" Regina asked.

"Stay in the carriage with Hadley." His face was pale and stricken. "Something up ahead lies in wait for us."

"Philip, wait," she shouted as he rode off.

Hadley slid out of the seat to join her. "Stay still an' quiet, mistress."

Regina closed her eyes and focused on Philip. She saw a flash of dark fur and sharp teeth in snapping jaws and trembled. *Wolves.* She knew he couldn't face these shifters alone.

She made up her mind at once. "Hadley, you must drive me onward, or so help me, I will climb out there and drive myself."

Hadley's mouth opened in shock. "Nay, mistress. You heard 'im. I will not put ye in danger. Not in yer... condition," he said, flushing with embarrassment.

Regina's anger had worn her patience thin. She had to coax out her magic, but in doing so, she put it to use. "Hadley," she said, enchanting him in a few words to do her will, "you will drive this carriage until I say halt."

Hadley got out and climbed at once back into the driver's seat and flicked the reins, sending the horses tearing down the track. Regina braced herself as they raced to catch up with Philip. When he saw them approaching, he halted Amis and turned toward them with a murderous glare.

"I thought I told you to stay with the Mistress!" he bellowed.

"It is no use, Philip. I have enchanted him."

His face flushed with anger. "You *foolish* woman! You have put yourself in danger. And not only yourself, but *my* child. Is there no end to your desire to ill-use me?"

"If you would govern your anger, you would see that I am *trying* to protect you. Look."

Just ahead, the scrub parted, and two wolves stepped out. Their fur was oddly mottled, giving them a frightening appearance. A third wolf, darker in coloring, joined them. Philip stilled. His eyes tracked their movements while he formed a plan.

Regina's breath quickened as the shifters moved to surround the carriage. The horses' eyes rolled, and they stamped at the ground, snorting uneasily. Hadley kept his hands tight on the reins. Just then, Regina felt a surge of her sisters' magic through her crystal and nearly shook with relief.

"They are men cloaked as wolves," Regina told Philip quietly. "My sisters are protecting us, but you will need my magic if we are to prevail."

One of the wolves moved to lunge at Philip, and Regina instinctively sprang into action. Siphoning her sisters' magic into her own, she formed a shield of energy against two of the wolves. She flung out her other arm, but before she could hurl her magic at the third wolf, Philip reached out and made a twisting motion with his hand. The wolf's neck turned sharply, and it fell to Philip's feet mid-jump, shifting back into human form. The dark wolf returned to human form, his expression shocked at his fallen companion.

A loud growl, sounding like a bellow of rage, came from the remaining mottled wolf as it morphed out of form. "You killed my brother," the larger man roared. "For that, you shall pay."

Regina flung her arms forward as the men lunged, freezing them where they stood with a flow of magic. "Now, Philip! Do it!"

Philip pulled his sword, and using his magic, he rushed over in a blur, striking both men dead. He stood still, breathing hard, gazing down at the bodies.

"You knew what those creatures were even before they shifted." He looked up at her with a gaze as firm as his tone. "Who sent them and why?"

With the danger now gone, Regina felt her sisters' magic retreat. She sighed. Her body felt weary from the strain of tension she had carried during the fight. "It was Mathilda's half sister. She is evil and seeks to destroy any happiness that Mathilda has found in life."

Philip ran his hand over his face. "Peace of the Goddess... What kind of person has that much hatred in their soul?"

"She is the worst kind, I am afraid."

Philip's eyes flickered briefly to hers, and she sensed him soften towards her, but the moment quickly vanished as he put up the wall again. "You had better be on your way to your father's house. I will get rid of the bodies and join you shortly."

21

Regina's footsteps fell hollow down the long hallway. Flames from the iron torches hanging on the stone walls flickered in the draft. Aside from Clovis, no one had spoken a word to her. Not even to offer condolences. She was met with scornful silence by the servants at every turn. *So, they would turn a blind eye to her being a witch, but not to her pregnancy.* A bubble of laughter over the absurdity of it arose, and she quickly tamped it down. Her heart grew heavy as she wondered what her father would say when he saw her swollen belly.

She turned at the end of the corridor and came to an ornate wooden door. Pausing, she took a breath before going into her father's bedchamber. At her entrance, a young maid Regina did not recognize bobbed a curtsey and slipped from the room. Two tall braziers against the wall burned brightly, casting a soft glow on her father's sleeping form.

As Regina approached the bed, she nearly flinched from shock. Her father's once robust figure had diminished; he was a gaunt shadow of his former self. The large, canopied bed seemed to swallow him. Her restrained emotions slipped, and she choked on a sob.

His sunken eyes fluttered open and lit on her face. He smiled weakly. "You came."

"Oh, Father." Regina took his hand and pressed it to her lips. "How long have you been ill?"

"Since shortly after our last visit."

"Why did you not send for me? My sisters and I could have healed you or eased your pain."

His eyes softened. "My fate is just that. Mine. I did not want magic to dictate what was meant for me. Now, I have little time left, and I will spend it speaking on matters of importance, not my illness."

"But Father—"

"Listen to me, Daughter," he said, willing strength into his words. His fingers squeezed around hers, and a fierce look of determination shone from his eyes. "I know of your condition. I also know that Philip is the father. You are my only heir, and I wish I could leave my property, my title, and all that goes with it to you, my child, but Philip has no title, and so the estate will return to the king. You have your mother's inheritance, but I have still set aside means for you to live by. Nonetheless, you *must* marry Philip, else the king will choose a husband for you. Once he learns of the child, he will not use you as his pawn. Your marriage to Philip will ensure your protection."

Regina's thoughts churned frantically. She would not be the king's pawn. She would rather die first. And Philip made it abundantly clear he wanted nothing more to do with her. "Father," Regina tried, "I can—"

He cut her off again with a dismissive wave. "I do not wish to hear of it. Philip is a good man. I want your promise to marry him so that I may die peacefully." Her father's eyes were steely with determination.

Regina gaped at him. He did not know what he was asking. It was not possible to marry Philip. Not now.

Outside the bedchamber, someone cleared their throat loudly. Grateful for the interruption, Regina turned and saw Philip lingering at the door. He beckoned for her to join him.

"Father, I need a moment. You rest, and I will return to you." He closed his eyes in response and sank into his pillow as if their talk had taken a great deal of strength from him.

Regina stepped out into the dim hall and closed the door. The torchlight behind him cast a golden hue on Philip's pale hair. A flicker of an emotion, too quick for her to decipher, flashed in his eyes before an odd expression came over his face. "I am sorry to take you away from your father, but I must speak with you." There was no warmth in his tone.

She braced herself, planning for some fresh hurt. "Go on," Regina said.

"It is your father's dying request that I marry you. He does not wish to leave you a pauper."

Regina clasped her hands around her belly, forcing herself to speak evenly. "Yes, he just told me. I care not about what happens to his wealth. I am no pauper. I inherited my mother's fortune, and I have earned more still from my skill at weaving."

"Your father has shown me great kindness," Philip continued, as if she hadn't spoken. His gaze was fixed on the wall just above her head, and she wanted to shout at him to look at her. "For his sake," Philip said, "we shall lie and say that we will wed. I do not relish the thought of misleading him, but it is not my wish to break the man's heart upon his deathbed."

Regina's heart crumbled. Philip did not love her. If he had, he would have wanted to wed her in truth rather than lie about it. She shut out the hurt and clung to her anger instead.

"Nor is it my wish," she said coldly. "I will go to Father and give him the words he so desires to hear."

Philip nodded curtly and turned to go back down the hall. Tears slipped down her cheeks despite her effort to force them back. She wiped them away and returned to her father's side.

~

CRICKETS SANG LOUDLY outside the window, a soothing song for Charles as he nursed drowsily at Ramona's breast. Isobel had just delivered her daughter, a beautiful miniature of herself. The baby was named Sunniva after her paternal grandmother.

With the newest mother and child peacefully resting, Mathilda was preparing herself and little Charlotte for sleep, while Ramona gave Charles his last feeding before bed. "What are you going to do about Cassandra?" Ramona asked.

"I do not know." Mathilda lay Charlotte on the bed and settled in beside her. Kissing her head, Mathilda brushed aside the dark curls framing Charlotte's face and smiled as her eyes blinked drowsily up at her.

"Do you believe that she caused the widow's death," Ramona said, "or that the wood is as bad as Larson described?"

"Most likely. But we must go into the wood at dawn to see for ourselves the damage she has done." Mathilda pulled her covers more tightly around her and Charlotte, as though it could shield them from the fear looming around them.

REGINA LAY in the bed of her childhood room, gazing into the shadows of the canopy overhead. Nothing had changed. The same deep-emerald curtains surrounded both sides of her bed, and matched the blanket she was nestled in. The same pastoral tapestry covered the narrow window. Regina felt her mother's touch everywhere, and her heart ached fiercely. Tired from the day's exertions, she slowly drifted to sleep.

The room grew warm, and her mother's familiar presence surrounded her.

Regina, your father will be with me this very night. Do not fret or be dismayed. Everything is as it should be...

Regina jerked awake. Sensing she was not alone, she turned and saw her father's maid standing in the doorway. A flame danced atop the wick of the iron cresset she held.

"My Lady, you must come at once. Your father is asking for you."

Regina pulled the covers back and eased out of bed. Philip and Clovis were standing by her father's bedside when she entered. Their faces were stricken with concern.

The heavy tapestry on the window had been pulled back, and a draft wrapped around her, chilling her beneath her linen chemise. "Father, I am here," she said, taking his hand.

"Swear to me," he said, his breath coming in laborious heaves, "swear before Clovis that you will wed Philip." He broke off in a fit of coughing. Clovis held a chalice to his lips, but he refused it.

Regina had already given her promise. Was he making her swear before Clovis as witness, or did he not remember she had already agreed? She bit down on her lower lip, trying to contain a sob. "I promise, Father. I will marry Philip." She glanced at Philip, but he refused to look at her.

A weight seemed to lift from her father's shoulders. "All is well," he said, barely a whisper. He smiled at her and quietly passed on. His spirit lingered briefly around her before it left.

Clovis saw what Regina already knew. "He is gone," he said gently. "I am so sorry, my lady."

Regina stared numbly at her father's hand still enclosed in hers. The familiarity of the room suddenly stirred a childhood memory: her mother singing by the hearth, her father lifting Regina into the air and twirling her beside the bed, their laughter ringing out. She would never see her family again. She let go of his hand and stumbled back. With a wail, she rushed out of the room.

In that moment, her mother's words suddenly filled her mind again. *Everything is as it should be....*

Mathilda kissed Charlotte and placed her on Gertrude's lap. Charlotte whined and reached for Mathilda, but Gertrude was quick to distract her with the wooden spoon Charlotte loved to hold.

"We will return soon," Mathilda promised.

"I am sorry I cannot go with you," Isobel said, cradling Sunniva closer in their bed. "Are you sure you do not want to wait for me to recover?"

"No, you stay here and rest without worry for us. We will be fine."

The outlying landscape of the small peasant village had drastically changed. What should have been dense green thickets and trees, full of life, was bare, as though in the throes of late autumn. Mathilda reached for an ash limb. Only two mottled, yellow leaves remained on the tree, and a sickly ooze seeped from their veins.

Katrina stared at the withered landscape in disbelief. "What has happened to this place? Everything is dying. Not even the birds sing here."

"Cassandra's black energy is taking its toll on far more than the villagers, it seems." Mathilda released the sickened limb. "My sister has lost all connection with humanity and nature. Her magic is poisoning the land."

"Up ahead is the old miser's place," Ramona said. "Let us call on him and see if he can tell us more than what he told Larson."

The small timber structure was situated right at the edge of the wood. It had a single tiny window opening covered with an oiled cloth. Mathilda noticed some daub had cracked and was in danger of falling away as she approached. She made a mental note to put aside coins for the repairs as she knocked on the door. No answer came, but she sensed the man's watchful presence inside. "Goodman Bradbury?" she called. "It is Mathilda. Are you home?"

She heard a slight shuffle before the door opened a crack, just enough for the old man to see out. "It *is* you," he said with relief. "Come inside quickly and close the door."

The tallow candle on the table flickered in the draft as Ramona closed the door. Mathilda stepped around the stone ring surrounding the open hearth in the center of the floor. A mattress was situated against the side wall, neatly covered with a woolen blanket, and the women stood near it. "What are you afraid of, Aemon?" Mathilda asked.

"The red-haired woman," he said, cautiously looking toward his window. "She is a witch, she is! And she knows you look after us. She came here a few nights ago and demanded the name of the man who fathered your child, but none of us knew of such a union, or a child for that matter, and the Widow Douglass said as much."

Ramona exchanged a troubled look with Mathilda.

"The witch looked right at the widow and squeezed her hands together. We didn't know what was happening until the poor widow clutched at her heart and fell dead before us. The witch just laughed." He suddenly grasped for Mathilda's hand. "Please do not speak of your life to us, or tell us anything that might give the witch power over you. She is evil. She warned us that if we kept secrets from her, she would find out, and we would be sorry. It is best that you leave this place and never return."

The threadbare tunic he wore, loose on his frail frame, made him look small and helpless. It was not right that he should feel this fear. Mathilda bristled with anger. "You are right, Aemon. She is evil. For your safety, I will no longer come to call on you or any of the others in my care. But do not worry; I will find another way to get supplies to all of you. I must go for now. Once matters are resolved, then I shall return to my visits."

"Go with care, mistress."

Mathilda was moved by his concern. "Do not worry for me. And should you ever need my help, tie a white cloth on a limb of the druid tree. I shall come with haste, no matter the danger."

~

WATCHING the shovels of dirt tossed over her father's grave had been difficult. Not because she stood alone, ostracized by her former house, callously ignored by Philip, but because she was now deprived of both her loving parents. Regina longed for her sisters' comfort and Hilda's faithful care. She had reached out with her mind to inform them of her father's death, and now she longed to be amongst them once more.

Hadley loaded her belongings into an inconspicuous cart and secreted her away, again under a heavy enchantment since he refused to drive her without permission from Clovis. For extra measure, she had spelled him to keep silent about her departure. As they lost sight of her father's manor, a horse galloped from behind them, quickly gaining ground.

"Halt!" came a call.

Regina poked her head out of the cart. Clovis waved and called again. "My Lady, *please!*"

She ducked back under the cover. "Keep driving, Hadley."

"Lady Darnley! I must speak with you at once," Clovis pleaded.

Regina felt a sick pit in her stomach. She knew Clovis meant to ensure she kept her promise to marry Philip. Now that the faithful steward had found out she had fled, he at least deserved a small explanation. "Oh, very well. Hadley, please halt."

Clovis reined his horse along the side of the cart as they slowed. His face was flushed and stricken with concern.

"My Lady, why have you stolen off like a thief?"

Regina crossed her arms, indignant that she had to explain herself to any servant, even Clovis. "If you must know, Clovis, I have no intention of marrying Philip. It was all a ruse for my father's benefit."

Clovis looked as if he would choke. His voice rose several octaves. "But, my lady! You gave your word. You cannot renege on your promise."

"I can and I will. I loved my father very much, Clovis. And I would have done anything for him, but not this."

"You would do this to your father? To his loyal servants who depend upon you to keep them employed?"

"Clovis, what nonsense is this? I have no rights to my father's home or property. It belongs to the king now."

"My Lady, your father has bequeathed to you a considerable fortune. He secured a grand home south of here and gave instructions to a certain number of trusted servants."

Regina's eyes stung. Her father had gone to such lengths to ensure her safety and prosperity. Guilt stabbed her. "I have no intention of taking the house, Clovis." She thought quickly. "But I will send word to Sir Reginald, my father's cousin. I know he would appreciate taking the house, as it would bring him closer to court. He is kind, and I will speak to him personally to ensure he retains all my father's servants. I assure you, he will not refuse me."

"But, my lady, it was your father's most ardent desire to see you and Philip settled at Wickshire House. And most advantageous for Philip. He would gain the eye of certain neighbors who could introduce him to court." Clovis's eyes softened, and the lines on his face relaxed. The earnestness in his gaze moved Regina. "Your father hoped," he said softly, "that eventually, Philip would earn a title."

Regina was torn between grief and frustration. She could not do what Clovis asked, and Philip did not even want her, but she was denying her father his last dying wish. She held back tears by a force of will.

"Clovis, you have been my father's most trusted man and a close friend for as long as I can remember. You knew my mother's secret and kept it in your heart." She reached for his hand and clasped it between hers. "You know my secret. I *cannot* resume my old life and my title. It would be dangerous for me to do so. You know this." Understanding dawned on Clovis's face. "I promise to speak to Reginald and ensure the house and servants stay with the family. Should he wish to part with even one among you, send word to me at once."

Clovis met her gaze. After a long moment, he gave a conceding nod. "My Lady, it has been my greatest honor serving your family. I pray for your continued safety and good health."

"Thank you, Clovis." With a heavy heart, Regina bade Hadley onward and sank back into the cart, releasing her tight hold on the tears.

∼

THE SIGHT of the little cottages, bathed in the warm, golden light in the verdant clearing, was a tonic for Regina's soul. The sound of the cart drew Hilda and her sisters out. Hadley had barely helped Regina down when Mathilda reached her and folded her in an embrace.

Standing in the peaceful clearing with her head on Mathilda's shoulder, Regina remembered that she still had a family that loved her. "It is good to be home," Regina said, regaining her composure.

Isobel stepped outside with a bundle wrapped in her arms. Regina pulled back the cloth and smiled. Sunniva had thick, dark curls and was fairer in coloring than her mother. Dark lashes fanned her little cheeks, and she sighed softly in her sleep. "She is beautiful, Sister," Regina said. "I'm sorry I wasn't here to witness her birth."

"Do not worry yourself over that," Isobel said, tucking the cloth back around her daughter. "I was well-tended. I am glad you are home. How are you feeling?"

"I am weary," Regina said, bracing her hands on her sore back. "And I would like a bath."

Hilda said, "I will go make one ready for you, mistress." She started back toward the cottage, but Regina called after her, "Hilda?"

"Aye?"

"I have missed you." Regina couldn't keep her voice from cracking with emotion.

A bright smile swept across Hilda's aged features, and tears shone in her eyes. "And I have missed you, my lady. Terribly so." She quickly turned away and went inside.

Katrina took Regina's arm. "How were things at your father's house?"

"Quite strained," Regina admitted, as they moved slowly toward the cottage. "The servants all felt I had deeply shamed my father with my 'indiscretion.' But the most shocking matter was my father's dying wish that I marry Philip. He made me promise on his final breath that I would agree. Of course, I gave my promise, a lie, but it eased his passing."

"Did Philip know of this?" Isobel asked. "He would have married you; I am certain."

Regina shook her head. "It was Philip's idea to lie to Father. He does not wish to marry me. Now, enough of this conversation. I have grown weary of these tears."

Regina drew her arm out of Katrina's, and caught the look of pity Katrina shared with Isobel as she turned toward the cottage. "And I'll *not* have your pity," she added firmly, over her shoulder. "Soon, I'll hold my daughter, and my heartbreak won't matter."

Mathilda stood with the other women, watching as Regina disappeared into her cottage. It pained her terribly to think Philip had treated her sister so callously. Had her instincts about him been wrong? She had been certain he was in love with Regina.

Isobel said, "Poor Regina. Do you think it is true? I saw Philip's affection for her. How could he have lost those feelings?"

"Philip is headstrong," Mathilda said. "He feels wounded and betrayed. However, I had expected him to come to his senses by now. I, too, find it hard to believe that he no longer carries affection for our sister. That kind of love does not fade so quickly."

"And what of your love?" Isobel asked, catching Mathilda off guard. "It has been months now, and Lughnasadh is upon us. Let us not forget what Duncan's grandmother foretold, that he should stay away until then. Should you inquire of him in a letter to his aunt?"

"I appreciate your concern, Sister, but writing to her would not be prudent. These are trying times between our country and his, and I would not wish to cause trouble on Margaret's behalf should the letter be intercepted. Duncan will come when he is able." Even as she spoke the words, she still knew in her heart that he would not come, yet something inside her could not let go of her hope.

~

THE SUN SLIPPED BEHIND the trees, adorning the sky in rich vermilion with undulating clouds, molten and fading pale toward the eastern horizon. Mathilda's gaze remained fixed on the scene, as she held tight to Charlotte, until the quieting of birdsong and darkened purple clouds were all that remained of the brilliant sunset. Sated, she crossed the clearing and joined the others at Regina's table to tell her sister of all that had transpired in her absence.

"Larson is fortunate indeed to return home unscathed," Regina said. "Especially after the open attack on my journey to my father's house and poor Widow Douglass's demise."

Mathilda felt her sisters' distress, especially Ramona's. She pulled Charles tight against her chest as she gazed absently beyond the window. Mathilda disentangled Charlotte's fingers from her hair and gave her the wooden spoon to hold instead. Looking up, she noticed how tightly Isobel and Katrina nestled their children now.

Regina suddenly paused, with a look of alarm. "Do you think Cassandra knows of the other babes?"

A tiny warning tickled the back of Mathilda's mind at Regina's question, and something forgotten unfurled. She suddenly saw herself lying before the Beltane fire during her coming-of-age ritual. Of all the whispered voices she had heard, one just became clear. A spell had been given to her. A powerful binding spell. Realizing Regina was awaiting her reply, Mathilda shook herself from the memory. "She was unaware of their births when we last parted," she said, "but she could very well know about them by now."

"This leaves me deeply unsettled," Regina said. Her delicate mouth tightened with worry. "I have never pushed you to take action against your sister, Mathilda, but I think the time has come to put forth a plan. I will *not* bring my daughter into the world, knowing the danger Cassandra poses to her, without preparing some kind of plan for her protection. You have access to vast knowledge. I am certain that somewhere there is a spell to destroy Cassandra, despite her immortality."

"Yes, there is a spell," Mathilda replied. "It was shown to me when we went through our coming-of-age ritual. At the time, I wondered about its use, but it finally became clear just now. We will need to look to the earth for assistance. We must have a moonstone for this spell."

"Where will we find such a stone?" Katrina asked, looking discouraged. "Moonstones are rare."

"I do not know," Mathilda replied. "It is for the Goddess to reveal. In the morning, I will spend time alone in meditation and seek her guidance." Relief settled over Mathilda as she realized she could protect her sisters and their children.

22

*D*awn came dismal and gray in the clearing. A thick fog shrouded the cottages. Mathilda finished nursing Charlotte and placed her alongside Charles. Ramona covered the sleeping children and closed her eyes, intent on gaining another hour of rest. After fastening her pattens over her shoes, Mathilda slipped outside into the melancholic bleakness.

Overhead, a blanket of clouds hung oppressively low, dampening the earth in a misty rain. Mathilda pulled her hood up as far as it would go and took the tiny footpath leading to her sacred place by the ancient beech in the wood. Once there, she took shelter in the hollow of the towering relic. Inside, the air was crisp and cool, and the earthy scents of decaying leaves and old, brittle bark thrilled her senses. These scents were familiar on a deeper level, in a way Mathilda could not readily explain. They were infused with something ancient and wonderful that lingered in the air and in the ground, older than humanity itself.

Resting her back against the bark, she closed her eyes and silently asked for guidance. She drifted into the clearness of her mind. At first, she only saw the dawn light filtering through her eyelids. Inhaling, Mathilda allowed herself to slip further into the recesses of her mind. She felt light, as though she were drifting beyond her body. Then, something in her mind began to take form. The small glade where her mother had led her for the Beltane ritual flickered behind her eyes.

Go to the place of the fire....

Upon hearing these words in her mind, Mathilda opened her eyes and eased out of the vision. She had her destination. She and her sisters must lose no time. She would hasten back now and tell them that the Goddess had revealed what they must do.

THE CART BUMPED through the wood. With Katrina in the driver's seat, the only one with experience driving a cart—and only twice at that, the journey was not as smooth as it would have been had Larson driven. But for this outing, they did not wish to have anyone witnessing their magic.

Regina closed her eyes and squeezed her hands together in her lap, gritting her teeth against the discomfort.

Katrina glanced over her shoulder and saw her. "Sister, you should not have come with us," she scolded. Then, kindlier, she said, "I'm sorry. I am trying to be careful."

Mathilda helped Regina shift back against the wooden slats. "I am fine," Regina said, looking pained. "I want to be with all of you."

With a light tug on the reins, Katrina carefully guided the horse away from a muddy rut, trying to spare Regina further unpleasantness.

Mathilda was relieved when they finally arrived at the Three Paths. Her teeth hurt from clenching them during the jarring ride. She and Ramona helped Regina get out of the cart. Regina held tightly to Mathilda's arm as they took the smaller, hidden path through the dense brush.

Pushing through to the other side of the hedgerow brought back a flood of memories for Mathilda. Her life had completely altered since the Beltane ritual. She felt years older than she had been when she last stood here.

Her eyes fell on the charred ground and the blackened remnants of their long-dead fire. Images of her mother flooded Mathilda's mind. She knew she could not allow herself to dwell on them; she and her sisters must accomplish what they had come here to do.

"Let us join hands," she said, "and ask for guidance to the stone."

Before Mathilda even opened her mouth to utter her plea for help, a ray of light pierced a hole in the tenebrous clouds as they stood, surrounding their mothers' old bonfire. The ground trembled and heaved. Isobel helped Regina keep her footing as the shaken group backed away from the gaping maw in the earth. A flash of silvery blue gleamed in the light, catching Mathilda's eye.

"There it is," she said. Reaching for a broken limb, Mathilda began digging the stone free. It was much larger than she expected and required a great deal of effort to get loose. Katrina found a jagged rock and bent to help Mathilda dig away the rest of the earth, still holding the moonstone. Together, they heaved it to the surface.

"I do believe this thing is bigger than my Rowan," Katrina said, speaking of her daughter. She rubbed her nose, leaving a streak of dirt above her lip that gave the look of a mustache. Mathilda and Ramona began laughing.

"What?" Katrina said.

"You have a dirt mustache," Isobel said, causing the women to laugh even harder.

"*Sisters!*" Regina shouted. She let out a sharp cry that echoed across the glade.

Mathilda turned with alarm. "Oh, dear." Regina stood white-faced, clutching her middle. A dark liquid streaked her dress and pooled at her feet.

Mathilda brushed the dirt from her hands. "Katrina, our hands are soiled. Help me brace her up. Isobel, you and Ramona will have to help Regina deliver her child."

Ramona squatted and pulled Regina's skirts up for Mathilda to hold. "We'll be returning with a moonstone and a baby," she said, as calmly as if she had expected nothing less on this particular day. "And very soon, from the looks of it."

"I don't think I can do this," Regina said, drawing in a sharp breath.

"I know you're frightened," Mathilda said, "but I promise you will be all right. We will help you through it."

Regina seemed to take courage. She cried out once more, and Ramona said. "The head is already showing. You will need to push now. Bear down..."

With a final push and a piercing cry from Regina, the babe slipped into Ramona's arms. "We shall have to use magic to sever the cord," she said, turning to Isobel.

Isobel's fingers moved in a cutting motion, and the cord separated. Ramona lifted the babe to Regina. "Here you are, Sister: your beautiful daughter."

Mathilda watched her sisters share in Regina's joy. They were all mothers now. The line would continue. She couldn't help but think of how her sister had just delivered her daughter in the place where their journey had first begun.

Ramona was asking Regina, "What name shall she have?"

Regina's hair was plastered against her forehead. She was pale, but there was a flush of color on her cheeks as she smiled tearfully at her daughter. "She shall be called Wren."

Mathilda pulled Regina's kirtle up around Wren, wrapping her in the folds, then lowered her sister's chemise and smoothed it around her ankles as best she could. "Regina, can you make it to the cart?"

"I think so. My desire to bathe is enough to get me there."

"Good." Mathilda took hold of Regina's arm and turned to the others. "Let us get our sister settled into the cart before we get the moonstone."

~

THAT EVENING, the women gathered around Regina's hearth, their children babbling cheerfully as Regina sat nursing Wren. It would have been a peaceful moment had the topic of Cassandra not ruined it.

"I sent for Master Bainard," Mathilda said. "I will entrust him to carve out a portion of the moonstone for us to use in the spell. We must first bind Cassandra. Her power is vile and far too dangerous for us to try to manipulate, so we shall transfer it into the stone and seal it away. This spell is 'ad mortem,'" Mathilda went on somberly. "And it must be completed on a full moon."

"To death," Regina translated. "Can you go through with killing your sister?"

A knot settled in Mathilda's stomach. It was not an easy decision, but she knew what the Goddess required of her. "I will do anything I must to fulfill my role as Guardian," she replied.

THE LIGHT of day suddenly winked out, leaving startling darkness in its place. No sound came from any direction in the blackened void. A piercing pain came in his chest, a memory of pain, really, causing Duncan to look down for evidence of a wound. Seeing nothing, he began to feel his way through the dark. How he came to be in this place, he could not remember, but one face drove him onward. Golden hair and eyes a deep blue-green: his love.

Onward he went, feeling nothing before him. The memory of pain was now gone, replaced by a surge of panic. He had to find his way back to his love.

"Mathilda!" he called. "Where are you, lass? Mathilda!"

Suddenly, a brilliant light cut through the darkness, temporarily blinding him.

"This way," a voice beckoned.

Duncan shielded his eyes. Suddenly, he understood. He was no longer amongst the living. "No!" he cried. "Mathilda! Lass, where are you?"

Mathilda jerked awake. She had accidentally fallen asleep in the chair. Instinctively, she looked in the cradle and saw that Charles and Charlotte were still napping. She rested her forehead against her hands, shaken by the dream.

"Are you ill?" Ramona asked. A needle was in her hand, paused above a cap she was sewing for Charles.

"No." Mathilda sank back against the chair and gazed out the window. Five weeks had passed since Lughnasadh. The words of Duncan's grandmother still haunted Mathilda, and her unease grew with no word from him or his aunt. Perhaps that was what had brought on her dream.

Ramona laid aside her sewing. "You have been growing more silent with each passing day. What troubles you?"

Mathilda sighed, meeting Ramona's worried eyes. "I fear that something terrible has happened to Duncan. I have seen him in my mind for many days. I dreamt of him just now."

Ramona's brows furrowed. "Tell me of your dream."

"Duncan was in a dark, cold place. He was calling out to me, but then he was silenced. It cannot bode well, I fear."

"Perhaps you should send someone to his aunt to inquire about him."

Mathilda gazed down at her lap. She realized her skirts were clenched tightly in her hands. She released the fabric and smoothed it. "I did send a letter to her," she admitted. "Several days ago now. I hope Margaret responds soon, for I fear the worst."

The door banged open, startling both women. "Mistress Mathilda, come quickly," Gertrude said, out of breath with hurry. "There is a strange man across the way."

Mathilda was on her feet at once. Gertrude would not react so strongly unless she felt the man seemed a threat. "Where is he?"

She and Ramona followed Gertrude outside. "There," Gertrude said, pointing toward the woodline. Standing by the large yew was a man Mathilda did not recognize. Even across the distance, she could see his sneer.

"How long has he been there?"

"I cannot say for certain. I saw him as I went inside to help put the children down for their naps. I thought at first that it was Larson, but Larson is over there, by the stable."

"Go inside with Hilda, and do not come back out," Mathilda said. "Ramona, stay here with Charles and Charlotte."

"I'll not leave you out here with that man," Ramona argued.

"If there is trouble, you can help protect me from the safety of the cottage. The children are more important."

Ramona's lips thinned. She nodded and stepped back inside the cottage, closing the door.

Mathilda strode toward the man. She sensed Cassandra's magic wrapped tightly around him. He stood, self-assured and unmoving, as she approached.

"Who are you?" she demanded.

An ugly smile crept across his face. In the next moment, he shifted into a black misty form and disappeared along the breeze.

"Sister," Katrina called from her doorway. "Who was that man?"

"A spy. No doubt Cassandra sent him," Mathilda answered.

She would find out more about him. First, to get all the children safe in one place. She and Ramona brought Charlotte and Charles over to Regina's cottage. Then Mathilda took a jar from her own mantel and went back outside. She bent and collected dirt from the place where the man had stood.

When she straightened up, Ramona was beside her. "May I join you in this?"

"Yes," Mathilda said. "I would be glad for the company."

In Mathilda's bedchamber, the two women pulled back the mat. Mathilda said, "If there was ever any doubt whether Cassandra knew of the children, she certainly does now." She placed a mirror in the center of the circle, along with the jar of dirt, and sat down.

Ramona said warily, "What will you do with the mirror?"

"Something risky," Mathilda admitted. "Hand me my mother's oak rod. And the bowl of holly berries," she added.

Ramona's brows arched. "Sister, why do you need these protective charms?"

Mathilda ignored the question and placed the rod and berries in front of herself as a shield. "Now, do not make a sound."

She gazed into the mirror, focusing intently. Carefully, she sent the slightest trickle of magic through it. After a moment, the surface rippled, and she saw Cassandra, her back facing Mathilda, working with her potions. Without the tight grip of magic that usually veiled Cassandra's emotions, Mathilda felt her sister's overwhelming jealousy. Malice was also present in the feelings.

Suddenly, Cassandra stiffened. She turned and faced a mirror in the room. She had a contemptuous smirk on her face. "I know you are watching me. How very clever of you to spy on me through a mirror. Now I can use your own trick against you."

Mathilda felt a quick surge of rage from Cassandra right before a blast of magic came through her mirror. She moved aside just in time. The jar of dirt bore the brunt of the energy instead, shattering from the impact. Mathilda waved her hand across the mirror and shoved it away. Her heart raced, and she took a long breath to calm herself.

"That was very dangerous," Ramona scolded. "What are we to do about our mirrors now? I'll not be able to trust my own image after this."

"I put a ward on this one," Mathilda said. "If Cassandra tries to spy through it, I will know. We must tell the others to ward their mirrors as well."

"Regina will not like this." In spite of everything, Ramona's mouth twitched. "She does like to check her reflection quite often."

The loose dirt and jar fragments lay scattered in the circle. Mathilda said, "We can still find out more about our visitor. Let us see what you and I can discover together."

Ramona took Mathilda's hands. As they spoke their magic, the dirt began to swirl on the floor. Mathilda reached over and touched it.

The energy of the man still lingered in the dirt. She felt his mortality, a relief, though her sister's magic was also present in what she sensed.

"It appears Cassandra has kept her word, at least. The man is mortal. However, she has enhanced his powers. We must be careful of him should we ever meet again." She met Ramona's eyes. "And I learned something else."

"Which is?" Ramona asked hesitantly.

"Cassandra is planning something against us. Something darker and more frightening than anything I've encountered from her before."

Mathilda lay in bed, smoothing her hand over Charlotte's back as she gazed into her night-darkened room. Cassandra's plotting, and the deep-seated hatred behind it, had shaken Mathilda. Her sister was working on something terrible indeed.

Mathilda now realized something. The simple binding incantation she intended to use on Cassandra most likely would not be enough to allow her and her sisters to complete the ritual. If Cassandra was anticipating anything at all, she might already have in place spells of protection. Mathilda would have to get around them with careful thought and planning, but she would have no time for that once she began the binding.

Suddenly, her mind opened; she saw herself and Ramona standing before Cassandra, and she was shown what it would take to secure the ritual. Her heart began to race. Could she keep her beloved sister safe while she obtained what she needed? Mathilda gazed at Ramona's sleeping form and Charles asleep at her side. *Goddess, please keep her safe.*

As Mathilda rolled onto her back to try and salvage some sleep, she felt a sudden pressure at the top of her head. Her body tingled all over as a presence came into her mind. She had met this spirit once before. Agnes Blàr. Her voice suddenly came clear, and as gravelly Mathilda remembered.

Duncan is dead, lass. He is with me. Have no fear; I will guide his way into the afterlife. He sends you all his love, eternally.

A burst of warmth flooded Mathilda's heart: an all-consuming love that swept away every obstruction in its path, even the bounds of mortality itself. It was devotion as deep as any sea and as gentle as a lapping wave. Mathilda tried desperately to hold on to the warmth surging through her heart, this final gift from Duncan before the torrent of grief crashed over her, drowning her in its depths.

Agnes's spirit began to fade. *I must now leave you, lass.* Mathilda was overcome with panic. She wanted to call out to the woman, to beg her to remain, but, like a snuffed candle, she was gone, and Mathilda was left hollow with pain.

The pain grew sharply, as if part of herself had been violently ripped away. Anguish tore like claws at her heart, and she shook with wracking sobs. Charlotte, asleep beside her, sighed softly at the movement.

Mathilda buried her face in her pillow and tried to contain her sorrow in silence. After some time, her eyes closed, and she slipped into unconsciousness.

SOMETHING GENTLY NUDGED HER SHOULDER. Mathilda's eyes felt heavy, as if she had swallowed one of her mother's sleeping draughts. She forced them to widen and saw Ramona standing over her. Charlotte fussed in her arms.

Ramona said, "I am sorry to wake you after the night you had, but Charlotte is hungry."

Alarmed, Mathilda sat up. "I do not understand how I slept through her wake time. Lay her down with me," Mathilda said, pulling her chemise off her shoulder. She lifted Charlotte to her breast and smoothed the baby's head, fighting back her grief as the memory of Agnes's vision reawakened.

Ramona sat on the mattress beside her. Mathilda said, "What did you mean by, 'after the night I had'?"

"You sobbed throughout the night. Aside from your mother's death, you've never been so distraught. I knew you must have received news of Duncan, so I put a sleeping spell on you. Forgive me."

"There is nothing to forgive." She swallowed roughly and met Ramona's gaze. "Duncan's grandmother came to me in a vision. He is dead." Another wave of sorrow threatened to consume her.

Ramona laid her hand on Mathilda's arm. "I am so sorry. Is there anything I can do?"

Mathilda tried to smile. "Thank you, but I think I only need time to myself. I will join you and the others shortly."

Ramona nodded and left Mathilda to her solitude.

Spending quiet time with Charlotte lifted her spirits. Mathilda recognized a sound she kept repeating and knew she would not be content for long. Mathilda finally gathered Charlotte in her arms and emerged from the bedchamber, urged by hunger.

Regina held out her arms for Charlotte. "Have some breakfast, Sister," she told Mathilda.

"She is fussing for her spoon," Mathilda said as she passed Charlotte over.

"Let us go get it, then," Regina said. She peeked inside the wicker cradle at Wren before heading toward the larder.

"There are fresh berries and some tarts," Ramona said, drawing out a chair for Mathilda.

"Thank you."

"Ramona told us the sad news," Isobel said, shifting Sunniva in her arms. "I am truly sorry, Sister."

Mathilda didn't trust herself to speak. Ramona held out a sheet of parchment tied with a simple woolen string. "This letter came for you earlier," she said.

Mathilda took the parchment. She untied the string. The lettering was thin and wavered as though written by a shaking hand.

> *I am writing to inform you that Duncan has died in battle. He asked me to give this to you some months back, but I kept it out of anger toward you. My conscience has bothered me, and so it is yours now.*
>
> *Margaret*

Mathilda touched the enclosed lock of hair to her lips. "It's true, then," she said, more to herself than her sisters. She hadn't dared to believe her vision might be false, but any last fragment of hope had now gone. "Duncan is dead."

Ramona took her hand. "Tell us how we can ease your grief."

Mathilda laid the parchment on the table next to her plate. She ought to eat, she knew, but her throat closed over at the thought. "I think I must weather the grief," she said. "Allow me this day, and I will be well."

"Of course," Ramona replied. "We will keep Charlotte entertained."

"Yes, we will, sweet girl," Regina soothed, bouncing Charlotte in her arms. Charlotte let out a squeal, bringing a smile to Mathilda's lips.

~

THE COTTAGE WAS quiet the following morning, save for the occasional shuffle from Gertude in the main room. Mathilda lay in bed, waiting for Charlotte to stir. She was ready to leave her chamber. These walls had seen her tears for too many hours.

She had done one thing yesterday. She closed her fingers around the locket she now wore and turned it over. On the back, engraved with her magic, an English rose and a Scottish thistle were entwined. Inside the locket, Mathilda had placed the precious lock of hair Duncan had sent to her, to keep close to her heart always.

Sometime during the night, Mathilda had put aside her grief, tucked it down deep alongside her abiding love for him. She had no other choice. The task she must complete this day would require careful focus, and she could not afford her grief to distract her. Ramona's life might depend upon it.

Charlotte suddenly opened her eyes. In the baby's flow of indecipherable chatter and giggles, Mathilda let the locket go.

"What are you so happy about this morning?" Mathilda asked, pressing kisses all over Charlotte's cheeks, bringing on another eruption of giggles. "We had better get ourselves out of bed. Your mother has much work to do."

Having dressed and fed Charlotte, Mathilda left her in Gertrude's capable hands and set off to find Master Bainard. Larson informed her that the stonemason had already departed, but had left something for her in the outbuilding. He went to fetch it and brought back a wooden box. Mathilda brought it into the cottage to inspect.

Master Bainard had carefully chipped off a portion of the moonstone, leaving Mathilda with a large chunk that filled both her hands. He had smoothed the edges on the cut side. The smoothed stone was silvery blue in the light. A golden hue ran along its rough top edge, catching Mathilda's eye. She shivered as she recalled the purpose of the moonstone. Such a beautiful thing for such a dark deed. She set it back in the box, closed the lid tightly, and went back outside to find Ramona.

Ramona sat on a blanket at the base of the knotty elm that protected Maelen's grave. Charles kicked his legs happily beside her, gazing up at the swaying limbs. Ramona was leaning against the tree's bark, doing nothing aside from enjoying the stillness of the moment, if the contentment on her face was anything to go by. "You look well," she said when Mathilda came up.

Mathilda thanked her and greeted her mother's grave. She sat down by Ramona on the blanket. "Master Bainard has prepared our portion of the moonstone. I have it in the cottage."

"That is good," Ramona said. She seemed eager to proceed with their plan.

Mathilda dreaded her following words. "There is something I must speak to you about."

Ramona looked at her warily. "Go on."

"It came to me in the night that there was a flaw in my binding spell. Cassandra may very well have some potent wards of protection already in place that could prove problematic when the time comes to bind her. As I reflected on this, I saw a way to ensure she would not escape our binding, but I will need your help. And it will be dangerous."

"I do not expect anything less concerning your sister. Continue." Ramona brushed a fallen leaf from her skirt and looked expectantly at Mathilda.

"I need a drop of Cassandra's blood and your protection whilst I obtain it." The words came in a rush, and she waited for Ramona's reaction.

Ramona's eyes widened. "Well, I wasn't expecting *that* much danger."

"I have a plan that will get us quickly out of Cassandra's reach once I obtain her blood. It will be a new use of my magic."

Ramona's brows rose. "Well, I can only imagine, but I trust you, Sister. When are you planning to go?"

"Just before sunset."

Ramona's jaw set, with a resolve Mathilda knew very well. She pushed away from the tree and got to her feet. "We had better go and tell the others, then."

Mathilda had braced herself for an argument, and it came at once. "I do not like you going without us," Regina said. She laid Wren in the wicker cradle by her chair and pinned Mathilda with a firm look. "What if something goes wrong?"

Mathilda spoke with more confidence than she felt. "The children must be protected. Ramona and I can handle ourselves with your help. You'll focus your power through the crystals. It will be no different than the other times we linked in this way." She saw Katrina shake her head across the table from her.

"I hope you know what you are doing, Sister," Katrina said. The firm set of her mouth said she didn't approve either. "We do not fully know the depth of Cassandra's evil, as she has kept to herself these past months. You could be walking into disaster."

Mathilda had considered this frightening possibility, but she trusted the Goddess and her sisters to see them safely through. She could not afford to let fear distract her. "I understand your worry, Katrina, but have some faith in me."

"Are you certain that going on foot is the best way?" Ramona asked. "It will be dark soon." She drew her cloak tightly around herself as if it were a shield of protection.

"Yes," Mathilda replied, forcing confidence into her words. "The cart would only slow us in the end, and the twilight shadows will help hide our departure."

"I suppose I will just have to see your plan in action to understand."

The woodland surrounding Cassandra's house was far worse than what they had encountered outside the village. Here, the trees and vegetation were blackened with rot, and a fetid stench made Mathilda want to gag. She covered her nose with her sleeve.

"Cassandra's evil has sickened the wood," Mathilda said sadly. "It is much worse than I feared."

Ramona's face went white, and she bent to retch. Mathilda hated that she had to put Ramona through this, but it was the only way. Ramona straightened, looking as determined as ever, and they continued.

The growl Mathilda had anticipated came as they neared the

clearing where Cassandra's house stood. A large wolf emerged from the shadows to flank Ramona. Another closed in on Mathilda's left.

"Tell your mistress that her sister wishes an audience," she said coolly, despite the anxiety pounding in her heart.

The wolf closest to Mathilda whirled into human form, the man who had spied in her clearing, and went into the house.

Several moments later, Cassandra strode out. Her black dress made her look pale and more sinister than ever. She eyed Mathilda with open hostility as she lingered just outside the door. "What do you want?"

"I must speak with you about some matters of importance," Mathilda said. She had anticipated that Cassandra would have stepped out further from her door. She had to get closer.

"Speak, then."

Mathilda eased ahead. "Have you been in the wood?"

"*This* is your important matter?"

"The woodland is dying. Of course, it is important. People are taking notice of it."

"I care not what others may notice," Cassandra said with a mouthful of disdain.

"It is not right, Cassandra." Mathilda inched closer still. Her heart was racing from fear, and before her sister could sense it, she forced it away, adding firmness to her voice. "Your festering hatred is causing it."

Cassandra scoffed. She looked toward the woodline as if noticing it for the first time. Mathilda took the opportunity to glance over her shoulder to ensure Ramona was still close behind her and said, "Your hatred of us is sickening the land. Why do you hate us so, Sister?"

Cassandra's eyes gleamed with malice. "It is *you* who hate *me*," she spat.

"You are wrong," Mathilda said, more gently now, preparing to step closer. "I do not hate you. I never have. You refuse to allow any kindness from me into your heart."

"Why should I," Cassandra demanded, "when you do not trust

me? It is you who cut me out of your life." She surprised Mathilda by closing the distance between them, giving her the advantage. Her heart pounded. She sensed the energy shifting around Cassandra. It was gathering, and Mathilda did not trust it. She had to act. "No! I am finished with you and your assurances of peace. You have your own family, and now you seek to destroy me—"

Now! Mathilda commanded from her mind.

Ramona's protective magic wrapped around her. Mathilda closed her hand around the knife she had kept hidden in the folds of her dress. In an instant, she had drawn it and pierced Cassandra's arm with the tip of the blade. Red blood gleamed on the steel. Mathilda felt her sisters' flow of magic strengthen through the pendant. She touched Ramona's arm, gathered her magic, and let it lift and carry them away in a thrilling rush. As the trees blurred at the edges of her vision, Mathilda heard Cassandra's scream trail along the wind behind them. "You will pay dearly for this!"

23

***

The mood at their table was somber. No one spoke. Even the children were subdued on their nearby pallet, where Gertrude and Hilda fed them mashed vegetables. It felt as though everyone was waiting for disaster to strike.

"Cassandra will no doubt seek to retaliate after my deed this night," Mathilda said. "We must prepare our minds for what we must do next."

She forced herself to take a swallow of wine. "My sister is probably beside herself right now, wondering why I took her blood. The full moon of Mabon gives us an advantage; Cassandra will not expect us to act against her so soon. We have always held fast to the feasts and rituals that come with the turning of the wheel. She will expect us to uphold this one, too. She will not anticipate our attack until after the feast."

"And your sister might use the full moon to her advantage as well," Regina said sharply. "Especially if she thinks we will be occupied with the festivities."

"I have considered that," said Mathilda. "Cassandra will no doubt be spying. That is why we shall give every indication that we plan to celebrate. We will visit the peasants, masked of course, to share our abundance of crops, and we will talk of nothing, unless we are safe indoors and shielded with our own magic, except the festivities and the Mabon feast. If she does have her eye on us, she will learn very little."

Regina gave a curt nod. "Very well. If we are to look as though we are preparing for a feast, I shall have Hilda send a letter first thing tomorrow to a few trusted servants from my father's house. It will look more convincing to have the extra help about."

"That is wise, Sister," Mathilda said. She felt assured that with the false plans to celebrate in motion, Cassandra would not see their attack coming. Her sister was sharp, but her hatred blinded her from seeing things clearly.

❧

AFTER DAWN BROKE, Regina helped Mathilda prepare the provisions. She tied a sack filled with several blankets and a few tunics she and the others had made for the upcoming cold season and set it aside.

"I am thankful for this diversion," she said, filling a basket with apples. "I needed a respite from the incessant thoughts of your sister."

"Yes, it does my mind good, too," Mathilda agreed. "Please insist that Aemon Bradbury keep the tunic *and* blanket. I am sure he will refuse. Humor his pride on my behalf."

"Pride?" Katrina scoffed. "I would describe it more as a nasty demeanor, only the old miser does not show it to you." She shoved the loaf of bread she had wrapped into a sack, and Regina just knew it was smashed.

"Sister, he has recently lost his loved ones," Mathilda said. "Surely you can relate and have sympathy."

Katrina flushed. "You are right. I shall try to be kind."

Regina heard wheels outside and glanced out the window as the cart drew up. "Larson is ready," she told her sisters. "Let us make haste."

"Yes," Katrina said, wrapping herself in her cloak. "Rowan did not eat well this morning. I have a feeling she will need me sooner than usual."

Mathilda walked outside with them. "Keep up your guard—and don't forget to alter your appearances," she said. "Ramona and I will keep the children entertained while you are away."

It was a chilly ride to the village despite the thick blankets. The crisp autumn air made everyone sniffle and tinted their cheeks pink. As before, they disguised their faces as women from their childhood. Larson steered them off the track and halted the horses toward the back of Aemon Bradbury's small wooden dwelling.

"Wait here with the cart, Larson," Regina said. "We will not be long."

Katrina got out the blanket and tunic Mathilda had sent. "I do hope Bradbury will be gracious," she muttered, climbing out of the cart.

"You'd best be kind," Isobel smirked. "Though Bradbury won't recognize you through the disguise, he will still inform Mathilda about you if you do not."

"Yes, yes." Katrina bundled the items in her arms and strode around to the front of the house.

Regina hesitated as they turned the corner. "Where is everyone?" The village seemed much too still, the quiet suddenly threatening.

"Look," Isobel whispered, close to Regina's elbow. "Aemon Bradbury's door is ajar."

Something was wrong. Regina crept toward the door. "Stay close," she whispered to her sisters.

She pushed the door open with a cautious hand. The room was dark, no lantern or candles lit. Regina stepped inside far enough to see a small lantern hanging on a hook by the door. At her focused glance at the wick, a flame shot up. As her eyes adjusted to the sudden burst of light, she caught sight of Bradbury's dark-clad figure crumpled beneath the window. In her shock, she let go of her disguise, prompting her sisters to release their masks, too.

Katrina ran to him. She dropped to her knees and placed her ear against his chest. "Goodman Bradbury!"

"Is he breathing?" Regina asked. She feared the worst as she hurried over to kneel beside her.

"Barely. Let me get his tunic open," Katrina said.

She worked the strings loose and pulled the tunic open. Regina caught her breath. Blackened streaks ran from the old man's neck down to his chest, as if someone had held a burning brand against his naked body.

Isobel drew back, visibly frightened. "He has been touched by dark magic."

Katrina listened to his chest again. "We must hurry and draw the magic from his body, Sisters. He is fading fast."

Regina laid her hands over Aemon's chest and watched with alarm as veiny black streaks of magic seized hold of her fingers, staining them as if she had dipped them into an ink pot. It was all she could do to sit still and let the dark magic seep further into her body, like a veil of filth settling over her. She felt as if she would be ill. Her body screamed in protest at the violation, but she forced herself to sit and draw in the final remnants of the evil spell.

Slowly, the old man's eyes fluttered open. A look of panic flooded his features. He struggled to rise.

"You are safe," Katrina soothed, putting a hand on his shoulder. "Goodman Bradbury, can you tell us what happened?"

He stared up at them, wide-eyed, and then sank back in relief. "Mistresses. 'Tis you."

"Yes," Regina said gently. "Who did this to you?"

He focused on her with an effort. "It was the red-haired woman." His voice was thin and feeble. "She came with two men this time. My door burst open, and there she was, smiling maliciously. I saw her men through the door, opening the animal pens. I got up to rush out and stop them, but I couldn't breathe. It felt like I had swallowed fire." A tear streaked down his face as he recalled the memory. "They took everything. My cow, the chickens, everything is gone. My stock was all I had. What will become of me?"

Katrina took his hand. "Aemon, do not distress yourself over your livestock. I will replace your animals myself, every last one. You will have your livelihood back."

The old man looked startled. "You would do so much for me, mistress?"

"I would," Katrina said firmly. "I will."

Regina felt a burst of pride at her sister's compassion and thoughtfulness. "We will see to it at once, Aemon," she said. But they must also learn more about what Cassandra had done. Where are the other villagers?" she asked. "We saw no one when we arrived."

"If they had the chance to escape, they would have taken to the wood."

"Let us help Goodman Bradbury to his bed," Katrina said.

They got him to his feet and onto the small bed against the wall. Katrina retrieved her bundle from the floor and shook open the blanket.

"Here is a blanket Mathilda made just for you. I want you to promise me you will get some rest and recover fully from this day." Katrina tucked the blanket around him and reached for the tunic. "And this is a tunic Mathilda also made for you, and Regina has a basket of fruit and tarts. There is fresh bread, too. I made it myself. We will leave the basket by your bed so you do not have to get up should you get hungry."

The old man wiped his tear-filled eyes with a shaky hand. "I do not know why you young women care for the likes of me, but I could not manage without you."

Katrina patted his hand. "You get some rest. We will be back soon to check on you."

Regina pulled the door closed behind them. "Well done, Sister. I have never known Aemon Bradbury to speak so kindly to anyone but Mathilda."

They all heard a twig snap, somewhere close by. Regina whirled around. She saw a tattered-looking group making their way through the wood. From the frightened faces she recognized, it looked as if most of the villagers had escaped Cassandra. Relief crossed several of the women's faces as they caught sight of Regina and her sisters, and they hastened around the trees, looking eager to relay what had happened.

"We had better go find out what losses they have suffered and head back," Isobel stated.

"Yes," Regina agreed, looking at the blackened effects of the filthy magic on her hands and fingers. "We need to release this dark magic to the Goddess."

A SMALL FIRE burned low in the hearth, casting a dull red gleam toward the table and the array of foulness that littered it. Cassandra lifted a piece of bark, careful not to touch the maggots that crawled amongst the rot and decay. She lowered the bark into the mazer and spoke the words of her spell. A brown sludge bubbled up to the edge of the bowl and slowly oozed back down. She placed a sleeve against her nose until the stench subsided.

Cassandra glanced up as Geoffrey stepped into the room. Her anger flared at the interruption. The light caught the blue-black hues of his raven hair, a feature she once found attractive. Now she could barely tolerate the man. If it weren't for his usefulness, she would do away with him. He approached her, eyeing the table in disgust.

"I thought you already had your enjoyment torturing the peasants."

"I have not yet begun my enjoyment, Geoffrey. Some of them got away." She carefully filled a vial with the putrid potion. She found herself smiling as she thought of its purpose. "This is sure to bring my sister here to my doorstep."

"But why seek her revenge? She is immortal, yes? What can you do to harm her?"

Cassandra recalled the cut on her arm, still raw and burning with pain. She had not healed herself, leaving the gash instead to heal on its own and scar as a reminder of what Mathilda had done. She would pay for her betrayal. What Cassandra had been working on would assure that. "I need not harm her body to make her suffer," Cassandra said now. She lifted the vial toward the light, pleased she had conceived the idea to make such a spell, and held it out for Geoffrey to take. "See that Ralf and Emory deliver this to the village."

Geoffrey's eyes widened. "But that will mean their demise as well."

Cassandra fought the urge to strike the man down in her frustration. She needed him willing to do her bidding. "Indeed, it will. Ralf and Emory have served their purpose, but now I am ready for more capable help." Cassandra glanced up at him, smiled seductively, as she ran her finger along Geoffrey's arm. "You have two brothers, do you not? Perhaps they might find themselves replacing those boorish fools."

By the time Katrina, Isobel, and Regina returned to Mathilda's cottage, the blackness that had started in their fingers now streaked up into their arms. Ramona eyed the discoloration in horror. "What has happened to you?"

"Cassandra had her men take anything of value from the peasants, leaving them without any means of support," Katrina explained. "Poor Aemon Bradbury took a nasty blow from her magic. We were able to draw it out, as you can see, and he is recovering."

Mathilda poured a jar of moon water, already enhanced with her magic, into a wooden mazer and added a pinch of salt. "Dip your fingers into the water," she said, passing the bowl to Katrina first. "It seems my sister hopes to punish me. She is reckless, but that's all to the good. Her anger blinds her, so she cannot sense our plans to end her vileness."

"Let us hope she remains blinded until we *are* ready to search her out," Ramona said.

"Yes," Mathilda said. She watched the final blackened remnants on Regina's fingers leech away into the water. "Take the bowl outside and pour the contents into the earth. You are now cleansed."

THE MIDMORNING SUN slanted through the window as Mathilda sat cross-legged on the floor, staring at the moonstone by her feet. Tomorrow would be the end for Cassandra. It had been two days since the attack on the village. The ruthlessness that she had shown to the peasants would be nothing compared to what she would unleash on Mathilda's sisters. Mathilda had caught a glimpse of the blackness in Cassandra's soul the day she collected her blood. Blackness and death. Cassandra was planning something terrible, but Mathilda still could not see what it was.

The terrible not-knowing was nearly too much for her. She could not bear the thought of harm coming to her sisters. They were her family now, and she needed them dearly. She could not afford to let her mounting fears take root, so she did all she could to shake herself free of them.

The door to her bedchamber suddenly burst open. Regina stormed in, eyes blazing. "Was it you who sent for Philip?" she demanded. Wren began to fuss in her mother's arms at the sudden outburst.

Mathilda sighed as she recalled writing the letter. After the attack on the village, Mathilda realized she would need Philip's help, but she was afraid Regina would forbid her from sending for him, so she had secreted the letter away with Larson to deliver.

"Yes," she answered, getting to her feet. Regina's anger washed over

Mathilda in waves, and she flushed with guilt. "I know you're angry, Sister, but please listen." She took Regina's silent glare as permission to proceed. "When we go up against Cassandra, the children will be here alone with Gertrude and Hilda and with no protection. I wrote to Philip, telling him of Wren's birth, hoping that once he saw her, he would want to stay and care for our children in our absence—and Goddess forbid—should anything happen, Philip could protect them with his magic."

Regina's face was stony and unreadable. The angry blooms of color still stained her cheeks, although she seemed to consider Mathilda's reasoning.

"Mistress," Hilda said, stepping into the doorway. "He is just outside, getting down from his horse.

"I will deal with you later, Mathilda Longhurst." Regina passed Wren into Hilda's arms and stalked out of the room.

Hilda gave Mathilda an apologetic look as she tried to soothe the fussing babe. "Mistress, I hope you'll forgive her sharp tongue."

"It's quite all right, Hilda." Mathilda made herself smile. "Regina will have her happy ending. I am certain of it."

Regina went outside, intending to forbid Philip from seeing Wren. As soon as she saw him, though, she knew he must have run into trouble. Blood dripped from a gash on his hand, and another cut stood out livid on his cheek.

Her anger evaporated. "Philip, what has happened?"

"I have much to tell you. Can we speak?" His gaze was imploring and held none of the bitterness he'd shown her recently.

"Of course." Despite her anger at her sister, she led him into Mathilda's cottage. Whatever trouble Philip had run into likely involved Cassandra. Mathilda would want to hear what he had to say. Hilda gasped at the sight of him. "Master Philip, whatever's happened?"

Regina answered first. "Hilda, please fetch me clean linens and some water."

Hilda gathered herself. "Yes, mistress."

Regina was relieved to see Philip hadn't noticed Wren sleeping in the wicker cradle near the hearth. She drew out a chair for him to sit and angled it away.

Mathilda poured a cup of wine and placed it before Philip. He took a long drink before turning to Regina. He looked pale and shaken. "Where is my daughter?"

"She is sleeping. Now, tell us what happened to you."

"I came upon two men on my way here. One of them was a witch. He attacked me, unprovoked. As we fought, a woman approached me from behind and commanded the men to leave. I turned then, seeing a red-haired woman, and felt the most powerful magic I'd ever encountered, aside from yours, Mathilda," he said, looking up at her, "though the woman's felt tainted and wrong. As the men took their leave, she transformed into a raven and followed above me as I went on my way. Once I was close to your cottages, she turned back."

Regina glanced worriedly at Mathilda. *Why had Cassandra let Philip pass unharmed?* Regina thought to herself. This unsettled her.

"Who is the woman?" Philip asked.

"She is my half sister, Cassandra," Mathilda replied. She looked as shaken as Regina felt. "I am certain she only allowed you to escape so that she could learn of your purpose here with us."

"I fear I have more to tell you," Philip continued. "There is pestilence in the little peasant village."

"Oh, dear," Mathilda said. "Did you go near it?"

"No. I overheard your sister's men speaking about it. The pestilence was caused by her spell. It seems she sacrificed two additional men to unleash it."

"What are we going to do?" Regina asked.

"*You* are going to do nothing," Mathilda said. "I will go. Stay here and look after the children."

Before Regina could try to argue, Mathilda took her cloak and stepped out the door with it. Regina stared after her a moment before her thoughts turned to the man beside her. She had mixed feelings about being in his presence again. She dipped the cloth into the water and washed the blood from Philip's face, noticing how he, too, stared at the door Mathilda had just gone through.

"I shall accompany her," Philip said.

"No," Regina said firmly. "Mathilda is quite powerful. She can handle herself."

Philip did not seem ready to accept her answer, and she could not divulge Mathilda's immortality.

"Would you like to see our daughter?" she quickly asked, hoping to distract him.

A look of vulnerability came over him. "I would like that very much," he said softly.

Regina smiled and rose from her chair. Wren woke as soon as she lifted her from the cradle, blinking against the light.

"You mean to tell me she was there the whole time?" Philip said from behind her.

"She was," Regina answered. She returned to her chair and pulled the blanket away from Wren's face so Philip could better see her. "Would you like to hold her?"

Philip nodded, as if he didn't trust himself to speak.

Regina settled Wren into his arms. At first, he just gazed at her. Then, his face twisted, and he released a broken sob. He pulled Wren close and kissed her, and Regina became overwhelmed with emotion. In that moment, there was no bitterness of wrongdoing between them, just the three of them and enough love to erase months of hurt.

MATHILDA PULLED the sleeve of her dress over her nose. The awful stench of rot and death was everywhere. The households she had visited so far had no survivors, and the Tinson family was near to embracing the Mother. Numb with shock, Mathilda tried repeatedly to draw out the pestilence, but whatever foul spell Cassandra had unleashed prevented Mathilda from healing the family. She collapsed against a wall, overcome with helplessness, then remembered she still had to check on Goodman Bradbury. Mathilda pulled herself together and left immediately for his house.

She found him lying on his mattress with weeping sores, covered in his own filth. He struggled to breathe. Her sorrow nearly gave way at the sight of him this way.

"Aemon, it is Mathilda. Can you hear me?"

A faint gurgling sound came from his throat.

Mathilda wiped her tears. She knelt by his bedside and took his hand in hers. "No, do not try to speak. Just rest. You are about to go to a beautiful place, Aemon. There, you will find no suffering, and those whom you love will welcome you happily. Think of them now and be at peace."

Mathilda sat with him until the last breath left his body. She said a prayer for his soul and went outside, too numb to even cry.

Across the way, she saw a man leaning heavily against a tree and knew him to be one of Cassandra's men. She could see by his weakness and sores that he had the pestilence. Even near death, he still looked at her with malice. Another man approached her from the right. His face was pale with fever, and his empty eyes stared with hatred at her. Surprisingly, the men had enough strength to attack. Their magic came at her, though with little force, given their weakened state. Mathilda sent out a burst of her own magic, pinning them against a house to stay until the disease could take them both.

A sudden idea struck her. She knew these men were doomed, yet they could be used for a greater purpose. Mathilda ran back inside Aemon Bradbury's house to search for a vessel. Having found one, she darted outside to watch the men. With her back against the door, she waited. Tree shadows began to bend along the wall behind the men as the sun slipped closer toward nones.

When the men finally collapsed to the ground, drained from their illness, she stood over their bodies, waiting. As they gave up their last breath, Mathilda was ready. She quickly spoke her spell and opened the lid of the vessel. The dull light of their souls streaked out from the men's bodies and into the container. Exhausted and heartbroken over the loss of so many beloved families, she put the lid back on and went to check on the Tinsons.

The four children had already passed on since she had found them earlier, and the remaining three adults were not far from joining them. Mathilda waited in the darkness of the room, sobbing, until they gave up their souls. She only took the energy of these souls, allowing them to pass on to the other side.

She dashed away her tears, went outside, and faced the little wooden dwellings—the homes of the dear families she had grown to love—and, with sadness in her heart, she raised her arms—a spark caught, soon burning every home. Mathilda set a protective barrier against the wood, keeping it safe from the fires. She stripped out of her clothes and cast them into the flames, then, using her power, she streaked away in a blur of magic that sent her quickly home.

Regina stood by the table, watching Philip as he gazed down at Wren. His gentleness touched her. He was caught between silent awe, as though he could not fathom the tiny being he held so dearly to himself, and smiling with joy, as if she were the most precious thing he'd ever beheld. He seemed so natural at being a father that she could almost imagine the three of them as a family, but she could not allow such hope. Philip had not even hinted at reconciliation. And besides, Wren belonged to the Goddess. Her daughter's life would be for a greater purpose than uniting her parents.

Regina was already planning a spell to send Philip on his way when something by the window nearest the hearth caught her attention. Her eyes widened. Mathilda stood outside, arms wrapped tightly around herself, without a stitch of clothing on. Mathilda caught Regina's eye and motioned for her to come outside.

"Philip, I will just be a moment," Regina said, excusing herself. She walked around the side of the cottage and found Mathilda crouched behind the wall. Her hair had mostly fallen from its braid, and her face was blackened with filth or soot; Regina could not tell, with tracks from where tears had streaked. She was unusually pale, and a haunted look shadowed her eyes. Regina wondered what Mathilda could have possibly encountered to bring so much distress.

She held out a hand as soon as Regina was within earshot, before she could take one step nearer. "Stay back," Mathilda urged. "I am unclean."

"Where are your clothes?" Regina asked, overcome with the fear that her sister might have somehow been assaulted.

"I had to burn them." Something terrible shone from Mathilda's eyes, and Regina shuddered at the magnitude of it. "I have been exposed to the pestilence. I cannot risk getting near anyone, especially the children. I need my jar of moon water, a candle, and a sprig of sage." She paused, as if struggling with her thoughts. "And the soap," she went on, "and some clothing before I can come before any of you." Her voice, though flat, shook as though she were holding back tears.

Regina hurried inside to collect everything.

"Is something amiss?" Philip asked.

Regina didn't take time to explain. "Mathilda has returned," she said. She took a basket into Mathilda's bedchamber to gather the needed items. "Would you watch Wren a little longer while I speak with my sister?"

"I will." He shifted Wren in his arms and smiled at the soft sounds she made. As Regina passed by him, Philip eyed the kirtle hanging over the edge of the basket curiously but said nothing.

Regina hurried back outside with it, and Mathilda said, "Would you carry it down to the pond? I must bathe."

Regina walked at a safe distance behind Mathilda down the

slope. When they reached the water's edge, Regina set the basket down and stepped back from her.

She dared herself to voice the dreaded question that had been in her mind since her sister's return. "How are the villagers?"

"Everyone is dead, including two of Cassandra's men." Mathilda's voice broke as she relayed the news.

Regina could not form words. It could not be true. "Everyone?" she finally managed to ask.

"All of them," Mathilda said, her voice dead.

Regina thought of the village children and of Aemon Bradbury, whom they had just helped. Tears welled in her eyes, and she choked on a sob. "How awful. The entire village is lost? Because of your *wretched* sister?"

The numbed shock Mathilda had carried since she returned suddenly vanished. She looked up with a hardness Regina had never seen in her before.

"Yes. I never imagined Cassandra could be so cruel. But I have something in store for her—something that she will not expect. I will never allow her to hurt anyone that I love again."

The venom in Mathilda's voice jolted Regina from her sorrow. "What do you mean?" she asked, dabbing her eyes with her sleeve.

"I will explain everything once I rid the remnants of death from my body." Mathilda took the candle from the basket and pressed the sprig of sage into the wick end. Regina heard her utter a spell to slow the sage's burn. Then, a spark of Mathilda's magic lit the candle. Thrice, she passed the candle across herself, the smoke from the sage wrapping around her like a film before dissolving into her skin. When she had finished the purification, she reached for the bar of soap and stepped into the pond. Regina winced on her behalf, knowing how cold the water was, though Mathilda showed no outward signs of discomfort.

Regina's thoughts turned to Philip. He was likely wondering what was keeping her away so long. "What shall I say to Philip? He will want to know how you fared. I cannot tell him you came in contact with pestilence without raising his suspicions regarding your immortality."

Mathilda rubbed the soap over her arms. The water rippled around her waist as she scrubbed her skin. "We will say that I destroyed the village from a distance once I discerned no life remained. Now, hurry inside before Philip decides to come looking for you and sees me unclothed."

Regina turned and went back up the slope, feeling uneasy. Mathilda's anger had frightened her. Cassandra's attack on the village went beyond all her other evils. Whatever plan Mathilda had must be equally devastating.

MATHILDA SAT on the bed as Ramona stood behind her, drawing the comb through the damp hair that lay loose down her back. The bath and purification had relieved her fears of exposing her sisters and the children, but no amount of bathing would ever cleanse her from what she had seen in the village. Images of Aemon Bradbury, his hand in hers, as he took his final breath, and the flames that consumed the village by her hand kept flashing through her mind. She heard her sisters talking in the other room and their children babbling their own conversations, and a fiery determination settled over her. She would do everything in her power to protect them.

"I am so sorry," Ramona said. "You had a deeper connection with the peasants than any of us, and I know how much you are hurting."

Mathilda twisted the ends of her belt as she thought about what she would do next. "Those dear souls did not deserve their fates. It makes me terribly angry. They were senselessly murdered because of my connection with Cassandra. Their deaths will not go unavenged, however. The Tinson family has helped ensure our victory against Cassandra." The twisting fabric on her belt rubbed her skin nearly raw, and she dropped the ends.

"What do you mean?" Ramona asked. She placed the comb on the table, gazing warily at Mathilda.

"Come with me. I have much to tell you all."

In the main room, Philip lay on the floor with Wren perched on his chest. Mathilda smiled. "She has taken up well with you in such a short time."

Philip grinned proudly. "It seems she has."

"Hilda, would you and Gertrude please take the children to Regina's cottage? And Philip, would you accompany them? I must speak with my sisters. Afterward, I would like to have a moment of your time."

"Of course." He tucked Wren into his arm and reached for Rowan with the other.

Once she and her sisters were alone, Mathilda waved her arm in an arch, casting them under a dome of silence.

"Why did you take such care to mute our conversation?" Regina asked.

"Because what I am about to say is for us only, and I do not know if Philip can control his curiosity."

"I see."

They settled around the table, the hearth flames cracking with new logs behind them.

"As you all know, Cassandra's men perished with the villagers. When they passed away, I took their souls and contained them in the vessel I brought home. I also took the soul energies from the Tinsons."

"Mathilda!" Katrina gasped. "Why would you do such a thing? It is... it is wrong!"

"I can imagine what you must think of me, but it is for a greater purpose. I know that you all have been worried about going against Cassandra. I, too, have worried. After what she did to those in the village, I decided I could not stand by and allow Cassandra to destroy anyone else that I love."

Mathilda dropped her gaze, hesitating before meeting their eyes again. "I want to recreate the immortality spell for all of you—if you will allow it, of course."

No one spoke. Mathilda took in their shocked expressions and began to fret with the cords of her belt again. Had she gone too far in her desperation?

"I think I would like to go through with it," Isobel finally said. "I do not want to die going against Cassandra, and I cannot help but fear that I *will* die if we do not allow Mathilda to bestow us with immortality."

"Isobel," Katrina scolded. "Do you not have faith in our circle?"

"Of course I do, but I am a mother now, and I have many fears I had not known before."

"She is right," Regina agreed. "What is your view on life now, Sister? You never speak of your immortality. Do you fear you will someday tire of this existence?"

Mathilda's throat felt tight with emotion. She took a breath. "I find it hard to imagine I'll tire of living, but I do fear a life without all of you in it." She couldn't bring herself to meet her sisters' gazes while she awaited their answers.

Ramona broke the silence. "Oh, Sister. I never considered that before. I can only imagine how lonely that thought makes you."

Mathilda raised her head. Speaking about her fear was a relief. "I am sorry I have not been more open with my feelings. I did not wish to burden any of you."

"Your burdens are *our* burdens," Regina said. "I cannot imagine the grief of watching loved ones die throughout a life of immortality. It is unimaginable." Katrina shook her head in agreement. "However, I would not want you to be alone. I will gladly take your spell. What we could do together with our infinite lives," she said wonderingly.

Mathilda imagined traveling to distant lands, exploring and discovering new plants for magical uses, and the people they could help. She found herself laughing. "I can always depend upon you to lift my spirits, Regina."

"I will also take your spell," Katrina said.

"As will I," Ramona added.

Relief flooded through Mathilda. Having her sisters, her allies, with her throughout eternity brought about a fierce determination. "Good. Cassandra will not stand a chance. Once she realizes that you are immortal, her ego will be undone. She would not consider that I would bestow immortality on another after chastising her for granting it. She is already jealous of our bond. When she discovers what I've done, she will become reckless... unfocused, and I will destroy her. Now I must speak with Philip about watching over our children," she said, rising from her chair.

Regina's pale-blue eyes met Mathilda's. "Sister, I am glad that you sent for Philip, though I am still angry you did not discuss it with me first." A teasing smile tugged at her lips.

"You are right. I should have told you of my intentions."

Regina smiled fondly. She kissed Mathilda's cheek and said, "All is forgiven, Sister."

MATHILDA FOUND Philip in Regina's bed with all five children snuggled against him, sound asleep. He returned her smile.

"Come with me," she whispered. Hilda slipped into the room as he left.

When they were seated by the hearth, Mathilda said, "You seem very well adapted to fatherhood."

"Thank you," he said, his face turning regretful. "I always hoped for a family of my own, but I fear it is too late."

"Why do you say that?"

"I do not think Regina would have me now." He looked toward the fire, avoiding Mathilda's eyes, but she did not miss his hurt.

"I would not be so sure of that," she said.

"She has been trying to get rid of me since I first arrived." A smile edged his mouth, and he shook his head. "I have sensed it."

A corner of Mathilda's lip twitched. She did not doubt Philip's words for a moment. "Perhaps it's best you speak with Regina. She thinks that *you* do not wish to be with her."

Philip suddenly looked embarrassed, remorseful even as his gaze dropped to his hands.

"Forgive my meddling," Mathilda gently said, "but after what transpired between you on your last visit, she was crushed and will not allow herself to be hurt again. I am afraid you will have your work cut out for you—and I warn you, Regina can be quite stubborn."

"Yes," Philip said, looking slightly amused. "She certainly can be." He turned inward, and Mathilda saw a flash of hope in his eyes. She studied him a moment, considering her following words carefully.

"Philip, I know you have questions regarding me and my sisters." Those questions shone in his eyes again, and she could sense his struggle to keep them to himself. "Believe me when I tell you our intentions are pure. I am dealing with a family matter that has been worsening for quite some time. I believe my half sister, Cassandra, has some vile deed planned, and my sisters must go with me on the morrow to find out what it is. I need your help. Given the magnitude of the situation, I cannot leave the children unprotected. I would be grateful if you could stay with them while we are out. Hilda and Gertrude will tend to their needs."

His mouth parted in surprise before a deeply humbled look settled over him. "I consider it an honor that you would place your children in my care," he replied. "It would bring me much joy to be with them."

Mathilda smiled. It seemed fate had brought Regina the perfect mate.

"You are a good man, Philip. I earnestly hope you and Regina can find your way back to one another."

"As do I," he wistfully replied.

24

The dawn half-light was nearly upon them as Mathilda stepped out into the chilly air with her sisters. A low fog hugged the ground, eddying around their ankles and pooling in the shadowy places between the trees.

Mathilda chose a tiny glade just off the path for her ritual and cloaked the women's presence. "Are you certain this is your wish?" she asked, disturbing the stillness surrounding the glade. "There is no going back."

At their nods of acceptance, she placed the vessel on the ground and asked her sisters to lie down. Their movements disturbed the fog, and it swirled languidly in the brightening dawn. Mathilda spoke a spell that wrapped around her sisters' minds like a gentle blanket, sending them into peaceful sleep. She fell to her hands and knees, speaking fervently.

"Great Goddess, I humbly come before you with a request. You know what we must face, and I beg that you grant my sisters immortality." Her fingers clenched in the dampened detritus as fear overcame her. The reality that she could one day lose them—maybe soon if Cassandra had her way—was overwhelming. Mathilda could not keep the brokenness from her voice as she humbled herself before the Goddess. "I could not bear it if anything were to happen to them, and I cannot face an eternity without them. Please, *please*, do not take my sisters from me." A sob escaped her lips, and she put strength in her final plea. "Search our hearts. I swear that we will remain devoted to you—to our purpose, and that we will not abuse our immortality."

A strong force seized Mathilda's mind. She sucked in a gasp at the magnitude of it.

The Goddess spoke to her in a voice of thunder and beauty. *"I see you, Daughter. You have lost much, yet you have remained pure. I will grant your request, but you shall all spill your blood upon this sacred ground and swear your fealty to me. If ever one of you should abuse your gift, my punishment will be swift."*

The pressure in Mathilda's head eased as the voice left her. She had heard the Goddess's voice before, but never with such magnitude. She sucked in air, gulping it in, and pushed herself back up to her knees. Relief came at once, leaving her trembling with gratitude. She took a calming breath and looked at her sisters.

"Awaken."

"Is it done?" Regina asked, stirring.

"Almost," Mathilda replied. "We must swear our fealty and promise that we will never abuse our immortality or else face punishment."

She pulled out her knife and took a breath, slicing the blade across her palm. Wincing, she turned to Ramona. Taking her hand, she cut Ramona's flesh, repeating the process until she finished with Katrina.

"Do you swear fealty to our Goddess?" Mathilda asked.

"We do."

"Do you swear never to abuse your power?"

"We do."

Mathilda pressed her hand to the ground, sealing her promise with her blood. As the others touched the earth, the vessel shook, and immortality flooded their veins, surrounding them with a brilliant light. Then, the light winked out. Birdsong suddenly filled the forest, hundreds of songs that only came in spring. Mathilda and her sisters gazed in wonder as they listened. Quickly, the birdsong faded.

A long, white feather glided overhead on the breeze. It drifted slowly, landing amidst the center of the women. Isobel ran her fingers over it. Wonder lit up her face.

"It is an omen," she said. "The spirits support us in our new endeavor."

"Yes." Mathilda picked up the feather and tucked it into her pouch. "How do all of you feel?"

"Strong. As if my magic could move every tree in this forest," Katrina said in awe. "Is this how it is supposed to be?"

"Yes," Mathilda replied. "You will need to accustom yourselves to it, but after some time, it feels natural. You must be careful not to abuse this new power, lest you find yourself like Cassandra and out of favor with the Goddess."

Regina scoffed. "We swore a blood oath. We are not reckless, Sister. And we are certainly not like Cassandra!"

"No, you are not," Mathilda agreed. "But the spirits required me to speak it, nonetheless. Now, we must get back before the children wake, crying with hunger."

As the others walked on, Mathilda linked her arm through Regina's. "May I speak openly with you?"

"Of course."

"I know you do not like my meddling where Philip is concerned, but I must speak my heart in this matter. Philip is a good man, and he loves you. Much more than you know. I have seen his heart, and it is pure. He desires to be a family with you and Wren."

Regina said nothing for a moment, and Mathilda sensed her tumultuous emotions.

"I do not think I can entertain such thoughts," Regina finally said. "Especially now. My role as Guardian is not for him to know. I cannot involve him."

"Perhaps he is meant to be involved," Mathilda said. "Not as

Guardian, of course, but as someone devoted to you and who would protect you and Wren for the duration of his natural life."

Regina stopped and faced Mathilda. "That is another problem I foresee. How can Philip see us like this? Never aging. He will know we are immortal."

Mathilda smiled. If that was her only remaining concern, it was easily remedied. "Then we shall age. We can enchant ourselves to look older as time passes."

Regina shook her head. "We would have to enchant ourselves anew each day. That would be difficult."

Mathilda's smile broadened. Regina's thoughts were complicating the matter. "Sister, if you can alter your appearance to that of a black-smith with a crooked nose, you can manage a few wrinkles and gray hair."

Regina's distress eased then. "You must truly wish me to grant Philip my heart."

"I do," Mathilda said, resuming their walk. "After losing Duncan, I cannot watch someone throw away love so recklessly. Please allow him to at least prove himself to you."

A softness settled around Regina's eyes. "Very well. I will not send Philip away just yet. But I will guard my heart. I do not imagine this will end well."

Mathilda kept silent at that. She had felt the Goddess had a hand in guiding Philip to Regina. If this were indeed true, perhaps in time, the Goddess would allow them to tell Philip the whole truth.

As the day progressed, everyone made a spectacle preparing for the Mabon feast. The servants Hilda had sent for arrived and were immediately put to work. Larson loaded the cart with clothing and provisions to take to the less fortunate in Whitsby Village and prepared a cover for the women to hide beneath.

Mathilda stood by the window watching him work as dusk settled around the clearing. Charlotte squirmed in her arms, and Mathilda shifted her to her other hip as she absentmindedly ran her hand over her daughter's back. Her unease grew as she thought of what she and her sisters must do this night. Mathilda had searched for any signs of goodness in Cassandra but had found none. The Goddess required retribution. With a heavy heart, she turned from the window.

"It is time," Mathilda said to her sisters. She snuggled Charlotte close, breathing in her sweet essence before passing her to Gertrude's outstretched arms. *Please protect our children,* Mathilda silently prayed as she watched Philip and the servants carry their babes into Regina's cottage. When the door had closed behind them, Mathilda reluctantly led her sisters into the bedchamber to prepare the spell for Cassandra.

Ramona drew back the rush mat and laid it aside as everyone settled on the floor. Mathilda felt heavy-hearted—she knew her sisters did, too. She sensed their worry as it mirrored her own. Words seemed too burdensome suddenly, so Mathilda got to her knees and reached across to rest her fingertips on Regina's temples, embedding the spell and the necessary steps they would need to take. Then, she moved to Katrina and repeated the spell until she finished with Ramona.

When it was completed, Regina got to her feet first. "I will tell Hilda we are to set out. She and the other servants know to go ahead with supper and make merry in our absence. If anyone is listening, they will hear a joyous occasion at my door. Philip has set wards. He will keep watch."

"Good," Mathilda said. She and Ramona dressed in simple kirtles of dark brown hues to better blend into the woodland, then they snuffed out the candles and waited in the waning twilight. The sack containing the moonstone sat at Mathilda's feet; its presence a heavy reminder of what was coming.

With darkness finally upon them, Mathilda cast a spell to mask her and Ramona under a shroud of magic, making them unnoticeable to watchful eyes on the clearing. She reached for the sack and slipped out into the night with Ramona, moving silently toward the awaiting cart. Larson had left a corner on the cover pulled back for them, and they eased beneath it. Moments later, the hushed movements of their sisters drew near. Isobel slipped beneath the cover, with Regina and Katrina following behind her. Mathilda had not sensed the presence of a spy, and she prayed they would go unnoticed throughout the rest of their journey.

With everyone wedged in amongst the provisions, Larson emerged from the stable and mounted the driver's seat, quickly turning the horses toward the track for Whitsby Village as planned.

The cart was filled with tension on the drive, easing only a moment when Larson stopped upon his arrival, and though he made quick work of unloading the supplies to the families, it felt like an eternity to Mathilda as she waited in the back for him to finish. With the last of the provisions delivered, he mounted again and steered them toward the track leading to Cassandra's home. Mathilda noticed the wary glances her sisters occasionally cast toward the sack with the moonstone sitting by her hip. She wished she could ease their worries.

The cart pitched roughly in the hardened ruts. Sensing they were close, Mathilda peeked out. Up ahead, the track narrowed. Dense brush hugged the edges of the cart, and she bade Larson to stop.

"We jump out here," Mathilda instructed her sisters. "Get behind the brush and do not make a sound."

With the five of them out of the cart, she sent Larson on his way. Mathilda's gaze fell on the sack clutched in Katrina's hands. She let out a shaky breath and quickly uttered a masking spell to conceal them for the rest of their journey on foot.

When they reached the border of Cassandra's property, Mathilda settled everyone into the hedgerow where they watched the movements of Cassandra's men. There were three of them, and they carried on in drunken conversation, oblivious to the women hiding in the wood near them. They spoke of a tavern and wenches, then ambled away toward the path leading to town.

"Well, that just made our night less difficult," Isobel said, watching the retreating men.

"What do we do now?" Regina asked.

"We wait a bit longer," Mathilda replied. "Cassandra is busy with something. I can sense her magic."

Light filtered around the door of the stone outbuilding, and shadows fell as Cassandra moved within its walls. Mathilda closed her eyes and focused on the structure. Her sister's tainted magic made Mathilda uneasy. She steadied herself and prepared to move.

"Cassandra is intent on her spell. Let us go closer while she is concentrating on her task. We will speak only in mind now."

The darkness felt oppressive, and the short, nervous breaths of the others seemed exaggerated to Mathilda's ears. Their energy was electrifying. Mathilda's heart pounded as she neared the building.

Cassandra's footsteps shuffled about inside. Then, there was an ominous silence, one with teeth and claws that searched through the darkness.

Careful Sisters. She knows.

The door to the building blasted open with a force of magic so strong that it lifted them from their feet and hurled them backward. Cassandra stepped out, vengeance blazing in her eyes. Mathilda scrambled to her feet and joined hands with her sisters. Looking up at the moon, they began their spell.

"Five witches to gather. Five witches to steal. Five witches to bind. Five witches to kill."

Their magic wrapped around Cassandra, rooting her to the ground. A momentary look of shock came over her face. Mathilda and her sisters moved closer, just out of arm's reach of Cassandra. Fear and understanding flashed in her eyes before the anger returned.

"You think you can destroy me? You are not powerful enough." She sneered with confidence as she gazed at the women.

Mathilda did not answer. Determination steeled her. "Katrina, it is time for the moonstone."

Cassandra's eyes fell on the sack. "What are you doing?"

Katrina placed the moonstone on the ground and resumed her place with her sisters. The elements jolted awake, called by the women's magic.

A look of wildness came over Cassandra. She rounded on Mathilda. "*No!*" she shrieked. "You will not do this to me. I am your sister! Please, I beg of you." Her knees gave way, and she dropped to the ground, sobbing. "You are not like Father. *Please* do not do this to me. I do not want to die."

Mathilda paused her spell and took in her sister's shaking body, her fear. The pleading face of her mother, who once begged Aelle for her life, suddenly flashed into Mathilda's mind. Cassandra wore that same face now, helpless and terrified. Mathilda nearly choked from the memory.

Ramona squeezed her hand. "What are you doing, Sister?"

On impulse, Mathilda changed the spell. "I bind you, Cassandra. From doing harm to us and all others."

"Mathilda!" Regina shouted. "No! You must finish this."

Ignoring her, Mathilda continued. "I bind you, Cassandra, from doing harm to us and all others. I bind you, Cassandra, from doing harm to us and all others."

Cassandra seemed to realize, all in a moment, what was happening. Her fear and helplessness vanished in the face of rage. "No! You cannot take my power. How will I survive? You would send me into eternity like a mortal? You would not *dare!*"

Mathilda looked up at the dark velvet sky. "To the powers that be," she commanded, "I call on the power of the harvest moon: Take the magic of this wicked servant and seal it inside this stone."

Cassandra jerked as Mathilda's spell took hold. She fought against it, holding desperately to the last of her magic. Then she saw it—the immortality in Mathilda's sisters. Rage burned in her eyes as she looked from one to another and another. Something began to take form behind Cassandra's eyes, and Mathilda felt a horrible sense of doom.

"You have brought this on yourselves!" Cassandra screamed. "You have no one to blame for their deaths but *yourselves!*"

"What is she speaking of?" Ramona asked, her eyes wide with fear.

"You will know suffering like never before," Cassandra declaimed. "I, too, call upon the power of the harvest moon." She pulled a vial out of her tunic and flung it to the ground, shattering the contents onto the grass. "Death, I bring unto you. As you cannot taste it, then your children shall."

"No!" Regina screamed, lunging at Cassandra.

Mathilda pulled her back. "It is too late," she choked out. "It is too late." From the moment the vial had shattered, she had felt Cassandra's spell take hold. Mathilda could do nothing to stop it. She watched, helpless, as the contents from the vial spread out in thick, blackened veins.

Cassandra sneered. "I curse them to an eternity of death and rebirth. Your joy shall turn to agony as you watch your children die over and over. As I live this eternal wretched life, powerless, they shall die as babes, never living a full life with you." Mathilda's heart raced, and her breath came in bursts. She had known one day she would lose Charlotte to her mortality, but Mathilda had taken comfort in knowing she would watch her grow old. For Cassandra to curse their children so cruelly... A shred of hope bloomed in Mathilda's chest as an idea formed in her mind, but Cassandra must have seen her thoughts. She smirked in triumph before she spoke again. "And no spell of immortality you utter will take hold. *This* shall be your eternal punishment."

Isobel fell to her knees, sobbing. Katrina and Ramona stood as if they had been turned to stone.

Cassandra gave a vile laugh before doubling over. As the last of her power was drawn out, she collapsed.

Regina whirled around to face Mathilda. "*What have you done?*" she shrieked. Angry, red blotches stained her tear-streaked face, and she screamed her anguish into the night.

Mathilda choked back a sob. Her moment of weakness had cost them dearly. "I am sorry... I—I took pity upon her."

Regina looked conflicted. Less angry. But she turned away without a word of forgiveness.

Ramona came to Mathilda's side. "We can reverse this, can we not?" Hope and desperation shone in her eyes.

Mathilda's mind reeled; she looked inward, praying the spirits would bring forth some spell she had learned, but they revealed nothing. "I don't know."

Cassandra's groan drew their attention. Mathilda shook herself from her despair. She still had one final thing to do. The moonstone lay on the ground. The dew had settled over it, and moonlight reflected in its shimmering hues. Mathilda bent to pick it up. Cassandra's terrible power thrummed from inside the stone, and Mathilda shivered. It was a shame something so beautiful must hold such evil.

"What are you going to do with it?" Ramona asked.

"These powers that take life and give death are the reason for all of this cruelty. I want nothing more to do with them. We must hide the stone before Cassandra wakes. We shall let the earth choose the place." Mathilda glanced warily at Regina. She felt her sister's anguish at her betrayal. Would Regina forgive her? "We need you, Sister."

Regina's lips thinned to a hard line. "Very well."

They placed the stone at their feet and reluctantly formed a circle once more. Mathilda struggled to speak.

"Great Goddess of the earth, we beseech that you wisely choose a hiding place for these dark powers. Let no one find them. And should there ever be a search for the stone, grant us knowledge of it beforehand."

Mathilda bent and picked up a large rock. She used it to chip off a chunk of the moonstone. No sooner than she took up the broken bit, the ground suddenly opened, swallowing up the tainted stone and secreting it away.

"It is done. This piece I broke off is linked to the stone with Cassandra's powers. Should anyone seek it, we will know. Now, let us get home to our children. I will beg the favor of the Goddess to save them from this death spell."

Mathilda looked over at her sister's body, slumped on the cold ground, and turned away. She used her magic to rush them all home. It brought them there faster than ever before.

They heard a commotion as they stepped out from the wood.

"What is happening?" Katrina asked, her voice shrill from fear.

Mathilda's heart thudded in her ears. "Let us make haste to find out."

Hilda came running to meet them. Her face was white with panic. "Mistresses, the children," she gasped. "Something is wrong. They fell into a deep sleep. Philip is trying to revive them..."

Mathilda barely heard the last words. She ran into Regina's cottage. The children were lying on the bed. They might have appeared to be sleeping were their faces not ashen, as though on the cusp of death. Mathilda looked at Charlotte. Her curls stood out starkly against the pallor of her face. The wave of dread that settled over Mathilda threatened to send her to her knees.

Philip's voice brought her out of her spiraling emotions. He stood over the children, his palms out toward them, chanting a spell to keep them from crossing over into the spirit realm. Sweat dampened his forehead, and he began to tremble. His power was weakening. Mathilda knew he could not go on in his current state.

"Philip."

He did not hear her.

She moved closer. "Philip," she said again, touching his arm. "Go with Gertrude. She will fetch you something to drink. Leave us with the children."

Dazed, he looked from Wren to Regina, and to the rest of the women. He nodded and staggered from the room.

Regina gathered Wren in her arms and sobbed helplessly, and Ramona's anguish as she pulled Charles into her arms was unbearable for Mathilda to watch. Isobel and Katrina tried desperately to rouse their daughters, to no avail.

Regina looked at Mathilda, and her pain nearly tore Mathilda apart. "I did not think that it would happen so soon," Regina said. "I thought I would have more time with her. This cannot be."

Mathilda bent and kissed Charlotte. Her face was cold, startling Mathilda. She fought against her collapsing emotions. She could not help her daughter if she lost herself to grief. "Sisters," Mathilda said, straightening up. "We must be strong if we are to help them. Stand with me and join hands. I will cast a spell to keep our children in their slumber and away from death until I can speak with the Goddess."

One after another, they seemed to find strength. Gathering at the foot of Regina's bed, they joined hands with Mathilda, lending her their power as she spoke her spell.

When she finished, she said, "This will preserve them for only a little while. Stay with them. I must be alone. I will speak to the Goddess and our ancestors."

Mathilda kept up her stoic appearance as she hastened outdoors. Then she ran and flung herself over her mother's grave, sobbing in grief.

"Merciful Goddess, they are just babes. I humbly beg of you: Prolong their lives. Let them know happiness and devotion for you. They shall be promised to you, just as my sisters and I were, and all those before us. Please grant me this request. I have been faithful. Do not allow our children to suffer for my grave mistake. *Please* have mercy. I saw my mother's dying moment, and in the rush of my pity, my sister took advantage of me."

She paused for a moment and recalled her mother's face. "Mother, if you can hear me, I beg your aid. I cannot lose my daughter. She is the love of my life. Intercede for me—for all of us. We will bring them up in accordance with the old ways. Help me, I beg of you."

The door to the cottage burst open. Mathilda heard Ramona calling her. "Mathilda! Come quickly!"

Dread seized Mathilda in a choking hold. If her plea had failed… but then she heard Ramona's voice again. "The children. They are all awake!"

Mathilda felt a rush of relief. A broken sob released her fear. "Thank you," she whispered into the darkness.

~

GERTRUDE STOKED the fire to stave off the chill of the night air. The logs popped, sending bright sparks into the air.

Ramona and Mathilda sat beside the hearth in a mutual shocked silence; Charles sleeping in Ramona's arms, and Charlotte at Mathilda's breast. Time seemed to move slowly for the two women after they had left their sisters and returned home. "How long do you think we shall have with them?" Ramona asked, smoothing Charles's hair.

"I don't know," Mathilda replied softly. "It could be months, perhaps years, if we are so blessed." A tear streaked down her cheek. She wiped it away before it could fall onto Charlotte's head. "How could I have been so foolish? I vowed I would never trust Cassandra again, and yet I fell so easily into her trap."

Ramona rose from her chair. She handed Charles over to Gertrude and knelt by Mathilda's. "Do not blame yourself so harshly. Even I was moved by Cassandra's entreaty."

"I am so sorry," Mathilda said with a sob. "I hope that you all can come to forgive me."

"Come now, Sister. None of this. Of course, we forgive you."

"I am not certain Regina will. She hasn't spoken a word to me since the children recovered. Peace of the *Goddess*, what was I thinking?"

Charlotte jerked awake and began to cry. Mathilda drew her closer and soothed her daughter back to sleep.

"Calm yourself," Ramona soothed. "Regina will come around. She always does."

~

"Mistress, let me take her," Hilda insisted once again. "You should eat something."

"No, Hilda," Regina replied. "Wren is content in my arms."

"Very well." Hilda sighed, but left Regina and Philip to themselves.

"She is right," Philip said. "You need to keep up your strength after the day you have had. Besides, I would like very much to hold my daughter."

Regina tore her eyes from Wren. For the first time since she had returned from the disastrous venture at Cassandra's house, she registered Philip's steadfast presence. She realized the toll his spell had taken on his body as he tried to save the children. He looked worn and weary. She felt a wave of deep compassion for him.

"Of course. How selfish I have been." She settled Wren into his arms. She sighed sweetly in her sleep as he held her close and kissed her head.

A rush of anguish suddenly overtook Regina. For an endless, terrible time, she had believed her daughter was dead or dying. She could not stop her tears once they began. "It is too much to think about," she wept. How could she have done such a thing?"

Philip looked up in surprise at her outburst. "Who?"

"Mathilda. She brought this death spell upon our children. Our babes would not be cursed had she not been weak."

Philip gently placed Wren on the bed and took Regina in his arms. "I do not know all of what happened, but from what I have gathered, Cassandra was a master at deception, and Mathilda is a kind, loving soul. It is no wonder that she struggled with her decision." He smoothed his hand over Regina's back, a loving gesture that took her by surprise. "I do not know if I could have gone through with killing my sibling. And yes, there was a terrible price for her moment of weakness, but she is paying for it also, is she not?"

Regina thought of Charlotte, and her heart wrenched. Of course. Mathilda's suffering was as deep and real as Regina's own.

"Yes," she said. "I have been unfair to Mathilda. I must go to her at once." She paused by the door. "Philip, thank you for your wisdom."

He smiled. "You go. I will stay with Wren."

~

Mathilda gazed into the dying flames. Ramona had taken Charles and gone to bed some time ago, with Gertrude following behind her to lay Charlotte in bed for the night. Mathilda was weary but could not sleep for the despair that still gripped her heart. At the sound of the door opening, she looked up. As she laid eyes on Regina, her guilt flared. She had never felt so small and unsure of herself as in this moment. Regina rushed over and flung her arms around Mathilda. "I am sorry, Regina. Truly."

Regina dropped to her knees and gathered Mathilda's hands in her own. "Let us speak of it no more. From henceforth, we will spend every moment loving each other and protecting our children."

Mathilda nodded and managed a smile. "Yes."

"Thank you for interceding with the Goddess and our dear ancestors on our children's behalf. Your level head and quick thinking saved them all. Now I will treasure my time with Wren all the more. And I have decided to take your advice and include Philip in her life. It is only right."

Mathilda thought of Philip and the efforts he made to keep their children from death's door. She hadn't thought her heart could fill any more with love. Now she found she had room for him there, too. "This is wonderful news. I know you two will be happy together."

"I believe we will."

EPILOGUE

Do sit still, Charlotte," Mathilda scolded. "It is not every day a girl celebrates her tenth birthday. You must look your best."

Charlotte stilled her fingers, where they had been restlessly moving over the buttons on her lavender kirtle. She narrowed her eyes, and for a moment, it was Duncan's face looking up at Mathilda. "Mother, only the aunties are coming to celebrate. They have seen me looking far worse than this."

Mathilda paused with the comb midway down her daughter's dark waves. "They have, but let me enjoy this moment at least."

"Oh, very well," Charlotte said with a sulky sigh.

Smiling, Mathilda resumed drawing the comb down Charlotte's back to the ends of her hair. She had grown so much. Except for her eyes, which were the exact shade of Mathilda's, she had her father's looks. The hurt from the empty hole Duncan had left in Mathilda's heart flared, as it always did when she recalled him.

So much had changed in her life since that long-ago Beltane night when she first met him. Her life had begun then. She became a mother; her sisters did too. Since then, another cottage had been built to house Isobel, Katrina, and their daughters, and Philip had moved in with Regina and Wren. The years had been kind. Though Mathilda was happy, she wished Duncan could be here to watch his daughter grow.

The door to the cottage burst open. A red-faced Wren stood on the stoop, beaming. "Come quickly, Charlotte! Madge has had her kittens!"

Charlotte sprang to her feet and ran outside, leaving Mathilda standing behind the chair with the comb in her hand.

"Oh, Charlotte," Mathilda sighed. Her daughter was also impulsive, like her father.

Ramona stepped into the cottage with a bundle of freshly picked yarrow. "Where are they off to in such a rush?"

"The cat Wren found has delivered her kittens."

"Ah."

Mathilda watched Charlotte run toward the stable. She stumbled and fell hard on the ground.

"Oh, dear. I had better go check on her."

She got a cloth and a bowl of water, but as she walked outside, she saw that Charles was already tending to Charlotte. He gently wiped the little girl's tears and brushed the dirt from her dress. Charlotte smiled up at him. She took his outstretched hand and let him lead her into the stable.

Ramona stood beside Mathilda at the window. "Their bond grows stronger by the day," she said.

"So it does," Mathilda agreed. "So it does."

ACKNOWLEDGMENTS

To Kris Faatz, my editor: To quote Mathilda, a simple thank-you seems insufficient. Your insight during this journey was deeply appreciated. Thank you for the time and the care you put into all of my characters. This story would not be what it is without you.

To Debby Kevin, the gentle mastermind at Highlander Press: Thank you for absolutely everything! Your kindness and encouragement were invaluable to this anxious author. Forever grateful!

To my family: Thank you for all the behind-the-scenes support. I love you!

To the kind souls on Instagram who have supported me with encouragement and sweet comments: I adore you all!

And finally, to everyone who has read my books and taken the time to leave a review: Thank you! Your support means the world to me.

ABOUT THE AUTHOR

Kimberly Patton is a devout lover of cats, overcast autumn days, and the deep, shadowy places of woodlands. She resides in Virginia with her husband and two children, where she spins tales that rivet readers. *Eternal Enchantment* is her second novel. Learn more at <u>kimberlypattonauthor.com.</u>

Photo credit: Marjorie Stallard

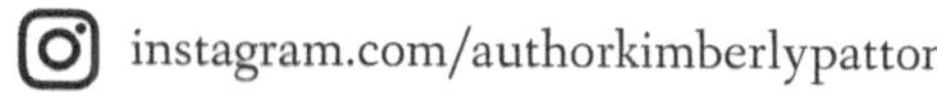 instagram.com/authorkimberlypatton

ABOUT HIGHLANDER PRESS®

Highlander Press® is more than a publishing house—it's a movement.

Founded in 2019, Highlander Press® exists to elevate powerful stories that inspire change, spark conversation, and expand what's possible. We specialize in guiding purpose-driven authors—from initial draft to beautifully published book—with clarity, confidence, and unparalleled support.

Our model is intentionally collaborative. We work hand-in-hand with each author to demystify the publishing process, champion creative integrity, and deliver top-tier results without the smoke and mirrors. Every author who walks through our doors is seen, heard, and supported—because we know that behind every great book is a courageous voice ready to rise.

At Highlander Press®, you're not just publishing a book—you're stepping into your next chapter as a leader, a visionary, and a changemaker.

facebook.com/highlanderpress

instagram.com/highlanderpress

tiktok.com/@highlanderpress

linkedin.com/company/highlander-press